A
Kiss for
Lady Mary

Books by Ella Quinn

THE SEDUCTION OF LADY PHOEBE

THE SECRET LIFE OF MISS ANNA MARSH

THE TEMPTATION OF LADY SERENA

DESIRING LADY CARO

ENTICING MISS EUGÉNIE VILLARET

A KISS FOR LADY MARY

Novellas

MADELEINE'S CHRISTMAS WISH

Published by Kensington Publishing Corporation

A Kiss for Lady Mary

ELLA QUINN

LYRICAL PRESS
Kensington Publishing Corp.
www.kensingtonbooks.com

LYRICAL PRESS BOOKS are published by

Kensington Publishing Corp.
119 West 40th Street
New York, NY 10018

All Kensington titles, imprints, and distributed lines are available at special quantity discounts for bulk purchases for sales promotion, premiums, fund-raising, educational, or institutional use.

Special book excerpts or customized printings can also be created to fit specific needs. For details, write or phone the office of the Kensington Sales Manager: Kensington Publishing Corp., 119 West 40th Street, New York, NY 10018. Attn. Sales Department. Phone: 1-800-221-2647.

Lyrical and the L logo are trademarks of Kensington Publishing Corp.

First Electronic Edition: May 2015
eISBN-13: 978-1-60183-456-0
eISBN-10: 1-60183-456-X

First Print Edition: May 2015
ISBN-13: 978-1-60183-457-7
ISBN-10: 1-60183-457-8

Printed in the United States of America

To my wonderful husband. You are my happily ever after.

ACKNOWLEDGMENTS

No book is written alone. Thank you to my critique partners, beta readers, my wonderful agent Elizabeth Pomada, and my fantastic editor John Scognamiglio for giving me the time I needed for this book, and last, but certainly not least, thank you to my readers. I hope you enjoy Mary and Kit's story as they find their way through misunderstandings and awkward moments to true love. If you have ever been in a situation where another person always takes what you say and do in the wrong way, you will have a great deal of sympathy for this hero and heroine.

PROLOGUE

The second day of May 1816, London, England
My dearest Constance,
I am distraught at the idea that you will miss another Season. London is always so diverting. However, I fully understand your concern over your granddaughter. It would be far better for her if we could get her settled. Speaking of which, Featherton has finally lost patience with his heir and is insisting he wed soon. We have long spoken of a match between our houses. Could it be the time has come for us to step in and arrange a union?
Your devoted friend,
Lucinda, Dowager Viscountess Featherton.

The tenth day of May 1816, Near Market Harborough England
My dear Lucinda,
I believe you are correct. I cannot think of a better match for my Mary than your Kit. We must plan carefully. There is also the matter of her cousin. He is still stalking her. If only there was a safe place for her to hide until her situation can be resolved.
Your friend as always,
Constance, Dowager Duchess of Bridgewater

CHAPTER ONE

April 1816

The Honorable Mr. Christopher "Kit" Featherton, heir to Viscount Featherton, waited behind a young gentleman at the entrance to Almack's. The other man was patting his suit, desperately searching for something. Kit, as he was known to his family and close friends, stepped around the individual, gave his hat, coat, and cane to a footman before addressing Mr. Willis, Almack's gatekeeper. "Good evening, Willis."

The older man bowed. "Good evening, sir. Her ladyship and Miss Featherton arrived not long ago."

"Thank you, Willis."

As Kit strolled into the assembly room, the young man complained, "I don't see why you didn't ask him for his voucher."

"Mr. Featherton is well known to us and all in the *ton*," Willis replied sternly. "You, sir, are not."

Kit couldn't help but feel bad for the gentleman, but the patronesses of Almack's were extremely particular about who gained admission to the rarified assembly rooms. He lifted his quizzing glass, surveying the attendees. Unfortunately, the one person he'd hoped to find was not present, and had not been for two years.

"Mr. Featherton, precise as a pin as usual." A light hand touched his sleeve. Lady Jersey, one of Almack's several patronesses, or Silence as she was called because she rarely ceased talking, smiled up at him. "Would you be so kind as to ask one of the young ladies to stand up with you?"

He inclined his head. Her ladyship had no need to ask. Unlike many gentlemen, he would do his duty. "Naturally. Is there anyone in particular?"

"Yes, Miss Caudle. The young lady in green next to the lady with the large red feather in her turban. She is painfully shy. I shall introduce you."

A few moments later Kit led the girl to join the group of gentlemen and ladies making up a set for a country dance. Bending his head slightly, he said, "Don't let anyone frighten you. This is really no different from your assemblies at home. You have only to stop worrying and you'll be fine."

A smile trembled on the girl's lips, and she nodded tersely. "Thank you."

Miss Caudle was light on her feet, managing the complicated steps perfectly. In a few moments, she began to enjoy herself. After the set he was pleased to see other men lining up to beg her to dance with them.

He made his way to his mother and sister Meg.

"That was well done of you, Kit." Meg grinned, and nodded to indicate Miss Caudle. "She was so afraid of doing something wrong, and I didn't know how to reassure her."

"I was glad to help. Do you require a dance partner?"

"No, mine is coming now." His sister's eyes twinkled. "Although if you could arrange to have Lord Beaumont ask me, I'd be forever in your debt."

"I hate to disappoint you, but there is only one reason he is attending." He motioned with his head to where his friend was standing next to a stunning woman with auburn hair.

"Oh, I know. Unfortunately, Lady Serena is too nice to be jealous of."

Kit glanced around to see a tall gentleman a few years younger than himself approach. "Swindon."

"Featherton." The new Earl of Swindon gave a short nod, before turning to Meg. "My dance, I believe."

His sister held out her hand and curtseyed. "Indeed it is, my lord."

After Meg left, he raised a brow to his mother. "Now that would be a good match, if he wasn't such a cold fish."

Mama gave her head an imperceptible shake. "She will pick when she's ready, and not before." She focused her steady blue gaze on him. "I'm much more concerned about you. It is all very well for you to be the perfect gentleman, but is there no lady who interests you?" He did not want to have this conversation now. "Perhaps you have a lady in mind?"

Her lips thinned. "You know perfectly well how I feel about match-making mamas. I shall not be one."

Thankfully, Lady Cowper, another patroness, intruded. "Mr. Featherton, I wonder . . ."

"I'll be happy to, ma'am."

He spent the rest of the evening doing the pretty, then retired to his rooms on Jermyn Street. Evening shoes off, brandy in hand, Kit stared into the fire. Until this past year, he might have gone to his club and enjoyed a night cap or two with his friends. But now they were mostly married. Late nights drinking brandy couldn't compete with the soft, warm arms of their wives. The others were either out of Town, or pursuing their lady loves.

Kit heaved a sigh. His mother was right. It was past time he'd thought of marriage. Still there was only one lady it had ever occurred to him to ask, and he hadn't seen her in a couple of years. Even then, she'd appeared in Town only briefly. Surely if she'd wed, he would have heard. Perhaps he should make a serious effort to track down Barham and asked him where his sister was.

September 1816, near Market Harborough, England

Lady Mary Tolliver heaved a sigh of relief. She'd been at her brother, the Earl of Barham's, dower house with her grandmother, the Dowager Duchess of Bridgewater, and her widowed aunt, Lady Eunice Phipson, for two weeks now. Thankfully there was still no sign of her cousin, Gawain Tolliver. Perhaps he'd finally given up attempting to compromise her. She'd been taking her regular walks after breakfast for the past week. But this morning she had remembered advice given to her by a friend to vary her schedule as long as Gawain was after her and had decided to go earlier.

She was about a half mile from the house when a familiar male voice asked, "How much longer?"

Mary stopped and scanned the woods. Suddenly, the dark green she'd taken for leaves ruffling in the slight breeze moved revealing a jacket.

Blast it all! It was Gawain, and she'd almost stepped into his trap. She'd known her luck wouldn't hold. She slipped behind a tree, and listened.

"About another half hour," a man with a rougher voice answered.

"Have the coach ready," Gawain ordered. "I want to get away as soon as we grab her."

She backed up carefully, keeping the dense foliage between herself and her cousin, until she could no longer see Gawain clearly.

"Did you hear something?"

Mary stifled a groan. How far was it to the house, and could she outmaneuver them? She glanced around. It was eight, maybe nine, feet to the old oak tree where, as a child, she'd won many a game of hide and seek. Gathering her skirts, she dashed to it and hid in the hollow part of the trunk. Gawain would have to know exactly where to look to see her. Still, she could not remain in the tree all day. She would have to hope they gave up waiting for her and left, planning to return another day.

"Nah, sir, just a deer or something."

Several minutes later, Mary shifted and dirt fell around her. This space had been far more commodious when she'd been younger. Something landed on her arm and began to crawl. Stifling a scream, she swatted at it, dislodging more debris. Her heart thudded, making it hard for her to breathe. It was certain her cousin wouldn't leave until at least the time when she normally passed by. She would just have to run. As they began to converse again, she picked up her skirts and dashed out of the home wood. Once she reached the outer part of the curtilage she raced through the rose garden, staying off the flagstone and gravel paths to the nearest door and darted in.

"My lady," Cook exclaimed. "You look like the devil hisself is after you." The old woman narrowed her eyes. "What have you got into? Shake out your skirts before you come in any farther. Is that a dead spider on your arm?"

Mary leaned back against the door, sucking in great gulps of air as she caught her breath. "That might be an apt description." She briefly considered asking Cook not to tell Grandmamma, but that would only insure her grandmother heard about it sooner. "I'll be down for breakfast as soon as I wash my hands."

"No rush, Lady Eunice isn't down yet either."

Attempting to avoid her grandmother and aunt, Mary made her way up the servants' stairs to her chamber. Her maid, Mathers, was waiting. "I saw you tearing across the garden, my lady. Did your cousin show up?"

"Yes." Mary's shoulders drooped as she removed her damaged bonnet. "I'll not have any more long walks now."

Somehow she'd have to find a way to avoid him for good, or at least until she could fall in love and wed.

"Thought it was too good to go on for long," Mathers said, as she took a sprigged muslin morning gown out of the wardrobe. "If you ask me, someone ought to do something about him."

"Someone" ought to be the eldest of Mary's brothers, the Earl of Barham. Unfortunately, he was much too good natured, not to mention concerned about scandal.

"When pigs fly," she mumbled.

"Did you say something, my lady?"

"Nothing of import." It was a shame there were no convents in England. She could hide in one of them rather than moving from estate to estate. Then again, it would be hard to meet an eligible gentleman, or indeed any gentleman at all, in a convent. On the other hand, it was proving impossible to meet a suitor under her current circumstance. "I wonder what Grandmamma will come up with this time."

A couple of days later, Mary joined her grandmother and aunt in the dower house's elegant but cozy morning room. Small paintings and miniatures encompassing generations of Tollivers covered the walls and surfaces. In the Queen Anne style, the furniture was old, but comfortable.

Long windows gave a view over the rose garden and the marble fountain in its center. The curtains had recently been changed from the velvet used during the colder seasons to a cerulean blue watered silk trimmed with gold braid. Even though they were experiencing one of their few warm days this spring, a log spat and popped in the fireplace.

In fact, the only disturbing part of the normally tranquil atmosphere was the conversation.

Doing her best to keep her jaw from dropping in shock, Mary stared at her grandmother. The older woman's thick silver hair was fashionably dressed, and even at more than seventy years of age, her face held few lines. Her gaze seemed as sharp as ever. Generally she was the picture of health, except for this recent burst of incipient insanity, for that was all it could be.

Mary opened her mouth, then closed it again. Several moments passed in silence as she struggled to make sense of what she *thought* she'd heard. After rejecting retorts such as, *Grandmamma, are you feeling quite well?* Or, *are you sure you wouldn't like a nice room in Bedlam?* And finally unable to come up with another way to ask her question, she simply voiced the nicest thought in her mind. "Surely I have not understood you properly. You want me to do *what*?"

"Well, I think it's a wonderful idea."

Mary shifted her gaze to her aunt. Perhaps madness had always run in the family and it had been kept a secret so as not to ruin them socially. After all, who would deliberately marry into a family where lunacy was rampant?

"He has a face like a fish." Aunt Eunice opened her eyes wide and moved her lips in a fair imitation of a fish.

"Hake." Grandmamma nodded decisively. "It's the way his eyes protrude."

Mary closed her eyes, repressing a shudder. "I agree, but surely there must be less drastic measures I can take."

Grandmamma leaned forward and pounded her silver-headed cane on the floor. "He may look like a fool, my girl, but he's canny, and, if what Cook told me is true"—Mary should have expected that—"which I have no doubt it is, he almost caught you a few days ago."

"Yes, well." Not the cleverest of replies. Surely, she could think of something more to say. "I got away from him," she ended lamely.

"This time." Grandmamma's lips thinned. She rammed the cane into the thick Turkey rug again.

"And every other time previously." Mary let out a frustrated huff. Unfortunately, her grandmother did have a point. It *was* becoming more and more difficult to evade her cousin. "Did Barham receive an answer to his last letter to Uncle Hector?"

After a few moments, during which Grandmamma turned so red it appeared as if she would have apoplexy, Aunt Eunice replied, "Yes. But it won't serve. Barham said Hector continues to insist your father promised you would marry Gawain, and he will not release your funds until either the marriage takes place—"

"In which case that spendthrift, Gawain," Mary almost growled, the anger in her voice surprising her, "would control everything."

Thus far she'd been satisfied to allow her brother to handle the whole ridiculous situation. Truth be known, she'd been so battered by her parents' successive deaths, she hadn't wanted to deal with it. Yet when Gawain had followed her to London for her first Season in two years and tried to compromise her, she had been jolted out of her complacency.

"Or you turn five and twenty."

Her aunt's voice interrupted her silent railing. "I'm sorry. What did you say?"

"When the trust ends," Eunice replied patiently.

Another two years of trying to evade Gawain. "Has there been any movement in our Chancery suit to replace my uncle as trustee?"

Eunice shook her head.

"Unless you plan to spend the next two years inside the house," Grandmamma said, emphasizing her speech with another loud thump of her cane, "you will do as your aunt and I advise."

Mary eyed the silver headed stick. What would her grandmother do if she hid it? Still, what they were suggesting was complete insanity. "But I—"

"He's found you everywhere we've tried to hide you, my dear." Eunice stared at Mary, a compassionate look on her face. "Drastic times call for drastic measures."

Mary slowly shook her head. "I don't think I could pretend to be someone else for that long a time."

"But you won't have to pretend." Her aunt beamed. "That is the brilliance of the plan! You can be yourself . . . with a slight change in your last name for the time being."

This—they were impossible. Mary threw her hands up in frustration. "And what, pray tell, am I to do if the gentleman who owns the property discovers my deception? Anyone could find out, then I would be completely ruined and no one would want to marry me."

"Don't you trust me?" Grandmamma raised one brow in the way she always did when she wanted to badger others to her way of thinking.

Mary seriously considered answering in the negative, not that it would help. Grandmamma was a force of her own. Why else would Barham allow her to remain here when she had a perfectly good dower house of her own at Bridgewater?

"Most of the time," Mary answered, drawing the sentence out. Though now wasn't one of them.

"We've been very careful," her grandmother said as calmly as if she were choosing a dinner menu, "to select a remote area where there are no important families."

There was something very wrong about all of this. "May I ask who the owner is?"

Her grandmother waved her hand as if dismissing her question. "The less you know for time being, the safer you'll be if Gawain comes sniffing around."

"Besides"—Eunice's already wide smile broadened—"I'll be with you acting as your companion. It will be such a lark."

Mary stifled a groan. All the cousins had heard about Eunice's larks. She'd been the youngest and wildest of Grandmamma's children, and had apparently not outgrown her previous tendencies. Mary had to find a way out of this harebrained scheme. "Won't your children wonder where you are?"

"Oh, after a while, I suppose." Eunice shrugged lightly. "But they'll think I'm with Mama and probably be happy I'm not around to corrupt their children." She took a sip of wine. "How Roger—the greatest rake in England and on the Continent, before our marriage of course—and I ever managed to produce such dullards, I shall never know."

Those were also tales Mary and her brothers had grown up hearing, at least the ones mild enough to tell children. She never had understood how her aunt had been allowed to wed Uncle Roger. "I think that type of thing skips a generation."

"One can only pray it is not gone forever." Eunice sighed.

"So then." Grandmamma tapped her cane for at least the fourth time. Mary's fingers itched to grab the thing away and throw it in the fireplace. "It's decided. We'll leave early tomorrow morning."

"That soon!" Mary had to stall them. Given just a little more time, she might be able to think of a better scheme. "It seems a little precipitous."

"Better to get it done before you have a chance to change your mind." Eunice rose, smoothing out her skirts. "I must see to my packing."

Mary suppressed her frustration. It was as if she were bashing her head against a stone wall. That actually might be more productive than conversing with her aunt and grandmother.

She considered denying she had agreed to anything. Not that it would matter. The problem was they'd want an alternative, and she couldn't think of another course of action. Yet she wasn't stupid; certainly something would come to her before she and her aunt actually reached wherever they were going and the deception began. If anything went wrong her life would be ruined. If only Grandmamma would see reason.

CHAPTER TWO

Mr. Gawain Tolliver, not even an *honorable* to use in correspondence, stood impatiently in the woods and scowled at the moderate-sized dower house. If life had been fair, his sickly uncle would have succumbed before fathering so many children, including the necessary heir and numerous spares. Who knew he'd had it in him to keep going for so long?

There was certainly no counting on the current Earl of Barham dying young. He'd been blessed with the same rude health as his mother. Not that it mattered. Barham had already fathered two sturdy boys. No, the only way for Gawain to get what he wanted and what was rightfully his, was to somehow wed his cousin Mary. She would be the very devil of a wife, but sixty thousand could make up for an awful lot, and by God, he'd not be cheated out of that. The only other option was to hope she fell in love and married without his father's permission, but he couldn't see her family allowing that to happen. Once he got her alone, all it would take was a few minutes to tie her up, keep her alone with him for a day or two, long enough that even her bloody brother would insist she marry him, and her money would be his. Not that he wanted an unwilling wife, but needs must, and at least consummation wasn't required for the marriage to be legal.

Masking his unhappiness with a smile for Sally Athey, the young maid who'd just arrived from Barham's dower house, he asked, using a gentle tone, "Do you have news for me, sweetheart?"

She fluttered her pale lashes at him. "I might, but if I tell you I could lose my position here."

Gawain brushed the backs of his knuckles gently over her rounded cheek. "Don't you remember my promise, sweet? I told you I'll set you up as soon as I'm married. You'll never have to worry about working again."

At least not on her feet.

"Well in that case . . ."

Thank the devil for gullible women. "Come now, I cannot stay here for long. Someone may discover me . . . and you."

She glanced hastily over her shoulder. "Her ladyship and Lady Mary are going to Bath to-morrow."

Bath! Who goes to Bath this time of year? "Is Lady Eunice going as well?" If he could get rid of Mary's meddling aunt, he'd be half-way there. As old as the dowager was, she couldn't possibly accompany his cousin everywhere.

"I heard her lady's maid say she was going to visit one of her sons in Suffolk."

He took Sally's hand, raising it to his lips. "You've done well, my lovely."

A pretty blush rose in her face. Perhaps he'd keep her as his mistress longer than he'd originally planned. A man needed someone to keep him warm, and it wouldn't be his hellcat of a cousin.

Sally snatched her hand away. "I must go. The housekeeper will miss me." She hiked her skirts and dashed hurriedly toward the house.

Gawain stared after her until she was out of sight, then mounted his horse and rode to the small lane not far from the dower house where his groom waited. "Whitely, let's go back to the tavern. The old lady and my cousin are departing for Bath."

"When do ye want to leave?"

"In the morning after breakfast. We're paid up with board until then." When they arrived at the inn, Gawain handed his reins to a stable boy, went into the common room and ordered an ale.

It wouldn't be hard to find his cousin in Bath. They were bound to register at the assembly rooms. He'd bide his time until Mary and the dowager arrived. After all, he still had almost a year to secure her as his wife. When he did, he'd never have to worry about money again.

Sally slowed as she reached a side door leading from the small formal garden into the back hall.

Mrs. Collard, the housekeeper, motioned her inside. "Well, Athey, was he there?"

Being called Athey, just as if she were someone important, was only one of the reasons Sally liked working at the dower house. "Yes, ma'am. I pretended to be interested in him, just like the other times, and told him her ladyship was going to Bath, just like you asked me to do."

"You didn't give him the tale too easily?"

She shook her head. "No, ma'am. I made him repeat all the promises." She wiped her hand on her pinafore. "He kissed my hand and got it wet."

Mrs. Collard harrumphed. "You're lucky he didn't try to kiss anything else." She narrowed her eyes. "He didn't, did he?"

"No, ma'am. I would never have allowed that. Not to mention his lips look flabby. It's no wonder Lady Mary don't wish to marry him."

"Bad business this is," Mrs. Collard said in a fierce tone. "Come along now. You must pack. Her ladyship said you could go to Bath with her and begin your training."

Sally almost couldn't speak. *Bath!* She'd never in her life been more than five miles from Market Harborough. Now she was to be taught how to be a lady's maid too, and all for helping poor Lady Mary escape that nasty Mr. Tolliver, which Sally would have done for nothing. "Yes, ma'am. I'll be ready!"

After dinner, Mary, her grandmother, and her aunt repaired to the drawing room for tea.

"There you are," Eunice proclaimed, handing Mary a cup.

It was time to beard the lion, take the bull by its horns, and any number of other things.

"Just how is it you know about this house you wish me to go to?" Mary asked.

Grandmamma sipped her drink, which look suspiciously like brandy. "The current steward of the estate is cousin to the"—she paused for a moment—"Bridgewater steward. I had a discussion with him during my twice yearly visit."

Mary had the distinct impression that her grandmother wasn't being truthful. "Go on."

"It seems the man's cousin has been in poor health and could use some help."

"I am to act as the estate manager then?"

"No." Grandmamma pounded that infernal cane on the floor.

"You are to act as its mistress. This is the perfect solution to all of your troubles."

Her scheme had all the makings of a disaster.

After a restless night planning and rejecting ideas to stop her grandmother, Mary awoke to blackbirds bickering outside her window. Sitting up, she watched as the lady bird threw out the bit of moss her husband tried to place in the nest. It did not appear as if he was having any more luck in his task than she was having in hers. She hoped the poor male bird would win at least one argument. Before too long, the sounds of Mathers in the dressing room reminded Mary she must rise.

A few minutes later, slowly drinking the tea that had been placed on her night table, as if she could delay the inevitable, she continued to cast around for an alternative arrangement to the one proposed by her grandmother and aunt. Yet nothing came to her. If only she had some other place or person to go to where she'd be safe. Unfortunately all her friends were in Town for the Season, and it wasn't fair to burden them with her presence for a year, not to mention placing them in possible danger as well.

Mathers walked in from the dressing room. "I'll send for your wash water. I have just been informed that Her Grace wishes to depart within the hour. We will travel with her until she thinks it's safe for us to go north."

Flopping back against her pillows, Mary groaned. "Bring me some toast and an egg as well, please. Once she starts a trip, she doesn't like to stop."

"I'll ask Cook to make a basket." The maid turned to go, then stopped. "For all of us."

The twelfth of September 1816
My dear Lucinda,
Our plan has finally been set in motion. I sent E and M north to-day. They should arrive in no more than four or five days. With any luck at all, by this time next year our two dear grandchildren will be wed.
Yr faithful friend,
C.
Dowager Duchess of Bridgewater

The fifteenth of September 1816
My dear Constance,
I received your missive yesterday and immediately sent
a rider north with instructions and the additional staff you
sent. All shall be ready.
   Your dear friend,
   L.
Dowager Viscountess Featherton

Four days after bidding a tearful adieu to her grandmother and sneaking out of the inn they'd stayed in the previous night, Mary sat next to Aunt Eunice in her well-sprung yet nondescript traveling coach as they entered the bustling market town of Rosebury, Northumberland.

"See how lovely it is," Eunice enthused as they passed well kept buildings adorned with window boxes of summer flowers.

"Charming." Two days ago, Mary had given up arguing. The only thing she wanted now was to get out of this coach and go for a walk. She had never traveled so quickly in all her life.

Eunice, having learned the art of rapid travel from her mother, had stopped only to change horses, for which they never seemed to have to wait. Every day they had been in the coach until almost dark and rose with the dawn. Only the mail journeyed faster. "How much farther is Rose Hill?"

"Only a mile or so beyond the town to the east. Oh, look"—Eunice pointed as they traveled over a stone bridge—"there is the River Coquet."

Perhaps Mary could still get out of this ridiculous charade. Pretend they were stranded due to a lame horse. Beg shelter for the night and leave early in the morning. Even if she could persuade Aunt Eunice to agree, where would she go?

"Now remember, my dear, walk in with your head held high as if you belong there."

"I don't suppose Grandmamma could have merely leased a house for a year."

Eunice turned from the view out the window and peered closely at Mary. "Leasing might have left a trail. The fewer people who know about this the better. Trust Mama and me. This will all work out for the best."

Much too soon the coach turned off the lane leading from Rosebury onto a rutted gravel drive. They bounced and jolted so hard that it was amazing their teeth didn't chip. After being almost tossed off the seat, Mary grabbed hold of the carriage strap and held fast for at least ten minutes before they came to a stop before a lovely early Georgian manor. The house was built of sandstone. Columns and a portico graced the entrance. Roses scurried up the walls, almost obscuring some of the windows. The house was definitely in need of a mistress. A stately older man in a black suit stepped out, followed by two footmen who looked suspiciously familiar.

"Was this place fully staffed before?" Mary asked.

For the first time her aunt fidgeted, twisting the fringe on her shawl around her fingers. "Er, I'm not *quite* sure what arrangements were in place."

Mary pressed her lips together. "I could swear I've seen those footmen before."

"Well you see," Eunice made a fluttering motion with her hand as if to send the question away, "Mama handled the specifics."

Naturally. "I hope she remembered to hire some of the locals, or they will not be happy."

"There, you see, Mary?" Her aunt gave a sunny smile. "That is just what Mama meant when she said you would know how to go on. *I* would never have thought of hiring the local people." She patted Mary's hand. "You will do very well here."

Mary heaved a resigned sigh.

The coach door opened. One of the footmen lowered the steps then assisted her and her aunt to the ground.

The older man stepped forward and bowed. "My lady. Welcome home. Your lady's maid has already arrived, and Rose Hill awaits your inspection. I am your butler, Simons."

The rest of the staff lined up by rank. She scrutinized them, but they gave no indication they knew her. How in the world had Grandmamma arranged all of this in such a short time? Simons escorted her down the row of servants, making the introductions as Mary memorized each name and asked a question or two about their lives.

Finally the housekeeper, Mrs. Enderson, a short plump woman

with a ready smile whom Mary guessed to be in her early fifties, showed Mary to her rooms. "You'll find a small parlor through the door to the left. The dressing room is on the right. Attached to that is a bathing chamber. I'll send tea up while your bath is being made ready." The woman's smile grew larger. "My lady, may I say how happy we are to have you here? It is a shame Mr. Featherton has been held up in Town."

Featherton? The only Feathertons she knew were . . . No, surely not. Grandmamma had said the person was of no consequence. England must be littered with Feathertons who were no relation to *those* Feathertons. And who had written the senior staff? It might behoove her to discover exactly what had been said. The difficulty was that in asking she might give herself away.

Mary gave herself an inner shake, smiled politely and pitched her voice in a manner that would suppress any more questions about Mr. Featherton, whoever he was. "Yes, a pity."

Mrs. Enderson bobbed a curtsey and left.

Mary removed her bonnet and placed it on the dressing table. She'd hated using that tone with the housekeeper, who only meant well. Yet it would not do to have any of them questioning her so-called marriage. She would make it up to the woman later.

Much better to let them think she'd had a falling-out with the man whom she was pretending to have wed.

Mary shielded her eyes against the sun's reflection as she gazed up at the front of the manor house. The days were already shortening, and they'd had their first frost. Not surprising as they had barely had a summer at all. Soon the Harvest Festival would be upon them.

When she'd arrived at Rose Hill, her first tasks had been to order every single window washed and the climbing roses cut back. After that, she and the steward, Mr. Stuttart, had gone over the accounts, debating various ways to raise the estate's income. She had also hired more servants. Locals this time.

Grandmamma had been right. There was a great deal of work to do here. Shortly after arriving, Mary had vowed to do everything she could to earn her keep. Maybe then she wouldn't feel so guilty for the ruse, and if she really were Rose Hill's mistress, she would ensure the estate was in good repair. Aside from that, behaving in any other fashion might cause unwanted speculation. Mary sincerely hoped Mr. Featherton who owned Rose Hill never found out about her deception, or if he did, she would be long gone, and untraceable.

Thinking of one Mr. Featherton caused her to remember Mr. Kit Featherton. Mary sat back on her heels. Although they had never been properly introduced, during her one full Season, she had dubbed him Mr. Perfect. Perfectly dressed, perfectly mannered, a perfect dancer, and perfectly able to ignore her. The only time he had come close to her was when they happened to come together during the course of a minuet or a country dance. She sighed. Every time his gloved hand had touched hers, she'd felt a tingling sensation. He had caught her gaze, holding it as if he wished to spend more time with her. Yet he never did. He was the only gentleman she had wanted to dance attendance on her who did not. Of course, he had no need of her dowry, nor did he care that she had been the Incomparable of the Season.

Turning back to the matter at hand, Mary was less sanguine about Eunice's idea to attend church and be on friendly terms with the neighbors. Yet she was right. It would have appeared odd for them to remain in seclusion and it would have caused talk. Instead they became part of the community. Mary found it odd that after the first introductions, no one had asked about Mr. Featherton, not even the staff. On the other hand, having her aunt with her as a companion was as strong a sign as she could give that her husband was not expected to begin living at Rose Hill anytime soon.

Leaning heavily on his cane, Mr. Stuttart hobbled out the front door and directed his attention up. "It does look much better, my lady."

She studied him quickly. Poor Mr. Stuttart had had one illness or injury after another. He appeared to be doing better now. She followed his gaze. Once the roses had been cut back, the house and roof had been cleaned. Mary smiled. "Yes, it does. It is amazing how a little work can yield such an improvement."

"Speaking of yields, I have the numbers from the apple and pear sales. That idea you had to get all the local farmers together made quite a difference."

It had been the practice of her father's to combine produce from the local farms, marketing it as a whole. There was much less chance of anyone being undercut that way. Rose Hill had been barely self-supporting, and she hoped to increase the earnings per acre so that much-needed repairs on the estate could start being made before a roof fell in, or a family suffered because the estate could not afford renovations to its tenants' houses.

If the worst were to occur, and she was found out, Mary could point to the improvements she'd made.

CHAPTER THREE

Mid-March, 1817, Featherton House, London

K it sat behind the desk of his study in his father's house on South Audley Street. He'd always found it easier to meet with his man of business here than in his own rooms. That worthy, Mr. Baxter, now sat across from Kit.

Baxter rubbed his nose. "I can't account for the difference, sir."

Kit glanced at the column of numbers concerning a minor property he had owned for several years, but had not visited since his first and only inspection. Despite last year's bad weather, the small estate had shown an increase in profits at harvest time, and now there had been more income from an unexpected source. "Whose idea was it to plant winter rye?"

"It would have to have been Mr. Stuttart's."

Kit wondered what had got into the steward that after so many years he was making drastic changes to the property. The stimulus in the estate's revenues had allowed improvements to be made to the house and tenants' cottages. "You said that Stuttart wouldn't allow his wages to be raised?"

"No, sir. He said the extra was better spent on the estate and village."

This was all extremely strange. Kit had never known estate managers to be particularly philanthropic. It was almost as if the man had become a new person. Kit shrugged. "Very well, let me know if he changes his mind."

Baxter placed his hands on the chair arms. "I will. If you've no further questions right now . . ."

"You're free to go."

"Thank you, sir."

Leaning back in his chair, Kit tried to form an image of Rose Hill and could not. Perhaps he'd been remiss in not visiting the property, though he had given the steward a great deal of latitude in handling the affairs. This was the first time there had been a surplus. Well, as the man had written, pouring it back into the estate was probably the best idea. After all, Kit certainly didn't need the blunt.

He should make a point of planning a visit sometime in June after the Season wound down. He was tempted to go now. Unfortunately he'd promised his parents he'd start looking for a wife this year.

An image of laughing gray eyes floated through his mind.

Last year, Kit had been to every entertainment in both the main and Little Seasons and had not seen her. His inquiries about Barham produced the information that he was not coming to Town unless his vote was needed in the Lords.

Perhaps he should write to Barham, but God only knew how Mary's brother would take that, and Kit did not wish to approach the issue of Lady Mary in a letter. He could have stopped in at Barham's estate, but had not done that either.

Kit should have danced with her when she'd come out, yet how could he have known back then that years later she'd still be the only woman he was truly interested in, and she had always been surrounded by her court, never seeming to notice him. Nevertheless, he should have approached her or searched for her before now.

The devil.

Kit pitched his pen across the room. Why was he dithering? Even if Lady Mary was taken, surely he could find someone he could bear to look at over the breakfast table day in and day out. Year in and year out. All he required was a female who didn't twitter and could hold a conversation about something other than the weather.

He shuddered at the thought of marrying any of the young ladies he'd met over the past year. They'd bore him to death within a month. Probably a week. He almost wished his mother was the type who would make a list of eligible ladies, but she had married for love and expected her children to do so as well.

Damnation. He'd just have to put his mind to it. Someone was bound to come along. Or perhaps he should find an excuse to visit Barham.

A knock sounded at the door. "Come."

Marcus, Earl of Evesham, strolled in, a wicked grin on his face. Something was up. "Have you heard the news?" Kit waved his friend to a chair in front of his desk, then handed him a glass of wine. "What news?"

"Serena delivered a girl."

Kit spit his mouthful of wine back in the glass. Before Robert Beaumont had married the former Lady Serena Weir, he had been the most notorious rake in London. Now he would have a daughter to protect from men such as he was. "You're joking me?"

"Not at all. Phoebe received word to-day."

Kit gave a bark of laughter. "Cabined, cribbed, and confined. It serves him right. She'll run him ragged."

"Serena writes that the baby already has him wrapped around her fingers." Marcus chuckled. "And he's preparing to talk to Angelo about teaching her to use a short sword."

"I'd love to see Angelo's face when he receives that request." In fact, Kit would make a point of it. They could sell tickets.

If anything, Marcus's grin broadened. "They'll be in Town in a few weeks, and Phoebe is planning a small get together. Wively and his bride will be there as well."

Life for all of them was changing, and Kit was beginning to feel left out. He was the last of his Oxford friends who was unmarried. By the end of the year, he'd be the only one without a child. He'd have to decide on a bride soon.

Rose Hill, Rosebury

Mary laid down her pen and rubbed the bridge of her nose. Finally all the accounts were in order. She stood, arched her back.

Just as she reached for the bell-pull, a knock came on the door to the office, and Simons entered with a tea tray. "You've been cooped up here for so long, my lady, Mrs. Enderson thought you might like some tea."

"Indeed I would." Mary smiled. Since the first day, the servants had treated her as if she'd been their mistress for years. They'd wanted and needed direction, which unfortunately did nothing to ease the guilt she felt in living here. "In fact, I've just finished for the day. How is Mr. Stuttart doing?"

"Much better, my lady. The plaster you had Cook make seemed to do the trick."

The poor man had fallen ill with a series of lung complaints lasting all winter. Finally Mary had dug into the books her great-grandmother had kept on household remedies and come up with something that seemed to be working. "Please ask Lady Eunice to join me."

Simons bowed and left, closing the door behind him. A few minutes later, Eunice entered the room. "You wanted to see me?"

"Yes. As soon as Mr. Stuttart is able to work again, we should make plans to leave. The upcoming Season will be all the explanation we need."

Eunice sat, poured a cup of tea and handed it to Mary. "Are you sure you wish to go to Town this year?"

Mary sank into a large leather chair. "No, but I think I have been here long enough, and I have a feeling I should move on, before we are found out, or Gawain finds me."

Eunice stared out the window for a few moments with her brow furrowed before responding, "I see your point, but the fact remains that you are safe here."

Tears threatened to clog Mary's throat. She couldn't wait much longer. All her friends were married and having babies. If she didn't wed soon, the chance to have a family of her own might be lost to her. "Don't you see, Aunt Eunice? I want to marry. It is as if life is passing me by. If I can find someone to marry, once I am betrothed, the court will have to act. My uncle cannot arbitrarily withhold his consent."

"You could allow Mama to make a match for you."

"No. I want to fall in love. You had the opportunity to wed the one you loved, as did my mother and brother. I just want the same chance." Surely there was a man who could love her for herself and not her dowry or her face. Someone kind, who would love and cherish her and their children.

"Yes. I see your point." Eunice took a sip of tea. "I shall write to Mama."

Mary put her cup down. "I'm going into Rosebury. Would you like to come with me?"

Her aunt nodded distractedly, as if she had something important on her mind. "Shall we walk?"

What could Eunice be thinking of? Her late husband? Perhaps, Mary thought, she should not have mentioned him. "Unless you'd rather take the gig?"

"Not at all." Eunice rose quickly. "Give me a moment to change my shoes and I'll meet you in the hall."

After Eunice left, Mary called for her hat, cloak, and gloves. A brisk walk would do them both some good.

A half hour later they reached the edge of the market town. Mary waved at one of the ladies strolling on the other side of the street. If it weren't for her deception, she would have been happy to call Rose Hill and Rosebury home. The town was lovely and the people welcoming. This had also been the first time in two years that she'd been free from her cousin's harassment. Being able to walk and ride without fear of being abducted by Gawain had been a blessing. Still, she was sure he would eventually find her as he always had before.

A carriage carrying the squire's wife, Lady Brownly, her eldest daughter, Diana, and another lady, whom Mary was unable to see clearly, pulled alongside her and Eunice.

Lady Brownly smiled warmly. "If we had known you were also coming to Rosebury, I would have been happy to fetch you."

Mary returned the smile. The lady and her daughter had been the first ones to welcome her to the area. "Thank you, but it has been a while since I've had a good walk, and I needed it."

"My lady, I must tell you my news!" Diana Brownly practically bounced on the seat as she spoke. "My godmamma—actually she is Mama's godmother, but she seems like mine—is sponsoring me for a London Season."

"Not if you act like a jack-in-the-box I won't." The caustic voice belonged to the unseen lady.

Diana immediately settled down, but none of the joy left her face.

Mary laughed. "She is right. You must not act like a hoyden in Town."

Before she could be introduced to the other lady in the carriage, the rector of the local church, Mr. Doust, strolled up to them and said, "My ladies." He bowed. "Lady Eunice, may I ask your opinions on a pressing matter?"

Eunice glanced over at him. When she answered, her tone was light and somehow joyful. "We would be delighted, Mr. Doust." She turned to Lady Brownly. "I am very sorry, but I must excuse myself. Please, come for tea before you leave for London."

"I'm afraid it will just be me." Lady Brownly glanced fondly at her daughter. "Diana departs tomorrow. There is a veritable orgy of shopping in which she must partake before the Season begins."

"Then we shall have a comfortable coze," Mary responded as her aunt spoke with the rector. It was probably better that way. Thus far, she had been extremely fortunate that no one had questioned her living here, and that no one in the area actually knew Mr. Featherton.

The Brownlys' coach moved on, and when Mary glanced at Eunice she saw that her aunt had a cat-in-the-cream expression on her face. Could she be interested in Mr. Doust? Admittedly, he was quite good looking, but for the life of her, Mary could not see her fun-loving aunt as a clergyman's wife.

Still, it was very sweet and made her yearn to look at some gentleman that way and have him return her gaze. Not even all the aggravation her cousin had caused her could make her cease to wish to be courted by a man she loved. In fact, it made her more determined than ever to pick her own husband. She would not allow Gawain to destroy her life.

Eunice and the rector disappeared into the church, and Mary ambled around the small garden. When all this business with Gawain had begun, she would never have imagined that her kind, scholarly uncle would have insisted she wed his son. Not only that, but he wouldn't even speak to her brother about the matter. All communication was done via letters and through solicitors. Something about this whole thing did not make sense. If only she could figure out what it was.

After an early dinner, Almeria, Lady Bellamny, sat in the drawing room of the Brownlys' modest manor house. Thank the Lord that rector had interrupted before introductions had to be made. Mary would surely have recognized her name immediately and possibly panicked. She was almost surprised the girl hadn't recognized her voice, although she had tried to disguise it by lowering it a bit. Still, she should have cried off the trip to the town. It had been a stupid risk.

Almeria took the cup her goddaughter Phillice handed her. "Tell me, my dear, who is Lady Mary?"

"Why, she is Mr. Featherton's wife to be sure. Perhaps I should not talk of it, but . . ."

Ah yes, where there was good gossip there was always a "but." Almeria waited for Phillice to overcome her scruples.

"I believe there is some sort of estrangement. He has never been here, or at least not for many years and certainly not since her arrival. Thank goodness she has her aunt to keep her company. In any event, I do not remember meeting him, though I suppose Sir Howard might have. I must say, I do not think much of a man who would abandon his wife in such a manner, although Lady Mary is too well-bred to mention it. One would think she didn't care, except that the few times Mr. Featherton's name has been mentioned she quickly changes the subject, and once I thought I saw her flinch."

Almeria stirred three lumps of sugar into her tea. On orders of her doctor, a most superior man, she'd been on a reducing diet. Still, one must have sugar in one's tea. "How does Lady Mary get on here?"

Phillice's expression perked up. "Very well. Indeed, I do not know what we did before she arrived. We all love her. She has done so much for Rose Hill and the town. I do not know how she managed it, but she is paying for the roof of the church to be repaired and replaced. If her husband does appear, he'll find it necessary to prove himself."

Almeria nodded. "Excellent. Perhaps I shall put a flea in Mr. Featherton's ear. He really should not leave his wife alone."

Her goddaughter frowned. "We would not wish to lose her, or cause her any trouble."

Almeria raised her brows in an expression of surprise. "Of course not. I would never do anything to harm the poor lady."

After she'd ascertained that Diana was packed and ready to leave early the next day, Almeria repaired to the writing desk in her chamber.

The seventeenth day of March, 1817, Brownly Manor, Northumberland

My dear Constance,

I am happy to be able to inform you that M is doing well and beloved by all in the area. I depart in the morning but shall have this letter sent by messenger, so that it will arrive before I do. Soon it will be time to put the rest

*of our little scheme in play. It is a shame young people
need so much help these days.*
   *All has been quiet here. and M appears to be safe.
Have you heard anything of the ogre?*
      Your dearest friend,
      A. Bellamny

Bridgewater House, London

Constance Bridgewater and her dear friend Lucinda, Dowager Viscountess Featherton, were sipping tea in Constance's parlor when a knock came at the door.

"Your Grace." The footman bowed. "This came for you by messenger."

Constance flashed a grin at her friend as she took the proffered message. "Thank you."

Once the young man left, she broke the seal off the letter.

Lucinda moved to the edge of her chair. "Is it from Almeria?"

"Yes." Constance read the letter out loud, then handed it to her friend. "I knew Mary would carry it off."

"Yes indeed." Lucinda glanced up. "This is excellent news. *Have* you heard anything about the ogre?"

"No." Constance shook her head slowly. "I spent most of the autumn and winter leading Gawain Tolliver a merry chase. Eunice's children have reported seeing a strange man around who answers Gawain's description."

"How are they taking Eunice's absence?"

"Most of them think she is with me. Even if they don't, they may be dull, but they are not at all stupid. They know Mary has been persecuted by that cousin of hers and something is afoot. Eunice has had her correspondence sent to her solicitor, who forwarded them on." Constance sat back in the chair. "Have you told your son yet?"

"In a roundabout way. Well," Lucinda gave a sly smile, "truthfully, not everything. In fact, none of the details. I merely said I was looking for a good match for Kit. Although Featherton is in agreement that Kit must marry, and soon, he is fond enough of me to allow my folly, as he calls it." Lucinda took a sip of tea and sighed. "My poor daughter-in-law would not be at all happy if she knew we were arranging a match. She would be extremely angry if she knew the details. I believe she is better left in the dark for the time being."

"I take it she still doesn't know the part you played in her marriage?" Constance chuckled. "I understand. I don't think Barham has figured out that I arranged his nuptials. Fortunately he didn't ask why I needed a few of his larger footmen in addition to mine. Ha! They all want to make their own love matches these days, but they will see. We old women know what we are about. An arranged marriage with love is the best option of all."

Once again a knock sounded at the door. "Another letter for you, Your Grace."

Constance took it. "From Eunice." She perused the contents. "Mary plans to come to Town to husband hunt. Eunice will stall her as long as possible, but we need to send Kit up there sooner rather than later."

"I agree." Lucinda bit into a small cake. "I cannot wait until Kit and Mary realize they are just the thing for each other. I do think this is the best match we've planned so far."

"Indeed, my dear. After all these years, finally our two houses will be connected by more than friendship." Constance smiled to herself. "As soon as Almeria returns, we'll spring the trap."

CHAPTER FOUR

K it stood motionless as his valet, Piggott, adjusted the back of his jacket. Easter had come and gone, and the Season was in full swing. Kit barely had a moment to himself these days, and still not one likely marriage prospect in sight, nor had he seen hide nor hair of Lady Mary despite diligently searching Polite Society's entertainments without arousing unwanted interests. He heaved a sigh.

"Busy day, sir?" Piggott asked.

"Not as bad as some. I'll take luncheon at my club, after which I am promised to my grandmother. She's expressed a desire to be driven in my new curricle."

"The dowager, sir? In your curricle?"

The corner of Kit's mouth twitched in an attempt to curve into a smile. He was certain Piggott's jaw would have dropped, were such a display not beneath any valet of quality. "Don't sound so scandalized. She's not a day over seventy. Been full of fun and gig her whole life."

"Yes, sir. So I've heard."

Kit cracked a laugh. "M'father swears he's the only man he knows who got gray hair from his mother instead of his children." He grew suddenly tired of Piggott's fussing. "Finish up. I must be on my way. I don't wish to be late for my engagement. After I see my grandmother, I'll be at Dunwood House, then I have two balls to attend this evening. One is Lady Bellamny's."

"Everything shall be ready, sir." Piggott handed Kit his gloves, hat and cane.

Kit opened the door into the corridor to find one of his father's younger footmen getting ready to knock.

"If you please, sir, his lordship requests you attend him immediately."

How odd. He'd seen his father just the other day. Kit frowned. "Has anything happened to one of my brothers or sisters?" The lad shook his head. "Don't think so. I was told only to come and get you." "Yes, sir." The footman dashed down the stairs and out the front door. "I wonder what could be the matter." He glanced over his shoulder. "Piggott, send a message round to Lord Evesham telling him I'll be a bit late."

A quarter hour later, Kit entered his father's study. A decanter of brandy and a half-full glass sat before Papa on the desk. Kit had never known his father to drink this early in the day. At least not brandy. Something must be terribly amiss. "What's wrong?"

Papa ran a hand down his face. "You might want to sit, my boy."

If this had something to do with him, Kit thought he would rather not. "I believe I'll stand."

His father took a sip, then leaned back in his large, dark leather chair. The exact same position Papa had taken the few times Kit had ever been in trouble. His father cleared his throat. "I realize you have been reluctant to marry. One might say you've been avoiding choosing a bride. Is there a particular reason you have been so hesitant?"

Other than not having seen Lady Mary, the only woman with whom he could consider living the rest of his life, for a long time, no reason at all. It occurred to Kit that he'd never realized how important his marrying was to his father. Perhaps he should have been more assiduous about finding a mate. He would do so this Season.

He shrugged lightly. "Why?"

After taking another sip of the brandy, his father stared at him. "I want you to tell the truth. I do understand youthful indiscretions. We went through more than a few with Crispin. Too many of them, to be honest. You have not caused anywhere near the worry he did. In fact, your behavior has been exemplary, and I promise neither your mother nor I will be upset. We'll find a way to make the best of it."

Make the best of what? Why was Papa bringing up his dead brother? Unlike Crispin, whose behavior had been nothing short of scandalous, Kit had made a point of never courting any type of scandal at all. He would never willingly put his parents through that sort of anguish again. "Sir, I think you'd better just tell me what it is you're talking about, because I haven't the least idea."

"Kit, are you already married?"

His breath stopped as if one of Jackson's punches had landed square in the middle of his stomach. Hell and damnation. *"Married! What the deuce gave you that idea?"*

His father poured brandy into a second glass, pushing it across the desk to him. "You'd better have some of this."

Kit took a sip, then set the tumbler down. This was no time to have his brain muddled. That would come later when, for only the second time in his life, he would drink himself into a stupor. "Where did you get the idea I had wed?"

"Lady Bellamny was in Northumberland to fetch her goddaughter's daughter, whom she is sponsoring for the Season. While she was there—"

The hairs on the back of Kit's neck prickled. "Where in Northumberland?"

"Rosebury."

Rose Hill.

His father raised a brow. "May I continue? This will go much more quickly if you allow me to tell you what I know, and then ask questions."

A flush crept up Kit's cheeks. "Yes, sir. I'm sorry I interrupted."

"As I was saying . . ." Papa took another drink. "When Lady Bellamny was there, she met a female calling herself Lady Mary Featherton who is residing at Rose Hill. That's the property you inherited from your great-aunt, is it not?"

"Yes, sir." That told him nothing. Mary must be the most common name in England, if it was indeed her real first name, which it probably was not. That the impostor had used the name of the woman he wished to wed made him want to strangle her. A dull ache began in Kit's jaw and he unclenched his teeth.

"Have you been up there recently?"

"No, but that will change." *Immediately.* "When did you speak with Lady B?"

"I did not. She told your grandmother, who was typically cryptic when she spoke to me, after which your mother did a very good job gleaning all the pertinent facts from Lady B. I, therefore, felt no need to approach her." Papa took a sip of brandy. "I take it the lady is not, in truth, your wife?"

"Is she a lady?"

"From what I was told, there is no doubt."

Who the devil could she be? Kit couldn't think of any *lady* who would engage in such an outrageous stunt, and he certainly didn't want to think of the scandal this would cause if it got out. Particularly now that his sister appeared to have decided on a suitor at long last. "How do we contain the news until I can meet with the woman and discern what game she is playing at?"

"I've been assured Lady Bellamny will not mention it to anyone." All well and good, but what about the girl she was sponsoring? Young ladies were known to blurt out almost anything going through their heads. What if he were introduced to the young lady that evening? Or someone mentioned him and she happened to mention the person at Rose Hill? Beads of sweat broke out on his forehead as he imagined the scandal. He pushed aside the brandy and stood. "If you'll excuse me, I shall make arrangements to leave on the morrow at the latest, though I shall try to cancel my engagements for the next few weeks and depart this afternoon."

His father nodded. "You may take my new traveling coach and use the horses I have posted along the Great North Road."

He bowed. "Thank you. I'll have Piggott send word when the trunks are ready."

"Oh," Papa said. "Before I forget, your grandmother cried off from her ride with you this afternoon."

Now that was a surprise. Kit couldn't keep his eyes from narrowing a bit. "Did she give a reason?"

"I believe she knew you'd want to depart as soon as possible, and Lady B requires assistance in rigging out the young lady."

Relief swept through him, and he grinned. "Ah, yes, shopping over a carriage ride. Tell her it would be my great pleasure to tool her around when I return."

"Kit."

He focused on his father's grim countenance.

"Let me know if you need assistance."

"I will. Thank you."

He strode out of his father's office and house. How the hell could a woman just move in and pretend to be his wife? Well, she wouldn't be there for long.

Seething with anger, Kit clenched his fists as he left Featherton House and made his way to Brooks's, where he was meeting Marcus, Rutherford, and Huntley for luncheon. The footman led Kit to their usual table tucked into the far corner of the dining room, where their conversation was unlikely to be overheard.

Marcus glanced at Kit and waved him to a chair. "I ordered for you. I take it something is amiss?"

Kit pressed his lips together for a moment, trying to decide how much to tell his friends. "You could say that." He sat back as the waiter poured a glass of claret for him and refreshed the other men's glasses. Once the servant left, Kit said, "It appears I've picked up a wife without my knowledge."

Raised brows and silence answered him.

Rutherford took out his quizzing glass. "Indeed?"

Kit relayed the story, then said, "I'm off as soon as may be."

"Would you like me to give Phoebe your regrets?" Marcus asked.

"No, of course not. I want to meet W03Wively's bride, and would not miss seeing Beaumont and Serena's baby. Will Phoebe mind if I don't stay long?"

"Give me leave to tell her what has happened and she'll have your trip planned for you before your man can pack."

Low chuckles went around the table. Phoebe Evesham was a formidable lady, and a good friend. She'd never met her match, though, until Marcus had returned. Still he'd had his work cut out for him. Kit didn't ever want to have to work as hard to convince a lady to marry him as his friend had. All of his friends, it seemed, had spent an inordinate amount of time courting the ladies who were now their wives. Although they'd grown up together, Rutherford had had a devil of a time convincing Anna to wed him. Kit shuddered when he thought of what Huntley had gone through to make his forced marriage to Caro work. Kit wanted only to fall in love and wed without all the attendant drama.

Beefsteaks arrived for the table, and they spent the next hour or so discussing what they'd been doing during the winter and their plans for this Season. When they'd finished, Kit made his excuses. "I'll see you shortly."

He strode north on St. James Street, then turned right onto Jermyn Street. His rooms were in the center of the block. Taking the stairs two at a time he bellowed, "Piggott, get packed, we're leaving."

Wiping his hands on a cloth, Piggott stepped from Kit's bedchamber into the main room. "For how long, where are we going, and when do we depart?"

"About three weeks, perhaps more. Northumberland. It's going to take a week to get there. You will leave as soon as you've packed my father's traveling coach. I must stop by Dunwood House first. I'll find you on the road. I'm taking the curricle."

Piggott's jaw dropped. "All that way, sir?"

"Damned if I'll be cooped up in a coach for a week. No one would be able to bear me, not even myself."

"May I inquire as to the rush?"

"I'll tell you later. At present, I must cry off from all my engagements. Pack me a bag with what I'll need if we get separated, including my buckskin breeches. No need to wear Town togs while traveling."

Sitting at his writing table, Kit removed his gloves. Well, at least this got him out of Town and freed him from bride hunting. Guilt attempted to take hold, and he shook it off. Who the devil would have the unmitigated presumptuousness to pose as his wife? If she were not an actual lady—and it was difficult to imagine a member of the aristocracy behaving in such a way—she must be awfully talented to fool Lady Bellamny, and no matter what her background, the woman would have to be a bold piece. The sooner he got on his way, the sooner he would have the answers to his questions. Perhaps he would run down Lady B and try to pry more information out of her. On second thought, that would involve her more than he wished. She was trying enough. He certainly did not want her meddling in his affairs. Despite what he'd said to his mother, Kit did not wish anyone matchmaking on his behalf, nor did he want to run the risk of meeting the young lady residing with her.

He wanted to punch something or someone. It was a shame he did not have the time to go to Jackson's. He could not believe a lady was masquerading as his wife—only an experienced charlatan would be able to pull off a deception like that. Not to mention that no lady would demean herself so, and take such a risk with her reputation. Whoever she was, she wouldn't be there for much longer.

As he sealed the last missive, the clock chimed three. Piggott had departed at least half an hour ago. Kit would be another hour leaving London, but they'd travel until it was almost dark.

His groom, Dent, knocked on the door and entered. "All's ready, sir."

Kit picked up the notes and his bag, and followed the groom out to the street, where his curricle was waiting. After leaving the messages with his father's butler, he drove to Dunwood House in Grosvenor's

Square, where the Eveshams lived during the Season. Dent jumped off as Kit drew the horses to a halt before climbing down. "I won't be long."

As soon as he entered the house, he could hear voices and laughter, high and low, coming from the back.

"My lord." Wilson, the Dunwood butler, bowed. Kit was shown to a large, noisy drawing room filled with parents and children. Who would have thought his friends would be so prolific?

Phoebe took him by the arm, leading him into chaos. "Kit, I'm so glad you were able to come. Marcus told me you must be on your way soon."

"Yes, forgive me, but it is unavoidable."

She smiled. "It's no matter. If you need anything, send a message. Come and I'll introduce you to Eugénie Wively, and you must see Serena and Robert's little girl. She is adorable."

Kit hadn't realized how tense he was until the thought of Beaumont with a daughter made him want to laugh again. Eugénie, Lady Wively, turned out to be a stunning young French woman who obviously had Wively wrapped around her slender fingers. Kit had never thought to see his friend so besotted.

Little Miss Elizabeth Beaumont gazed at him with serious green eyes, but it looked as if she'd have her mother's auburn hair. She grabbed onto the finger he gave her. "It is my pleasure to meet you, Miss Beaumont." Turning to Serena, he smiled. "She is as beautiful as her mother. I predict she'll run Robert ragged."

Serena gave a peal of laughter. "She already is. I pity the man who falls in love with her."

He kissed Elizabeth's brow. A longing for a family of his own suddenly surged up inside him. As soon as he got rid of the doxy living at Rose Hill, he'd make a point of forgetting about Lady Mary and find a woman with whom he could share his life and raise a family.

Mary pushed back the wide-brimmed straw hat she wore for gardening, stripping off her gloves before taking the glass of lemonade from Simons. "I think it's coming along."

"Indeed it is, my lady. I haven't seen the garden look so good in a great many years."

Daniels, the gruff, wiry old head gardener, leaned on a shovel.

"Won't see all of what her la'yship has done 'til summer and next year, but she's got some talent, she has."

The warmth rising in her cheeks stopped as she realized she wouldn't be here to enjoy the fruits of her efforts. If only she could return here after her Season. Glancing up at the sky, she supposed it to be close to five o'clock. Past time she should be dressing for dinner. She finished the glass, handing it back to Simons. "Daniels, I think we had a good day."

"Yes, my lady. We're just about finished for now."

If only it were simply for now. This would be one of her last days in the garden. Keeping a pleasant expression pasted on her face, she made her way up the back stairs. The closer it came to the time she must leave, the more she wanted to remain. Would Mr. Featherton sell the property to her? Once her birthday had passed, she could well afford it. Yet that didn't answer the question of her name. He certainly would not allow her to continue to masquerade as his wife.

Hot tears pricked her lids. Taking a handkerchief out of her pocket, she dabbed at the corners of her eyes. There was no reason to become maudlin now. She would go to London and have her Season. She would meet a gentleman to wed. Then she would have a home she could make her own.

"Were you rolling around in the mud?" Mathers stood at the dressing room door, hands on her hips.

Mary gave a watery chuckle. "You might think so. I did remember to wear my gloves. And I have left my shoes by the garden door."

"Well, that's something. I'll get the shoes later. Come along now and get that dirt off you."

Soon Mary sank into the warm water of her bath. She hated having to deceive the servants, dependents, and all the local people. Unfortunately, there was nothing she could do about it. She gave herself a shake. Looking to the future would be more productive than moping and wishing things were different.

That evening at dinner Mary took a bite of the soup, new pea with just a hint of mint. The freshness practically burst in her mouth. "Give Cook my compliments, Simons."

The knowledge that once she left she would never see Rose Hill again had dogged her all day, and it hit her particularly hard at that moment. The soup turned to ash in her mouth, but she forced herself to eat it and a few bites of each remaining course as she smiled and did her best to act as if everything was all right.

After tea had been served in the drawing room, Eunice took Mary's hand. "Try not to be so down in the mouth, my dear. You must trust all will be well."

Mary blinked back her tears but couldn't stop her voice from wavering. "Yes, I must continue to believe that." She set her cup down and rose. "While there is still enough light, let me show you what I've done with the garden."

Once outside, Eunice linked her arm with Mary's as they strolled on the new gravel paths. "It looks wonderful."

"Yes. I'm very proud of it." Mary's throat closed painfully. "We planted over fifty new rose bushes. I've always wanted a rose garden." She wiped the moisture from her face. She would not cry. "I don't want to leave."

"I know, dear." Eunice touched her head to Mary's. "Neither do I, but we must look at the bright side. You have not been chased or harassed since we've been here, and you've improved the property beyond all measure. No one could possibly complain about your residing here for the year."

Except that it had been based on deception. If she wasn't to become a watering-pot, it behooved her to think of something else to discuss. "How is the new roof for the church progressing?"

Eunice grinned. "According to Mr. Doust, extremely well. It will be finished before summer."

Mary slanted a glance at her aunt. She had not asked about a possible understanding Eunice might have with the rector before now. "And you and Mr. Doust?"

"No matter how I feel about him, I'm afraid it cannot be." Eunice heaved a sigh. "The dear rector would be scandalized by our ruse. Even I cannot come up with a story he would accept. No, I'm afraid I must think of him as a lovely flirtation." Her lips twisted into a wry smile. "Until we began to make friends here, I did not understand your concerns."

It was a little late for remorse now. Mary repeated Eunice's words back to her. "Everything will work out for the best."

It had to.

CHAPTER FIVE

K it and his small group of servants had stayed the night in
Alnwick and got a late start in the morning. It would not do to
arrive at Rose Hill too early. After luncheon should be time enough.

God knew he didn't want to spend any more time than was necessary under the same roof with the female pretending to be his wife.
He'd had a great deal of time over the past week to plan how he would
arrive. In the end, he decided to do so in as impressive a way as possible. That ought to convey to the woman that he was serious about re-
covering his property. All his life he had worked hard to avoid scandal,
and he refused to have one touch him or his family now. He would
give no quarter. If she would not willingly pack her bags and leave by
morning, he'd help her out the door.

He glanced at his pocket watch again. For the past half hour he
had been waiting on the outskirts of Rosebury for Piggott to catch up
with him. Finally he spied a carriage being led by his father's coachman. Of all the bad luck. The wheeler had gone lame. At least it wasn't
one of his father's horses. Since they'd left York, he'd been on his own
for cattle. He'd have to get the poor animal looked after. He hoped
that Rosebury would have a decent hostelry. He would be damned if
Dent had to lead the carriage all the way to Rose Hill.

"Sorry, sir," Robins, the coachman, said as he approached. "He
threw a shoe. Shouldn't be too bad once we get it fixed."

"There's nothing you could have done to prevent it, but time is of
the essence. We'll have to find a replacement."

After they made their slow way to the center of the town, Kit located the blacksmith, while Dent went off to ask about a stable where
he could board the horse and hire another.

Kit stepped into the large stone smithy, peering through the dim light until he located a figure. "Good day. I have a horse that's thrown a shoe. Can you help me?"

A large, middle-aged man with coal-black hair materialized from the dark interior. "Aye, gimme time t'finish here." He retreated back into the darkness, and the next sound was the sizzle of hot iron being put in water. "Passin' through?"

"Here on business. Name's Featherton."

The smith stopped what he was doing and turned. "Be ye the Featherton what owns Rose Hill?"

Kit smiled. "I am."

The other man scowled. "See here, ya not plannin' on causin' trouble for our Lady Mary, are ya?"

Good God, what had that blasted female been doing? He wondered if Mary was even her real name. "Not at all. I'm just making sure she is doing well."

Not exactly a lie.

"We don't hold wi' wife beatin' here aboots."

"Why would I want to . . . ? No, of course not. I don't know who would. Can't a man visit his wife?"

Why the hell had he said that? He should not have given credence to her lie.

"Took yer sweet time," the smith said in an only slightly less belligerent tone.

Kit opened his mouth to respond in kind, then thought better of it. He had no wish to continue this conversation. "When you've finished, my groom will be outside."

What the devil had he walked into? Had that fraud been slandering him? He paced impatiently as he waited for the man to appear.

Five minutes later Dent ambled toward Kit with a sour look on his face.

"No horses?" Kit asked.

"Nah, he's got a horse. Interestin' thing, though. He asked what your plans with your wife are. Last I heered, you ain't got one."

Irritation flared through Kit. He wanted to shout out loud that he did not have a wife, but he had the distinct impression that if he renounced her, word would travel and the entire town would rise up against him. Unless, that was, Dent had already let the cat out of the bag. "You didn't tell him that, did you?"

"Nah, said my master don't talk about his private doings to me."

Dent speared Kit with the same glare the groom had turned on him when, as a child, he'd attempted to jump his pony over too high a wall. "Ye goin' to tell me what's goin' on?"

Kit could barely stop himself from spearing his fingers through his hair. "Yes, but not here. Do you know the way to the house?"

"My memory ain't failed me yet. I remember the road."

"Then tell me we have a wheeler."

"Aye, we got one, and he'll see the other gets shod. Gimme a minute and I'll tell the smithy."

"Good." One problem was settled. The sooner he got his conversation with his impostor of a wife over with, the better. "Let's go."

As Kit was about ready to climb into his curricle, a gentleman who looked to be in his late forties approached.

"Good day to you, sir," the stranger said.

Kit put his foot back on the ground. "A good day to *you*. May I help you?"

The man had a pleasant smile on his face, but it didn't reach his eyes. "I'm Mr. Doust, the rector. I understand you are Mr. Featherton of Rose Hill."

Doust. That name sounded familiar. Nevertheless, Kit did not want or like the interference. He inclined his head. "I am, sir, and I am anxious to reach my home. It has been a long journey."

"I was just on my way there. I shall do myself the honor of showing you the way."

The hell he would. "I'm sure I can find it without assistance."

"No problem at all." A young boy brought over a mare. "You see? My horse is already saddled. I'll not delay you at all." The rector put his foot in the stirrup. "We are very protective of our ladies at Rose Hill. Lady Eunice and Lady Mary, your wife"—the man paused as if waiting for Kit's response, then nodded—"have done a great deal for the town and your dependents. I don't believe the estate has ever been in better shape."

"Have they indeed?" *Two females?* There were *two* of them? No matter. They had probably done nothing more than knit scarves for the poor. "I'm sure the credit is due to my steward, Mr. Stuttart."

Which was deuced odd as it was.

Doust raised one brow. "I would have thought you knew that Mr. Stuttart has been ill since last summer. In fact, if it weren't for Lady Mary, he would probably have died. He is only now on the mend."

"Indeed." How else could Kit respond? Whatever the devil had been going on at Rose Hill, he'd better get to the bottom of it. "Let us be on our way."

He climbed into his curricle, while the rector mounted his horse. A deuced fine one at that. Doust, horses. Damn, that was the Earl of Marnly's family name. No wonder the rector had a sweet goer. The family bred some of the best horseflesh in the kingdom.

Ten minutes later, they turned off the main road and onto a well-maintained drive. The windows of the old sandstone house sparkled in the sun. Roses in pink and red climbed in an orderly fashion up the building. Kit noticed that the high stone wall at the entrance was in good condition, as well. He had to admit that the adventuress had maintained the property well, but if she thought to continue passing herself off as his wife, that was another matter entirely.

The front door opened as he came to a stop. Even the knocker gleamed. He tried not to clench his jaw as the rector came up beside him, a moment later, as they climbed the shallow stairs.

A servant—the butler, he assumed—bowed. "Good afternoon, Mr. Doust. The ladies are in the morning room. May I ask the name of your friend?"

Doust slid a look at Kit.

This got worse and worse all the time, Kit thought chagrined. His own servants didn't even recognize him. Why the devil had he waited so long to come here? He was beginning to feel as if *he* was the wrongdoer. "I am Mr. Featherton. You must be Simons."

The merest flicker of distaste passed over the butler's face. "Indeed, sir. I shall escort you to the ladies straight away."

As they followed the butler down a long corridor, Kit couldn't help noticing that the carpets were clean and in good repair, the woodwork gleamed, and the wall sconces sparkled. The walls appeared recently painted, as well.

Simons opened a door, and bowed as Kit and Doust entered the room.

"Lady Eunice and Lady Mary," the rector said, "how are you doing this afternoon?"

The older woman rose. "We are quite well, Mr. Doust." When her gaze lit on Kit, a line appeared between her brows, then disappeared. She smiled as if she'd been expecting him. "Mr. Featherton, how good of you to bring our dear friend with you."

A younger woman standing in front of the French windows started, then stared at him with the same silver eyes that had haunted his dreams. Her golden hair was dressed in a simple knot, loose curls framed her oval face, and her countenance had changed from a friendly smile to a mask of fear.

What, by all that was holy, was Lady Mary Tolliver doing pretending to be his wife?

Of all the females in England, she was the last one he expected to see at Rose Hill. Something was vastly wrong with this situation, and he had many more questions than answers. Prime among his concerns was why in the bloody hell she was here in the first place. Almost no one outside of his family even knew he owned this property. A rage he'd never experienced before rose within him. What a fool he had been, spending the past couple of years mooning over a fraud. Had she planned to trap him into marriage?

Keeping his eyes fixed on her, he set a pleasant smile on his face and strode toward her. When he was no more than a foot away, he took her hands, raising one then the other to his lips and placing lingering kisses on each palm. Damn the butler for having left the door open and Doust for being there at all. There was nothing for it but to play his part. "Aren't you happy to see your husband, my dear?" Lowering his voice so that only she could hear, he added, "And are you prepared for the consequences?"

Mary took in Mr. Featherton's broad shoulders, his fashionably styled chestnut-brown hair and piercing blue eyes. The most beautiful eyes she'd ever seen.

Of all the gentlemen who could have appeared, why did it have to be Mr. Perfect? If only she hadn't talked herself out of what she knew in her heart to be true.

Featherton. The one man who had completely ignored her during her only full Season, and here she was posing as his wife. A person of no importance, her foot! What had her grandmother been thinking?

The humiliation of that first Season came flooding back. That no one else knew about it mattered not at all. She knew that he'd danced with almost every young lady except her. She'd even saved dances, hoping he would ask her, but he'd never claimed them, forcing her to make excuses about needing a flounce mended in the ladies' retiring room, or being too warm and requiring a glass of lemonade.

How could she have been so wrong? More than once he'd been

heading straight in her direction, and each time she could have sworn he was finally going to request to stand up with her, but he'd always veered away at the last moment to ask another girl to take the floor or to speak with some gentleman. She must be the last lady he wanted to see at Rose Hill. It didn't matter. He had never cared about *her*, and she did not want *him*.

Still, she could barely breathe. It was a miracle she was not lying in a dead faint. His tone was soft, but menace and heat lurked in his voice.

She focused on his words. *Husband?* She drew a shallow breath. *Consequences?* Oh, Lord. What would happen to her now?

Remember your breeding.

She tried to smile, forcing the corners of her lips up. "Yes, of course. If only you had given me some notice, I would have been prepared."

His body blocked Eunice and Doust from seeing her reaction. Try as she might to remain calm, Mary could not stop herself from trembling. Fear of what Mr. Featherton might do to her warred with anger at her grandmother. Grandmamma must have known whose house this was. Mary raised her chin. If she wouldn't let Gawain trap her into marriage, she would not allow her grandmother to, either.

Yet perhaps Grandmamma wasn't aware Mr. Perfect was here. After all, he *should* be in London letting the *ton* fawn all over him, not at Rose Hill threatening her.

She slid a quick look at him. This was a scandal waiting to happen. Being caught by him ended her hope that no one would ever find out what she had done. Still, there had to be some way out of this situation. Surely Mr. Perfect didn't wish to be trapped into marriage with her, a woman he couldn't even bear to dance with, on the other hand, he was quite capable of ruining her.

He glanced over his shoulder and addressed the others. "If you could leave us alone for a while?"

"I shall show Mr. Doust out, but I shall not be far. You have only to call if you need me," Eunice said, casting a meaningful look at Mary.

Every nerve in Mary wanted to scream, *No! Don't leave me with him*, yet that would cause a scene, something she must not do if she were to escape this mess with her reputation intact. She must remain composed. Giving in to the vapors would not help. Now that he was no longer looking at her she found herself able to take a deeper breath. Unfortunately, that turned out to be a mistake, as she caught his scent. No perfume at all, just pure male musk and leather. His buttery-yellow buckskin breeches were cut to show off his muscular thighs. No padding there. No wonder women vied for his attention.

"Mr. Doust, if you would tell Simons we might want tea, or perhaps something stronger," Mr. Featherton said.

The words were phrased as a suggestion, but the tone made them a command. Oh Lord, what had she got herself into, all because she had given in to her grandmother?

He slid his arm possessively around her shoulders, and led her to the small sofa in the center of the room. "Sit here and breathe. You must not faint, it would give a bad impression." He grinned wryly, although the humor did not touch his eyes. "Even worse than the one the townspeople and servants already have of me. Are you responsible for that, or was it merely my absence?"

He was furious, but her heart was thudding so hard that she could not even respond. After the first few weeks at Rose Hill, she'd not thought about what would occur if the rightful owner appeared. She'd felt safe for the first time in years. Oh Lord. They were properly in the suds now.

"The property looks to be in much better skin than when last I saw it." His voice was hard, but at least he wasn't shouting. "I understand I have you to thank for the improvement."

Hardly surprising, considering it had been years since he'd visited. She opened her mouth, intending to tell him just that, but he continued.

"No need to speak now. My arrival must be quite a shock. Once tea is served, we'll discuss why you are here."

Fortunately Simons arrived quickly. He placed the tea tray on the low table in front of the sofa and gave Mr. Featherton a look, then turned to Mary. "My lady, please call out or ring if you require anything else."

"Thank you, Simons, I shall." Her voice resembled a croak, but at least she had produced words.

Once Simons left and closed the door behind him, Mary started to pick up the pot, but her hands shook so badly that she sloshed tea from the spout. She stopped and took a breath.

"Here"—Mr. Featherton took the pot from her hands—"allow me."

He was being surprisingly kind, considering how angry he was.

"Milk or cream?" he asked.

"Simons will have brought milk."

The corners of Mr. Featherton's well-shaped lips rose. "Sugar?"

"Yes. Two, please."

Now that she was sure he wasn't about to rail at her—at least not immediately—she allowed herself to study his features. His wavy hair was cut in the latest style, reminding her a bit of Byron, though his shoulders were much broader than the poet's. Mr. Featherton dressed in the mode of a country gentleman, though it was clear no tailor less talented than the famous Weston had made his clothing. Beneath a fine layer of dust, she could see her reflection in the high gloss on his boots.

"There now." He glanced up. His blue eyes caught her gaze. "Here is your tea, my lady."

"Thank you." Her hands still quivered a little, but the tension had begun to ease. She took a sip. She had to get control of this conversation. "I assure you I have said nothing about you to either the townspeople or the servants. I—I would not have slandered you. In fact, I did not truly know it was your property."

"Indeed?"

Unable to look at Mr. Featherton, Mary smoothed her skirts. "You must wish to know how this deception came about."

"That *is* what brought me here," he said in a dry tone.

She flinched. "Yes, of course."

Really, she told herself, she was acting like a fool. "This was my worst fear. Grandmamma and Aunt Eunice said it wouldn't happen, but it did, and I knew it would." Mary straightened her shoulders. "I am sorry. My aunt and I shall leave in the morning, or as soon after as may be."

He took a sip of tea, then placed his cup on the table. "I do not think that is the best strategy. Your immediate removal would cause unwanted talk. I would like to know how you came to be living here. After all, you do not resemble the typical adventuress."

He was taking it all so coolly that Mary relaxed even more. She surprised herself when a gurgle of laughter escaped. "Is there such a thing?"

He smiled, showing perfect white teeth. "A good question. I don't believe I've had the pleasure of meeting such a woman."

Given his straitlaced reputation, that wasn't startling. She took another sip of tea. "I said they should have leased a property, but my aunt said that would leave a trail."

He went still and stared at her, and there was an almost dangerous edge in his voice as he asked, "And just who are you so afraid of that your safest option was to masquerade as my wife?"

CHAPTER SIX

Mary knew that Mr. Featherton deserved to know the truth, and there was no point in hiding it now that she'd been discovered. "My cousin, Gawain Tolliver." She took a breath. "Since my mourning for my father ended, I have been moving from family member to family member hiding from him. His father, my uncle, is my trustee." Mr. Perfect—if she kept thinking of him by that name, she was going to slip and end up blurting it out—Mr. Featherton listened patiently while she tried to tell the story in a logical fashion. "That is how I ended up at Rose Hill."

He was quiet for several moments, his brows drawn together in thought. "Your cousin has not found you here, has he?"

"No." She heaved a sigh. "The months I've been here are the first time in years that I've felt safe from him. Being at Rose Hill has been like heaven." She smiled, remembering all she had done. "I was able to try new ideas for the estate and refurbish the formal garden."

Kit set down his cup. His anger rapidly drained as he considered Mary's plight. Now that he could see *her*, the only thing he could think was that Lady Mary had a beautiful smile and he was happy to finally see it aimed in his direction. In a rueful tone, he said, "Then I had to come and ruin everything."

Her gaze flew to him. "No, no, no, please don't say that. Even if I have enjoyed Rose Hill, this plan was folly, and I must leave soon in any event. I need to find a husband or Gawain will still attempt to . . ." Her face turned a lovely shade of pink.

Deuced strange that her father's brother had been chosen as trustee. If the matter had ever been taken to court there would have been no problem having the man replaced. "I thought you couldn't marry without your uncle's permission?"

She straightened her shoulders. "Once I am five and twenty, I will control my own fortune and may marry whomever I choose, and it will not be Gawain." Then she frowned. "Unfortunately, that will not be for another year."

No, but Kit was not so green that he didn't know very well that she must wed *him* or see her reputation ruined beyond repair. Her presence at Rose Hill could not be kept a secret forever, particularly with Lady Bellamny's goddaughter knowing. "It seems to me that if you met the right gentleman, he would not care about your money."

She picked up her cup and drained it. "Be that as it may, I shall not give up what is mine."

He couldn't disagree with her, nor would he try. "What happens if you marry without permission?"

Lady Mary pressed her pretty lips together. "My fortune goes to my uncle."

A lesser woman might have given up long ago and married as her uncle wished. Of course, this explained why he hadn't seen her for such a long time. He had always admired her beauty, now he respected her resolve and valiant nature. How odd that the Dowager Duchess of Bridgewater had chosen his estate, though it did meet all the requirements, being far from London and the prying eyes of the *ton*. Even stranger was Lady B's involvement. If she had not told his grandmother, Lady Mary could have left here and he'd never have known. However, the most important part of what she'd said had to do with marriage. . . . "Do you have a gentleman in mind?"

Her shoulders drooped. "No. I thought my grandmother would make up a list of suitable candidates, and perhaps my friends would help."

He opened his mouth, then closed it again. What he should do was demand she marry him. That, after all, would settle everyone's problems. This whole scheme would cause a scandal for them both. In fact, under the circumstances it was inevitable. And since her heart was not engaged elsewhere, he need not worry that he would be breaking it. Still, something told him that she was not in the right frame of mind for a proposal, no matter how practical. The problem was, he couldn't think of another way out of this mess than for them to wed. It appeared fate had neatly penned them in. Not that he minded all that much, given that he had been searching for her for years. But a nagging voice kept telling him it would behoove him to spend time getting to know her first.

"I saw how well the house looked from the front; would you show me the changes you've made to the rest of the property? We could start with the gardens."

A line creased her forehead. "Are you sure you would not rather rest after your long journey?"

Kit grinned and lifted her hand to his lips again. "I'm not at all tired, and I am rather interested to see what you've accomplished."

"If you insist." She allowed him to place her hand on his arm. "We can go out this way. I just replanted the garden this spring. . . ."

Lady Mary began detailing the repairs and changes she'd made. She certainly knew what she was doing, and appeared to be a sensible woman. Before long she would realize she had no choice but to marry him. It might not be a love match, yet she was not in love with anyone else, and he had not been able to get her off his mind. Kit could see them as a contented married couple. Perhaps in time they would grow to love each other. It would save him the bother of courting. The more he considered it, the better he liked the notion.

He lost himself in the music of her voice. Daffodils, hyacinths and other spring bulbs were making an appearance. Lilacs in bloom lined the garden on one side. New plants seemed to be everywhere. He took out his quizzing glass. Roses. Dozens of them, underplanted with lavender and probably other herbs. He wondered if she had added lamb's ears, as well. As a child, they had been his favorite. If not, he would suggest it. The property was much more pleasant than he'd remembered.

"I should have planted in autumn, but the design hadn't come to me then." She furrowed her brow, as if rethinking her decision. "Daniels assures me they'll be fine."

Kit remembered the name from the list of servants. Though there appeared to be many more than he was paying for. "Where did the footmen come from?"

"Grandmamma arranged for them. I hired more maids. Eunice and I share the cost."

He appreciated her frugality on his behalf, but it was not as though he couldn't easily bear the expense himself. "I think the estate can afford them."

Lady Mary shook her head firmly. "No, it would not be right. You should only have to pay for the staff necessary to keep Rose Hill running, not for the cost of my aunt and me being here." She paced along beside him, then stopped. "In fact, as soon as I come into my inheritance, I shall pay the past rent on the house. It is only fair."

Damn it all. He didn't want payment for her being here. "In that case, I shall pay you for the improvements you've made and for acting as steward, which will, no doubt, equal the rent, or"—he paused—"possibly more."

Placing her hands on her hips, she faced him squarely. "Now you are being silly."

He met her gaze and raised his brows. "No sillier than you. After having only servants living in it for so many years, I cannot imagine the estate was in the excellent condition I find it in now."

"No, it wasn't." She pulled on her bottom lip with her teeth, and Kit had trouble tearing his gaze from her mouth. "Very well, we'll call it an even trade."

"I agree." He took her hand, returning it to his arm as they strolled through the rest of the tour. He listened with part of his mind as she prattled engagingly about the garden and the changes to the estate, while with the rest he applied himself to the problem of her masquerade.

Kit was quite sure Lady Mary had been truthful with him, yet there was something else going on. Something of which she might not be aware, and there were the cousin and uncle to deal with as well. Her grandmother seemed to be the lynchpin of everything that had happened. Once he had all the pieces of the puzzle he would solve it, of that he had no doubt. He grinned. Even if they had to come up with a story regarding when they had married and why they had been so private, at least the problem of whom he would wed was resolved. All that was left was to convince Lady Mary that he was a good bargain as a husband.

Bridgewater House, Mayfair, London

"Are you sure it was him, Your Grace?" Constance's dresser, Anderson, asked as she stood beside a window in the first floor parlor, hidden from view by the drapes.

"Almost positive. A shame there are so many people in Berkeley Square. It makes it easier for blackguards to hide." Constance stared at the window from a safe distance. She did not dare look out again herself. If Gawain Tolliver saw her, he would realize that she knew he was watching the house. "Get that young maid. Athey, isn't it? She can recognize the scoundrel. By the way, how is she doing?"

"Picking up her duties quite well." Anderson pulled the braided bell pull three times. "I have her cleaning one of your carriage gowns. She'll be a skilled dresser in no time."

Not long afterward Miss Athey entered the room and curtseyed.

"Yes, Your Grace?"

"Find something to do around the window facing onto the square and tell me if you see Mr. Tolliver."

Miss Athey took a cloth from her pocket and pretended to clean the window. "Yes, Your Grace. That's him, all right. I'd recognize him anywhere."

"Well, drat the man. I can't lead him to Lady Mary." Despite Lucinda's faith in her grandson, it wouldn't do to have Gawain ruining any courting that may be going on. "I'll have to think of something else."

A knock at the door interrupted her.

When Miss Athey opened the door, the Bridgewater butler was there. "Your Grace, the Dowager Viscountess Featherton is waiting for you in the morning room."

"Just in time. Perhaps she will have an idea." Constance rose and picked up her cane. Getting old was the very devil. "You may help me down the stairs."

He held out his arm. "Yes, Your Grace."

When she entered the morning room, Lucinda was standing at the door to the garden. She turned. "Lovely this time of year."

"I agree. My granddaughter did an excellent job when she was here a couple of years ago. Come sit. We have a problem."

After Constance told her friend about Tolliver's presence, Lucinda asked, "Isn't Mary in correspondence with Lady Evesham and Lady Huntley?"

"She is. They have been friends for years."

"In that case," Lucinda said, grinning, "I have just the thing, and Kit won't even know he's been tricked. I am quite sure the ladies would be happy to help. I was at Catherine Beaumont's house the other day when her grandson and his wife brought the baby to visit. Such a beautiful little girl. They will be leaving Town in the next day or so. As I understand it, the Eveshams and Huntleys plan to accompany them. I believe there is some talk of going to Edinburgh. One of Huntley's aunts lives there."

There was no doubt both couples were discreet enough, and the gentlemen were friends of Kit's. In addition, in the event Mary balked, Lady Evesham and Lady Huntley were more than capable of convincing her that she must wed Kit. Constance walked to the writing table. "I'll ask the ladies to attend me immediately. Not only will they be able to help ensure that everything goes well, they can stay to witness Kit and Mary's marriage vows."

Eunice ambled toward the wood, her hand tucked in the crook of Mr. Doust's arm. Once she'd seen the look of recognition on Mr. Featherton's face when he saw her niece, she had been fairly certain all would be well. Mama and old Lady Featherton had been right when they said he had a tendre for Mary. Be that as it may, it wouldn't hurt to keep the rector near in the event of a problem. Besides, Eunice wanted to spend more time with him. Soon he'd be nothing more than a pleasant memory. Well, perhaps more than merely pleasant, but a memory nonetheless.

She'd not been as drawn to a man since Roger, and she didn't know why Mr. Doust interested her so. He was not much above average height, nowhere near as tall as her husband had been, or as flamboyant. On the other hand, she herself was short, so a man need not be tall to appeal to her. His eyes were a clear brown. Much like a horse's. He was stocky but had not run to fat, and he moved with a grace she would not have expected. At the local assembly in January, they had danced, and if he had tried to kiss her, she would have let him. If not for Mary and the May game they were playing . . . Eunice sighed. If, if, if. None of it mattered. She recited the story she had decided to tell him. "We will leave for Town as soon as my mother arrives."

His brow furrowed. "When will that be?"

"I'm not sure. Next week or soon thereafter. Before my niece's birthday."

"And what of Mr. Featherton?"

Drat. She kicked a stone. This was what came of allowing her mind to wander.

Before she could think of an answer, Mr. Doust said, "It is clear Lady Mary was not expecting Mr. Featherton, nor was she . . . best pleased to see him." The rector stopped, turning her toward him. "Lady Eunice, I hope we have become friends. If you tell me what is going on, I might be able to help."

Eunice repressed a groan. Should she reveal the secret and watch as Mr. Doust lost all respect for her? Yet when he gazed at her with those steady brown eyes, she felt herself wanting to confide in him.

"You do realize," he said quietly, "that even if I were prone to gossip, my vows prohibit me from doing so."

A smile tugged one corner of her mouth. She could not imagine anyone less disposed to tittle-tattle than the rector. She took a breath. "Very well, but you must promise not to say a word until I'm finished."

He led her to a wooden bench and waited for her to sit before he did, then he took her hand and held it. "I promise."

A light shiver ran through her. Why did it feel as if he were offering more than concern for a friend? "After Mary's father died, only a year after her mother, and the mourning period was up, her brother Barham and his wife removed to Town for the Season. Mary resided with them. Mama and I thought nothing of their cousin Gawain Tolliver being around, until he began pressing his attentions on Mary. Barham warned him off, but that just made Tolliver more devious about following her. Then one evening, during some entertainment or other, as she was returning from the ladies' retiring room, he tried to trap her. Fortunately she was able to get away, but he didn't stop his attempts to compromise her. Barham wrote to his uncle, Tolliver's father, and complained, but he received no reply. Soon it got to the point where Tolliver was popping up wherever Mary went, and . . ." Once she'd finished the story, Eunice waited as Mr. Doust sat quietly for a few moments.

"Why Mr. Featherton?"

"His grandmother, one of my mother's bosom friends, was sure he'd had an interest in Mary, and Mama thought that during Mary's first Season she had noticed him more than the other gentlemen. To hear Mama and the Dowager Lady Featherton talk, it is past time he was wed. Even his father, who has been very tolerant about his unmarried state, has begun pushing for him to find a wife. That was when his grandmother, Mama, and Lady Bellamny hatched their plan." Eunice glanced at Mr. Doust, but his countenance showed nothing but polite interest. "I must admit, I agreed with them. Mr. Featherton is a much better choice than Mr. Tolliver, who is a fish-faced cur who only wants Mary's money. Mama is a dab hand at arranging matches. Still, after being here, I do wish there had been another way. I did not appreciate how close to courting scandal this would be."

"How did you become so involved?"

She shrugged one shoulder. "I generally travel to visit my children and grandchildren, and cannot be pinned to one place. As I was the least likely to be missed, I agreed to remain with Mary."

Mr. Doust grinned, shaking his head slowly. "A conspiracy of old ladies—other than you, of course. I've often thought women should be given more to occupy their time. We gentlemen ignore a great deal of talent by not recognizing their skills."

Eunice couldn't believe he wasn't upset; in fact, she was stunned. "How can you think this situation is funny?"

He sobered immediately. "I don't. I do, however, admire you ladies. And if the young man is so inclined, this could all work out quite well."

She pressed her lips together. "You are as bad as Mama and her friends."

"Oh no." Then he did laugh. "Just an old war horse. I've seen far stranger things than this."

What did he mean by war . . . "You were in the military?"

He smiled. "Yes, as a chaplain. I was army mad, but my father insisted I go into the church. In the end, I managed to satisfy both his requirements and my desires. Once Napoleon was exiled at Elba in '14, I was offered a position with the Bishop of London, but I was not only sick of war but of politics. I asked for someplace quiet and was sent here. Despite being a market town, the living here is a pittance. They were having trouble filling the position. I accepted it as the money didn't matter to me. I have a comfortable independence."

Eunice had wondered at his seeming freedom to act in all matters. This explained quite a lot. "How nice it must be not to have to answer to anyone."

"It is, rather."

Rising, she placed her hand on Mr. Doust's arm. She felt good about telling him the truth and was ecstatic he had taken it so well. "Despite my mother's machinations, Mary has been insisting she'll have a full Season and be allowed to fall in love. That will create a problem."

"I don't see any way around a marriage with Mr. Featherton," Mr. Doust said, then was quiet for a moment, frowning. "Surely she'll see she's been outmaneuvered?"

"So one would think; however, Mary can be stubborn, inventive and, in many ways, naïve. Quite frankly, I do not expect her to simply fall in with Mama's scheme." Eunice glanced at the sky. She had been away longer than she had planned. "It is time for me to check on her and Mr. Featherton, and change for dinner."

Mr. Doust twined her arm with his, drawing her close. "Invite me, and I'll try to discover his intent."

She gazed up at him. "You would assist in this conspiracy?"

His eyes warmed. "My lady, I would have thought that by now you'd have realized there is very little I would not do for you and those who matter to you."

"Oh my." Warmth rose in her face. How long had it been since she'd blushed? "You have me acting like a girl again, and I must tell you, my salad days are long past."

He raised her fingers to his lips, kissing them one by one. "I think you are the perfect age. I would be honored if you will call me Brian, and may I call you Eunice?"

This was more than she had expected and everything she had wished for. Pulling his head down to her, she pressed her lips to his. He moved slowly, gently at first; then she touched her tongue to the seam of his lips and he opened his mouth to receive her. Frissons of pleasure shot through her as he tilted his head, deepening the kiss. She threw her arms around him, pressing her breasts to his chest. Who would have thought a rector could kiss like this?

Their tongues tangled and caressed. He tightened his arms around her. Oh, God. How could she have lived so long alone?

CHAPTER SEVEN

When Brian finally lifted his head, breaking the kiss, their breathing was ragged. He'd waited months to do that. He pushed a loose strand of hair away from Eunice's lovely face. She and her niece looked very much alike, with their golden hair and gray eyes. Eunice's complexion was still clear, but small lines had appeared around her eyes. Her figure wasn't that of a younger woman. It was mature and soft in all the right places, which suited him just fine. As soon as she was free of her responsibilities to her niece, he'd ask her to marry him. "Eunice, I have enough wealth to command some of the elegancies of life, including residing in Town for the Season, if that is important to you. Please tell me I may court you."

"I thought that is what we *were* doing," she replied in a slightly breathy tone.

She linked her arm with his. "I would like that extremely, Brian."

He had cleared that hurdle easily enough. Now he needed to know what Featherton was thinking. The sooner Lady Mary was settled, the sooner Eunice and he could be married. "I'll escort you back to the house before I return to the rectory to change."

As they retraced their way, Brian saw the young couple, though he supposed they wouldn't appreciate being called that, in another section of the garden. "They appear to be getting along fairly well."

"No doubt she told Mr. Featherton everything."

Brian lifted a brow.

"That is Mary's way. She is honest to a fault." Eunice smiled. "She wouldn't lie even to avoid a thrashing."

"She must have been very uncomfortable here, forced to deceive everyone around her."

Eunice nodded. "At first, yes. Then, because the steward was so ill, she took over the estate management and has been much happier for being employed."

"And what about you? Do you have a house? Do you want one?"

She had a contemplative look on her face. "I have the dower house, but rarely reside there. As I said, most of the time I travel to visit my family and friends. At first it was an adventure, being able to go where I wished, whenever I wished it, yet since I've been here, I have realized how nice it is to wake up and always know where I am."

They reached the shallow stairs to the stone terrace at the back of the house. He said, "I've had my eye on a place on the outskirts of Rosebury. The home is an easy walk to the church. It does not compare to Rose Hill, but neither is it a small cottage."

She gazed up, studying his face. "Perhaps we should take a look one day."

"I'd like that." He raised her hands to his lips. "I shall be back in time for dinner."

Brian's horse was quickly saddled, and he was on his way back to the small rectory. Now that he knew she had feelings for him, he was surprised at his eagerness to see Eunice again.

Mary left Mr. Featherton in the study where she kept the estate books. He had asked to see them, and there was no reason why he shouldn't. They were his, after all. She could not believe how well he had behaved. Would he remain here after she left? There was still a possible problem with Diana Brownly, but Mary would take Diana into her confidence and ask her to swear never to reveal the secret. The girl would probably think it was romantic. As for Gawain, Mary would hire armed footmen and never go anywhere alone.

She opened the door to her chamber and found Mathers frowning. "What is wrong?"

Mathers pointed to the door leading to the next room. "They are staying in there."

Mary shook her head. "Who?"

"Mr. Featherton and his man."

Mary stared at the solid carved oak door separating her room from the next. She had completely forgotten that the master's chamber was next to hers. Why had she not realized that the servants would of course put him next to his "wife"? She needed to come up with a reason to put him in the other wing or any place other than adjacent to her? "He must move."

Mathers shook her head. "Not unless you want to cause talk."

"But . . . but I cannot." A roar started in Mary's ears. "We are not married."

Nor would they be. Not unless he went back to London and paid court to her. Despite how pleasant he'd been this afternoon, after he'd slighted her that Season, she was not inclined to simply fall into his arms.

Her maid crossed her arms over her chest. "It's a shame Her Grace, your grandmother, is never around when her plans go to Hades."

Especially this time. "Are you sure the door goes directly into his bedchamber?"

Mathers shrugged. "To be honest, I haven't looked. The only time I saw the room I went in through the door to the corridor, but your dressing room is on the other side, so I assume his is, as well."

"Find out to-morrow." Mary couldn't keep her eyes off the door. It was almost as if she expected him to walk through it at any moment. "I'll keep it locked."

"Only at night. I'll make sure it's unlocked by the time the maids get up here."

She'd completely forgotten about that part of Mr. Featherton's being here. Who would believe she was still chaste? Everyone would . . . will think they were acting as a married couple. Well, perhaps not. After all, she'd not spoken one word about him since she arrived. Still, his visit was going to cause a goodly amount of speculation, not only here but in Rosebury and the surrounding area.

She removed her hat and threw it on the bed. Oh, why couldn't Lady Bellamny have waited another week or so to tell his father? Then Mary would have been gone, and where was Grandmamma? The Season had already begun. She should have been here by now.

Mary refused to have all her dreams destroyed. She would not be forced to marry anyone. What was she to do?

"Here, my lady. Let's get you cleaned up and dressed for dinner. There's nothing we can do about him being so close now."

"You're right." She looked away from the door. *Except leave as soon as possible.*

After she had washed, she donned a turquoise silk evening gown trimmed with ivory lace. A year old, but it was still in good condition. She wondered if her London modiste had completed her order for this year yet. Mathers threaded ribbon in the same color blue as the gown through her hair.

Mary clasped a single strand of pearls around her neck, then added the matching earrings. "The salmon and ivory shawl, I think." She stood as her maid draped the shawl over her shoulders. "Perfect. I'm going to my aunt so that we can walk down together."

Eunice would be able to help her figure out the problem with Mr. Featherton.

Mary had taken no more than five steps down the corridor to her aunt's room when the door to the bathing chamber opened, and out stepped Mr. Featherton. Though he wore a colorful silk banyan, he'd not fastened it all the way up, and a goodly portion of his chest stared her in the face. Dark curly hair dusted the part of him on display. He must not have been completely dry, as the fabric clung to his broad shoulders and hugged the rest of his body.

Mary's mouth dried. *Oh my!* She'd never seen a man's neck and chest before. Dragging her gaze up, she encountered his newly shaven chin and his mouth. For a moment, the corners of his well-shaped lips curved. Above his straight nose, his blue eyes darkened.

Oh dear. *That* was what was sleeping mere feet away from her. It wasn't only his manners that were perfect. Flames shot up her neck into her face, and she tore her gaze away. Her words came out more as a croak. "You should give a signal, or be dressed more properly."

Then, to her chagrin, she darted away.

Without knocking, she burst into her aunt's room, closing the door as quickly as she could and leaning back against it.

"Good heavens, Mary, you look as if you've seen a ghost." Eunice rose from the dressing table. "What is the matter?"

Mary's heart raced. "M-Mr. Featherton."

Eunice scowled. "If he touched you . . ."

"No no. He'd been bathing, and when I saw him . . ." Mary began to feel a little foolish. After all, she'd seen the Elgin Marbles. Granted, they'd not been damp, and dark curls hadn't adorned their bodies, making her want to reach out . . . "It was just that part of his chest"—her face burned—"was—was naked."

Her aunt covered her mouth with a hand. Laughter lurked in her voice. "Only a part?"

She nodded. "I'm being silly, aren't I?"

Eunice put her arm around Mary's shoulders, leading her to a small sofa against one wall. "Maybe just a little. Though you've been kept very close and have not been exposed to many men. I'm sure it must have been a shock. Sit for a moment, and I'll pour you a sherry."

The astonishing part was how much she'd wished to touch him. She wanted to know what his chest felt like. Would it be hard or soft? Would the curls be silky or springy?

She raised the glass of sherry, taking a sip. How was she to go on with him at Rose Hill? His simple presence in the corridor seemed to have robbed all the surrounding air. "I'll be fine in a few moments. I never expected to see him there."

"Well, Mary, it is his house."

"Yes, but it's been my home!" And her safe haven. She blinked back the tears blurring her vision. She was the one who'd cared for it, and improved the property, and—and now none of that mattered. "Why isn't Grandmamma here yet?"

Eunice sat while her maid finished dressing her hair. "She must have been held up. Until she arrives you will have to find a way to deal with Mr. Featherton."

Mary took another sip of sherry. "If only I had more experience engaging with men rather than running from them."

Eunice glanced at Mary from the mirror. When she spoke, her tone was as dry as dust. "It is a little difficult to do that when almost every Season you've had has been either interrupted or cancelled by someone's illness, death, or harassment."

"I suppose you have a point. I shall learn. I must if I am to have a Season."

Eunice turned to face Mary. "You have a great deal of common sense. Do not allow yourself to be led astray by fanciful thoughts or desires, and all will be fine. When it comes to selecting a husband, my only advice is to follow your head as well as your heart." Her aunt rose. "Let us go. Mr. Doust is joining us for dinner."

Mary linked her arm with Eunice's. "I'm surprised you are encouraging him."

A sly smile graced Eunice's lips. "I think I may have been mistaken about how easily he shocks."

That could only mean one thing. A chill ran down Mary's spine. Soon the whole world would know, and she'd be ruined. "You told him!"

"He realized at once that you did not recognize Mr. Featherton until I said his name. Don't worry. He is still the rector. He'll not tell anyone."

This situation was untenable. Mary chewed on her bottom lip. "Entirely too many people know already."

The more people who knew, the harder it was to keep a secret. One that would ruin her.

As Lady Mary fled down the corridor, Kit groaned. That was not well done of him. He should have known she might see him. His behavior had always been above reproach. Unlike some of his friends, young ladies hadn't even attempted to trap him, simply because no one would believe he'd misbehaved.

Still, when Mary had stared at his chest, his partially bare chest, his body reacted as it never had before. He'd wanted to crow when desire lurked for a moment in her lovely silver eyes. Or had it been fear? *Damn.* This would not do. Their position was untenable enough without him lusting after her. He'd have a word with Piggott. Another post-bath chance meeting must not happen again . . . at least not until they were married; then, he hoped, she'd consent to bathe with him.

Kit stepped into the drawing room a moment before the rector was announced and shown in. He wondered if Doust dined here on a regular basis or if he had been invited because of Kit. "Good evening. I was about to pour"—he glanced at the sideboard—"a glass of sherry. Will you join me?"

The rector inclined his head. "I'd be happy to."

He motioned the other man to one of the chairs in front of the fireplace, taking the one across from it for himself. "Shall I take it you wish to discuss my presence?"

"I think I have already figured out the truth of it." Doust grinned. "I won't let the cat out of the bag, if that's what you're worried about."

Interesting. "Pray continue." Kit cocked a brow. "Other than knowing Lady Mary's grandmother is involved, I am at sixes and sevens."

The man settled back, crossing his legs. "It all seemed a bit strange to me, at first, when the ladies arrived." Doust took a sip of sherry. "Yet for at least a month beforehand, the servants had been talking about their arrival and the new servants who were expected."

Kit had to force himself not to interrupt with questions.

"The scheme," Doust continued, "had apparently been well planned to appear completely natural, and, by the time the ladies reached Rose Hill, it did. Until to-day when you arrived, and I could see Lady Mary had no idea who you were at first, I believed what the rest of the area did."

"And that was?" Kit sipped his sherry, wishing it were brandy.

"That you had married, there was a falling out of some sort, and you sent her to your northernmost property. As far away from London as possible."

"Damn. No wonder the servants and townspeople are all suspicious of me." Doust studied him as he took another sip of sherry. Kit took a much larger one. Did this house have no brandy? He had a feeling he wasn't going to like what was next. "Continue, please."

"Once you got a look at Lady Mary, you appeared to know her."

"Yes. I remembered her quite well. Though she did not appear to remember me much at all." He grimaced. That had been a blow to his pride. "But considering I spent most of my time doing the pretty with other young ladies and watching her from afar, I should not be amazed."

Doust's eyes widened a bit. "You surprise me, sir. I have heard your address is excellent. You are the prize every hostess wants at her entertainments."

"Ah, yes"—Kit saluted the rector with his glass—"but I have also been, shall we say, marriage shy."

"And Lady Mary was too much temptation."

He clung to as much dignity as he could under the man's scrutiny and inclined his head. "In my defense, I was barely eight and twenty, but you have the right idea."

"And now?"

He took another drink. "Now I am commanded to marry, and the only woman who has ever inspired me with the least desire to join my wedded brethren is Lady Mary. She has been on my mind a great deal of late. Though, I must admit, I did not expect to meet her here."

That was either a blessing or a curse. He just wished he knew which.

Doust drained the glass then set it down. "Fencing with you is entertaining, but may I be blunt?"

Kit tossed off his sherry, then poured two more. "I wish you would. It would help to finish this conversation before the ladies are down."

"I wish to marry Lady Eunice, and she will not do so until Lady Mary is settled. Do you know who the grandmother is?"

That was what he should be applying his mind to, rather than Lady Mary's charms. "Lady Mary's surname is Tolliver. I cannot remember if her paternal grandmother is still living, but her maternal grandmother is the Dowager Duchess of Bridgewater"—he slammed the glass down on the small side table, sloshing the liquid. *Damnation!*—"one of my Grandmother Featherton's oldest friends, and Lady Bellamny with them! I have been played for a fool."

"You're not the only one. While Lady Eunice and I strolled in the gardens to-day, she finally took me into her confidence." Doust leaned back in his chair. "Lady Mary has no idea of the scheme either."

Being in hiding as she had been, she most likely didn't even know of their grandmothers' friendship. Kit was not looking forward to her finding out, and he certainly was not going to be the one to tell her. She would have to figure that out for herself.

CHAPTER EIGHT

K it took out his handkerchief and wiped the wine off his hand. "No, I could see that when I spoke with her. What I don't understand is how she thinks to get out of this without a scandal unless we wed."

"Though I agree with you that your marriage was the purpose all along. She has great faith in her grandmother, and it might not occur to her a match had been planned without her knowledge and consent. Nonetheless, I wouldn't tell her. According to Lady Eunice, Mary wants a Season and to be able to choose her own husband."

Kit had never known his grandmother to act stupidly. Hadn't she and the dowager duchess even considered Lady Mary might very well balk? "That will make things more difficult than they already are. With that goddaughter of Lady Bellamny's in London, I cannot take Lady Mary there and court her. Still and all, I have no intention of enlightening her as to the scheme." He almost growled. "The only thing that would accomplish is to set her against me. I had a friend who tried to force a marriage, and it did not go well for him." At least not at the beginning. Robert did finally end up wed to his Serena. Kit rose, careful to put his glass down lest he smash it against the fireplace. "This will require a much finer hand than I expected when I spoke to Lady Mary earlier."

The door opened. Doust stood and bowed. Kit moved toward Lady Mary. "My ladies, we've been waiting impatiently for you to join us."

Mary had never appeared so beautiful. The turquoise of her gown brought out the golden hues of her hair. He fought to keep his eyes on her face when all they wanted to do was rove over her shapely form.

When he kissed her hand, she blushed. If anything, she was as innocent as Serena Beaumont had been when she first came to Town, but in a different way. Mary would have been educated in the ways of Polite Society, yet had not had much of an opportunity to wield the knowledge. He wondered how much time he had before their grand-mothers appeared. Then the devil would have to be paid. Mary would not appreciate having her choice taken away from her. He needed to secure her hand before she understood how limited her selection of husbands was.

As Mary strolled down to the drawing room with her aunt, she'd decided her only option while they were at Rose Hill was to play the dutiful wife, to a point. There was no reason to raise the suspicions of the servants. She wanted to speak with her aunt about what her alter-natives were, yet each time she brought the subject up, Eunice seemed determined to change the conversation. The growing unease Mary felt that she might be forced to wed Mr. Featherton to avoid a scandal was not comforting. There must be an alternative.

Not that she didn't like him. He was Mr. Perfect, after all, and he'd been very kind, except when he'd been so angry at first. Still, she did not wish to be forced into marriage and did not want him to feel trapped either. She could not imagine a worse way to begin a wedded life. Yet it had worked for her friend, Caro Huntley. But her situation wasn't the same. She had been in danger. Mary was not, at least phys-ically. What a bumble-broth. If there was a way out of this mess, she vowed she would find it. Until then, she would stick to her purpose.

Though she did rather wish Mr. Featherton would like to court her. If not, there were other gentlemen who would wish to marry her, of that she was certain. All she needed was sufficient time for them to find her.

He came forward when she and her aunt entered the room, and bowed over their hands, kissing hers. She tried to fight the image of his naked chest and failed. Opening her fan, she applied it vigorously. "My, it is a bit warm in here."

If he had any idea she was still affected by him, he did not show it; instead, he cupped her elbow in his hand. "Is it? Come nearer the windows. I'm sure the air will be cooler." He escorted her to the win-dow seat she frequently sat in. "Would you like a sherry or wine?"

It had been hours since she'd eaten, and with the two glasses of sherry she'd already had, Mary was becoming a bit tipsy. "Nothing, thank you. I believe Simons will soon announce dinner."

"As you wish." Mr. Featherton leaned elegantly against the window embrasure. His dark blue coat fitted so well there was not even a crease. He wore an elegant buff waistcoat with gold and rose embroidery. His breeches were the same color as his coat. His evening pumps were so shiny the candle light was reflected in them. He made poor Mr. Doust appear a bit shabby in comparison, although he had looked fine enough before. Was it only Mr. Featherton's clothing, or was there something more catching her attention?

"I apologize," Mr. Featherton continued, "for not having your maid notified about my bath. It will not happen in the future."

Mary fanned herself again. It wasn't any cooler here. If anything, the room had become increasingly warmer. "I appreciate your thoughtfulness."

Fortunately, before this embarrassing conversation could go any further, Simons announced dinner.

"Please allow me to escort you, my lady," Mr. Featherton said in a low voice.

Mary took his hand and rose. "Thank you."

He leaned his head close to hers. "You must show me where the dining room is. I do not remember."

She gave him a small smile. "Since Eunice and I have never entertained, other than the tenants, we use the family dining room. There is no reason to use the formal one."

"Very wise and doubtless easier to heat."

"Yes, although all the windows are in good repair, as are the chimneys," she responded, unable to hide the pride in her accomplishments.

"And the accounts are in excellent shape. I could not have done better myself."

This time when she colored, it was from pleasure and not embarrassment. She hadn't expected his approbation and was glad he had appreciated her efforts. "Since I am the only daughter in my family, I was taught alongside my brothers."

"Did they learn music and deportment as well?"

She slid a quick glance at him, but he wasn't laughing at her. "Not when it came to music, they had no talent, but they did take lessons in deportment from my governess. She left when I was nineteen to marry my brothers' tutor. They started a school in the Midlands." Of course her family had thought Mary would soon be wed. "Here we are."

The room was one of her favorites. Long windows lined two walls facing south and east, providing light for most of the day. She had chosen a cream-colored silk wall covering with a loose pattern of roses and vines. Glancing at the table, she made a mental note to speak with Cook regarding changes in the menu now that Mr. Featherton was here. "You must tell me your favorite dishes or if you have any dislikes. I am afraid I have arranged the meals to please myself. Aunt Eunice will eat almost anything."

He dismissed the butler, instead holding out her chair at the foot of the table himself. "I will think on it and let you know. I'm fairly easily pleased. Like your aunt, there is not much I dislike." After she was seated he sniffed the air. "Asparagus soup? I thought the season wasn't until May."

"We have some planted in the succession houses."

He bowed. "I commend you on your housekeeping, my lady." Then he whispered, "If you will play along, I have an explanation for my absence." Her brows came together slightly. What could he be planning? "It is entirely self-serving." He gave a boyish grin that appealed to her immediately. "I would wish to be at least tolerated by my servants and the town."

This was a slippery slope. Would it not be better to feign coldness? No, that wouldn't help. It would only make everyone even more uncomfortable. "I shall do my best."

When he smiled his whole face lit up. He'd always appeared a bit remote, but he really was quite nice.

"Thank you."

Once Mr. Featherton took his place, she signaled for the meal to begin. After the soup was removed, he raised his wine glass. "To you, my lady."

Aunt Eunice and the rector raised their glasses as well. Mr. Doust said, "To reunions."

Mary tried not to choke. "Yes, indeed."

As plates of roasted lamb, French beans, sole in lemon sauce, and a salad of early greens and cucumbers were being served, Mr. Featherton glanced down the short table at Mary. "Please forgive me for not giving you notice of my arrival, my lady. Once the ship arrived I went straight to London, then came here. I hope you've forgiven me for leaving so soon after the wedding, but it did turn out to be necessary, and you would not have enjoyed the journey."

For several moments she was struck speechless. How much bolder could he be, and how was she to respond? "I know you believe I would not have been happy, but that was for me to decide, sir. Nevertheless, I have been exceedingly well employed here and am quite content."

Let anyone hearing that decide for themselves if she was satisfied with making her way without his interference or not.

His eyes sparkled with mischief. "I see I have my work cut out for me. I do wish to be in your good graces, my lady."

What in God's name did he mean by that? Yet perhaps it was all playacting for the servants and, notwithstanding their loyalty, it would be all over town by to-morrow. She gave her attention to her food. At least she had given as good as she'd got and would continue to do so. Thankfully, the rector turned talk to the needs of the town.

It was not until they were in a lively discussion over how much the estate should contribute to additional repairs on the church and the local school that Mary realized she had no place at all in this conversation. Regardless of how attached she was to it, Rose Hill was not hers and probably never would be. Needed or not, she hated this pretense of being something she was not.

Through a haze of despair, she heard Mr. Featherton say, "Very well, it shall be as you wish, my dear."

Any other woman would probably have smiled smugly, but this was all too much. The charade had been bad enough when he wasn't here. Now that he was—and worse, was acting as if he were her husband when she didn't know if that was what she wanted—the walls seemed to close in on her, and she couldn't breathe.

She set her serviette by her plate and rose. "Thank you, sir. Aunt Eunice, we should leave the men to their port."

As the final course had only been served moments before, Eunice gave Mary a startled look before rising. With a growing panic, Mary left the room, not even looking to see if her aunt followed. She strode back down the corridor, across the hall, and into the drawing room before stopping.

Eunice shut the door behind them with a snap. "Mary, I have never seen you act with such intemperance. Compose yourself this instant."

"I cannot do this." Mary paced back and forth across the room. She wanted to rant or run away. Why could no one understand? "Now that he's here, I can't pretend. I cannot even look the servants in the eye." She had to leave before the gentlemen rejoined them. "I'm sorry."

She fled up the stairs to her chamber, yet even there she was not alone. Her maid was laying out her nightgown. "Please undress me, then you may retire."

Mathers began unlacing Mary's gown. "You look as if a cup of warm milk wouldn't be amiss."

Her temples throbbed and her throat ached. "I'm not a child anymore."

"No one said you were, my lady, but a bit of warm milk is good for calming the nerves. You've had a difficult day."

That was one way of putting it. "I just want to go to sleep."

Once she had donned her nightgown, she climbed between the sheets. All she wanted was to fall in love as her friends had done. Why was fate conspiring against her? With any luck she'd wake up to-morrow and this would have all been a bad dream.

Kit caught a glimpse of the back of Lady Mary on the stairs. Her skirts moved rapidly upward as she fled. "That didn't go quite as I had planned."

"Does it ever when dealing with women?" Doust said drily, shaking his head. "You didn't really believe she'd simply fall into your arms, did you?"

She was probably one of the few ladies who wouldn't. Kit gave a rueful smile. "I had hoped to show her that I am a reasonable man, and by marrying me she'd be fully involved in most of my decisions. I thought it would put this situation in a better light."

The promise of a partnership had worked for Marcus and Rutherford.

The rector was silent for a few moments. "You know what Lady Mary wants. If you do wish to marry her, you need to find out how to give her at least as much of it as you are able under the circumstances."

The devil! It wasn't as if she had a choice. For that matter, neither did he. Yet did she realize it, or did she think he was trying to trap her as well? Kit ran a hand over his face. Subterfuge was what was needed. He'd have Piggott talk to Mary's lady's maid, but first Kit would speak to her aunt. "You are correct, of course. Lady Eunice might have some ideas."

Kit and Doust entered the drawing room. Lady Eunice was staring into the fireplace, a glass of wine held loosely in her hand. Kit took the chair on the other side of the small table from where she sat on the sofa.

Her lips pressed together, she glanced at the two of them. "I've never seen her behave in such a manner before."

Doust handed Kit a brandy, a decanter of which had miraculously appeared on the sideboard, then sat on the sofa next to Lady Eunice, as she said, "It has been a trying day."

He took a sip, savoring the burn as it traveled down his throat. "What can I do to help?"

"I don't know. Mary is generally a sensible woman. She wants a husband and children. Yet I very much fear she has deluded herself into thinking she has a choice about whom she will wed."

Kit wanted nothing more than to hit something. "If you have any ideas at all as to how I can bring her around, I'd appreciate hearing them."

Lady Eunice shook her head. "At this point, I don't know what to do. Perhaps sleeping on the problem will help." She set her glass down on the table and rose. "Gentlemen, I shall see you in the morning."

He and the rector stood. "Good night."

Doust reached out, taking her hand. "I'll take my leave now. Walk me to the door, if you will, my lady."

She smiled. "Gladly."

Cursing Mary's and his grandmothers, Kit made his way to his bedchamber. He began engaging in what-ifs. What if they'd brought Lady Mary to Town, where he could and would have courted her? But that wouldn't do anyone any good now. He'd have to deal with what he had, and she wasn't going to make this easy for him. "Piggott," Kit said, opening the door, "I have a job for you."

His valet paused in the midst of polishing Kit's boots. "What would that be, sir?"

"Have a talk with Lady Mary's dresser, and find out what her lady-ship's tastes are."

"Are you planning to court her ladyship?"

Kit drained his glass. "I am, and I must do so quickly."

Before word got out and there was a scandal that could not be contained.

CHAPTER NINE

The next day turned to rain. Feeling as low as the clouds overhead, Mary decided to remain in her room and pretend she had the headache. Mathers ferried messages from Cook and her housekeeper, brought meals on trays, and made cryptic remarks about those who should know better. Mary did not ask, indeed she didn't want to know. Instead of hiding away and moping, she would be better occupied doing something, anything. Making plans, writing lists. But the more she considered the problem, the harder it was to see her way out of this mess without creating just the sort of talk that would ruin her.

On the afternoon of the following day she sat on the sofa pretending to read as she gazed out her window over her newly planted garden. Perhaps a ride would help. She could sneak down the back stairs and out the side door. What she couldn't continue to do was stay in her chambers, yet neither could she face Mr. Featherton. What had possessed her to behave so rudely? Oh yes, her sensitivity. There was only one thing to do, and the sooner the better.

The door opened. Eunice entered, followed by Simons with a tea tray.

Mary waited until he'd left, before announcing, "We shall depart early to-morrow."

"No, we will not." Eunice sat on a chair next to the sofa where Mary was ensconced. "Where would you go?"

"London. I'll join Grandmamma at Bridgewater House."

"What if Gawain is watching it? He must be in a panic by now, and what if you run into Diana, and she tells someone you are Lady Mary Featherton?" Mary shuddered as her aunt continued without mercy. "Mr. Featherton's departure during the Season is probably a topic of discussion. He is quite well-known."

Everything her aunt said was true. Still... "Then I'll go elsewhere." She fought the tears threatening to fall. "I just cannot stay here. It is impossible!"

"You must." Eunice's tone was as cold as ice. Lines bracketed her mouth. "The servants are already beginning to talk. You are a Tolliver. Behave like one and not some missish—"

"That is enough." Mr. Featherton's firm tone caused Mary to jump and Eunice to stop talking. He strode across the room to them. "Lady Mary, allow me to call your maid. We shall say you are still in bed with a sick headache."

That wasn't far from the truth. Her nose started to run, and he handed her his handkerchief. At least she wasn't weeping.

Her aunt's lips formed a thin line. "She must realize . . ."

Mr. Featherton glanced over his shoulder. "She will, but this is not the way to do it." He pulled a chair to the other side of the sofa from Eunice, then rubbed his large palms up and down Mary's arms, warming them. "Lady Mary, will you drink some tea? It might help."

Trapped, she was completely trapped, but at least he wasn't yelling at her. "Thank you."

He poured, adding milk and two lumps of sugar. She couldn't believe he'd remembered how she liked it.

The rector had entered as well, and took her aunt to the far corner of Mary's parlor, where they spoke in hushed tones.

Mr. Featherton turned back to her. "I can call your maid, or we may address your concerns now. Tell me what you wish."

She drained the cup, and he filled it again. "I don't know what I want. It's all so confusing. I—I feel as if I should leave here as soon as possible." She heaved a shuddering sigh, then voiced the doubt that had crept into her reasoning. "But that won't help, will it?"

Kit took his time pouring a cup of tea for himself, wishing it were brandy. No wonder men drank so much of the stuff. What he said next would lay the foundation for their lives together. With wide, frightened eyes, she gazed up at him. She was so pale, and appeared appallingly fragile. Yet to have lived the life she'd led for the past two or more years, as she hid from her cousin, refusing to give up what she desired—she had to have steel in her. He respected her for that, but it wasn't helping them now.

Fortunately, Mathers had been more than forthcoming with Piggott. All Lady Mary had ever longed for was to be courted and desired for herself, not her money or her beauty, and she wanted to attend the Season. He might not be able to give her a Season until after they were married. That he had no need of her money was probably one of several reasons her grandmother had selected him. Yes, she was the loveliest woman he knew, but judging by her accomplishments, she was so much more.

It was time she faced the truth about their situation with no roundaboutation. "It would probably make matters worse." He wanted to put his arm around her; instead he took one of her hands, intertwining her fingers with his. "The other day you told me how you came to be here, but you didn't ask me how I knew to come."

She was still for a moment as her brow furrowed. "I'm not sure I wish to know."

He reached out to touch her, to smooth her forehead, but stopped. "The time for ignoring realities is over."

She took a breath and nodded. "Someone told you."

"Someone told my father. He told me."

She tensed again. "Who?"

"My grandmother heard it from Lady Bellamny. Did you know she was here?"

Lady Mary took another drink. "Not until after she'd left. Lady Brownly came for tea, and told me that out of the blue, her godmother offered to sponsor Diana for the Season." She bit down on her lip so hard he thought it would bleed. "Do you know if our grandmothers are close?"

"They have been for years."

Then, in a preternaturally calm voice, she said, "They planned this. Our grandmothers and Lady Bellamny were in it together."

"Lady B was most likely a willing accomplice rather than an instigator," Kit agreed. Lady Eunice was probably involved as well, but he'd keep his own counsel regarding her.

The crease between Lady Mary's brows deepened. "But why?"

"Considering what you've told me about your cur of a cousin, they had probably hoped to protect you."

She stared at him as if grasping for the missing piece of a puzzle. "No. I meant, why you and not another gentleman?"

"I have no idea." He tried to remember if he had ever mentioned Lady Mary to his grandmother. The woman had an uncanny way of ferreting out information, not to mention a long memory. "I have been notoriously difficult to please when it comes to choosing a wife. I believe my grandmother tired of waiting for me and determined to make a match." Her eyes widened, and he hurried on. "She is correct, I must marry, but I have never been a loose fish, and attempting anything like this would never have occurred to me."

A gurgle of laughter escaped Mary, and a small smile appeared on her lips. "Are you calling our grandmothers loose fish?"

He frowned for a moment. It was extraordinary what old women left to their own devices could get up to. "Yes, I believe I am. When I was told a woman was here portraying my wife, I was furious. Everyone agreed that I should make haste in traveling to Rose Hill. It took several moments, but then somehow I knew you did not come up with this outrageous scheme."

Her countenance relaxed, even as she sobered.. "It was—is nothing short of shocking. I argued with Grandmamma before we parted ways and then with Aunt Eunice the whole journey north. Yet every point I made was pooh-poohed, as if I had no idea what I was talking about." Her chin took on a mulish cast. "But I was right."

He raised her hands to his lips, kissed her fingers, and tossed away any loyalty he had for his grandmother. "You were completely in the right. We ought to insist they be locked up somewhere. Still"—thank God he hadn't said *unfortunately*—"it has left us with no reasonable choices." Mary ceased to look at him and instead stared at her lap. Kit placed one finger under her chin, raising it. "Despite our innocence in this plan, we have been put in a disgraceful situation. Would being married to me be such a hardship?"

"It's not that." Her eyes swam in sudden tears. "I don't *know* you. This . . . this type of arranged marriage is what I do not want."

"We can grow to know each other." He handed her his handkerchief, and he knew his chances of settling this situation were rapidly slipping away. Still, he had to try to make her see reason. "I'm considered to be an easygoing sort of fellow."

She closed her eyes and a small tremor ran through her, not, he knew, of passion. "I do not believe we were even introduced."

"We weren't." He grinned, attempting to lighten the mood and the circumstances in which they found themselves. He couldn't bring himself to let her know how much failing to arrange a proper introduction had bothered him. "I was studiously avoiding a leg shackle at the time." A tear drifted down her cheek. Oh dear God! She really was weeping. Before she could use the handkerchief, he wiped away the drop with the pad of his thumb. "Please say I'm at least tolerable." "You are being very kind to me. The thing is, and you may think it silly, particularly under the circumstances, but I have always wanted to be courted." Mary blinked quickly and swallowed. "I want to fall in love."

Kit searched her lovely silver eyes. "I want that as well." The only difference was he was already on his way to falling in love with her, and they must marry. Since he'd been fifteen, he'd led an exemplary life. What trick of fate had decreed that he must suffer before he wed? Yet Mary was hurting as well, and the least he could do was to attach her affections. "Allow me to court you."

She seemed startled. "You would do that? Even after all that's been done to you as well?"

He raised one of her hands to his lips, brushing his lips slowly across her knuckles. "Gladly, if you'll permit."

This wasn't at all how Mary had planned to meet her future husband, and she was not happy about it. Though she did appreciate how hard Mr. Featherton was trying to please her, not to mention his having been trapped as well. Yet, if they did not suit, she would not, could not marry him. As for now, it was time to start behaving like a lady of breeding. "If you wish." Her cheeks warmed under his steady blue gaze. "Under the circumstances, I think it would be proper if you called me Mary."

He grinned. "My name is Christopher, but most call me Kit."

That was one thing in his favor. She had always liked Kit as a nickname. "Very well."

A knock sounded on the door, and Simons stepped in. "My lady, sir, you have received correspondence."

Mary held out her hand. "Probably my grandmother."

Kit did the same. He received two letters. Both with seals. "And mine." He added in a dry tone, "I wonder what they have to say for themselves."

She was tempted to giggle again, then she glanced at the seal. "It is not from Grandmamma. It's from Phoebe. Lady Evesham now." Mary popped off the wax, and read. "*Oh my word*, she writes that they are passing through and wishes to visit, but how . . ."

Aside from Caro Huntley, Phoebe was Mary's closest friend, but how did Phoebe know Mary was here? She had been careful to never put her whereabouts in a letter.

He'd opened one of his missives. "From my mother. I'll read it later." When he spread out the sheets of the other, his mouth opened, then closed again sharply. "Passing through, my foot. Meddling more like, and it's not just Phoebe and Marcus. How did they get up here so quickly?"

"No, you're right." Mary read down the page. "Anna Rutherford and Caro Huntley are traveling with them. I know Caro quite well, but I've only met Lady Rutherford a few times."

"At least the others had the sense to go elsewhere."

This sounded suspiciously like another conspiracy. "What others?"

"My friends and their wives. Though I don't suppose you know Lady Beaumont and Lady Wivenly."

Mary cast her mind back. She'd heard about them, naturally, from Phoebe and Caro, but had never met the ladies. "No. Why would they . . . Good Lord, you said something!"

His head shot up. "*I?* No. I told Marcus about the pretense, but he was out of the country when you came out, and you've been in hiding since he returned. He could not have known it was you."

That left only one explanation. Her friends would never have revealed her problems, not even to one another. "One or the other of our grandmothers is involved. I can feel it in my bones."

"Probably both; that's the only thing I can think of that makes sense." His tone was grim. "They must be in collusion."

Mary had appreciated her grandmother's help over the past few years, but if she had known what Grandmamma was capable of, Mary would not have been so sanguine. This interfering had to cease. The time had come for her to take control of her life. "I'll murder mine."

"We will make it a double . . . What is the term for killing one's grandmother?"

"I have no idea."

"A double homicide then," he added in a dry tone. "Is the nursery in as good a shape as the rest of the house?"

"Why do we . . . ?" She glanced back at the letter. "Phoebe says . . . yes, here it is. She'll have Arthur, he is almost two, and Anna is bringing

Benjamin. I recall him being a few months younger. They are traveling with their nurses so as not to impose on us." Mary frowned. "Us?"

He raised his brows. "They definitely know I'm here."

"We have a lot to do to prepare." Mary rose and went to the lovely rosewood inlaid desk her grandmother had sent for Christmas. She hadn't thought of it at the time, but this should have been her first hint that Grandmamma had no intention of Mary leaving Rose Hill for a long time to come. What did Phoebe and Caro think of all this? "We might have to bring in more servants to serve the visiting servants."

"Nursery maids, maids, valets, and grooms, if not furniture as well." Kit rubbed his chin. "You are in charge here, my dear. I am still an interloper."

She pulled a face. "Not for long, you aren't. We have a few days before their arrival. They are at Lord Beaumont's home north of York, and will visit Edinburgh after leaving here. I'll start a list."

Kit took another sip of tea. This was becoming deuced complicated, and now he'd only have four days to court Mary and convince her to wed him before their friends arrived. He had little doubt if Phoebe put her mind to it, she would find Mary a way out of marriage. She had almost done the same for Serena, and he didn't want her interference.

If only he'd tried to fix his attention with her earlier; then again, there was the uncle to deal with. *Damn*, he must discover where the devil the man was. Mr. Tolliver might refuse to talk to Barham, but he damn sure wouldn't be allowed to ignore Kit.

As it stood now, they'd have to wait for her birthday before they could marry, and that wouldn't do. He wanted to wed her the moment she said yes. In addition, he was extremely concerned how long they had before the whole world knew they were not yet husband and wife. Good God! They couldn't have the ceremony here. "We may have to make a trip across the border ourselves."

She dropped her pen, and her eyes widened. "Whatever for?"

When had he become such a dolt? She hadn't agreed to have him yet. He picked the pen up and mended it for her. "If you decide we should wed, we can't have anyone here know we are not already man and wife."

She bit her bottom lip. "My grandmother has a lot to answer for."

He wasn't going to argue that. So did his grandmother. "Parricide."

"What?"

"The killing of a close family member. That's the best I can do."

"I like the sound of that word." She gave a curt nod and went back to her lists.

Murder was looking better every minute. "It is almost time to change for dinner. Unless you wish to deal with the servants this evening, I propose you wait until morning before you advise the staff what is coming. In the meantime, we can take ourselves off for a tour of the estate and a picnic."

"You might have a point." She passed the feather end of the pen over her lips, and he found himself envying the pen. He'd much rather have his mouth in its place.

"The staff," she continued, "has not had guests here since before your aunt died. There will be a great deal to do. I am more than happy to have a good night's sleep instead of remaining up late to answer questions concerning beds and the like. I'll tell them I want an accounting of items we must have and menu suggestions prepared for when we return."

He glanced over his shoulder. "Where are your aunt and the rector?"

"They must be playing least in sight." Mary giggled, and Kit hoped it was a good omen. "You do know he is courting her?"

"I was made aware of that fact." Kit drank the rest of his tea. "Shall I see you in the drawing room?"

She slid a look at him. "Yes. I promise not to run off again."

Thank God for that. "I know you won't." He placed a kiss on her palm, then closed her fingers around it. "We will make this work. I promise."

A small sigh escaped Mary, and she gave him a tremulous smile. "I'll see you in an hour."

This must be more difficult for her than for me. He already knew what he wanted. He'd just have to bring her round.

If only he knew how to court a lady. Kit gave himself a shake. He was bound to come up with something, and it had better be soon.

CHAPTER TEN

K it closed the door to Mary's parlor. The picnic was a start. Ladies loved eating out of doors. Being alone with her in a romantic spot would be the perfect way to begin their courtship.

He made his way down the stairs, opened the green baize door, then descended to the lower level. Simons and the housekeeper were sitting around a long dining table in close conversation. The cook supervised a kitchen maid turning meat on a spit in the fireplace, while keeping her attention on numerous pots on the stove.

"Excuse me for disturbing you." The housekeeper's eyes grew wide and she shot out of her seat. Though the butler's expression didn't change, he was standing before the housekeeper. Kit waited for the woman to compose herself, then said, "I have planned an outing for her ladyship to-morrow." He focused on the cook, who stood arms akimbo with a wooden spoon in her hand, glaring at him. He eyed the spoon warily, remembering exactly what it felt like to have his knuckles whacked with one of those, and he didn't wish to repeat the experience. Not that the cook would. He was the master here . . . Still, it didn't hurt to tread lightly. "If you could make up a picnic basket to be ready in the morning, I would be in your debt."

The woman's countenance softened a bit. "Yes, sir. I know just what her ladyship likes."

He noticed the cook didn't ask what *he* liked. Ah well. As far as the staff was concerned, he was the errant husband and Mary a paragon. "Simons, send a message to the stables to have my curricle ready after breakfast."

The butler bowed. "Yes, sir."

Kit inclined his head slightly before retracing his steps and reaching his bedchamber. Hopefully Piggott had had the forethought to have a bottle of brandy ready. Nevertheless, considering how it could have gone, it had been a successful day, and he was looking forward to spending time alone with Mary.

"Sir." The valet handed Kit his letters. "You left these in her ladyship's parlor."

"Thank you." He opened the letter from home.

> *My darling Son,*
> *Your father told me* all*. I have never been so shocked in my life. Your grandmother is completely unrepentant, and I have suggested that if she wishes to organize the lives of others, there are several very good charities who would appreciate her efforts. I sincerely hope she does not attempt to arrange marriages for your sisters or brother. They would not take it nearly as well as I know you are.*
>
> *Your father asked me to relay to you that he has involved himself in the Chancery case and will bring pressure to bear. He asks if there are any other offices he may perform to assist you.*
>
> *Please tell your wife to be, for I will not mention names, that we welcome her into our family and look forward to meeting her. Poor girl!*
>
> *With much love,*
> *Mother*

Leave it to Mama to get to the heart of things, and relieve him of two concerns. She would now probably busy herself concocting some believable story for the *ton*. He'd write back, asking her to send him a selection of family rings suitable for a wedding ring and have Papa search for Mary's uncle as well as contact Barham about the marriage settlements.

"Do I have time to bathe?"

"No, sir, her ladyship is in the bathing chamber. I'll have one drawn for you before you retire. I have water set up for you to shave."

Kit thought back to Mary's reaction at seeing him in the corridor, before she scurried off. He'd like to see that look again. Even more, he would like to join her in the bath. First things first. "Find out for me her ladyship's favorite area, or the most romantic one for a picnic."

"Of course, sir. I shall ask Miss Mathers."

All Kit required now was a bit of luck and his famous address. He'd be leg-shackled before he knew it.

"Gawain, it is not good enough!" Cordelia Tolliver's shrill voice cut through the cool air of her modest Cambridge home. Red splotches mottled her normally perfect complexion.

"Mama . . ." As much as he loved his mother, Gawain would have been happy to strangle her at this point. "I have searched everywhere. Lady Mary has disappeared. As I told you before, by the time I ascertained she was not in Bath, more than a month had elapsed." Unfortunately, the maid he'd used for information was now never alone. Someone must have discovered she had been meeting him. "When I returned to the dower house, she wasn't there, either. Nor is she in London."

His mother glared at him without saying a word.

"Then I chased the old lady to every watering hole in England." Something had to satisfy her. After all, he wanted the marriage as much as his mother did.

"Did you look for her at Lady Eunice's residence and at all her children's estates?"

"Yes."

"Gawain, the longer you wait, the more we risk your father discovering what we've been doing, and then she will slip through your fingers. Not only that, but the Chancery court is bound to rule before too much longer," his mother ended on a sob.

At least she'd stopped screeching. "I am well aware of that." He rubbed his temples. "It's as if she has dropped off the end of the earth. Perhaps she went abroad."

Mama cast her eyes at the ceiling. "With whom? Her allowance would not cover extensive travel." Her face brightened. "Unless she ran off with some man and married. Then the money is ours."

Even his father would not allow such a blatant disregard of Mary's father's will. Gawain stopped scowling. He wanted Mary as well as the money. How else was he to gain entry into the upper levels of the *ton*? On the other hand, once he had the funds he would be a good catch and might not need his cousin. That would make his life easier. He could marry the daughter of an impoverished peer. A calm, biddable lady who would be happy to have him as her husband. "If only she had, but she's not stupid. The gentleman would have to be as rich as Croesus to make her give up her inheritance." But . . . the money . . . Of course. Why in the bloody hell hadn't he thought of it before? "How does she get her allowance?"

"I'm not sure." Mama turned a blank face to him. "I would imagine she draws on her account at Hoare's."

The ache in his head eased. "Then we must discover a way to find where the funds are sent."

A smile lit his mother's still lovely countenance. When she was young, she had been called *The Incomparable*. The only way his father got her to marry him had been by lying about his expectations. "Oh, my love. That is an absolutely brilliant idea."

"You keep Papa busy, and I shall go through his papers this evening. Then I shall write to the bank in Papa's name, asking for the information."

"Oh, no need, darling," Mama said with a wave of her hand. "He's off chasing rocks somewhere."

His father was always off somewhere studying giant stones. If it hadn't been for that, this whole scheme Mama had hatched would have fallen apart. He leaned down and bussed her cheek. "I'll find Cousin Mary."

Mama squeezed his hand. "Soon you'll be married, and we'll have what we were cheated out of all those years ago."

He couldn't give her the title she had coveted for so long, but he could get the money. Perhaps then she would finally be happy.

Mary paced her parlor. It had been extremely nice of Kit to offer to court her. Even though she knew he could not be, he had even acted as if he was interested in her. Still, she must have a plan in the event she and Kit did not suit. After he left her parlor, she studied her copy of *Debrett's* and confirmed her suspicion that Mary was the most common girl's name in England. It was then the solution to her problems came to her. Not a perfect one, a better option than being forced into a loveless marriage.

She'd been out of Polite Society for so long, few would recognize her, and other than her very close friends, it seemed no one in the *ton* knew exactly who Lady Mary Featherton was. She could go abroad and live. She would need a companion, but that shouldn't be a problem. Her brother supported dozens of poor relations. She would merely hire one of them. Once she came into her inheritance, she would find a way to tie it up in a trust so restrictive that no fortune hunter would want her, including Gawain. After a couple of years, if she hadn't met a gentleman she wished to wed, she could return to England. Her grandmother had assured her not all men wished to marry young women. She only hoped Grandmamma was right.

Mary penned one letter to her brother's man of business and another to Barham, explaining everything that was going on, what she wanted done, and authorizing him to act in her behalf. That was much better than waiting until her twenty-fifth birthday. When she'd sealed them into a packet, she summoned her groom, Terrey.

A few minutes later, a knock sounded on the door. "My lady, you wanted me?"

She handed him the package. "I need this sent to London as quickly as possible."

"I'll get them off to catch the mail coach right away."

He closed the door behind him, and it was as if the weight of the world had lifted from her shoulders, almost as if she could float in the air. For the first time in years, she felt free. Now she could be courted without knowing whether or not she would actually marry Kit. What a wonderful position to be in. And if she was unable to love him, Mary would make plans to travel the Continent. Phoebe and Caro would help her make the arrangements.

An hour later, Mary stared into the mirror, fidgeting as her dresser arranged her hair.

"Do be still, my lady."

"I am."

Mathers huffed, but didn't speak again. Once she was done, she handed Mary her spangled shawl.

Mary arrived in the drawing room to find Kit already there. She briefly considered telling him what she had decided. If he was serious about courting her, it wouldn't matter, and if he wasn't, then she wanted to know immediately. She could always change the orders regarding a trust if she decided to wed him. On the other hand, perhaps it was best to say nothing. For the time being, she'd enjoy her independence.

She smiled as he greeted her, raising her fingers to his lips. His breath hovered over them, and a tingle started in the tips, moving up through her arm. She'd felt a warmth before, but, oh my, that was very nice indeed. She'd always known she would enjoy being wooed. Her breathing hitched as he gazed into her eyes. "Good evening, Kit."

"Good evening, my dear."

Oooh, an endearment, and he sounded sincere. He was certainly moving this courting business right along. She wondered how soon he'd kiss her, and if the kiss swept her away—just as she had always dreamed of—she'd know it was love.

She chewed her lip, wondering what he'd do next.

When he led her to the window-seat, she noticed two glasses of sherry on the table next to it as well as a chair. He'd also done his research as to what she liked to drink and where she preferred to sit.

Kit placed one of the cushions behind her, before sitting in the chair. "I think your rector may be joining us as well."

That shouldn't surprise her. Even though Mr. Doust had been very helpful when he took Aunt Eunice away this afternoon, and Mary had made the decision her aunt would have expected her to make, she dreaded seeing her aunt and Mr. Doust this evening. "He has been fond of Aunt Eunice for an age, and she of him. I wish them well."

"As do I." Kit leaned back in his chair, idly twirling his glass.

Mary took a sip. "I wish I knew more about him."

He flashed her a smile. "Worried about your aunt?"

"Perhaps a little. You must admit, he is not your normal run-of-the-mill rector. He seems different somehow. Have you seen his horses?"

"It was one of the first things I noticed." Setting his glass down untouched, he took her hand. "I don't think you have much to worry about. I would wager he is a close relation to the Earl of Marnly. They are famous for their cattle. The earl is quite elderly. Mr. Doust may be one of his sons."

"Then his horses make sense." Eunice would be happy to remain in the area. She had mentioned something about it being like home. Mary felt the same, but she could not allow that to influence her choice of husband. She would wed for love and nothing less. "I suppose there is nothing to be concerned with after all." Mary took a sip of her wine. "Tell me about yourself. I only know that you spend most of your time in London, own Rose Hill, and our grandmothers are friends."

Kit stood, lounging against the side of the window seat. He truly did look magnificent. "I generally spend only the Seasons in Town.

The rest of the year I reside at our principal estate, or travel to the lesser properties. As you might know, I am heir to Viscount Featherton, whom I sincerely hope lives to a ripe old age." He grimaced a bit. "I have a sister who is two years younger than I. She has three children. A brother who will finish at Oxford this year, and is pegged for the foreign service. A younger sister who has been out for a couple of years now and appears to have finally settled on a gentleman. Two more sisters who will make their come outs next year and the year after, and a younger brother. Family tradition has him going into the army, but he's much too bookish. I expect he'll go to the church. Fortunately, my father holds several livings."

Mary grinned. "I can understand why you wish him a long life."

Kit raised his glass in a salute. "Indeed. Just the thought of having guardianship over the children has me in a panic. Though, we generally get along well. Have you only Barham?"

"No. I'm not actually the only girl. I have an elder sister, Osanna, but she has been married and living near Land's End since I was nine. We are not close. She is the oldest. Barham also has several years on me, yet he has always been around, thus I know him better, and we rub along quite well. The twins, both men now, are close to my age, but they've left home. Our family traditions are not so different from yours. One is in the army, and the other in Vienna with the foreign service." She had always wished for a sister closer to her age. "Do you know Barham?"

Kit had been in the middle of taking a sip of sherry when she asked. He swallowed. "We were in Eton together. Afterward he went on to Cambridge, and I attended Oxford."

"Yes, he was always more interested in the sciences. In some ways he is very like Uncle Hector." She paused, still attempting to make sense of the change in her uncle. "Until my father died, and Uncle began insisting I wed his son."

Kit gazed at her steadily as if he too knew something was wrong. "Tell me more about your uncle."

The line creasing Lady Mary's forehead deepened, and Kit wanted nothing more than to smooth it. Truth be told, he'd just as soon take her in his arms and kiss her witless.

"He was always very kind, but absent-minded. His primary love is for rocks, the large ones that one finds in circles. He's a well-known petrologist, but he is also extremely good with numbers and investing. Papa told Barham that our fortune would not be nearly so large if it weren't for Uncle Hector. I do not understand what has changed him so."

Kit wondered if his father knew Hector Tolliver; at least having the uncle's name and interests would aid in finding the man. "It does sound as if something is not right. I understand Barham has not spoken to him?"

She shook her head. "Uncle Hector is never available. All communication is through letters. Although I'm quite sure he is the one egging Gawain on. Who else could it be? My cousin didn't pay the slightest bit of attention to me until after Papa died."

That's the other thing Kit must do: find this Gawain and put an end to his persecution of Mary. "If you will tell me what your cousin looks like, I shall ensure he can no longer bother you."

She stared at Kit for several moments. "How can *you* stop him? No one else has been able to."

"Believe me, I have my ways." He tried but failed to keep his tone light.

Lady Eunice and Doust entered the drawing room just ahead of Simons. She had the look of a well-kissed woman, if Kit knew anything about it, and he did. The urge to pull Mary into his arms, taste her lips, and kiss them until they were plump surged through him again. How long would he have to wait before Mary had the same appearance?

During dinner it appeared as if they were all focused on keeping the conversation light. Doust was encouraged by the ladies to tell them about Ireland and the horses.

"Mr. Featherton had already guessed who you are." Mary smiled shyly. "I think it was clever of him."

"Indeed it was." Doust saluted Kit. "It has been a very long time since anyone put two and two together."

Kit smiled and accepted the compliments. He was more interested in knowing if Mary's accolade meant that she was softening to him. He hoped so. They could not go the way they had been much longer. To-morrow, on the picnic, he'd make his first concerted effort to claim her affections and her hand.

CHAPTER ELEVEN

The next morning, wanting to ensure all was perfect for his outing with Mary, Kit awoke as the sun crested the tree tops. Not a half hour later, he strode to the stables on the other side of a macadam courtyard. Even here he could see Mary's handiwork. The semi-hard finished surface had not been there previously. The last time he was at Rose Hill, it was mostly dirt and mud. Roses that must have been replanted from another location, scrambled up the wall, creating the impression the stables were part and parcel of the house. The roof and outside of the building were in pristine condition. A low "moo" drew his attention to the other end of the long structure that now stretched to a stone barrier, incorporating what had once been separate smaller stables. All in all it was a vast improvement, and she'd only been here a few months.

Damn, the woman was a wonder. Exactly the sort of wife he needed. He must take care not to step over the line and frighten her away. He would not make the same mistakes some of his friends had.

Last evening, he had found himself touching her whenever possible. Kit would have to keep his growing attraction for her under control. To do otherwise would dishonor her. Marriage before lust.

All he'd have to do is keep repeating that mantra.

Dent called a greeting. "Looky what I found. Two of the most beautiful steppers I ever seen."

Kit ran his hand over one of the matched, dark-bay geldings harnessed to his carriage. "What handsome gentlemen. They must be out of Lord Marnly's stables in Ireland."

"Ain't no doubting it. Her ladyship's groom told me they got them from the rector." Dent scratched his head. "Found two good hacks as well. Someone other than the rector has a good eye for horseflesh.

Don't suppose you got a hankering to add to the stables? We got plenty of empty stalls." Dent gestured with his chin in the direction of the stone wall. "Dairy and buttery's down that way, and the coach house is now the first building ye come to from the drive."

The whole arrangement was pleasing to the eye as well as sensible. "I just may discuss additional cattle with the rector, but for the time being, I should inspect the estate. Did you get the hamper from the cook?"

He pointed under the curricle's seat. "Right there. I was just gettin' ready to bring it around."

"I'll go back in the house and fetch her ladyship."

"Ah, sir?"

Kit turned to his groom. "Yes?"

"It would mean a lot if you kept on her ladyship's good side. Mrs. Gregson, the cook, keeps a fine table, but our fortunes are tied to yours."

Wonderful. All Kit needed was more pressure. After having met the woman, he could see her attempting to get back at him through his servants. "I'll do my best. By the way, make some inquiries about a Mr. Gawain Tolliver. He is a sort of relation to Lady Mary. I want to ensure he's not been around."

"And if he has?"

"We'll find another place for him to be." Kit would not tolerate the scoundrel's harassment of Mary. How no one else could get rid of the man was beyond him. Barham might not want to be ruthless with Tolliver, but Kit had no such compunctions.

He made his way to the front of the house where a neat trellis of yellow roses was just coming into bloom. Mary stood in the doorway speaking with Simons. "Good morning, my lady."

Smiling, she gracefully descended the steps and held out her hand. "Good morning to you, sir."

Kit thought he saw the butler's lips tilt up the tiniest bit but couldn't be sure. No matter, soon he and Mary would be wed, and the staff would have no cause to worry about her. Simons entered the hall, leaving Kit alone with her. "Allow me to help you into the carriage."

She started to place her foot on the step when he suddenly gave in to the need to lift her into the carriage, depositing her gently on the seat.

Her eyes widened. "Goodness. No one has ever done that before."

He had never done that before either, and in future he'd ensure no other man ever had the opportunity. "I hope you don't mind my groom appropriating your horses. Would you like to drive?" Mary settled her skirts. "Thank you for asking, but maybe later." "Ah, you are going to assess my skill. I do not suppose you'd be impressed if I told you I am a member of the Four Horse Club?" "Are you really?" she asked in an amazed tone. "Barham has wanted to be a member for years. Unfortunately he's a bit ham-handed. My father was a member, though." "Yes." Kit coughed. Should he tell her he'd been one of those blackballing poor Barham? "I am aware of your brother's attempts." "Oh no!" Mary's light laughter filled his soul. "I know it's terrible, but even his wife won't allow him to drive her. He sulked for days when she agreed to allow me to tool her around in my phaeton." Kit threaded the ribbons through his fingers. "In that case, I definitely wish to see your skill."

As they drove around the estate, she introduced him to his tenants. Everyone, it seemed, knew he was here and took their cues from her. Once they saw she was friendly toward him, their skepticism turned to acceptance. From the way all and sundry were acting, he could not imagine either the Rose Hill servants or his dependents believing he and Mary were not husband and wife. If he didn't soon win her agreement to wed him, there would be the devil to pay.

Toward midday, he directed the carriage to a wooded area by the river. After unhitching the pair, he led them to a shaded spot where the horses could drink and munch on the spring grass.

He took out the hamper and blanket and carried them to a flat area near the water. Mary helped him spread the blanket out on the ground and soon the food was unpacked. Cook had given them enough for days: Cheeses, bread, hothouse grapes, cold beef, and chicken made up the meal.

"This is my favorite spot on Rose Hill." Mary gave a small sigh as she settled elegantly on the blanket.

He reclined on the other side of the dishes, finally able to relax a bit. It appeared his plan to woo her was working. "That is what I was given to understand."

A light pink colored her face. "Thank you."

"It is my pleasure." He accepted a piece of cold chicken from her and bit into it. "This is excellent."

Her blush deepened. "Do you like it? It's an old receipt I found. The chicken is soaked in herbs over night."

"I have never had chicken that was so delicious." He didn't know any other woman, not even his mother or grandmother, who knew as much about cooking as Mary appeared to.

As she nibbled on a piece of local cheese, Kit couldn't keep his eyes from straying to her lips. A sudden and almost overpowering urge to push her down to the ground and kiss her senseless coursed through him.

Which was exactly what he should not, could not do.

He was not a barbarian. Thus far he'd successfully ignored the fact that Mary slept mere feet away from him, that he could hear her sing when she was in the bathtub and naked. He couldn't ruin everything now. Mary may have to wed him, but he would court her properly.

Her small, even teeth bit into a piece of bread, and the tip of her tongue licked a crumb from the corner of her lips. His heartbeat quickened, and Kit stifled a groan. When had eating become so erotic?

No kissing until you are betrothed.

Reaching over, he grabbed the jug of wine and removed the cork. "Would you like some?"

She sat up straighter, cleaning her fingers with a serviette. "Yes, thank you."

Rather than actual glasses, the cook had packed old-fashioned pottery wine cups. He filled one for Mary, bending sideways to place it next to her. At the same time she moved to take it. Their fingers brushed and their lips were only inches apart. She stilled, her eyelashes fluttering down.

Kit's heart thudded as he backed up slowly, attempting to get his baser instincts under control. No matter how much he wanted her, there would be no sampling the wares. Everyone around her was trying to manage her life. He must allow her to make her own decisions . . . to a point.

Mary waited and waited as time seemed to stand still. Kit was so close. She'd been sure he was going to kiss her. Then he moved away. She could have screamed with frustration. This was so unfair! The first time she wanted to be kissed, and the blasted man didn't even try. How was she to determine if she could love him if they didn't kiss?

Stamping down her annoyance, she took a sip of chilled white wine. She would be reasonable. They'd only known each other a few days. Perhaps he thought it was too soon, yet Grandmamma had said men always took what was offered and sometimes what wasn't. Mary remembered catching Barham kissing his wife during the house party at which they had met. They hadn't thought it was too soon.

Maybe Kit had not wanted to kiss her. Perhaps he was willing to wed her only to stop a scandal. He could go jump in the river if he thought that.

Mary opened her mouth to ask, then shut it again. She would wait a while longer, but if he didn't do something by next week, she'd call this courtship off. There was no point in being wooed by a gentleman who didn't truly want her.

She tried not to frown as he tossed off his cup of wine and immediately poured another. She hoped he did not always drink so quickly. She'd never heard of him being a drunkard, but some hid it well.

Perhaps it was something else. "Kit, is anything wrong?"

"No." He set his cup down. "I was merely distracted by the view."

Trees lined the area in which they sat, framing the vista across the narrow river. On the opposite bank was a meadow dotted with sheep, across the fields to the hazy blue hills beyond. "It is beautiful."

And she would miss it if she had to leave. Yet now was not the time to grow maudlin. Her friends were coming, and anything could happen in a week. She tucked into her meal. There was no point in hurting Cook's feelings. Kit was eating as well, and silence fell, but it was not uncomfortable.

Once she'd finished, Mary wiped the corners of her mouth with a serviette and searched for conversation. "Have you seen Phoebe's little boy, Arthur?"

"Yes. I visited them before I left to travel here. He is the image of Marcus, but with Phoebe's eyes."

That told Mary nothing as she hadn't yet met Marcus. "He must be a handsome little boy."

Kit grinned. "The ladies think so."

"I don't doubt you are correct. I cannot imagine a baby of Phoebe's not being beautiful." Mary checked her watch brooch. "It is almost two. We'd better return to the house soon."

Kit sprung lightly to his feet, holding out a hand to her. As she clasped it, warmth filled her, and she scrambled up quickly but none too gracefully. When he didn't release her, she glanced up and their gazes caught for a moment before he seemed to recall himself. Something had lurked in his eyes. If only she had the experience to read them.

Her heart sped as he once again placed his hands on her waist and lifted her into the carriage. That . . . her reaction . . . had to mean something.

He strode around to the other side, climbed in, and took the reins. "I believe it is your turn to handle the ribbons."

"I'd love to. It has been a long time since I've tooled an equipage this fine." Joy filled her as she threaded the leather through her fingers. He released the brake, and she gave the horses their office.

They were moving at a brisk pace when a rabbit suddenly darted out from a hedgerow. One of the horses shied. In an instant, Kit's arm was around her shoulders as she struggled to control the pair.

"Can you manage?" he asked, his tone on edge.

"I think so."

"Let me know."

Mary tried to ignore the feel of his large body touching hers from hip to shoulder. He had tensed, and his hands were ready to seize the reins if required. She was impressed that he hadn't just taken hold of the ribbons. Most men would have assumed she couldn't handle them.

Finally she got the team to a walk and Kit eased back. She wished he hadn't. On the other hand, maintaining such close contact was not prudent. She liked it much too well.

"Excellent job." His deep voice caressed her. "I'd let you drive any of my cattle."

She didn't even attempt to hide her smile as she slid a glance at him. "They are yours. The other pair was too old, and I had to put them out to pasture."

"You don't say?" A boyish grin appeared on his countenance. "I admired them earlier. If I'd known, I would have spent more time looking them over. I heard you got them from the rector. Did Mr. Doust help you with the two cover-hacks as well?"

"No." She shook her head. "We didn't know Mr. Doust well at the time. I bought them at the horse fair in Edinburgh. I did not think there would be much chance of meeting anyone there who knew me."

"You are resourceful, and you've got a good eye for horseflesh."

A rush of pleasure rose in her. "Thank you." It was nice to be admired for her abilities. She feathered the turn onto the drive. "I do love driving."

Her neck and shoulder began to tingle as his arm slid along the top of the seat behind her. She wanted him to touch her again, just a little, and she was surprised to discover how disappointed she was when he did not.

"I've had a wonderful day," he said as they entered the carriage yard an hour later. "Please compliment the cook for me."

Was that all he could say? A pout began to tug on her mouth, and she made herself smile politely. Perhaps she was expecting too much too soon. After all, his reputation was that of a perfect gentleman. Yet did that mean he was passionless? She could not imagine living without passion. "I will. I'm sure she'll be pleased."

He jumped down and waved away her groom as he reached out for her. Once again Kit's large, warm hands circled her waist, lifting her to the ground. Mary pretended to stumble, and he pulled her closer. Less than an inch separated her chest from his. The pulse beneath his jaw jumped. Did that mean he felt something for her after all? How was she to know for sure?

Phoebe, Countess of Evesham, stood on the bottom step of Robert and Serena Beaumont's home in York with a list in her hand, ticking off items as they were loaded on the six large traveling coaches lined up in the drive. "I think this is the last of it."

Her husband, Marcus, shook his head. "This reminds me of setting off for France with Serena. Have you warned Lady Mary we're coming?"

"Of course." Phoebe pinched the bridge of her nose. "I still cannot believe their grandmothers did this. It was all I could do not to give them a piece of my mind. How unfair to both Kit and Mary. I only wish I had known how desperate the situation with Mary had become. If she wants out of this arrangement, I shall do my best to find a way."

"What about Featherton?" Her husband's tone was gentle but firm. "He's just as trapped as she is, and his reputation is equally at risk."

Phoebe gazed at Marcus and became distracted by his turquoise eyes. He grew more handsome every year. Tucking her hand in his arm, she said, "We shall help both of them."

"And pray to God their interests are not opposed."

Phoebe sighed. *Now wouldn't that be a pickle.* "Indeed."

"Mamma, Papa." Almost two years old, Arthur broke away from his nurse and pelted down the steps.

Marcus caught him, throwing the child up in the air as Arthur squealed. "Are you ready for a journey?"

Arthur burrowed his head in Marcus's shoulder. "I ride with you."

"Only if you behave."

His son nodded. "I be good."

"You do realize," Phoebe pointed out, "Ben will now wish to ride with Rutherford."

Marcus shrugged. "I doubt Anna will object." A wicked glint shone in his eyes. "In any event, Rutherford probably needs the practice."

The other two couples who were traveling with Phoebe and Marcus—the Rutherfords and Gervais and Caro, Earl and Countess of Huntley—made their way down the stairs, followed by Robert and Serena Beaumont. Rutherford held his son Ben's hand. Huntley had his arm around Caro's ever-increasing waist.

"I so wish we could accompany you," Serena said, hugging Phoebe. "You'll let us know if we can help."

"I shall." She embraced her cousin. "Take care of my goddaughter."

Serena glanced over at Robert, who was holding the baby. "I don't think you need to worry."

Marcus grinned. "I'm trying to figure out who's more besotted."

"You're jealous," Robert retorted, "because I have two beautiful ladies and you have only one."

A few moments later, three horses were brought round. Marcus settled Arthur on a large roan before swinging up behind him and attaching the belt Marcus used to fasten his son securely to him.

"Papa, I go with you," Ben demanded, holding up his hands.

Rutherford heaved a sigh. "Very well, but I'm not changing your clout."

Once Anna and Caro were settled in the lead coach, Phoebe allowed herself to be handed up. "Sam," she called to her coachman, "we're ready."

She settled back in her seat, and Caro asked, "Have you heard from Mary?"

Phoebe shook her head. "Only the one letter welcoming us and letting me know all would be ready."

"Well"—Anna turned from the window—"we shall simply have to wait and see what we have when we arrive. Caro, you know her the best of all of us, do you not?"

"Most likely." She rubbed her hand over her stomach. "We grew up on neighboring estates and kept in contact after I left for Venice. The two things she always looked forward to were the Season and a love match."

For at least the hundredth time in a week, Phoebe shook her head. "I cannot believe her grandmother did this."

Caro raised a brow. "I can. According to my godmother, Horatia, the Dowager Duchess of Bridgewater has arranged all her children's and most of her grandchildren's marriages. Albeit she has been extremely cunning about doing so, and many times the couple wasn't even aware they had been matched."

"In that case," Anna said, "I'm surprised at how ill they handled Mary and Featherton."

"I'm sure it is due to the cousin." Caro's brows furrowed. "I remember him as a child and didn't care for him then. Loose fish doesn't begin to describe the man."

Phoebe glanced at her friends. "In that case, we shall ensure that Mr. Gawain Tolliver doesn't get anywhere near Mary."

"I do not doubt we'll have plenty of help from the gentlemen for that." Caro frowned. "My concern is for Mary and Kit."

"I am positive," Anna said, giving Caro a reassuring smile, "we'll think of something."

"I hope you're right." She rubbed her stomach again. "I have a feeling this isn't going to be easy."

CHAPTER TWELVE

The next morning, Kit strolled into the breakfast room and found Mary already reading a gazetteer while she dug into a dish he'd never seen before. "Good morning."

She glanced up, startled, as if she had not expected to see anyone else. "Good morning to you as well. I thought you'd still be asleep."

Apparently she'd taken him for an idleby. Though in fairness, they had not met at breakfast before. Yesterday, not wishing to spoil their fragile accord, he'd had his valet bring him a tray, and the two previous days, Mary had broken her fast in her room. "No, it's my habit to rise early." He took the chair next to hers. There were no dishes set out on the sideboard as he was used to, but a pot of tea was on the table. "Is the tea fresh?"

"Let me ring for more."

She jiggled a small silver bell and Simons appeared immediately. "My lady?"

"Bring a fresh pot of tea, and"—she turned to Kit—"what else would you like to eat?"

Ah, this was his opportunity to discover what she had. "Whatever you're having is fine." He took out his quizzing glass. "What is that?"

Mary grinned. "It's a bacon floddie. They are usually served with eggs and the local sausage, but I'm not fond of any sausage."

"I'll have two of those with their full accompaniment, and toast."

Her butler bowed again and left. Why he thought of the servant as hers when he'd been paying the man's wages for years, Kit didn't know.

A few minutes later Simons returned. "Your breakfast will be ready shortly, sir."

"Thank you."

As the door closed behind the butler, he considered opening it again for propriety's sake, but that would appear odd as everyone thought they were married. Why the devil wasn't Lady Eunice down here playing gooseberry? He'd have to have a word with her. Craning his neck, he attempted to read the paper over Mary's shoulder. "Is there anything interesting?"

She swallowed and glanced up. "This is the *Post*. We won't receive the *Gazette* until later in the day. Are you still interested?"

That was a challenge if he'd ever heard one. Perhaps she didn't like to share her newspaper, or did not like to be interrupted when reading. "I'm as prone as the next person to want to know what is going on in the *ton*."

She handed him one of the pages that she'd already read. It was probably good to know she was proprietary over her reading material. "It's too early in the Season for much to occur, but there is one engagement announcement. A Miss Charlotte Manning has accepted Lord Peter Marshall."

Simons brought the tea and a stack of buttered toast. Mary poured Kit a cup, adding cream and one sugar. Brilliant woman to have remembered how he liked his tea. Then he focused on what she'd said. "Poor Stanstead."

She looked over the top of the newssheet. "A friend of yours?"

"Yes." Kit took a sip of tea. "He is Robert Beaumont's cousin."

"Was Lord Stanstead in love with her?"

"I don't know." Kit leaned back in his chair. "He was infatuated, and he had hopes in that direction. They met at Robert and Serena's wedding last year, yet I never thought she was right for him."

Mary placed the paper on the table, and met Kit's gaze. "I wasn't aware men had thoughts on matters of the heart."

In that case, she had a great deal to learn. Perhaps now he could make some inroads with his lady. "Stanstead has recently attained the grand age of two and twenty. It's not time yet for him to marry."

Her brows rose. "I must agree. It is young for a gentleman. Yet he wished to wed?"

Kit cradled his tea-cup, taking a sip and savoring the taste. "Apparently. He had an unfortunate family life, but his mother remarried last year to a man Stanstead admires greatly. She just gave birth to a baby boy shortly before Serena had her girl, and he wants the same type of life."

"What do his friends think of him wanting to settle down?"

That was an interesting question. Kit shrugged. "I'm not sure how many of his friends are his age. He appears older than two and twenty and takes all his responsibilities seriously."

"Hmm," was all Mary said before burying herself behind the newspaper again.

He quickly demolished two pieces of toast before his food arrived. The floddies looked almost as good on his plate as they had on Mary's. He eyed hers, just as she glanced over her paper, and she gobbled up the last bites on her plate. Apparently she didn't like sharing her food any more than she did her reading material. Using his fork, Kit cut a piece of the floddie and tasted. "Heaven."

"I agree." She eyed his plate. "Aunt Eunice doesn't like them at all."

Based on his memory of yesterday's chicken, he asked, "What are they made of?"

"Potatoes, eggs, onions, flour, and bacon."

"You are the only lady of my acquaintance who would know that." He finished the one and made short work of the other. Perhaps he should request more. Kit wondered what it would be like to feed her.

Mary's chin rose a bit. "I make it my business—"

"No no." He held up his hand and chuckled. "Don't pull caps with me. I admire you greatly for it. My great-grandmother used to know all manner of useful things."

She picked up her cup and sighed. "My great-grandmother did as well. I do not understand what happened."

"The same thing that occurred with landowners." He wanted to sigh himself. "There was a time when the typical gentleman knew much more about husbandry than most do now. Although there is a growing movement to recover the knowledge and find new ways of making estates more productive without harming one's dependents."

She stared almost longingly at his plate. "Eat your eggs before they become cold." Mary refilled her cup. "How do you feel about farming?"

He did as he was told before answering. How pleasant it was to break his fast with her. "I believe one should know as much and more than one's steward."

She raised the most eloquent and skeptical brow he'd ever seen.

Now how would he explain why he hadn't been here in years? "I am kept busy going to my father's estates, and I've spent time in Norfolk at Pope's farm. But you are in the right of it. I should not have neglected Rose Hill."

She took a piece of fresh toast. "No, you should not have, but at least you are learning what you need to know. Are your family's properties extensive?"

"In a word, yes. I've been told the only reason we hold a mere viscountcy and not an earldom or higher is that my ancestors knew better than to curry too much royal attention. Instead, they concentrated on building up their holdings."

She studied her cup as she asked, "Does that include recent generations?"

Ah, he'd forgotten she was an heiress and had probably been courted for what she could bring to a marriage rather than for herself. Not an intelligent way to treat a progressive-thinking lady. "No. My parents married for love, and my mother expects me to do the same."

The corners of her lips curved up as she took a drink. "My parents wanted that for me too. That is one reason I know Papa would never have arranged for me to marry my cousin."

If that was the case, then why the devil did their grandmothers cook up this untenable scheme? Those two old ladies had some explaining to do. Normally he greatly admired and was very fond of his grandmother, but right now, he could wring her neck.

His stomach still rumbled. "Shall I order more floddies?"

"If you wish. You're sure to get on Cook's good side if you do."

Mary discovered she enjoyed having breakfast with Kit. Unlike her father and brothers, he was not at all grumpy in the morning. For a few moments she thought he'd attempt to take the newspaper, but he hadn't. That had surprised her. And he was interested in trying new foods. She couldn't imagine most of the gentlemen she knew doing that so easily. Still, she had not trusted him when he glanced at her plate. He was probably one of those people who thought everyone should share. Harrumph. The twins used to think that as well, and learned better. He might get a fork in his hand if he tried to take any of her food.

He rang the bell and when Simons appeared he ordered more bacon floddies. "I take it Barham's holdings are extensive?"

"Not so much in land as in other investments. My father said my uncle helped build back the family fortunes after my grandfather depleted much of it."

Kit's tea-cup hung suspended between the plate and his mouth. "The same uncle who is insisting you marry his son?"

For a moment she'd forgotten about Uncle Hector's role. Really, Mr. Featherton's presence had a derogatory effect on her brain. "Yes," she said slowly. "Which is yet another reason his insistence there was a betrothal agreement does not make sense. He built his own fortune as well. Why would his son have any need of marrying an heiress?"

"I have people looking for your uncle. When we find him, we'll make a point to ask." Kit drained the last of the tea.

Mary appreciated his concern, but doubted he would have success where her brother had failed. She glanced up to find his plate already clean. He must have polished off the last of the toast as well. She would have to ensure there was more food on the table to-morrow, or have a few serving dishes set out. That would please Cook. "What are your plans for the day?"

"I thought I'd leave it to you. What would you normally do?"

Simons reappeared with floddies, toast, and another pot of tea.

"Yesterday, I was making assessments. To-day is when I take the tenants items they need or could use. I detest those ladies who ride out bestowing their bounty, never knowing what a family truly requires." Try as she might, Mary couldn't keep the hard edge from her voice. But what did it matter? He should know how she felt.

"You make a good point." Kit cut his eggs, and held the fork out to her. "You looked as if you wanted more."

She opened her mouth, closing it around the savory dish. "I love this." As she chewed, he poured her another cup of tea, adding milk and sugar. "You really don't have to do that."

"But I like to," he said, feeding her another forkful.

Soon the floddies, toast, and tea were finished. He put his serviette on the table and stood. "I'll go with you. Although you have left me little to be concerned with when it comes to the farming. I recently heard of a new plow that might be helpful here."

Ooh, it would be beyond anything if he really knew about . . . "The one with the self-scouring moldboard?"

He looked almost like a peacock preening. "Exactly."

Talk about prayers being answered. "I wanted to buy one, but we have not been able to afford them for all the tenants."

"If you agree"—he gave her the warm look that she was coming to like so much—"I'll make arrangements to have one delivered for every tenant and the home farm."

Before she could stop herself, Mary jumped up and wrapped her arms around his neck. "That would be wonderful."

He stood, his arm snaking around her waist. When he gazed down at her, she was sure Kit would kiss her. She puckered her lips and . . . The door opened. "Oh, excuse me, my lady."

Drat, drat, drat. She dropped her arms, and Kit stepped away. "It's all right, Simons. Mr. Featherton and I were just leaving." All she wanted was a kiss. Was fate scheming against her? "I'll meet you at the stables, sir."

"I won't be long, my lady."

She hurried out of the room. Somehow, she must find a way to give him another opportunity to kiss her, and she would tell Simons from now on to knock if the door was closed. Especially at breakfast. She remembered Phoebe writing that her husband had accomplished a great deal of important courting at the breakfast table. Caro had told Mary that her husband fed her. Mary might not have croissants and chocolate, but she had floddies and tea.

Damn, that was close. Kit resisted the urge to swipe his hand across his forehead. Her joy had been so real, her lips so tempting, he'd almost forgotten his vow. Kissing and the rest would have to wait until after the betrothal.

Thank God, he knew they would marry. He didn't think he could manage it if that wasn't already settled. He had scorned Beaumont for trying to trap Serena, but if it weren't for Kit's grandmother's machinations . . . He could understand why his friend had been so desperate. The more he came to know Mary, the more he liked her. Not only was she intelligent and practical, but she seemed to become more beautiful each day. How that was possible, he wasn't sure. She'd already been the loveliest lady he knew. Not to mention his desire for her was growing by leaps and bounds. He'd never been so attracted to a woman before. He wanted her; no, he needed her. In his home and his bed. He had one, now he needed to work on the other. How long would it take before she agreed to be his wife?

He made it out to the wagon mere minutes before she appeared. Why it was so important for him to be there first, he didn't know. Nineteen baskets were already loaded. Strange, he'd thought he had more tenants than that. Not wanting to ask her, he reviewed the names in his head. Twenty-one. She walked out with Cook, carrying two bags.

"Ye tell 'em that was the best batch of barley I ever had," the older woman said.

"I won't forget. They will love your spice loaves. Mrs. Davies says you make the best ones in the county and England."

Cook blushed. "G'an on with ye, ma lady."

Mary smiled. "It's the truth."

Not wanting to disrupt the moment, or, more likely, ruin his cook's mood, Kit waited until she was next to the wagon before saying, "Do the last two tenants not need a basket?" She gave him "the look." The very one his mother gave his father when he'd said something dim-witted. He hated having to dig himself out of a hole. "I'm sorry. I didn't mean to suggest . . ."

Maybe he should just stop now.

"In fact, two of the families normally do quite well. I have included hard bonbons for the children and a tisane for one of the ladies who suffers from flatulence."

He reached into the pouch he carried, pulling out a handful of candy. "Such as these?"

"Yes." She rewarded him with a smile. "I predict you'll become popular with all the children."

As long as he could please her, he would have achieved his purpose. He handed her into the conveyance. "Will you drive, or shall I?"

"You may. I find I like being a passenger. Aunt Eunice never likes to tool the wagon."

Now that she had mentioned her, Kit had noticed Lady Eunice had been absent of late. "Where is your aunt?"

Mary's brow crinkled. "I'm not sure. Normally she is down for breakfast before I leave."

The woman damn well needed to be there during breakfast. Especially after what almost happened this morning.

Less than fifteen minutes later, they arrived at the Robson cottage. The children, remembering him from yesterday, ran out to greet them. Although they were too well mannered to ask for the sweets, the youngest, whom Kit judged to be around four years old, wrapped her arm around his leg and beamed up at him.

"Annan," a frustrated voice called from the cottage, "git yer hands off the master."

Lifting the girl into his arms, Kit called back, "Please, Mrs. Robson, don't let it bother you."

He reached into the purse he'd left in the wagon, drawing out a handful of the bonbons. He handed one to her, then divided the others among her brothers and sisters. Eight children—the house didn't seem large enough. Still holding Annan, he whispered in Mary's ear, "Do they require an addition?"

She smiled. "If you look in the back, you will see it has recently been enlarged."

"Thank you."

A sudden blush infused her cheeks, and she grabbed the basket, hurrying toward Mrs. Robson. Now, if he only knew if she was pleased with his approbation or he'd embarrassed her.

It took most of the day to complete their rounds, but since they were offered everything from tea to cheese and bread at every stop, neither of them was hungry when they returned home.

Home.

Kit had never before thought of Rose Hill as his home, yet Mary did, and even if he had a choice, he would not take the property away from her.

All day long he'd fought himself from taking her into his arms. He lifted her down from the wagon and struggled to remove his hands from her waist. She stared up at him, her gray eyes searching his, and his chest tightened. God, how he wanted to kiss her, run his hands through her golden hair.

One finger at a time, he released her. "We should go in now."

Her lashes lowered and she turned toward the steps. "I shall see you before dinner."

What he needed was a cold bath. That evening he made sure he was the last one down. Kit no longer trusted himself to be alone with his prospective wife. No matter how drawn to Mary he was, he would not behave as his brother had.

* * *

Shortly before seven o'clock in the evening, Gawain Tolliver entered a clean, neat tavern in the City, not far from the 'Change. He understood why bankers would patronize the place. It reminded him of an orderly account ledger. Spying an empty table in the back, he strolled to it and ordered a coffee.

Late yesterday, a clerk who worked at Hoare's Bank, Mr. Beacon, whom Gawain convinced to help him find Cousin Mary, had sent a note around. The man had been reluctant to assist until Gawain wove a story telling the man that her family was concerned, as Lady Mary had not been in touch with anyone for several months. Thankfully, Mr. Beacon's opinion of females' abilities to take care of themselves was not high.

As the church bells of St. Paul's tolled the hour, a spare, middle-aged man entered the tavern. Beacon slid onto the seat across from Gawain. He took off his spectacles, wiping them thoroughly with a cloth before replacing them on his face. "I do not know how much help the information I have found will be to you. The funds are transferred to the Bank of Scotland in Edinburgh. You would need to contact them to be provided with more information as to your cousin's whereabouts."

Gawain wiped his brow and heaved a huge sigh. That was more information than he'd had in months. "I thank you. The family thanks you. Surely we will be able to discover her whereabouts now."

The clerk stood and bowed. "It was my pleasure to assist. I trust her elders will give the young woman a good talking-to when you find her."

"Yes, they certainly shall." He rose, and shook the man's hand. "Again, you have our thanks. You were our last hope."

Mr. Beacon flushed. "I wish I could have been of more aid. Well, good-bye and good luck."

Gawain retook his seat and slowly drank his coffee. Was Mary really in Scotland? Or was this simply another wild-goose chase to keep him busy until she could find a husband? If his cousin weren't so headstrong, he would suspect the dowager of making a match for her. Then again, she'd need to be somewhere there was at least some sort of Marriage Mart, and surely the dowager would insist on being there with Mary. After all, an established lady with connections had to sponsor her.

Edinburgh had a Season. Not as large or refined as London's, but

Mary might think it was better than nothing. He'd just have to wait until the dowager made a move and led him to his soon-to-be wife.

"Sir."

Gawain glanced up. His groom had a wide grin on his face. "The old lady is getting ready to leave. I sent a message to have your things packed."

"Finally. Get the boy we've had watching the house. We'll take him with us. He can be useful. It won't do to let her know I'm following."

The George Inn, Stamford, Lincolnshire, England

"Is he still following us?" Lucinda lowered herself carefully into a chair in their private parlor. A fire roared in the fireplace, and the room was warm enough, but her old body wasn't what it used to be. Riding in a coach for hours over the past week hadn't helped either. Blasted roads. One would think with the tolls the government charged they would be in better repair.

"That's what Athey said," Constance replied, leaning on her cane just a bit too heavily.

"You are making sure she is in no danger?" Not that Lucinda thought the girl would come to harm, but when her friend was focused on something . . .

"She is well protected. There is at least one footman with her at all times."

"I don't believe I've ever seen a more tenacious young man."

Constance gave a basilisk stare. "With sixty thousand at stake? I'm only surprised he hasn't done more."

Lucinda took a sip of the excellent claret. The George was known for the quality of its cellars. "I'm wondering if we haven't been the slightest bit ham-handed with Kit and Mary."

"What do you mean?" Constance sniffed her wine before taking a sip.

"Well, dear, we were both able to arrange matches for our children and many of our grandchildren without anyone being the wiser . . ." Lucinda left her sentence hanging. It was always better to allow Constance to figure things out for herself.

"I see your point. They will come to the conclusion that we masterminded the scheme." She heaved a sigh. "I know Mary has romantic ideas, but honestly, I do not know what else we could have done. Allowing Gawain Tolliver to get his hands on her was not an option."

"I would like to see my great-grandchildren," Lucinda prodded gently.

"Never fear. Once they discover they were meant for each other, they will come around." Constance's tone was bracing but not convincing.

"I do hope so. From the last letter Featherton received from Kit, it appears he is not happy with the situation."

A sharp tap sounded on the door and dinner was brought in. Footmen assisted Lucinda and Constance to the dining table. Perhaps she was right and the children would forgive them. Now, if they could only get rid of the ogre. Mayhap they could arrange for young Mr. Tolliver to have a carriage mishap someplace in an area several miles from a coaching house. In fact, that was an excellent idea. She'd speak with the coachman after dinner.

Gawain sat in the common room of the inn across from the George. Even if he'd had the funds, he couldn't have stayed there. Hell, he couldn't even afford to bring the boy he was using to watch the duchess. Who would have thought the lad's mother would demand twenty-five pounds for the urchin. Five days and the dowagers had only traveled thirty miles from London. Where the hell were they going? It couldn't be back to the dower house; he had bribed one of the villagers to watch and there were no preparations being made.

Even his mother agreed that Mary wouldn't go into Polite Society until her grandmother was with her. Unless she planned on joining the old ladies somewhere along the road. Now that would be convenient. He'd follow them and snatch her the moment she was alone.

He took a pull of the bitter local ale. If only his mother was right and Mary had taken up with a man. That would settle all their problems. Even if she waited to wed him, he'd be able to blackmail her. Not everything he wanted, but a damn sight better than nothing. He took another drink and frowned. He wished he didn't have to marry her, but the money would make up for a lot. Perhaps he could find a gentleman to seduce Mary and convince her to wed him before her birthday? Then he'd have the money. He'd have to pay a goodly sum, but it might be better than having a shrew to wife. Yet, who could he get to do it who would wait for payment?

CHAPTER THIRTEEN

Mary sat in the window seat of her parlor, staring out at the garden. It had been three days since she and Kit had gone on the picnic, and although he was very attentive and everything one could expect from a gentleman, something was wrong. She had made sure he'd had several opportunities to kiss her, and just when she thought he would, nothing happened. He had to kiss her. Otherwise she wouldn't know if she could love him or he could love her.

This was very much the same as when she'd thought he would ask her to dance during her first and only full Season. If he was finding it that difficult to like her enough to kiss her she didn't want him. She'd be no man's penance.

Was it only the possibility of scandal that made him want to marry her? She cast her mind back over all their conversations. He apparently didn't require her money, albeit no one would turn down such a fortune. He'd complimented her housekeeping, but never her appearance. Even her blackguard cousin had done that, for all the good it did him. Perhaps Kit didn't find her pleasing. She'd always been held to be pretty, some had even said beautiful. Two gentlemen had offered for her that Season only because of her appearance, or at least that was what all the poems they had written to her had been about. Papa had been alive then to protect her from the fortune hunters, and there had been several of them. What a lowering thought that Kit may not think her even passable. Maybe he preferred ladies with dark hair and eyes.

What else had he praised her for? He loved what she'd done in the garden and the property. *Her estate management.* Kit remarked on that more than anything else. He had said Featherton wives always brought something to the family. Was that the reason he was content to wed her? If so, he was no better than the others who wanted her solely for her looks or her dowry. Why couldn't a man love her for herself? Why did there always have to be another reason? Well, she would not be married for her housewifery.

Still, that begged the question of whether she loved Kit or could love him. She liked that he took responsibility. He had even owned up to neglecting Rose Hill. He had a good sense of humor. He enjoyed gossip and admitted it. Not many of the gentlemen she knew, the number being pitifully small, would ever disclose that. He was kind to her and to their tenants, especially to the children, and the servants. It must mean something that she wanted to kiss him. If only he would oblige her by kissing her, she would know if she loved him, and more importantly if he loved her.

"My lady?"

"What is it, Mathers?"

"It's time to dress for dinner. Shall I put out the deep rose?"

"That's fine."

"What's got you so blue deviled?"

"Nothing. I'm just trying to figure something out."

"Mayhap Mr. Featherton could help."

No, no, no! He was the last person she could turn to. Mary frowned. "I don't think so. That is who I'm having problems with."

Mathers stilled. "He hasn't—"

"Oh, good gracious no!" Mary shook her head. "That's part of the problem."

Her dresser sniffed. "I think you've been reading too many of those romance novels."

She would not go round and round with her maid about that. The only things Mathers read were sermons and improving works. "I do not wish to discuss it."

Her maid muttered something about young ladies going to the devil. "Let me untie this gown and get you into the other."

When Mary entered the drawing room, Eunice and Mr. Doust were in conversation, and Kit stood off by himself, holding a glass of sherry loosely in his fingers. She pasted a smile on her face. "Good evening."

He came to her immediately, took her hand, and raised it. "I was beginning to worry something might be amiss."

Mary met his gaze as he searched her face. He *had* been concerned. Did he really care about her? "I could not decide what to wear." A small smile appeared on his lips. Oh, those lips. She'd dreamed about them last night and had woken kissing her pillow. He touched them to her fingers, and she thought she'd gone to heaven. "I am sorry for being late."

"You could never be late. I told Simons to put dinner back for a quarter hour."

No wonder her dresser had been in a hurry. She was always on time. What was happening to her? "Thank you."

Wrong. This was all wrong. She thought she might be falling in love, and he did not love her at all. Perhaps she should tell him she had found a way out of their grandmothers' trap. But then everything would be even more uncomfortable than it already was, and their friends were arriving soon.

What a pickle! Perhaps when Phoebe, Anna, and Caro left for Edinburgh, Mary would go with them. Away from Mr. Perfect and all her less-than-perfect feelings.

Kit placed Mary's hand on his arm. Damn if he hadn't fallen in love with her. He dreamt of nothing else but her. He couldn't even remember what had occupied his dreams before Mary had come into his life.

Last night he'd wanted to open the door between their chambers and show her how much he desired her. If they had been alone, he would have run his fingers through her hair, allowing it to fall down her back. That it was long, he'd surmised, but did it flow to her waist or her hips? How he wanted to feel its silky texture, bury his nose in it and fill his senses with her scent.

He would have fused his lips to hers, nipped and licked his way down her graceful neck, then to the sensitive base. Kit wanted her more than he'd ever wanted a woman before. How many times now had he almost kissed her? But to act on his desires would be to dishonor her, and he could not do that to the lady for whom he cared so much. If only he knew she had the same feelings for him as he did for her, then he could propose and put himself out of this misery. "What do you have planned for dinner to-night?"

She dropped her gaze, and when she spoke, her voice was toneless. "I only remember we have cockle soup to start."

Drat it all, somehow he'd hurt her. He'd rather take a knife to his gut than injure her in any way at all. "It sounds wonderful."

When Mary tugged her hand, he let it go. "As you are aware," she said in a sour tone, "I am a good housewife." She turned to Doust and smiled. "What a pleasure to have you join us again."

He slanted a glance at Eunice. "The pleasure, my lady, is all mine. I hope I have not outworn my welcome."

"No, indeed. We enjoy your company."

At least Doust and Lady Eunice were happy. Kit was about to drag Mary out of the room and find out what the devil he'd done, when Simons saved Kit from himself. "Dinner is served."

Kit placed Mary's hand on his arm. She shivered as a spark ran up his arm. "Are you cold?"

"A little."

He wrapped his arm around her, drawing her to his side. "I am told I'm a warm fellow."

The jest appeared lost on her. "You are. I should have brought my shawl." She moved away. "We should go in. I do not want Cook to be upset."

The soup was good, as was the rest of the meal, yet with Doust and Lady Eunice making sheep eyes at each other and in general behaving like April and May, and Mary avoiding meeting Kit's eyes, it was the longest meal of his life. For the first time, he was relieved when she stood, signaling an end to dinner. By the time he entered the drawing room, Mary had gone.

Perhaps it was a good thing his friends were due in a day or two. Somehow he'd managed to get on her bad side, and he didn't even know how he'd done it.

Hell. This courting business was a deuced sight harder than he'd thought it would be.

Around eleven in the morning the next day, one of the younger footmen skidded to a stop on the polished oak floor in front of Kit. "Sir, there's a mess of coaches coming up the drive."

Reinforcements. Finally. He was fully prepared to be the butt of his friends' jokes if they could just tell him how to go on with Mary. "Go find her ladyship and tell her she is wanted in the hall."

The lad bowed. "Right away, sir."

Several minutes later, Mary came from the back of the house. Kit was at the door when she joined him. "What is it? Jemmy was out of breath when he got to me."

Moving to her side, Kit placed his hand on the small of her back. For a moment she leaned into it, then stopped. If only he could ask her what was wrong, but he doubted she would tell him. "It appears our guests have arrived."

Mary's face lit up like the fireworks at Vauxhall. "I can't wait. It has been so long since I've been able to spend any time with them. All I've had is letters."

Kit hadn't before considered how lonely her life must have been during the past few years. If she gave him the opportunity, he would ensure she was never isolated again. "Simons, open the door." He placed her hand on his arm. "Shall we, my lady?"

"Yes, let's." Her smile grew wide, and he ground his teeth, wishing her happiness was directed at him.

They strolled through the doorway just as a team of gleaming, perfectly matched blacks came stamping to a halt. Three gentlemen on horseback rode up to the wide, shallow granite steps. Two had small children strapped to them. He grinned. That was one way to do it. When the third carriage stopped, the door opened and two women piled out, quickly making their way to the horses.

Simons was about to open the lead coach's door when Marcus called out, "Here, take him and give him to his nurse. I'll get my lady."

Kit fought the urge to chuckle as Arthur was handed to the butler.

Mary giggled, covering her mouth as she did. "I should not have laughed."

"I don't know." Kit bit off his laugh. He doubted the butler would enjoy being the object of amusement. "The sight of your butler holding Arthur out as if he doesn't know what to do with the lad is quite entertaining."

Fortunately, the child's nurse was right there to take him.

"It is. Oh no, now he has the other one."

"That's Ben. Anna and Rutherford's boy."

By the time Ben was in Simons's hands, Marcus was handing Phoebe down from the carriage.

Mary rushed forward. "Phoebe."

Soon Mary was crushed in her friend's embrace, then handed off to Caro and Anna. As the ladies hugged and kissed, the gentlemen came to greet Kit.

He clasped Marcus's hand. "How was the trip here?"

"About as expected with two young boys. How goes the courtship?"

Kit grimaced. "For a day or two I thought I was doing well, then something happened yesterday, and she's been distant ever since."

"Women are the very devil to figure out." Huntley clapped Kit on the back. "But we're here to help."

"That's the truth." Rutherford shook Kit's hand. "I'm sure the ladies will aid the cause as well. They've been worried about Lady Mary."

"They are not the only ones." Kit ran a hand over his face. "Come in and get settled. I'm sure Mary will have ordered tea." He lowered his voice so that only his friends could hear. "Remember the servants believe us to be man and wife."

"That has got to be awkward for you," Huntley said.

"You have no idea," Kit responded in an undervoice. It also might be one reason this courtship was not going as well as it should.

The ladies joined them, and they made their way into the hall.

"The house is cozy in a way that reminds me of Marsh Hill." Anna turned to Mary. "It's wonderful."

"What a lovely abode," Caro exclaimed. "It is the perfect size. Large enough to entertain friends yet small enough to not become lost in."

Huntley put his arm around his wife's waist, and shook his head. "That is a story for another time. You'll note this house was not added on to, higgledy piggledy."

Mary's lips twitched. "Your home in Suffolk?"

"The very one." Caro closed her eyes for a moment. "Apparently no one thought to build up, rather than out. It rambles so badly we can use only half the rooms, if that."

"Can you remodel?" Mary signaled for everyone to follow her.

"Therein lies the problem. It is not ours to do with as we wish. Gervais is in delicate negotiations with his father, who, unfortunately, likes the building as it is."

The conversations on old houses and the best way to modernize them continued until Kit's and Mary's guests were settled in their chambers.

In the corridor outside of her chambers, Kit took one of her hands and kissed the palm, curling her fingers around it. "The drawing room or the morning room?" She glanced down at her fist then looked up, searching his face as if confused. "The drawing room. I'll show them the rest of the house to-morrow. Unless you'd rather—"

"It is your home," Kit said, meaning every word. He had never been drawn to this property before, but Mary had made it into a warm, welcoming home. Of its own volition his head bent to kiss her. He pulled it up sharply. What the hell was he doing? "It would probably confuse the servants if you did not do it."

The soft expression left her countenance, and she pressed her lips together before turning on her heel and marching back down the stairs. "Naturally, we would not wish to upset the servants."

He gave thanks to the Deity he'd not given in to his impulse. She probably would have slapped him.

"Ooooh, of all the infuriating, godforsaken men. Why did he have to come into my life?" Pacing the length of the drawing room, Mary ranted to herself. "Well, that's a stupid question. My grandmother is to blame, and once she arrives, I'm going to give her a good piece of my mind. I never should have gone along with this—this stupid idea." She turned to pace back down the room when the door opened.

Simons gave the most formal bow she'd ever seen him perform. "My lady, the Countess of Evesham, the Countess of Huntley, and Lady Rutherford wish to see you."

Once the door was closed, Phoebe glanced around. "We heard you talking and did not know if you were alone. Yet before we could knock, your butler showed us in."

Caro took Mary's hands. "He will bring tea soon unless you require something stronger. Come, sit, and you can tell us what has happened."

She glanced at the door. "Where are your husbands?"

"In the nursery making sure the children are settled." A sly smile appeared on Anna's face. "If they arrive too soon, you will show us around your garden."

Caro sank into the sofa in front of the windows, which was part of several seating areas in the long room.

Shoving a small pillow behind her friend, Mary sighed. "I am a terrible hostess, paying more attention to my concerns instead of my guests."

"Nonsense," Caro responded. "We came to help you."

"Because of my grandmother?" Mary knew it was so; still, she had to ask.

"Both of the grandmothers," Phoebe said, taking a seat in a chair. "They were about to leave Town and come here when the duchess caught your cousin watching the house."

Mary dropped onto the sofa next to Caro and covered her face. "Shall I never be shut of him?"

Simons entered, placed the tea tray in front of her, left, and closed the door behind him.

"I don't know how much time we'll have before the gentlemen join us." Anna chose a chair and settled her skirts. "I realize you do not know me that well, but it would help if you told us everything from start to finish."

Phoebe and Caro's trust in Anna made Mary resolve to ask for the help she needed. Taking a breath, she straightened her shoulders. "Caro, you know when my cousin began to bother me?" Her friend nodded. "Barham's first child had just been born, and he didn't wish to remain in London but would not leave me alone. I went back to the estate with him, but Gawain followed." She told them about each time she'd thought she had escaped him, only to discover he'd found her and tried to bribe the servants and others in the area. "Finally we let him think he had, and the maid gave him false information. That was when I came to Rose Hill."

Caro shifted her position so that she faced Mary. "I wish I had known. But you have been safe and contented here?"

"I've been happier than I've been in a very long time." She was so thankful to be able to unburden herself. "As all of us were, I was raised to run a great estate. Rose Hill is not quite that, but it gave me an occupation." Yet another reason Papa would not have betrothed her to Gawain. Uncle Hector did not have a large holding for his son to inherit. She told her friends about her early fears and doubts about the name Featherton, and what occurred when Kit arrived. "He was enraged, as he well should have been, and I was devastated. He was the last person I wanted to see."

And it didn't make it easier when he said Rose Hill was her house. He, of all people, knew how untrue that was.

Caro took Mary's hands. "I remember how you seemed drawn to each other and I was surprised nothing came of it."

"I had no idea I was so obvious." Her grandmother had been in London then. Had she noticed Mary's attraction as well? "I did try to hide it."

"It was not just you," Caro said, squeezing Mary's hand. "He could barely keep his eyes off you."

That she had not expected to hear. After he ignored her she'd thought him indifferent. "But what am I to do?"

"We know the match was planned by your grandmothers." Phoebe's lips formed a thin line. "I do not agree with how they went about it; nevertheless, we must work with what we have."

Mary pleated and unpleated her skirts, praying that her friends would agree with her plan to avoid an unwanted match. "At first I thought there was no way out of it, but if we find we do not suit, which is beginning to look like the case, I have hit upon a scheme to avoid marrying him."

The ladies exchanged glances; finally Caro asked, "What is your idea?"

Mary glanced down at the hand Kit had kissed. "I have decided to go abroad to live for a few years. In the event some man attempts to force me to marry him, I've instructed my brother and his man of business to draft documents not allowing my husband to have access to any of my property for the duration of his life. Barham has permission to act for me. I realize that is premature, but I would rather have the provisions put in place as soon as I inherit."

For several moments, the room was so quiet the sound of the clock on the mantel ticking sounded as loud as church bells.

Caro's brow creased as she pressed gently on Mary's hand. "Living abroad is not always the answer."

"Nor is running away," Phoebe added.

"I must agree." Anna nodded. "Your best course of action is to confront him with your doubts." She cocked her head for a moment. "I believe the gentlemen are coming. Let us continue this conversation in the garden."

Thank God for Anna's hearing. Mary did not wish to see Kit before she knew what she would do.

* * *

Kit opened the door to the drawing room. The tea service was on the table, untouched. Where the devil had the ladies got to? He strode to the window seat and looked out. The women were strolling the garden, two by two, their arms linked.

Huntley came up beside Kit. "Must be a serious discussion if they've left without drinking a cup of tea."

His friend was right. He caught a glimpse of their profiles as they turned a corner. None of them were smiling. "I honestly do not know what I have done."

"Do you mind if I pour?" Rutherford asked. "I'm a bit peckish."

Kit shook his head. "Not at all. Once we've finished what is on the tray, I'll ring for something more sustaining."

"Why not call for it now?" Marcus asked, filling his plate.

"I don't want the servants to know the ladies did not partake."

Huntley pushed Kit down onto the window seat. "Give over, man. What the hell is going on here?"

The others pulled up chairs, until they were seated in a semicircle. Marcus sat. "That's what I'd like to know as well."

Taking out his quizzing glass, Rutherford went to the French window. "Agreed. The sooner we know what the problem is, the sooner we can be with our wives."

It felt strange sitting in Mary's favorite place. Kit rubbed the back of his neck. "I don't know."

Rutherford's quizzing glass focused on Kit. "Unfortunate, but not surprising." He waved his arm to include Huntley and Marcus. "However, you have with you those who have battled the female mind and won." Huntley rolled his eyes as Rutherford continued. "I believe you must begin at the beginning."

Huntley pressed a cup of tea into Kit's hands.

He took a sip. It was better when Mary made it. "I had not visited Rose Hill since I first inherited it . . ."

As he finished the tale, Huntley polished off the last biscuit. "You wish to marry her?"

"In a word, yes." Kit put down the cup of cold tea. "I've been attempting to woo her, but, as I said, I've done something wrong and do not know how to get this courtship back on track."

Rutherford went to the door and spoke to whoever was in the corridor. Kit almost grinned at his friend taking charge of the food. At least he didn't have to worry about them making themselves at home, and considering the problems he faced with Mary, that was good.

Marcus sauntered over to the sideboard, filled four glasses, and came back with two, one of which he gave to Kit. "Sherry. I have found it is better for cognition than brandy."

After the other two men had their drinks, Kit continued. "Just when I think we're becoming closer, she backs away."

"What does she do when you kiss her?" Marcus asked.

"*Kiss her!*" Kit jumped up and began pacing the room. He was at the end of his rope. "I've been doing my best *not* to kiss her. Good Lord. Mary has been through enough without me acting like a raging beast. Look at what happened when Beaumont followed his basest instincts and compromised Serena." He shook his head. "No, I will not do the same. I have vowed not to touch her until she agrees to marry me."

"In case you haven't noticed"—Huntley held his glass up, tilting it, looking at the amber liquid—"she has already been compromised. One word to the wrong person, to anyone in the *ton*, and everyone will know she has been living here as your wife. With your reputation as the perfect gentleman, the gossip will be vicious."

"You don't think I know that?" Shades of his dead brother rose in Kit's mind and he downed half of his glass in one gulp. It was time to admit what bothered him the most. "Mary has no interest in kissing me."

His friends stared at him, stunned. He drained his glass, waiting to hear what they'd advise him to do next.

CHAPTER FOURTEEN

"Kit will never fall in love with me." Mary blinked away the tears pricking her eyelids. She'd wanted to be able to talk about how she felt, but now every nerve was stretched to the breaking point.

After a few moments, Phoebe slowly shook her head. "I do not believe it."

"Neither do I." Caro pulled a branch of a lilac bush down, inhaling. "He still looks at you the same way he did before."

"I agree with Phoebe and Caro," Anna said. "What makes you think he's not interested in you?"

"Most of his compliments are on how well I have managed the estate. He has never told me I look pretty or even nice."

"I realize Kit is reserved, but that is ridiculous," Phoebe said with disgust.

Anna cast her eyes at the clouds. "What a slow-top."

"I'm not so sure." Caro ran her hand over the privet hedge, releasing its fragrance. "By praising you on what you've accomplished, rather than your beauty, such as another man might, he probably does think he *is* being considerate of you."

"Kit is very proper," Anna added. "Other than his mother and sisters, I doubt he has told any lady that she looks pretty. He might be waiting for a sign from you."

"But he hasn't even tried to kiss me." There, it was out. What a horrible admission to have to make even to one's friends. Men were supposed to want to kiss women.

This was too much. Mary plopped down on one of the new benches she'd had built. "I've all but thrown myself at him. I don't know what more to do."

Phoebe raised a brow. "Are you saying you have attempted to kiss him, and he has refused?"

"No. Of course not." Mary hated pouting and that's exactly what she was doing. "What do I know of kissing, other than being slobbered upon by Gawain or some other man in an attempt to compromise me?"

Anna grinned. "I have a book—"

"*No!*" Phoebe said firmly. "You and Rutherford had done much more than kissing when you started with the book. You would give poor Kit apoplexy."

Caro's eyes widened. "Book? Why haven't I heard about the book?"

"Anna can tell you about it later." Phoebe's lips curled up into a smile. "It is very interesting, but this is not the time for it."

"Very well." Anna heaved a sigh. "I still think Mary should attempt to seduce Kit."

"You know," Caro said thoughtfully, "that is not a bad idea."

Mary's face was heating to the point that she knew she was bright red. "Sed . . ." Suddenly her mouth was dry. "Seduce him?"

"Only if you love him." Phoebe let the words hang in the air for a few moments. "You did say you like him a great deal."

"Well, I think—just think, mind you—that I may love him a little." Mary desperately wanted one of her grandmother's teas with brandy. "Do you truly think he likes me?"

"I believe he's in love," Phoebe said.

Anna nodded. "Or very close to it."

"I agree." Caro glanced toward the house. "Shall we join the gentlemen?"

Mary couldn't very well protest when it was clear by the expressions on her friends' faces they wanted to see their husbands.

If that was love, she wanted it, desperately. Still, if her friends were right and Kit loved her, that changed everything. Never let it be said a Tolliver allowed love to slip through her fingers. Now all she had to do was to figure out how to kiss him, or get him to kiss her. Then she'd know if they would suit. Though the fact remained, he had to at least give her a sign he would welcome her affection.

Kit looked out the window as Mary and the rest of the ladies returned. Her chin had a mulish cast, and he wished he knew what the others had said to her.

"Have you told her how lovely you think she is?" Marcus asked as he glanced out the window.

Kit dragged his gaze from her. "That would be forward."

"Good God, man." Huntley dropped his head into his hands. "Every woman likes to be complimented."

That wasn't fair. Kit did flatter her. He sniffed. "I do. I tell her what an excellent job she's done with Rose Hill."

"We could just take him out and shoot him now," Rutherford said to no one in particular. "It would put him out of his misery and ours."

"It's a good thing"—Marcus gave a rueful smile—"you have us here to help you."

Huntley refilled Kit's glass. "When being courted, a lady wants to be told she is beautiful and desirable, *not* that she is a good land steward."

"They also need to be kissed." Rutherford shook his head in disgust when Kit scowled. "I think you're making a mistake. The normal rules of polite behavior do not apply to courting, but if you're not going to kiss her, then you must figure out some way to be more attentive. She probably doesn't realize you're even interested in her."

It wasn't that he didn't want to kiss Mary. Her lips drew him like a siren's call, but he'd made a habit of correct behavior, and his friends' advice went against everything he considered honorable. On the other hand, he was becoming desperate, and they could be right. What if he had given her the wrong idea?

"Very well." Kit took a swallow of the sherry. "I will do as you suggest. If she slaps me, I'll blame it on you."

"Here they come." Huntley grabbed the tumbler from Kit's hand. "Now tell her how much the fresh air agrees with her. That she has roses in her cheeks or something like that."

The door opened and the ladies strolled in, all of them but Mary with broad smiles for their men. Kit moved toward her, took her hand, and gave her his most charming smile. "How lovely you look. The fresh air agrees with you."

God, he sounded like an idiot.

Her eyes widened, and her cheeks turned a pretty shade of pink. "Thank you."

Well, perhaps not so much of an idiot. She seemed to enjoy the accolade, and she hadn't even looked as if she wanted to hit him. This wasn't so bad after all. "I'm afraid we finished off the tea. Would you care for some more?"

He curled her fingers around his.

She glanced at the remnants of the tea tray. "I am a bit sharp-set." A quarter hour later, another pot of tea arrived accompanied by some sort of grilled cake. "What is this?"

Mary's eyes danced. "Cook must have thought we were hungry. They are singing hinnies, and this"—she pointed at a slice of cake—"is a spice cake. Cook is famous for it."

Their friends gathered round for tea and food.

Once Kit had passed cups and plates to everyone he bit into the singing hinny. It tasted of butter, fried scone, and raisins. Could anything be better? "These are wonderful. I'm so glad you encourage Cook to make local foods." Damn. Now he was complimenting her for her housewifery. "I mean—"

Mary put her hand on his arm, and her voice was soft, as if she wanted only him to hear her. "It's all right. I know gentlemen love their food."

Ah, progress. She'd never touched him first before. Who would have believed a compliment could accomplish so much? He'd have to do that more often.

"That is not the only thing we love." Where in the hell did that come from?

She gazed at him quizzically, but before either of them could respond, Rutherford called out, "These are excellent. We must have this receipt."

"I shall have Cook write it out for you." Mary glanced at her watch, and rose. "If we don't prepare for dinner soon though, we'll be in her black books."

Confound it all. The moment was lost. Kit stood as well. "We will be along shortly." He waited until the last skirt disappeared out the door. "I'd say that went well."

Marcus raised a brow. "You'd better fix her attention soon."

"Of course I shall. The quicker we're married the better this situation will be."

"I don't think that is exactly what Marcus is saying." Huntley rubbed his forehead. "If you cannot convince her being your wife is a better option, your Lady Mary has a plan to avoid the parson's mousetrap."

"*Not wed?*" The ramifications were too horrible to contemplate. Not only would she be ruined, he would be as well, and that would affect his sisters, particularly Meg. "That is not possible. My mother is already at work smoothing over any hint of a scandal."

Rutherford groaned. "Have you told Lady Mary that?"

"Of course not. I saw no need." And he damn sure wasn't going to tell her now. She'd consider it part of a trap. "What did she say?"

Huntley explained her idea, and Kit felt the blood draining from his head. If she ran off he'd have the devil of a time finding her. Just the thought of her alone in a foreign country chilled him. Damn it all, they would marry, and soon. Either that or he'd make his Grand Tour chasing her around Europe.

Mary sipped her sherry. "I just want to go to Paris for the Season."

After the ladies had bathed and changed, they'd reconvened in her parlor.

"Gossip and other news travels very quickly between Paris and London. With your cousin lying in wait for you, he could easily discover your location," Phoebe stated firmly. "Being in a foreign country with him would only add to your problems."

There were times when Phoebe could be annoyingly right, and Mary knew she was acting childishly. Still, it was difficult to give up something she'd had her heart set on for years now: A Season where she could fall in love.

Caro's brow pleated as she studied Mary. "Does it have to be in Paris?"

Other than London, Paris was the only place she'd ever considered. She took another sip of sherry. "Where else could I go? Vienna? I hear many of the *ton* like it there."

"Edinburgh," Caro said. "Of course the Season is not as large, but it *is* an option, and not as far as France or Austria."

Anna moved to the edge of the wide cane-backed chair. "That's perfect. Your cousin will never find you in Scotland."

Mary had never even considered Edinburgh. Before Lady Bellamny had offered to take Diana for the Season, the Brownlys had discussed Edinburgh. There were balls and assembly rooms, and who knew what else. Except . . . "I don't know anyone there. Where would I reside? Who would sponsor me?"

Caro set her glass down and leaned slightly forward, hindered by the child she carried. "We are going to visit Gervais's aunt and uncle, Lord Titus and Lady Theo Grantham. Lady Theo is the youngest daughter of the Duke of Gordon. They have a large house in the new part of the city." Caro grinned. "From my correspondence with Lady Theo, I'm sure they would welcome more company." She glanced at Phoebe then Anna. "In fact, we can all go. I shall write to her immediately after dinner and should receive the answer in a day or so."

Mary stared at Caro. Her eyes glowed and excitement swirled around her. She had been denied a whole Season, but had still found love. The scheme had much to offer. Granted, Edinburgh wasn't London, but it was a capital. Mary would have her friends with her; she wouldn't come across anyone who knew her as Lady Mary Featherton; and they were correct, Gawain would never think to look for her there. Not only that, but she'd heard interesting things about Scottish men. If she and Mr. Featherton didn't suit . . . Perhaps this was meant to be. "What a wonderful idea. If you wish you may use my escritoire and write the letter now."

Once Caro had sealed the missive, Mary sent it down to be posted by special messenger. She wondered what Kit would think of the plan. No matter, she was going in any event. If he chose to come, he was welcome to accompany them.

The next morning, Kit was in the game room organizing the fishing rods, when Huntley joined him. "The gear looks to be in good condition, and I have enough rods for everyone."

"Any idea what fish is most prevalent here?"

"Mostly trout," Kit said over his shoulder as he fixed a hook to one of the lines.

"I don't suppose you've spoken with Lady Mary this morning?"

He turned. When he'd received the message the ladies were breaking their fast in the nursery, he'd not thought it strange, yet now . . . was something wrong? "No, I have not. If you have something to say, open your budget."

"Caro wrote to my aunt yesterday. She and I were already going to Edinburgh. Now there's a plan afoot for all of us to visit the city for a few weeks."

Which meant Mary wasn't bolting to the Continent, at least not yet. "Indeed."

Huntley lounged against a wall, swinging his quizzing glass. "You're invited as well. It might be to your benefit. No one can deny you show to advantage at entertainments. She'd see you at your best."

As if Kit was a horse on sale at Tattersall's. "You might have something there." Mary was an Incomparable, and Kit had no doubt the Scottish men would be all over her. Competition, but nothing he couldn't handle. Surely she wouldn't actually want one of them as a husband. In any event, he'd make sure none of them got too close to her. "When do we depart?"

"I expect an answer by late to-morrow. I'm sure the ladies will wish to leave a day or so afterward."

"Is there a possibility your aunt will not be able to accommodate us?"

His friend grinned. "Not a chance in the world. Uncle Titus has had her trooping all over 'those blasted rock sites,' as she calls them. Although she enjoys it immensely, she's more than ready for female companionship and parties." Huntley stopped playing with his glass. "Aunt Theo will also be extremely happy to try to find a match for Lady Mary."

Kit wasn't aware he'd clenched his jaw until a dull ache began. "Your aunt needn't bother. Mary will wed me."

Huntley grabbed three of the fishing rods and strode to the door. "Naturally. Just like the biddable lady she is."

Kit slammed his fist on the table. "Hell and damnation!"

Huntley's laughter floated down the corridor. Lady Mary Tolliver would marry Kit no matter what. She cared for him, and he more than cared for her. Somehow he'd bring her up to scratch.

Eunice tripped lightly down the steps to the hall where Brian awaited her. "I can't tell you how glad I am that Mary's friends are here. It relieves me of all my chaperone responsibilities."

Her heart fluttered as he smiled down at her, placing her hand on his arm after he'd slowly kissed each finger.

"I share your joy." They walked out to the drive where his curricle stood.

She could scarcely breathe, her heart was galloping so wildly. She wanted him to kiss her lips and so much more. Oh my. Imagine being affected like this at her age. She was sure someone would say it was inappropriate. "Where are you taking me?"

"I thought you might like to see the property I mentioned." He helped her into the carriage, climbing in the other side. "Unless it is too soon for you, that is?"

"No, your timing is perfect." Having her niece's friends here and watching how happy they all were had given Eunice time to think of hers and Brian's marriage. She really did not wish to wait much longer.

They were half-way down the drive when he asked, "Have Mr. Featherton and your niece decided when the marriage will be?" She tried to stifle the sigh but was unable to. "No. The truth is, Mary says she will not wed if she's not sure she is in love."

"It creates a problem, but I can't say that I blame her. I'm surprised Featherton hasn't been able to get her to agree." Brian was still for several moments as he feathered the turn onto the road toward Rosebury. "Didn't you tell me you and your husband had a love match?"

"Indeed we did. Yet unbeknownst to us, the marriage had been arranged." Eunice thought back ruefully to the day she had confronted her parents. "I was young and very rebellious. When I discovered there was a plan afoot to marry me off, I was certain my father had chosen another gentleman. Someone the very opposite of me, who would try to tame my spirit." She couldn't help grinning at the memory of her young self. "Consequently, I very dramatically stormed into his study and announced I would wed Roger or no one. Papa nodded calmly and said that was a fortunate circumstance as he'd signed the betrothal agreement the previous day."

Brian let out a bark of laughter. "That took the wind out of your sails."

"It did, rather." She smiled. "I'm not sure I ever remembered to thank him."

"Did their other matches turn out as well?"

She thought back to her other brothers and sisters. "Yes. Those who are alive are still very happy. I believe Mama had something to do with Barham's marriage, as well as the eldest girl's. Still, she's never been this obvious before. The only reason I can think of for her behavior is that the cousin must be a much more serious threat than we'd previously thought."

A comfortable silence fell, until Brian turned into a well-maintained drive lined with hedgerows. "Here we are."

In a few moments, an elegant manor house built in the local, light yellowish-brown stone appeared. "It's lovely. How clever to have placed a round flower bed in the middle of the drive."

"I was told the owner built the house for his grandson who, instead of marrying a local girl, wed a young woman whose father owned a shipping company and had no son. The man has made Bristol his home." He drew the gig to a halt at the Georgian-style portico. "There is apparently every modern convenience."

"That, I'll be interested in seeing. I suppose it's one of the advantages of building a house rather than having one handed down over the centuries." Eunice put her hands on his shoulders as he lifted her down, setting her lightly on her feet. She stood still for a moment, breathing in his very male scent of leather, horse, and musk.

"Eunice, my love." His voice was low and seductive. "If we remain here, I'll kiss you in front of God and whoever is here."

Although she couldn't see anyone . . . he was the rector and they shouldn't take the chance. "Lead on, sir."

The house was indeed modern, with Rumford fireplaces in all but the main drawing room, where two marble fireplaces intricately carved with Greek figures anchored each end of the room. The dwelling had been tastefully and expensively furnished. "Does the furniture come with the house?"

"I believe the owner is willing to sell it as part of the whole."

Crystal sconces lined the walls. "These almost look like the new gas ones."

"They are, but they've been altered so that candles can be used until we get gas up here."

"How forward thinking. Is there a ballroom?"

"I don't know."

They walked through all the ground floor rooms, impressed by the pocket doors used so that rooms could be combined if needed. A ballroom was found on the side of the house with most of the formal rooms. It jutted out into a garden, and gave the appearance of a conservatory with three glass walls set at angles. She was surprised to find that the panes of glass opened. "How lovely and clever. Just what one needs on a warm night."

They didn't spend too much time looking at the bedchambers on the first floor until they got to the master's bedchambers. The apartments included two bedrooms, each with its own dressing room. She glanced at a door that did not lead into either of the bedrooms. "What is this, I wonder?"

Brian opened it, allowing her to enter first. Light flowed through windows built high on the walls, which were covered in pale yellow glazed tiles. A stove, covered in elaborately decorated multicolored tiles stood centered on one wall and next to it was a large, pink marble shell-shaped bathing tub complete with pipes for water. It was as if the Romans had constructed it.

Brian flushed, and when he spoke his voice was gravelly. "The birth of Venus."

"I've never seen anything so decadent in my life." Eunice laughed. The sound echoed around the chamber. "I'm quite sure my dresser would declare this scandalous."

"No wonder the price is so low." He ran a finger under his collar. "We probably ought to see the remainder of the house."

She whirled around, unable to resist teasing him. "Perhaps we should give it a try. You know, just to make sure the water pipes work."

"Eunice." Her name came out in a strangled tone.

"What?"

He turned toward her, backing her up to a wall. Leaning in, he anchored his hands to the tiles on either side of her head. "I'm doing my very best to keep from taking you here, against the wall. The least you could do is not tempt me. Unless"—his lips touched hers, and she could feel his barely repressed lust—"this is where you want our first time to be?"

Her breathing quickened. Was that what she wanted? Her nipples ached for attention, and need coursed through her. It had been so long, so very long. She took a breath. This was the first time she'd seen him out of countenance, and she loved that he had such passion for her. As to the bathroom, definitely sometime but not their first mating. "Oh, very well. Though I do want this house. If you don't buy it, I will."

He straightened, hustled her out of the room, and quickly closed the door behind them. "If you want it, you shall have it."

"Wonderful." She turned to him, went up on her toes, and kissed him. "How soon may we wed?"

"Considering I can barely keep my hands off you, we should let it be known we are betrothed and will marry almost immediately."

"Come to think of it, with Mary and her friends going to Edinburgh, we can put it about that she and Mr. Featherton are leaving for an unknown period of time, making it necessary for us to wed soon." She tilted her head, watching him study her. "To-morrow perhaps? I've always wanted to elope to Scotland."

Brian caught her around the waist as she danced away, bringing her flush against his hard body. "You, my lady, will be the death of me. The morrow is not possible, but in a few days we can leave. Fortunately, the rector in the next parish owes me a favor. He can stand in for me on Sunday."

"What a fabulous idea." Their lips touched, and she opened to him, slowly stroking his tongue with hers. "I have plans for our new bathing vessel."

He nipped her ear. "You're not the only one."

CHAPTER FIFTEEN

Mary was with Kit and their friends, on the terrace discussing possible entertainments in Edinburgh. Huntley knew there was a theater, and she hoped they could attend a performance. It had been so terribly long since she had been.

The weather had warmed nicely, and the stones of the house radiated the sun's heat. She sipped a glass of chilled champagne, the first she'd had in ages. This was a celebration of sorts. It was time for her to move on with her life.

Kit hovered near her, as if he knew her plans might not include him.

Eunice strolled out through the French windows holding hands with Mr. Doust, who snatched two glasses from the footman, handing one to her aunt.

He cleared his throat. "We have an announcement. Lady Eunice has done me the great honor of agreeing to be my wife."

A cheer went up from the men, who descended on Mr. Doust, congratulating him on his lucky catch. The ladies joined Mary in hugging her aunt.

"Oh, I'm so glad for you." Mary kissed Eunice's cheek. "You've never looked happier."

"I never thought to be this blissful again." Eunice returned Mary's embrace, blinking back tears of joy. "You will be shocked, but we plan to leave in the morning, and wed in Scotland. I don't think it is appropriate for me to remain here alone with you away. You have your friends; you don't need me. As luck would have it, when we stopped in at the rectory, a friend of Brian's, who is also a clergyman, had arrived begging a place to stay. If not for that, we would have had to wait a few days longer."

"I shall miss you, but I don't want you to delay your happiness because of me." The one thing she couldn't see was her aunt residing in the rectory. It was much too small. "But where will you live?"

Eunice's smile grew larger. "We've only just come from viewing a house for sale not far from town. Mr. Doust has already made an offer for it. Although he didn't tell me that until after I threatened to buy it if he didn't."

Kit was again next to Mary, handing her another glass of champagne as he addressed the rector. "If Mary agrees, until the property transfer is complete, you may both stay here. No one will think that at all improper."

Mr. Doust inclined his head. "Thank you. We'll take you up on your very kind offer. I don't know what they were thinking when the rectory was built. The residence is more suited to an office than a home for a couple."

"How soon will you depart?" Kit asked.

"To-morrow." Mr. Doust raised Eunice's hand to his lips. "I'll see you at dawn. It will take the better part of the day to reach Coldstream."

"Is that the closest border town?" Mary asked.

"Indeed." His eyes never left Eunice's face as he continued. "The road going there is not as good as the North Road, but it's ten miles closer, and there is a decent inn."

"Unless you'll upset your cook," Kit said, "you are invited to dine with us this evening."

"Yes, please do," Mary added.

Mr. Doust still held Eunice's hands and gazed at her face as if she were the most important thing in his life. If only a gentleman would look at her in that way.

Finally he glanced at Mary and Kit. "As I've no cook to offend, I'd be pleased to join you. My housekeeper makes meals for me a few days a week, and that keeps me for several days."

"Then it's settled. I'll tell Simons to set another place." She signaled to the footman, giving him the message.

Kit poured more champagne for everyone. He stared at her, and his brows quirked as he raised his glass. "To marriage and new beginnings."

Was something wrong with her? When he turned to Mr. Doust, Mary surreptitiously ran her hand down her bodice, making sure she hadn't spilled any of the wine. It was dry. How very strange. What could he have been looking at? How could she think of seducing him, when he peered at her as if she had something between her teeth? Rutherford held up his glass. "Here's to the parson being caught in the mousetrap." Kit's fingers curled into a fist. He'd attempted to catch Mary's gaze so that she'd know he meant to include them in his toast as well, but she acted as if there was something amiss. This wooing wasn't going at all as he'd intended. Instead of becoming closer, she was slipping away from him. Somehow he had to find a way to stop her from getting away. He sidled next to her. "Is everything all right?"

Her startled gaze flew to his. "Yes, of course. I'm very happy for Eunice. It is what she wanted."

He bent his head so only Mary could hear. "Would you like to be there when she marries?"

Her shoulders drooped. "I would. Though I understand her desire to wed as soon as possible. If only we would hear from Huntley's aunt, but that's impossible."

Receiving an answer so quickly would be impossible, yet he'd do everything in his power to make this right for her. There had to be a way. "If your aunt and Doust could put off the trip for a day or so, we could all travel together. In fact, now that I think about it, we'd be much better off departing before Sunday. Otherwise we shall be expected in church. Your aunt said you attend services regularly."

Mary's fingers toyed agitatedly with her long pearl necklace, drawing his attention to a curl dancing near her delicate shell-like ears.

She gave him a small, tight smile. "I hadn't thought about that, nor should we be seen traveling on Sunday."

It was the same thing his mother would say. Kit was glad he'd guessed correctly. "No."

She cut a worried glance at him. "Still, we must wait to hear from Lady Theo."

Kit wanted so badly to take her in his arms and kiss away her concerns. "Let me see what we can do. Why do you not ensure everyone is ready to go in the morning, while I discuss our problem with Huntley?"

"Of course. Though I think we are mostly packed."

Kit watched Mary rejoin the ladies before he sauntered over to Huntley. "How soon do you think we'll hear from your aunt?"

"Caro said the letter was sent by special messenger shortly after breakfast." He thought for a moment. "Assuming he has no trouble finding her house, and she is home, I'd say the earliest we'd receive an answer is to-morrow late afternoon. Why?"

"Mary wishes to see her aunt wed. If at all possible, I'd like to depart in the morning. That way Lady Eunice and Doust can have the ceremony when we reach Scotland."

"Hmm." Huntley rubbed the side of his face. "I can't see the messenger going cross-country until he reaches Alnwick. Before then, he'd stay on the Great North Road. If we leave early enough, we can catch him. As I said, I do not believe my aunt will say no to the additional company. If she does, I'm sure we can find an inn or hotel large enough to accommodate our party."

Kit called Doust over. "We are thinking of going with you so that Lady Mary can support Lady Eunice. If I recall correctly, there is a small village, Lamberton, which is directly across the border north of Berwick-upon-Tweed. Its tollhouse is a well-known wedding spot. Would that disrupt your schedule too much?"

"Not at all." He grinned. "As a matter of fact, if we're going to have an irregular marriage, we should have as many witnesses as possible. Though my original plan of Coldstream will be faster."

Thankfully, the matter was decided quickly. Before Simons had announced dinner, all and sundry had agreed to escort Lady Eunice and Doust to Scotland and attend the wedding.

A part of Kit had expected and wanted Mary to fall upon him with gratitude.

He smiled when she came up to him. She gave him a polite smile in return. "Thank you for arranging for me to be with my aunt when she marries. It was very kind of you."

Kind! A tick began in his jaw. He was starting to hate that word. He'd never before wished to break something, but he did now. Somehow he maintained a pleasant countenance and gave a slight inclination of his head. "It was my pleasure."

Damn and drat. That hadn't worked either. All they were doing was leaving for Scotland sooner. Now what the deuce was he supposed to do to attract her? Other than take her in his arms and maul her, and that he would not do. Maybe Huntley was correct; Edinburgh would give Kit an advantage he did not appear to have here. No Scot alive could match him in polite behavior. He would devote himself to her and keep the Scottish rascals away.

Swan and Talbot Inn, Wetherby, England

The bedchamber Constance had been given overlooked the main street and one side of the inn. Stars still twinkled in the antelucan sky. Lately it wasn't only Gawain Tolliver who was watching wherever she and Lucinda were staying; another man was, as well. Unfortunately, Lucinda had been unable to find any way to disable the blackguard's carriage long enough to escape for more than an hour or so. He must be getting desperate. Be that as it may, Constance was heartily sick of being the subject of his attention. She and Lucinda must be on their way north without Mr. Tolliver in tow.

"Do you see him?" Constance asked her dresser.

Anderson glanced back over her shoulder. "No, and he's not been skulking around in the past day or two. Leastwise not so I could see."

Perhaps Gawain had gone, and that was the reason for the other man. The problem was, Constance didn't know if that was good or bad. Surely he couldn't have discovered where her granddaughter was. At the same time, she did not think he had given up his hunt. He must be planning something else, and she did not wish to remain here until she knew what his next step was. "I think we should make a dash for it."

"I'm not sure any of us are dashing around these days, Your Grace. What do you have in mind?"

Constance tapped a finger against her chin. "You take the other servants and the luggage while Lady Featherton and I walk around the town. To-day is market day. There will be a great deal of traffic. Then, when we're sure he's not watching, she and I will slip away."

Anderson pulled out the traveling trunk from the corner. "Maybe have the coach meet you at the other end of the town."

"Excellent idea." Constance tapped her cane on the floor. "I've been saving my horses, but both Featherton and Barham have cattle stationed along the Great North Road. We can keep going as long as need be."

Her dresser narrowed her eyes in thought. "If you're planning to move fast, you should keep a couple of the footmen with you, Your Grace." Anderson's lips twitched. "Just to make sure you can make it to the other end of town."

Constance hurled a pillow at her maid, missing when the woman ducked. "I should send them with you," she retorted. "You're not that much younger than I."

"That may be true." Anderson sniffed. "But I haven't taken to using a cane to walk. I told you before you'd start relying on it."

Drat the woman if she didn't have a point. Constance glanced at her elegant swan-headed cane. She had started carrying it as a small conceit, but lately she'd been having to depend on it too much. All this traveling probably didn't help either. Mayhap when all this was over, and Mary and Kit were safely wed, Constance would take the time to learn to walk without it again. Bath would be a good place for that. The waters were vile for drinking, but bathing in them seemed to help people.

"If you want my advice," Anderson said, "you'll let me get you some plainer clothes and you could walk without your cane. You'll want the footmen to be in street clothing as well. That way the blackguard might miss you if he's still around."

"Go in disguise?" Constance stared at her dresser. "What a brilliant idea. I'll talk Lucinda into it as well." An image of two old ladies in faded black came to her. "Get us some widow's weeds. That ought to work."

Just over an hour later, Constance and Lucinda were dressed as middling country ladies. Their coachman had suggested blacking the gold crest marking the coaches, and Constance agreed. Their lady's maids left with the first carriage, and the baggage coach departed a half hour later. The footmen were dressed in clothing bought from the landlord. She twined her arm with one of the young men. "I haven't had a lark like this in years."

Constance headed off first out the back of the inn, down the alley behind it, and thence to a small road full of traffic going into the town. Lucinda would meet her at the butcher's shop. From there they'd act like old friends meeting unexpectedly. Even that would be a new experience. Neither of them had ever been in a butcher's shop before.

Constance and her footman followed the directions the landlord had given them. "Do you see anyone pursuing us?"

"No, Your Grace. I had a look out the common room's window before we left and saw the man, but I haven't seen him since."

"Let's hope he'll still be there waiting for a long time to come." Before they reached the butcher's, people were staring at them. "What do you think is wrong? I look like everyone else."

"Beg'n your pardon, Your Grace, but you don't sound like them, and you walk different. Not like an old country woman."

So much for her ruse. "Let's find Lady Featherton and depart. I don't want to leave a way for *that man* to find us."

A few moments later, she saw a female who looked like Lucinda peering into a shop window. Her shoulders were hunched a bit, and when she spoke it was not with her usual clipped consonants. How had she known to do that when Constance had not?

As soon as they were close enough, Constance whispered, "We should depart immediately."

Her friend raised a brow.

"I'm drawing attention."

Lucinda linked arms with her. "Then let me do the talking. Round your shoulders a bit, and shuffle your feet some more."

"Where did you learn to do that?"

"Oh"—her eyes twinkled with laughter—"my eldest sister and I used to escape from our governess and learned to blend in with the locals. It came in very handy on May Day when we attended the festival to look at the handsome local boys."

An hour later, Constance and Lucinda settled into the soft velvet squabs of the coach. They were on their way north, and, as far as they could tell, no one was following.

"You're sure they aren't still at the inn?" Gawain's groom had been across the street from the posting house since early morning. Gawain arrived a few hours later when the dowagers usually took a walk after breakfast. It was now mid-afternoon, and they were nowhere to be seen.

"As sure as I can be. I went in just like you told me and said I had an urgent message for the Dowager Lady Featherton." Whitely held out the sealed missive he'd used. "The landlord said they'd left before noon." He spat on the ground. "Couldn't get more than that out of him. So's I went around to the stables and sure enough, the coaches was gone."

Bloody hell! Gawain ran a hand through his already unruly hair. "Let's go. Even with several hours' head start, at the pace they travel we won't have a problem catching up with them."

* * *

Close to dinner time, Gawain stopped at one of the larger inns. "Find out if they've been here," he instructed Whitely. "I can't believe we lost them somewhere along the road. I hope they didn't turn off to visit someone."

A few minutes later, his groom returned. "No one ain't seen hide nor hair of them."

Where in the bloody hell could two old ladies have got to? "They had to have come through here. I'll wager anything the servants have been paid not to tell." Gawain ran his hand over his face. What was he supposed to do now? "We're going to Edinburgh. Perhaps I can find something out at the bank. We'll travel until dark. They can't be that far in front of us."

It was a damned good thing he hadn't gone out gambling since before quarter day, and his father paid for his servants and living expenses. All this traveling around wasn't helping much, but it was strange, he seemed to have more money than usual. Gawain grinned to himself. He'd have a lot more money after he married his cousin. Every penny of it would be his, and she wouldn't have any say at all how he spent it. All he had to do was find her. Unfortunately, he'd just lost the dowager. The one person who knew where she was, and he was running out of time.

As usual, Kit escorted Mary to dinner, bowing gracefully after tucking her chair in before taking his place at the head of the table. Ever since he'd stared her out of countenance earlier, he'd been more attentive. Reminding her why he was called Mr. Perfect. Perfect to every lady except her, that was. Well, she had said she'd give him a chance, and she would.

After dinner, instead of remaining with their port in the dining room, the gentlemen rose to accompany the ladies into the drawing room for tea. Once more, he joined her, remaining by her side. She found herself relaxing around him.

She stifled a yawn. "If we wish to make an early start, we should retire soon."

He leaned his head close, as if making their conversation private. His breath touched her ear, and she fought not to sigh at the warmth. His voice was seductively low. "I agree. Have you ever visited Edinburgh?"

She fought the impulse to lean into him. "No, but I've heard it is lovely."

"If you wish, we may discover it together. I'll bring my curricle, and we can take trips around the area."

He should not do this to her. One minute he was praising her housekeeping skills and the next he acted as if he really intended to court her. "That sounds lovely."

When they entered the drawing room, Mary glanced around. This was another of her favorite rooms, and she would miss it. An ache began in the area of her heart. He was always so considerate and easy to get along with, except he wouldn't kiss her. If only she knew she and Mr. Featherton were meant to be together, she need not feel as if she were leaving her home.

After about a half hour, she called for tea. One cup later, the married couples excused themselves and made their way to their chambers.

Kit walked with her up the stairs. They stopped outside of her parlor, and he kissed her knuckles. "I'll see you in the morning, my lady."

"Good-night, sir."

She entered her room and heaved a frustrated huff. If only he would have kissed her lips instead of her hand. If her friends were right and he liked her, then it followed that he would kiss her on the mouth. She would wager that her friends' husbands had kissed them. Maybe not Huntley, but that was different. He and Caro had hardly known each other when they'd been forced to marry to protect her from a madman. Their story had been too much like a romance novel for comfort. Mary knew Kit was reserved, but why did he have to be so very proper? On the other hand, he had complimented her on her person to-day. She sighed. Falling in love was rather difficult.

A few moments later, Mathers helped Mary out of her gown and stays, combed her hair, then helped her don her nightgown. Too excited about the trip to sleep, she went into her parlor. A small stack of mail she'd not got around to earlier lay on her desk. On top was a letter from her brother. She popped off the seal, read it, and laughed. Typical of Barham not to have dated the thing.

Mary,
What the deuce is going on with you?
Shortly after I received your last missive regarding a
trust—thank you for not crossing it, by the way—Viscount

*Featherton contacted me regarding marriage settlements.
I was never so nonplussed. He wants me to come to Town
to discuss them. I'm trying to put him off, but are you
going to marry Featherton? I have nothing against the
match. In fact, it would be a deuced good one. He's almost
as rich as the Golden Ball. I tried asking Grandmamma,
but she's as close as a clam and won't tell me a thing.
Practically patted me on the head and told me not to
worry.*

*It's the devil of a hard thing being the head of the fam-
ily when I don't have a clue what's going on. Well, whatever it is, just don't create a scandal. Haha, I know you
won't.*

*I'm to remind you that Osanna's eldest will come out
next year, though what that has to do with anything, I vow
I don't know.*

*Where are you? What do you want me to do about
Featherton?*

B.

Mary's temples started to throb. If Barham knew how close she
was to doing just that, her easygoing brother would have her in front
of a clergyman. If she did create a scandal, because it would be her
decision that caused it, her niece and her whole family would be affected. Was she being selfish in wanting to pick her own husband?
Everyone else had made love matches. Why shouldn't she be allowed
to do the same? If only she were certain of her course, this would be
so much easier.

She poured a glass of wine and stood gazing out the window. Finally the aching stopped, and a sort of peace settled over her.

The night-blooming nicotiana glowed softly. The small bits of
quartz in the gravel reflected the moon's beam as it traveled across
the path. The rest of the garden, the one she'd rescued and renovated,
was in shadows. This whole estate had been virtually hers for almost
a year. Did she really wish to cast it away? Would she be better off
marrying for safety and position? And children. Ever since her friends
had arrived, the nursery was alive with laughter and affection. Their
husbands were with the children as much as the ladies were. She
wanted that for herself, and she also wanted a loving husband. Not

just someone who would give her children, but one who would help raise them. She wanted a man to gaze at her the way the others looked at their wives, not as if there were something wrong with her. A light knock sounded on the door before it opened. Caro, dressed in a frothy turquoise wrapper, strolled in. "I saw the light and thought you'd be awake."

Mary poured another glass of wine, handing it to her old friend. "It's been an eventful few days. I'm trying to catch up with my correspondence. Come and sit."

Her family's and Caro's family's estates marched along each other, and, being of an age, they had become close. Even Caro's flight to Venice had not lessened their friendship. Mary almost wished her friend was still abroad, so that she could flee to Venice as well. Yet that was selfish. Caro had found true love with Huntley, and Mary could not begrudge her friend that happiness. Not when she wanted it so badly for herself.

Caro curled up on the sofa, tucking her slippered feet under her. "Since our conversation yesterday and this morning, I've been studying you and Kit."

Mary sat in the French cane-backed chair. Her heart started to quicken. Was this bad news? "And?"

"You seem to not understand one another."

She shook her head, not understanding. "Could you explain more fully?"

Caro tilted her head to the side. "You are both so frightened of doing the wrong thing, that you do exactly that. Phoebe and Anna said they have never seen him so out of countenance. You do know he is famous for his address?"

Mary took another sip of wine. "Yes, but I do not understand what they mean."

"That he cares enough not to want to place a wrong foot." Caro straightened. "If a gentleman doesn't feel anything for a lady, he does not change his behavior; but if he does, then he is unable to act as if she doesn't matter. We have told you we think he's in love, and yet you prickle up like a hedgehog around him." She grinned. "Though I have to say, this evening you were nicer."

Mary shoved a stray curl behind her ear. "But he does not do anything to indicate his feelings for me."

"He might be afraid of being rejected. After all, he wants to marry for the right reasons as well as you do."

Perhaps she had mistaken the look he'd given her. "I was thinking about that before you knocked. Other than love, what are the right reasons?"

Caro smiled softly. "Well, in my case it was to protect me not only from being abducted but from scandal, much as in your situation. Though I had neither the time nor any choice. You, my dear friend, at least have some time. Allow him to woo you. Mayhap being in Edinburgh will be easier. No one will know you are supposed to be married, and there will be no pretense to maintain."

Exactly what Mary had hoped. "I want it to be easier. I do realize that even if no one knows who I am, word will eventually get out that Mr. Featherton is married."

Caro gave Mary a knowing look. "Back to Mr. Featherton, are you?"

She felt the heat rising in her face and took a sip of wine. "It seemed better to keep a distance."

Despite being several months' pregnant, Caro rose with all the grace she had before, crossed to Mary, bent down, and kissed her cheek. "Kit has a very mild manner, but do not mistake that for weakness. I shall leave you now, or Gervais will come looking for me."

Once the door closed, Mary considered what her friend had said. Was that part of the problem? Aside from the gentlemen of the *ton*, who had offered her empty flattery, she was used to large, physically powerful, bluff men, such as her father and brothers, who were Corinthians who engaged in every sport.

Could someone like Kit, the perfect gentleman—her cheeks warmed again—be as strong? What kind of man did it take to hold the *ton* in one's palm? And what would he do to obtain what he wanted?

CHAPTER SIXTEEN

K it poured a glass of brandy. He should probably be in bed trying to sleep, but the Featherton estate waited for no one, and he'd been slacking on his work since arriving at Rose Hill. He'd have to have the mail forwarded to him in Scotland. Shuffling through the letters, he found one from his father.

> *K,*
> *I have contacted Lord B with a proposal but have not heard from him yet. I shall give him two more days before seeking him out.*
> *Your grandmother has absconded with the Dowager Duchess of Bridgewater to parts unknown. I assume they are traveling in your direction.*
> *The only good news concerns the court case. There will be a hearing next week. I shall keep you advised of the out-come and inform Lord B. That, if nothing else, should bring him to Town.*
> *Keep me apprised.*
> *F*

Kit blew out a large breath. Thank God for his father. Mary having control of her own funds would make her feel better, more powerful. He picked up his quill, dipping it in the ink.

> *F,*
> *Please offer to place LM's funds in a trust for her use only.*
> *By the time you receive this, or near to it, I will be in*

> *the other capital at the home of Lord Titus Grantham. I*
> *trust you to find his direction.*
>
> *Yr Servant,*
> K

Kit addressed the missive, then pressed his signet ring into the hot wax of the seal. Dent would be able to take it to the mail and meet up with them on the road to-morrow.

Placing his elbows on the desk, Kit formed a temple with his fingers. Unlike every other woman he had ever met, Mary had not responded as he'd wished. It was becoming clear she wanted something more, but what? Were his friends right? Did she wish to be more aggressively courted? Even kissed before she decided to marry him? If that was so, he'd have to readdress his methods. He rubbed his hands over his face. How would he even know? He might end up giving her a disgust of him.

By his estimate, he had two to three days until they reached Edinburgh. He'd have to plan his siege on Mary. With any luck at all, he'd have her promise to wed before they reached Lord Grantham's house, and he wouldn't have to worry about Lady Theo's potential schemes to find a husband for Mary.

Kit strolled out of the house the next morning. The sun was barely above the horizon as he stared at the mass of vehicles. He didn't know why the addition of two extra coaches and his curricle made the cavalcade seem so much larger than when his friends had arrived, yet they did.

Mary stood by the other ladies, who were checking items off their lists as they sent the coaches holding their personal servants and luggage ahead. Huntley's inestimable valet, Maufe, assured his master all would be ready at their first stage of their journey.

The cerulean-blue carriage gown Mary wore caused her eyes to appear even more silver than usual. The garment was topped by a spencer which enhanced the finest bosom Kit had ever seen. Somehow he had to ensure she rode with him for as long as possible.

He was barely able to drag his eyes from her when Rutherford sauntered up. "Reminds me of our travel in France when we helped Serena escape Beaumont. That actually worked out well for both of them. Perhaps this trip to Edinburgh will have the desired results for you and Lady Mary."

Kit refused to equate his situation with Beaumont's. Mary was not fleeing Kit. He took out his quizzing glass, affecting to survey the seeming chaos, yet found himself focusing on Mary again. "I'm beginning to think we *are* going abroad and for an extended period." Phoebe and Anna fussed with something in the coach that would carry their children. "We're missing something or someone." Mary went back into the house, and he glanced around. "Where is the groom?"

Rutherford pointed to the end of the row of coaches, where a brown-and-gold painted curricle had just pulled up behind the last coach.

A few moments later, Doust strode up. "I'm glad I'm not late. I had an emergency with a parishioner. Fortunately, I was able to hand it over to my rector friend who is standing in for me." He grinned. "He even made a point of telling me to take a few days for a honeymoon."

Kit hadn't even thought of his own wedding trip. He supposed he had better come up with something, and Mary might have ideas as well. "Let's see if the ladies are ready."

After Lady Eunice settled in with her betrothed, Kit turned to Mary, who was now standing with Caro and Phoebe. "I would be honored if you rode with me until we get to the Great North Road."

Her eyes widened as if his offer was the last thing she expected.

"What a splendid idea." Caro beamed. "Phoebe was just saying that little Arthur was a bit out of sorts and wished to travel with his mama. It will be much more comfortable for Mary to be in the curricle."

Mary stared at Caro for several moments, as if she was holding back a retort, before facing him, her countenance schooled into a polite smile. "I'd like that extremely. Thank you for offering."

"If you wish, you may drive." Without waiting for her answer, he lifted her up, trying to ignore the urge to pull her against him. He satisfied his desire to touch more of her by settling the rug over her lap and legs. "Let's be off so that we're not catching the dust from the coaches."

"That's a good idea. The road will be bad enough without that." She took the ribbons, threading them expertly through her fingers. "Thank you."

Laying one hand on her arm, he leaned closer to her. "You never have to thank me. I enjoy seeing your happiness." She blushed charmingly. When Kit straightened, he added, "And I have every expectation you will do an excellent job."

Suddenly she stiffened. "I'm glad you have confidence in my skill."

What the hell had happened? One moment Mary had been happy and smiling, and the next she froze again. If only he knew what he had said. Was he not supposed to compliment her skill at all? She'd been happy the last time he'd done it. Then again, he had failed to tell her she looked pretty.

She gave the horses their office and off they went, tooling down the drive toward Rosebury.

Skills! Mary thought. All he could ever think to compliment her on were her skills. All the other men had praised their wives' beauty this morning, even when they were yawning, but other than greeting her, Mr. Featherton had said nothing. Even after she'd taken such care to look particularly attractive, all he could say was she drove well.

Caro's words came back to Mary. Perhaps he was afraid of offending her. If only she knew what to do. Unfortunately she couldn't think of the problem now. They were entering the town, and she had to attend to the team. She inclined her head to people as they waved. Her throat tightened. No. She would not think of this being the last time she would be here.

When they'd reached the road toward Alnwick, Kit said, "I had a letter from my father. Your case to terminate the trust will come up next week."

Her heart stopped, and she dropped her hands, almost losing her hold on the horses. Finally she remembered to breathe again. "How? I mean, I've been waiting for so long."

She slid a quick look at him, and his lips had curved up in a smug smile. "My father has some influence, and I asked him to use it on your behalf."

Mr. Featherton took her breath away. He had done what her brother had not been able to accomplish in two years, and in such a short time. "But why? I do not understand."

"Because you wanted it. I could see the restraint chafed you."

Oh my goodness. What did one say to that? "You have my deepest appreciation."

"I'd rather have your trust."

Unable to think of a response, or do more than give him a quick glance, she applied herself to the pair.

"Would you agree to start anew?" he asked.

Her heart thudded against her chest as she fought to keep her voice from trembling. "What exactly do you mean?"

"I believe we have both found it difficult to enter into a courtship in the presence of those who thought us already married. In Edinburgh you will be known as Lady Mary Tolliver and be properly chaperoned. I would like you to allow me to be your suitor, as if the deception had never occurred."

She couldn't believe they were having this conversation now. Right when she dare not take her attention off the team. Still, that was what she had wanted, to be wooed and not trapped into marriage, but could it work? Thus far it had not. Was he right? Would things change between them in Edinburgh? Her friends' conviction that he loved her flitted through her mind, and she had to admit, even when she was angry with him, she was still very much attracted to him. "Very well," she said evenly, trying not to appear too eager. "Let us proceed as you suggest."

"Thank you." He sounded relieved; if only she could see his expression she'd know whether she had made the right decision.

At least in Edinburgh, if they truly did not suit, she would have other choices. The chance that it might get out that someone had posed as his wife nagged at her. She didn't want either of them hurt. Perhaps Caro was correct, and Mary's behavior was making the courtship more difficult. She was still so angry with her grandmother, was she truly not giving Kit a chance? It really wasn't fair to take her fury out on him. If that was indeed what she was doing.

Marcus rode up next to them. "Doust suggests we take the route he mentioned before. Going north through Coldstream, and from there on to Edinburgh. He says it will cut twenty miles from our journey. The road might not be as good, but it won't be as crowded either. I've already sent a rider ahead to notify the baggage coach. We'll stop at Wooler, about ten miles or so from the crossroad."

She stole a quick glance at Kit, who nodded. "Very well. When do we turn north?"

"There is a major crossroad with an inn. Apparently it cannot be missed."

"We shall see." Kit laughed. "Generally when one says that, missing the object is the easiest thing in the world."

That was a true statement, but when had she begun thinking of him as Kit again? Mary gave herself a shake. She needed to stop being such a pea goose.

Marcus left, leaving her and Kit alone again. After a few miles of skirting lakes, barely visible through the trees, on one side and pastures on the other, they entered dense forest.

She shivered.

"Are you cold?"

The horses must have felt her unease as well, as they picked up their pace. It couldn't hurt for them to trot for a bit. A nervous laugh burbled out. "No. It's just that the road reminds me of all the stories I've heard of highwaymen."

"It is rather dark." He edged closer to her, and despite her confusion about how she felt for him, she was grateful for his warmth.

A half hour later, the view opened to cultivated fields, and a large fortified building stood at the crossroad, proclaiming itself to be the Runside Inn. She and the horses heaved a collective sigh of relief. "Ah, here is our turn."

Mary guided the pair onto the road going north.

She anticipated Kit would move away from her, but he did not, instead remarking, "I expected more sheep in this area."

"Not at all. We have good soil in this part of the county. Wheat and various types of corn are grown here. I believe the closer to Scotland we travel, you'll see more sheep."

"You are . . ." He stopped, and cleared his throat. "We have another hour at least until we reach Wooler. Are you still comfortable driving?"

That hadn't been what he was going to say, which was most likely something about the land. *Drat! She was doing it again!* Why could she not simply appreciate his kindness for not saying anything and accept his concern for her? "I'm fine for the present. I shall give you the ribbons when we make our pause."

Until now, the only travel she'd experienced were the mad dashes her family made from their estate to Town, and the one to Rose Hill. It seemed none of them were capable of leisurely journeys. Cattle had been always stationed along the route and teams changed out with great speed and regularity. It was nice to finally be able to enjoy the scenery and stop at an inn for more than a quick night's sleep or a cup of tea. There would be no changes of cattle on this road, and a couple of times, she had to remind herself to nurse the pair along so as not to blow them.

Kit entertained her with comments on their surroundings. At times comparing it with other places in England, he drew her out about her home county, which he had visited only briefly. As much as she wanted to be in a city now, Mary came to realize how much she loved being in the country. "Which do you like better, Town or the country?"

He took a few moments before answering. "Although there is much to recommend Town, the theater for example, I am more at home in the country. Each time I visit one of my father's properties, the people in the area always make me feel welcome. I like the closeness."

Hmph. The country ladies probably looked forward to a chance to show themselves off to him.

"What about you?" he asked.

"I love the country. Though I wish I'd had more of an opportunity to shop and visit the theater and opera."

"I recall Huntley saying Edinburgh has a theater. It would be my pleasure to escort you." His voice trailed off as if he didn't know how she'd respond.

She had never heard him so unsure of himself. That must be part of what Caro had noticed. In the past, Mary would have thought Kit didn't truly wish to accompany her. Now she saw it differently. Was it true that he was no more sure of her than she of him? "I would love it."

Each time they passed another vehicle or a person walking along the road, Kit inclined his head and called a greeting. She had never been around anyone so genial to his fellow man as Kit was, and it gave her a warm, joyous feeling that she was with him.

Not more than two hours later, they reached the outskirts of the market town where they were stopping, and she was more than happy to pause for a while. Mary pulled up beside a footman in Huntley's livery who had waved at them. "My lady, Mr. Maufe said to tell you we are at the Red Lion, which has the advantage over the Black Bull."

"Thank you." She started the horses again. They too would be pleased to rest for a while.

"I'd be interested to know," Kit said, "what the difference is."

She might like to know as well, but not right now. "As long as I can walk for a while and have something to eat and drink, I do not think I care."

"There on the left." He pointed.

Kit's groom was ready to take charge of the horses, while Kit lifted her down from the curricle, keeping his large hands on her waist until she got her feet back under her again. For several moments, she stared at his nicely tied cravat, which was a little silly. Mary raised her gaze to his. A smile hovered on his lips, and his eyes were as warm as his hands had been. Butterflies took up residence in her heart. "Thank you. I think I can manage now."

"If you're sure?" he said, not removing his hands.

"Mr. Maufe's waiting, my lady," Dent said, interrupting the moment.

"Positive." Yet she did not want Kit to move.

As they strolled to the door, she placed her hand on his arm. Once inside, Mathers was there to take Mary to a clean but sparsely decorated chamber. A long mirror filled one corner of the room. "Oh dear. I didn't realize how much dust I'd have on my gown."

"Thought that might be the case. I'll brush it off a bit now. I've got your pelisse for when you leave again." Mary stood still while her maid cleaned the worst of the dirt off. "How was your drive?"

"It was delightful." And it truly was. She'd had fun handling the pair, and Kit had been entertaining.

Mathers cut Mary a cryptic look.

"No, I am quite serious. I've never driven for such a long distance, but the fresh air and views made it a wonderful experience." Not to mention Mr. Featherton had been a perfect companion. After she'd stopped taking umbrage at everything and had given him a chance, that was. "I believe I'll see some of the town until the others arrive and have refreshed themselves."

Kit was waiting for Mary when she strolled out of the inn. He'd been pleasantly surprised they'd spent so much time together without him getting on her bad side. *That was the first time that had happened.* "I'd planned on exploring the town. Would you like to come with me?"

She placed her hand very properly on the top of his arm. "I had the same idea."

Damn if he'd allow her to keep putting distance between them. Considering he was wooing her, he tucked her hand securely in the crook of his arm as they turned right onto the busy main street and began snoodling toward the church. "The landlord tells me the town burnt down and was re-built about a hundred years ago."

"That would explain why it looks so modern, even the church. I don't believe I've ever seen a newer one."

They continued up a flagstone path lined with bushes just beginning to bud. He opened the door to the church and a wave of cool air rushed out. The interior was whitewashed plaster, detailed in the local stone. "Very pretty and peaceful."

"Yes, it is." She smiled softly, glancing at him. "The windows let in a great deal of light."

He could envision them standing at the altar, pledging their vows. "It makes me wonder if this plain and simple interior is the way of the future."

She raised a brow, but her eyes twinkled with wickedness. "Not if Prinny has anything to say about it."

This was the first time she'd made a joke around him. He laughed. "Have you seen the Brighton Pavilion?"

"No," she said, shaking her head. "I've heard about it. Grandmamma was not at all impressed. She also accused him of quacking himself."

He agreed with the dowager duchess. If Prinny didn't eat so many rooster stones, he probably wouldn't be so fat. "His physician should put him on a reducing diet. He would be in better health if he lost some weight."

"According to Grandmamma, he used to be quite handsome."

"So I've heard." He gave a shudder. "I will only advise you that unless you wish to hear the subject discussed ad nauseam, do not mention it around any older ladies."

Mary laughed, and the sound filled his soul. Kit wished she'd do it more often.

They strolled to the other end of the high street. By the time they returned to the inn, Kit was congratulating himself for remaining on her good side thus far.

He was glad the rest of their coterie had arrived so that they could eat. "I hope nuncheon is ready. I'm starving."

Mary nodded. "I'm feeling a bit peckish myself, and it is not even noon yet."

"We broke our fast much earlier to-day."

Caro and Huntley sat on the window seat of the large private parlor situated on the inn's first floor.

Huntley rose. "Good, you're here. Now we can eat."

"We were just saying something of the sort," Kit responded. He helped Mary to a chair next to Caro's at one end of the long table laden with meats, cheeses, bread, and two savory pies. He filled a plate for Mary, and Huntley did the same for his wife.

Mary poured glasses of lemonade for herself and Caro. She held out the jug. "Would you like lemonade or ale?"

"I'll take ale, thank you," Kit responded, pushing a mug across to her.

"I will as well," Huntley added. Once his mug was filled, Huntley took a long pull. "The others should be here shortly. They are giving the nursemaids time to eat and stretch their legs."

Caro grinned. "And letting the boys run off some of their energy in a nearby field."

Huntley reached across the table, covering her hand with his. "It won't be long before ours is doing the same."

While they gazed at one another, Kit glanced at Mary. If he hadn't been listening, he would have missed her small sigh. That was what he and Mary both wanted, and it was up to him to get them there. The only question was how.

At that moment, the door opened to a cacophony of high-pitched laughter. Phoebe and Anna strolled in, with Marcus and Rutherford following, bouncing the boys on their shoulders. Soon all that was left of the meal were crumbs.

"By the by," Kit asked Huntley as they watched Arthur and Ben finally succumb to Morpheus, "why *did* Maufe select this inn over the other?"

"The innkeeper here did not argue with Maufe when he explained what he wanted. The other one did."

Caro giggled. "I've always said Maufe adds to our consequence."

"Did I not hear that he and your lady's maid married?" Kit asked.

"They did indeed." Huntley grinned. "An unusual step, but one Caro and I supported wholeheartedly."

Forty minutes or so later, the group re-boarded their carriages. Kit half expected Mary to make her excuses to him and ride with the other ladies, but when she entered the yard, she gave him a small smile and made her way to his curricle. Before he could get there to hand her in, Dent had done it. Kit stifled a growl. He'd have to speak with his groom about being so efficient when it came to Mary. Disgruntled, he climbed up. At least he had her attention for the next two hours.

She gave him the ribbons. "It is your turn."

"Thank you."

They sat in silence while he maneuvered the carriage through the busy street and out of town. The landscape once again turned into gently rolling hills. Mary pulled a piece of paper from her pelisse pocket. "I purchased this from the landlord. It lists the towns and villages along the way. I thought it might be interesting."

He glanced over. She held a thick, brightly colored rectangular paper. He doubted it would be much help. "It might at that."

They passed the time commenting about the countryside, and when they entered a village, Mary brought out the map. "This is Akeld."

In a blink of an eye they were surrounded by fields again.

She frowned. "I must say, the map made it seem larger. I didn't even see the inn mentioned."

Kit had, and it was not more than a crofter's cottage. "We shall have to see what the next village brings."

But the next village was only slightly more prosperous than the first.

Mary shook the map. "And all this time I thought I was missing things when my family traveled so quickly."

Unable to help himself, he let out a bark of laughter.

Her head snapped around to him. "What is so funny?"

"I imagine"—Kit struggled to bring himself under control—"you were on large post roads, not smaller ones such as this, and passing through significantly larger towns and villages."

She gave a rueful smile. "You might have a point. Will it be like this until we reach Edinburgh?"

If he said it would be, she might abandon him for the ladies' carriage. His laughter died. "Not having traveled this way before, I can't say, but we shall find out."

They passed a signpost to Flodden, and agreed they did not need to stop at the famous battlefield.

Finally they were hailed by the same Huntley footman as before. "My lady, sir, you're to go to the Collingswood Arms on the main street through Cornhill. Mr. Maufe says we're stayin' there."

It was on the tip of Kit's tongue to ask why they were not finishing their trip to Coldstream, but he'd no doubt discover the reason later. He flipped the footman a coin. "Thank you."

They were almost through the picturesque village when he saw the hotel set back from the road. Now he knew the answer.

The Collingswood Arms, built of stone the color of sand, stood in its own park. Perfect for the children and their two-day stay, as they would not travel on Sunday. Liveried footmen were with Maufe as they came to a stop in front of the hotel.

Mary clasped her hands together. "How lovely. Maufe is truly a gem."

Kit grimaced. "If there was any way to hire him away from Huntley, I would."

"Perhaps a better idea is to allow him to train your Piggott."

When Kit turned to Mary, her eyes were full of mirth. A look he'd seen more to-day than in the past week they'd been together. "I might just do that."

Before Dent could reach the curricle, Kit hopped down and lifted Mary from the carriage. Even though he held her so that no part of her touched him, his blood heated. The moment her feet touched the ground she gazed up at him, her startled eyes deepening in color to pewter. What he wouldn't give to know what she felt at that moment.

"My lady," Maufe said. "Your dresser is waiting for you just inside the door. A bath is being prepared."

Mary gave an imperceptible shake of her head as if to clear it. "Yes, of course. I'll come directly." She turned back to Kit. "Shall I see you before dinner?"

"Yes." He took her hand, bringing it to his lips. "Perhaps another stroll?"

She stilled, like a deer uncertain of her surroundings. "I—I would like that."

Slowly, he let go of her fingers. "Send word when you are ready."

"I shall." She made her way into the hotel.

Though she hadn't looked back—and he really had not expected her to, she was too much of a lady—he'd made progress. Almost as much, if not more, than the day he'd first suggested a courtship. Now if only he could convince her to marry him.

CHAPTER SEVENTEEN

"The weather is being particularly fine for this time of year, don't you agree?"

Mary grinned at Eunice, who had been pacing the floor of Mary's chamber for the past twenty minutes at least.

"What in heaven's name could be taking so long?"

Eunice was as jumpy as a cat. Mary had never seen her aunt so nervous before. "You did say Mr. Doust had to track down the rector in Coldstream."

"Yes, but how hard can that be?" Eunice's arms flew up, then dropped again. "The town is not that big."

"Have some tea." Mary handed a cup to her aunt. "I'm sure he'll return soon."

Finally, Eunice sank onto the chair facing the fireplace. "Thank you. It is probably only nerves."

"What is there to be anxious about? You two have been smelling of April and May for the better part of a year, and you've been married before. It's not as if you do not know what to expect."

"Yes, but I was younger then, and my betrothed had the blessing of my family." Eunice screwed up her face. "This decision feels so much more important for some reason."

Well, she had a point. Mary took her aunt's hand. It must have been much easier to have had an arranged marriage with a man one already loved. "Perhaps because you are the one making the decision."

"You may be right." Eunice gave a tight smile. "If it goes wrong, I'll have only myself to blame."

"Come now." Mary used her most bracing tone. "That is quite enough of that sort of talk. At this rate, you'll convince yourself not to marry him at all." The sounds of horses and men rose from the front of the hotel. "That may be him now."

A few moments later, a knock sounded on the door. "Come." The door swung open. Mr. Doust clutched his hat in his hands and fixed his gaze on Eunice. "If we're to be wed by a clergyman before next Wednesday, we must go immediately."

Her eyes widened as she rose. "Now? But why?"

"The rector won't marry us on Sunday. He has to be out of the area on Monday and won't be back until late Tuesday. The only other option is to wed over the anvil." He swallowed. "This is what you want, isn't it?"

The worry in Eunice's face disappeared and she smiled. "Yes, it is. Let me get my things, and I'll be right down."

Eunice rushed off, and Mary dashed to the wardrobe where Mathers had put her jewel box. Her aunt may have been married before, but some traditions had to be maintained. She drew out an old pearl necklace with a sapphire pendant. Old, blue, and borrowed. Now to find something new.

Caro, Anna, and Phoebe entered one after the other, wearing traveling cloaks and bonnets.

"I take it we're all going to a wedding," Caro said.

"Yes." Mary rolled the necklace up in linen, then placed it in her reticule. "I need something new."

"New?" Anna's brows puckered for a moment before clearing. "Oh my. Yes indeed. Will a handkerchief do? I brought several new ones I'd just completed."

Mary gave her friend a hug. "Perfect. Bring them all. We'll probably need them." She donned her hat and pelisse. "Let's be off."

When they arrived in the hotel's yard, the carriages were waiting. No curricles this time. They couldn't afford to become dirty before the wedding. The ladies took the largest one, and in no time at all they were on their way, and crossing the bridge into Coldstream. The coaches pulled up at the western entrance of an old, gray stone church.

Mary took out the necklace, fastening it around her aunt's neck. "This is for you for to-day. Old, borrowed, and blue."

"And this"—Anna handed Eunice a handkerchief of fine white work—"is something new."

Eunice swallowed and blinked her eyes. "Thank you so very much."

The carriage opened, and Mr. Doust held out his bare hand. "My lady."

She removed her gloves, sticking them in her reticule before placing her much smaller hand in his. "Sir."

One by one, the gentlemen helped their ladies down from the carriage. When it was Mary's turn, Kit executed a short bow. "Shall we?" She watched as his fingers closed around her hand, swallowing it. When she looked up, he was smiling. She bit the inside of her cheek. How long would it be before she married? "It's been a long time since I've attended a wedding."

The corners of his lips quirked up. "In that case you should have your handkerchief ready. It's my experience ladies express their joy with tears at such events."

Her brothers would be in a panic at the proposition of a lady crying, even with happiness, yet Kit appeared sanguine. She stepped down to the dirt road. "That doesn't horrify you?"

"No indeed." He tucked her hand firmly in the crook of his arm. "Not when they are happy." He pulled a face. "Now tears of distress are a very different matter. I don't know a man alive who doesn't dread them."

They followed the others through the main door, making their way up the nave to where a sandy-haired gentleman busied himself in front of the sanctuary.

The man straightened as they approached. "Mr. Doust, my lady, welcome."

"My dear, ladies, gentlemen," Mr. Doust said, "allow me to introduce Mr. Creelman, who you have probably surmised is the rector."

Once the remaining introductions were completed, Mr. Creelman asked Doust and Lady Eunice, "Who will be your witnesses?"

Doust glanced at Kit. He nodded. "Lady Mary Tolliver and Mr. Featherton."

Mary started. She and Eunice hadn't discussed who'd attend her and her betrothed, but Mary should have expected she would. Still, she'd never acted as a witness and was a little unsure of what to do. Hopefully, the rector would tell her. "I'm happy to."

"If everyone else will take their seats," Mr. Creelman said, "we shall begin." Although the service was straight out of the Book of Common Prayer, and the newlyweds took communion, the service seemed rather short to Kit. He supposed his marriage to Mary would be much the same. He found himself looking forward to calling her his wife and hoped she'd soon feel the same.

During the wedding dinner at the hotel, he remained by her side, filling her plate from the numerous offerings at the table, and fetching her drinks. She had not exaggerated when she'd told him she was not a picky eater, and it pleased him to see her eat what he'd brought. Once Doust and Lady Eunice retired, the talk turned to Edinburgh.

While they'd been in Coldstream, the messenger, waylaid by one of their footmen, had arrived with Lady Theo's letter. Huntley handed Caro his penknife, and she slid it under the seal; spreading the single page out, she quickly perused it and grinned. "We are all welcome. She is getting the nursery ready as well. She already has a list of entertainments we might be interested in and will make up another list of suitable gentlemen for Mary."

Kit forced back a growl of frustration. He did not need Lady Theo finding another man for Mary. Thankfully she'd only blushed and not agreed with the suggestion. Now though, her eyes sparkled with excitement as Caro recited some of the outings and parties to which Lady Theo had accepted invitations on their behalf.

Kit had thought he'd understood Mary's desire for a Season; he did have sisters. But looking at her now, he realized he hadn't fully appreciated how much she looked forward to it. Had he become so jaded with the Season that he'd applied his feelings to her?

For years now, his role was to be the perfect gentleman and guest. After the first few years, he never even flirted with ladies. How had he fooled himself into thinking he could convince her to marry him with a picnic or two and compliments on her garden? Perhaps he needed to make his own compilation of what a lady being courted might wish to do, and, if Lady Theo was playing matchmaker, he'd better secure dances and appointments for other entertainments before he and Mary arrived in Edinburgh. Come what may, he'd ensure Mary had the best Season of her life.

He wondered if any of the ladies had brought a guidebook of the sights a visitor shouldn't miss in the area. If not, he'd procure one as soon as they arrived. It was a brilliant idea, even if he did say so himself. Whenever they were not at some event or another planned by their hostess, he would keep her busy with him. There was no way he'd allow some Scottish rogue to take Mary away from him.

Three days later, their caravan entered Edinburgh. Apparently the only one who'd visited the city before was Maufe, who sat with Huntley's coachman in the lead carriage. After winding through streets, they finally pulled up in front of a large town house on a corner of Charlotte Square in the new city.

A footman stationed on the stairs opened the door, and an elderly man dressed in a black suit stepped out and bowed. He called over his shoulder, and almost immediately, additional footmen poured out of the lower levels of the house. Several moments later, after the ladies and children had reached the pavement, a tall, elegant, middle-aged lady dressed in the height of fashion, appeared on the step. Surely this could not be Lady Theo. The woman who tramped through the countryside with her husband, looking at rocks.

Holding out her hands, she grinned broadly. "Huntley, I'm so happy to welcome you to Edinburgh." She glanced next to him. "And this must be Caro. How very pleased I am to meet you, my dear. We had quite despaired of ever finding him a wife." Lady Theo hugged Caro, then turned to the rest of the assemblage. "Welcome to my home. Please come in and rest while your maids and valets settle you in. I have a rather large repast waiting to be served to you in the back drawing room and for the children in the nursery."

"I'm glad to hear that," Mary said quietly. "My stomach has been grumbling for the past hour."

Kit smiled. "Mine as well." He led her up the steps and into a large hall laid with yellow marble that matched the Georgian columns. The grand staircase, done in a medium-colored wood, gleamed with beeswax. "If I were a boy again, I'd slide down that."

Next to him, Mary snorted. "I would have slid down it as well."

They followed their hostess into a rectangular room off the hall. Windows lined two walls, and fireplaces anchored each end. Once the company were relieved of their outer garments, tea accompanied by large trays full of food arrived.

"Where is Uncle Titus?" Huntley asked after they'd finished eating.

Lady Theo waved her hand around, fingers fluttering. "Here and there. He is preparing to submit a paper to the Royal Society and had a meeting scheduled with some of his colleagues. Not knowing when you'd arrive, I told him to go on. He'll join us for dinner."

"If no one minds," Marcus said, glancing at the rest of them, "Rutherford and I wish to take the boys out to the park."

"I think that's a splendid idea," Lady Theo said. "In fact, you gentlemen are rather *de trop*. After the ladies have refreshed themselves, we shall discuss our entertainments." She focused on Kit. "Mr. Featherton, your reputation precedes you. I'm quite sure we would not have received nearly so many invitations without your presence."

He stifled a groan and rose with the rest of the men. They recognized a dismissal when they heard it. He took Mary's hand, giving it a slight squeeze. "I'll see you before dinner then."

A lovely pink flooded her cheeks. "Of course."

He and Mary had been getting along so well. She had not turned away from him once during their journey to Edinburgh. Finally his courting of her was going well, but in order to forestall Lady Theo's plans, he'd have to move quickly.

A half hour later, Mary, Caro, Phoebe, and Anna joined Lady Theo in the morning room overlooking the gardens in the back of the house. As expected, more tea was served.

Mary twirled one of the curls framing her face around one finger. Ever since Lady Theo had singled Kit out, Mary had wondered exactly what the older lady had meant. Was it merely his reputation as Mr. Perfect, or was there more? Unfortunately, she could not bring herself to ask.

She almost fell upon Caro with gratitude when she did. "Kit Featherton, as you know, is extremely popular in London, but I'm surprised he is known here."

Lady Theo raised a brow. "You'd be surprised how far and fast news travels. The ladies here have heard how he's not only the perfect gentleman, but has, so far, avoided marriage. I know several young ladies who are already planning their weddings." She raised her brow, an amused expression on her countenance. "They have reasoned that as the missish English ladies did not appeal to him, the bolder Scottish lasses might."

Mary's hand curled into a fist, crushing part of her skirt. She didn't care at all if another lady was interested in Kit. Although he'd been very pleasant during their journey, perhaps more than pleasant, she'd had a truly wonderful time. That did not excuse the fact that Kit had not made any advances showing her he truly wished to marry her. He hadn't kissed her. The ugly specter of him kissing another woman raised its head, and Mary bit her lip. She was not and would not be jealous. They didn't even have an understanding. Stifling a sigh, she schooled her mien into a pleasant mask and hoped no one had noticed her initial reaction. Unfortunately, her fist still crushed her gown. *Drat.* She'd never hear the end of it from Mathers if she ruined it.

"To-morrow I shall take you on some morning calls." Lady Theo recited the entertainments she thought most appropriate for the rest of the week. A Venetian breakfast, a ball at the assembly rooms, dinner and cards, and a ball in three days' time. "We are not as busy as London, but I'm proud of our Season."

"I'm sure it will be lovely." Caro smiled at Lady Theo. "I must say, I am glad for something a little less hectic than London, and I've always wanted to visit Edinburgh. Thank you so very much for allowing us all to invade your home."

"Not at all. I am rarely around ladies, and you've given me the perfect excuse to host my own ball. Now"—Lady Theo turned her sharp gaze on Mary—"I understand we must find you a husband."

Thankfully, she'd just put down her cup, or it would have gone crashing to the floor. As it was, she barely swallowed her tea without spewing it all over. "I thought I'd let things happen as they may."

Lady Theo slowly shook her head. "It must only appear that way. As I told Caro, I have made a list of eligible gentlemen, including information on their families. You will not want for choice."

Mary fought not to drop her jaw. "*Their families?*" she squeaked.

That was a stupid thing to say. Families were important. One needed to know what one would be left to deal with after the marriage. Had she ever met Mr. Featherton's mother? She struggled to bring her wayward thoughts under control. What did it matter if she wasn't going to wed him?

"We have several gentlemen down from the Highlands," Lady Theo continued. "I'll not deny they are extremely impressive specimens, but if you should be interested, Lady Mary"—Mary snapped her attention back to her hostess—"you must remember most of them live in isolated areas which you may not like."

Such as Rose Hill. Actually, Rosebury hadn't felt isolated at all. Although from what she'd heard of the Highlands, one could easily be a day's ride or more from any kind of town at all. Still, if she fell in love . . . Who was she trying to fool? She'd never be able to live in the middle of nowhere. Very well then, no Highlanders no matter how remarkable they were.

"What is your portion, my dear?"

Bother. That was the second time she'd been caught woolgathering. "Er, I believe I'd rather say moderate. Nothing to get excited about."

Lady Theo nodded her head sagely. "Good thinking. There is no reason to encourage fortune hunters. Though in my experience, most of them go to London. How is your wardrobe?"

Thankfully Mary had been readying herself for London. "I received a package from my modiste in London before we left. All I require is a final fitting for some of the gowns."

"Excellent." Lady Theo tugged the bell-pull, and almost immediately a footman opened the door. "Tell Beattie to send a note round to my modiste. I expect her to attend me in the morning. The hour may be as early as she wishes. Oh, and it's time for someone to fetch the gentlemen."

The young man bowed. "Yes, my lady."

Lady Theo glanced at the clock. "We shall dine in two hours. Lady Mary, I'll advise you as to the time of the fitting."

"Thank you, my lady." There was, after all, nothing else she could say.

"If you'll excuse me, I have some matters to attend to. Please make yourselves at home." Lady Theo sailed out of the parlor, the door snapping shut behind her.

"Well." Mary glanced at her friends. "I didn't expect her to take charge in such a manner."

"I know what you mean." Caro grimaced. "On the other hand, this is her city, and she knows it well."

"The real question," Phoebe said, "is whom do you wish to marry? Has Kit done anything to fix your attentions?"

Mary pulled at a curl. "He is all that is exceptional . . ."

"But?" Anna prompted.

"He is Mr. Perfect, and he doesn't seem to feel anything particular for me." Mary gave an exasperated huff. "And I will not throw myself at him. I've given your suggestion a great deal of thought, and I cannot. I shall have to look elsewhere for a husband."

Her friends nodded. Thankfully no one brought up her living at Rose Hill. Well, this was up to Mr. Featherton, after all. If he wished to marry her, he'd find a way to show her. Until then, she planned to enjoy her Season without Gawain trying to trap her. That at least was something to be happy about.

CHAPTER EIGHTEEN

K it was in his chamber tying his cravat, as Piggott kept up a steady stream of conversation. Normally Kit was interested in the goings-on of the house in which he was visiting, but to-day he impatiently waited to hear what Lady Theo had planned for Mary. Kit vowed to thwart any attempt by the formidable female to match his Mary to anyone else. Yet asking his valet to just get it over with and tell him seemed a bit pathetic.

She was everything he wanted in a wife; they had never lacked for conversation, she was intelligent, resourceful, responsible, kind, and so lovely it made his heart and the rest of his body ache with longing. The depressing fact was, during the last three days of travel he'd fallen irrevocably in love with her, and she hadn't appeared to notice. He'd never before spent so much time in one female's company, never danced attendance on only one lady, and he'd damn sure never had to stop himself from pulling one into his arms. His fingers came close to trembling each time he touched her. Yet other than a few blushes, which were charming, she hadn't seemed to have been affected. He would like to take his friends' advice and kiss her, but first he must ensure she would welcome his advances.

Kit gave himself a shake, and Piggott cried out, "Sir, you've ruined another one."

Hell and damnation! Kit glanced in the mirror. "Well, it's not the Trone d'Amour, but it's not bad. The extra two creases are even interesting. I shall leave it at that. We'll name it 'The Featherton.'"

His valet came around and peered at his neckcloth. "You might have something there, sir, and I defy anyone to replicate it."

Kit doubted if he could tie it the same way again. "My jacket, please."

Piggott assisted Kit in donning his jacket. Tucking his watch and quizzing glass in his waistcoat, he should be just in time to escort Mary to the drawing room. If only he knew what Lady Theo had planned. Leaving his chamber, he headed toward the grand staircase. Fortune was with him. Mary turned the corner from her wing of the house. Lady Theo apparently didn't believe single ladies and single gentlemen should sleep near each other. Any other time he would have agreed, but now he was not so sure. "Shall I escort you, my lady?"

"Oh. I didn't see you." She gave him a tenuous smile. "Yes, thank you. I believe the others will be along shortly."

Something was bothering her, and he wished with all his heart she'd confide in him. "Did your meeting with Lady Theo go well?"

"Yes." Mary's finely arched brows drew together slightly. "She has a great many invitations all ready. To-morrow we ladies will accompany her on morning visits."

It was time to start ensuring she would not be spending all her time without him. "When you expressed interest in seeing the city, I borrowed a guidebook. If you like, we may walk to some of the closer sights to-morrow afternoon." She glanced up at him, confusion lurking in her lovely gray eyes. "Only if you won't be too tired after a round of meeting new people."

Finally Mary laughed. "I doubt copious cups of tea will tire me, and after three days in a carriage, even a well-sprung one, I'd love to walk."

"I'll arrange for a footman to accompany us. I imagine the proprieties are the same as in London."

"Yes." She heaved what sounded suspiciously like a sigh. "I'd forgotten."

She wasn't the only one. After living for a year as a "married lady," the constraints of being an unwed female might chafe. He should apply his mind to the best way to turn that to his advantage. By this time they'd reached the door of the drawing room. Lady Theo and Lord Titus stood by a window, talking. They turned when Kit and Mary entered.

He bowed slightly. "Good evening."

"Mr. Featherton." Lady Theo glided toward them. "Just the gentleman I need to speak with." She drew him away as Lord Titus engaged Mary in conversation. "One of my dear friends has a daughter who is painfully shy. I mentioned to her you were here, and we thought you might engage her daughter for a dance. I understand you have a way of drawing young ladies out."

Not what Kit wanted to hear, or do for that matter. "Of course, my lady. I am happy to be of assistance."

"Come, Mr. Featherton, what do you prefer to drink before dinner?"

"Sherry is my preference." He stole a glance at Mary, who was in discussion with Lord Titus. She already had a glass of sherry.

"I believe we can find some. I understand Lady Phoebe's uncle, the Marquis of St. Eth, is a connoisseur."

"As is the lady herself." If Lady Theo had another point to make, he wished she'd get on with it and stop this slow perambulation around the room, the sole purpose of which appeared to be to keep him away from Mary.

"Indeed. I do hope she will not be disappointed by my cellar."

Before he could answer, the rest of the group arrived. Lord Titus served them all glasses of sherry.

"This is fine for before dinner," Lord Titus said, "but afterward, I have some well-aged Scotch from my family's stock. In my opinion, it is better than the finest brandy."

"I've had the pleasure of sampling Scotch whisky a few times," Marcus remarked. "When it's well brewed and aged, it can indeed rival a fine French brandy."

Lord Titus, in the act of lifting a glass to his mouth, paused. "And where did you drink it? I thought you hadn't been to Scotland before, and to the best of my knowledge, no self-respecting Englishman would willingly partake of it."

Lifting his lips into a smile, Marcus saluted him. "In general, you are correct, my lord. My father would not have it in his house. I, however, traveled broadly for eight years and had the great good luck to come across more than one of your countrymen. They always seem to have a taste of home around. In parts of America and Canada, it's actually produced in small quantities."

Lord Titus laughed. "You've put me in my place, my lord. I should not make suppositions."

"Nor," Lady Theo said in a harsh tone directed at her husband, "do we wish to dredge up all the problems between England and Scotland."

He strolled over to her and kissed her cheek. "My apologies to you, my love, and our guests. In my defense, I'm suffering from political overstimulation."

Kit began to amble toward Mary, but before he could take his place next to her again, Lady Theo had the women in conversation at the other end of the long room. If he didn't know better, he'd think his host and hostess were purposely keeping Mary and him apart. That he would not allow.

Mary glanced at him. Yet the moment her gaze met his, she lowered her long, dark lashes and turned her head. What the devil did that mean? He never should have agreed to come here until they were married. After all, Huntley and Caro had wed before they loved each other. Kit could have made it work as well. *Damn it all.*

From the moment Lord Titus had drawn her aside, Mary had surreptitiously studied Kit from beneath her lashes. Then their gazes met. It never occurred to her he'd be watching her as well. She missed him by her side, and no matter what else she attempted to think about, it all came back to him. Next to her Caro laughed, but Mary had missed the joke. Surely, he'd escort her to dinner. He was coming her way, after all. Yet when the meal was announced, her host was bowing before her, not Kit.

Lord Titus held out his arm. "My lady, allow me." She placed her hand on his arm, and he escorted her to the seat on his left. Phoebe sat on his right, and Kit was at the other end of the table on Lady Theo's right. Not exactly the correct protocol, but it left Caro and Huntley together.

Well, drat it all.

Unless Scottish manners allowed shouting down the table, Mary was not even going to be able to talk with him until the gentlemen joined the ladies after dinner.

She made herself smile as Lord Titus recommended a dish. "This is baked salmon with tarragon, a particularly Scottish receipt."

Kit's deep, smooth voice carried lightly down the table. She would not look. She'd not make a spectacle of herself. "Thank you, my lord. It sounds delightful. I'm sure I shall love it."

It was the longest meal of her life. A thrumming started behind her ears and spread through her head. By the time Lady Theo rose, indicating it was time to leave the gentlemen to their libations, Mary had a rare headache. Once in the corridor, she caught Caro's arm. "I need to lie down."

Caro searched Mary's face. "You do look pale. Shall I come with you?"

"No, thank you. Mathers will know what to do. Please make my excuses to Lady Theo."

"Naturally, I will. Get a good night's sleep. I'm sure all will be well come morning."

Mary gave Caro a quick hug. "Of course. Thank you."

Several moments later, Mary entered her empty chamber. Not expecting her mistress to retire so early, Mathers was probably with the rest of the servants. Perhaps some time alone would help Mary think. She toed off her silk slippers, moved to the dressing table, took the pins and ribbon out of her hair, then dragged a comb through her curls. This visit was not going at all as she'd thought it would. She wished she was back at Rose Hill, or that she'd never gone to Northumberland in the first place. The only good thing that had happened was that she wasn't dodging her cousin.

Theo watched Mr. Featherton as he, once again, glanced around the drawing room, his frown deepening. All evening he and Lady Mary had been casting looks at each other when they thought no one else was watching. It would make short work of marrying them both off, if the young couple were enamored of each other, but before involving herself, Theo resolved to discover what was going on. She'd been on the wrong end of believing two young people were in love before. She was older and, hopefully, wiser now.

She strolled up to Huntley, who was standing with his wife. "Caro, my dear."

"Yes, my lady?"

"None of that now, we are of the same rank, and related. I know you are much too well mannered to mention the age difference. I insist you call me Theo." She linked her arm with Caro. "Come with me if you would. We've hardly had time to get to know one another, and I'd like to speak with you for a bit."

Huntley raised his wife's fingers to his lips. "I'll be here waiting for you."

Well, that was nice to see. Love was important in a marriage. She glanced at her husband. Which was the very reason she'd married the sometimes ill-natured younger son of a Scottish peer. What a row with her father that had been. "I'll come right to the point. Am I mistaken, or do I sense something between Lady Mary and Mr. Featherton?"

"You are perfectly correct." Caro paused for a moment. "The problem, as I see it, is that they are not only both reserved, but Mary is a romantic. You know Mr. Featherton's reputation."

"Ah yes. Mr. Perfect."

"Indeed." Caro glanced up with a disgusted look. "Mary is waiting for an overt sign from him, and he is too proper to give it. He says he will not insult her honor."

Theo couldn't stop a huff. "There are times when a lady's honor needs to be insulted. What a muddle."

"That is what we've been thinking." Her niece shook her head. "Nothing any of us says seems to work. I'm quite sure if we locked them in a room together, they'd end up playing cribbage."

This was the most interesting case of courtship going astray Theo had seen in years. "They do not appear to be dullards."

"No, not in the least." Caro's lips formed a thin line. "Both Mary and Kit, Mr. Featherton, are intelligent, well-informed individuals with a great many talents and interests. It's just, when it comes to one another, they don't know what to do."

"Love can make fools of greater people then they are. Let me put my mind to it. I'm sure I can come up with a solution. In the meantime, we shall go on with my plans."

"Of introducing them to other people?"

"Indeed. Come to think of it, a little jealousy might be just what is needed for at least one of them to forget him- or herself."

"I'll not disagree with you." Caro sighed. "But I know for a fact, Kit has never lost his temper in public."

"Well, then it's about time he did." And Theo knew just the gentleman to do it. As long as the rake remained a gentleman with Mary, the scheme forming in Theo's mind would do the trick.

Kit excused himself shortly after tea. Caro had mentioned Mary having a headache, and he wished he could make sure she was all right. He reached the top of the staircase and gazed at the corridor leading to her chamber. He was half-way to the end, and stopped. What the devil did he think he was doing? He couldn't very well enter her chamber, even if he knew which one it was. He ran his fingers through his hair. There must be some way to discover how she was doing.

Luckily for him, Mary's maid passed carrying a tray.

"Mathers?"

She turned and blinked. "Yes, sir?"

"I, er, I am concerned about Lady Mary."

The dratted woman stood stock still, obviously waiting for him to explain himself.

"I was told she wasn't feeling quite the thing." His neckcloth tightened, and he had an urge to loosen it. "If you could tell me whether or not she is better, I'd appreciate it."

The maid gave a sharp nod. "I shall inquire."

Kit remained where he was for several moments before Mathers returned. "Her ladyship says her headache is going away."

He waited for the woman to continue, but it became clear that he wasn't going to get anything more out of her unless he asked a great many important, not to mention impertinent, questions. "Thank you."

Mathers bobbed a curtsey. "Good-night, sir."

Every instinct he had urged him to go to Mary; instead he turned on his heel and stalked off to his own room. To-morrow, while the ladies were making morning calls, he'd scour the town for the best of the sights for him and Mary to visit. Together. Somehow he'd have to find a way to continue to court her and remain near her for the duration of their stay.

Kit woke early the next morning, arriving in the breakfast room moments before Mary entered. Covered dishes lined the sideboard, and sun streamed in through the east-facing windows. He held out a chair for her. "I'd be honored if you'd allow me to fetch your breakfast."

The butler set a tea-pot on the table in front of Mary.

"Thank you. I'll pour."

A footman brought in bannocks, which apparently took the place of toast here.

He smiled. "Excellent."

Surveying the offerings, he found salted herring, smoked salmon, beef, bacon, black pudding, and porridge, but no eggs. He filled two plates and two bowls, giving them both a little of everything. The servants were still adding to the dishes.

How were they supposed to discuss anything with footmen running in and out and the butler standing at the door? He almost wished they were still traveling. Well, he'd better do something fast, before the others got here.

He set her plate on the table, taking the chair next to her. "This afternoon, would you like to discover some of Edinburgh's sights with me?"

She spread butter and jam on a piece of the bannock she'd broken off. "What did you have in mind?"

"I thought we'd start with Holyrood Palace, unless you'd rather see something else." Kit had never felt so out of control of a situation in his life. Everything depended on Mary, and he never knew what she'd decide.

She chewed her bread as if she had something on her mind. If only he could get her to open up to him. "No. I'd like that extremely. The palace is said to be lovely."

He slowly let his breath out. "I'll order the carriage for after luncheon."

Lady Theo entered the room. "Lady Mary, I'm glad to see you are feeling better. We have quite a schedule this morning."

Mary hesitated the slightest bit before she smiled and greeted their hostess. "Thank you, my lady. I am much improved. I think all the travel finally caught up with me. I look forward to the visits."

"I'm glad to hear it." Lady Theo called for more tea before taking her place at the foot of the table. "We cannot have you looking poorly while showing you off to potential suitors."

"Like a blasted horse at auction," Mary muttered to herself.

Kit put his cup down with a snap and held the serviette to his lips. Mary quickly raised her cup to hide her smile before she broke out laughing.

"May I know what I said that was so funny?" Lady Theo asked.

"I'm sorry, my lady. It was not you. There is a"—Mary had to think quickly—"a couple of birds bickering outside in the tree. It reminded me of something my—my brother told me."

Lady Theo looked out the window just as a bird flew by. "I see."

When she went back to her tea, Mary slid a glance at Kit. That was the first time he had laughed since they'd arrived. Come to think of it, it was the first time she'd wanted to laugh as well. How had she not noticed before how they always found humor in the same things?

She hated not being in control of her life, and it had been going on much too long. Caro was right. Mary must do something if she wanted a happy ending. All she had to do was think of a plan, just as she had done to increase the profits at Rose Hill. Rather than telling herself she didn't care about Kit, it was time to admit she was falling in love with him. All she had to do was concoct a scheme that would make him fall in love with her as well. She gazed down at her plate and was surprised to find it empty. She had even eaten the black pudding albeit without tasting it.

Placing her serviette on the table, she rose. "If I'm to be ready, I must change now."

"No wish to desert you, my lady." Kit inclined his head to Lady Theo. "But I have arrangements to make."

"Go on with you, Mr. Featherton. My husband will be down shortly. I believe he is taking you gentlemen to one of his clubs or to a coffeehouse."

He bowed. "Lady Mary, may I escort you?"

When Kit straightened, his eyes danced with laughter. She had to keep her eyes lowered or she'd go into whoops. In her most demure voice, she responded, "Thank you, sir."

At the top of the stairs, she slapped her hand over her mouth as she began to giggle. "Oh my. I didn't realize you heard me."

His shoulders shook. "It's a good thing I'd finished swallowing or my food would have been all over the table."

"I remember something of the same being said when I'd first come out. I had hoped that part of the Season was over."

His hands clasped her shoulders, and he studied her with an expression she didn't understand. "Mary."

"Mr. Featherton?"

His smile died. "Have I fallen so far in your esteem?"

She glanced around. Servants appeared to be everywhere. "No, but we are not alone. I would not wish to cause talk."

A footman passed them.

"You are correct, of course."

She nodded. "If you'd like, I will still call you by your given name when we are alone."

"That is my desire." He appeared to focus on her lips for a moment, then said, "I wanted to tell you—"

Voices floated down from the nursery. If he didn't say whatever it was soon, there'd be no chance. "Yes?"

Too late, Rutherford entered the landing.

Kit bowed to her. "I'm looking forward to this afternoon."

Of course that was all it was. What had she expected? He was Mr. Perfect and would never have made a declaration at the top of the stairs in a busy household. Yet before she'd spoken, he'd appeared not to notice anyone else was around. Would she ever learn to hold her tongue? Now she might never know what he would actually have said.

Drat, drat, drat!

If only she could bring herself to at least kiss him.

CHAPTER NINETEEN

K it watched Mary stride away. All he had wanted to do was kiss her, and he'd stupidly picked the busiest part of the house. Then he'd forgotten to address her properly. What a sapskull he was turning into. What the devil was wrong with him? He'd never done anything so outré in his life.

"Featherton."

Rutherford's voice startled Kit.

"I'm sorry. I didn't hear you."

"That," his friend said dryly, "was apparent. Do you know if there are plans for us to-day?"

"Yes. Lord Titus is taking us around while the ladies pay morning calls."

"That might not be so bad. I have to admit that the Scotch whisky was extremely good last night. I never would have thought it."

Kit shook his head. "As long as we are not subjected to any separatist political talk, it will be fine. Living in England, one forgets how the Scots consider us."

"I believe we have worse relations with them than we do with the French."

"Considering we smuggle in brandy and have onerous taxes on Scotch whisky, I can see their point."

Still, as long as it didn't interfere with Kit's courtship of Mary, he couldn't care less about the cross-border enmity. Then he remembered that Lady Theo wanted to introduce Mary to prospective husbands. Scots or English, he'd protect her from all of the scoundrels.

An hour or so later, Kit and his friends were ensconced in a cozy building on St. Andrew Square called the New Club. The coffee was excellent. The latest London papers, albeit two days old, had been provided, as well as the Edinburgh newssheets. Several local gentlemen, as well as those visiting for the Season, stopped by to talk with Lord Titus and be introduced to Kit and his friends. He lifted his cup to find only dregs; then again, he'd had enough coffee to last him for at least a week.

After an hour or so, he felt as if he'd met most of Edinburgh's bachelors on the prowl. Most of them on the hunt for a wife. Which, according to many of the gentlemen, was the only reason to be in the city for an extended period of time. Some of the Highlanders acted as if they'd be perfectly happy to dispense with the courting and toss a lady over their shoulders for the journey home.

The thought of any of them focusing on Mary as their quarry, made the almost constant pain in his jaw even worse. He had to stop clenching his teeth. On the other hand, he was lucky he wasn't developing a tic.

Maybe he should just take Mary in his arms and carry her off. He tried to envision himself doing that, and the thought shriveled, flopped around a bit, and died. He had no doubts concerning his physical prowess. He'd even scored a few hits on the great Jackson himself, but that just wasn't his way. He had no need to strut around calling attention to himself and what he was doing.

The women he'd been with had always appreciated his discretion. Many in the *ton* didn't even realize he had had liaisons. Not the slightest breath of scandal had ever attached to him, and it could not. He had one sister out, another who'd come out next year, one the year after that, in addition to two younger brothers who looked up to him as a model for their own behavior. He'd already had long discussions with the boys about bullies at Eton and showed them how to handle such situations. He'd even taught the girls some defensive moves and ensured that all his brothers and sisters knew they could come to him about anything.

Kit had always held himself to a higher standard. It would never do for his behavior to be compared with that of his long dead older half-brother.

He prayed Mary didn't want or need the young peacocks swaggering around the club, especially the ones in kilts. If she did, that would present not only a problem but the potential of an extremely large scandal.

"I hear ye will be at the ball tonight." A tall young man with black hair and broad shoulders, whose name Kit had misplaced, stood next to Lord Titus's chair. "And ye have with ye a Sassenach lookin' for a husband."

Christ, they'd only been here a little over a day. Kit's fingers curled into a fist as the name came to him. *Lord Duff.*

"You'll have to discuss that with Lady Theo," Lord Titus responded smoothly.

"Aye, I'll do that." Duff stroked his chin thoughtfully. "Mayhap, my mother will know aught. Time and more I had a few bairns of my own."

Not with Mary, the coxcomb wouldn't. If this were London, the betting would have already begun. Damn, Kit should have thought of that before. "Lord Titus, is there a betting book here?"

"There is, but you have to be a member. Besides, it's not the same as in London. Bets here are normally for horse races and contests. Not raindrops racing down the window, or ladies."

Relief flooded in, easing the ache as Kit's jaw unclenched. "As it should be."

With the ball this evening, and the other entertainments, it appeared Edinburgh was going to be even busier for him than London. Not only would he be expected to dance with young ladies, he'd have to protect Mary as well. Perhaps it was time to stop being the most perfect gentleman guest.

Apparently the polite fifteen minutes rule did not apply across the border. They were at their fifth house on their visits. Here guests were meant to be fed well. Mary was going to float away or require a hasty trip to a water closet if she drank one more cup of tea. She'd consumed so many delicious local cakes and biscuits, she had no desire at all to eat luncheon. Which was fortunate, as it was long past the hour.

She'd been having a wonderful time, until some young ladies decided to focus all their conversation on Kit.

"I hear he's as handsome as can be." Miss Clara Ross opened her large blue eyes. "And he came here looking for a bride."

Where in all of Christendom had that rumor started? Had *Kit* given up on *Mary?* Or rather, she hoped, it was merely gossip.

She lifted her cup to her lips, pretending to drink, and lied. "You do realize that any lady Mr. Featherton married would be expected to live in London."

The girl's hopeful smile faltered for the slightest moment, then Miss Ross rallied. "Oh aye, but he's so rich a wife could travel, and he'll be a viscount."

Indeed he would, but this young lady would not be his viscountess. In her most bored drawl, Mary replied, "Indeed. After, that is, his father, who is in good health and of whom Mr. Featherton is quite fond, is dead. He will naturally ascend to the title."

That did the trick. Miss Ross shut her mouth and ate a cake. Mary refused to consider her own behavior. With these bold Scottish girls, Kit needed someone to protect him.

Lady MacDiarmid was announced. She entered the parlor, smiling like a cat who'd found a particularly juicy mouse. Behind her was a young lady who looked to be an exact replica of her ladyship when she was a decade or two younger. Rich brown hair, medium height, and slender build, but well endowed. Mary had rarely seen two more beautiful women.

The older lady, followed by the younger one, curtseyed. "I'm so pleased we're not too late to meet Lady Theo's visitors."

"You almost were, Morna." Lady Theo allowed the other lady to buss her cheek. "We are leaving shortly."

Undaunted, Lady MacDiarmid smiled and said, "You remember my daughter, Finella?"

"Of course I do." Lady Theo squinted at the girl for a moment. "Surely she is not old enough to be out yet?"

The other lady raised a brow. "Sixteen, the same age as I was."

A look of disgust passed so quickly over Lady Theo's face Mary almost thought she'd imagined it, except for what came next.

"Then you should know better."

The pleasant mask on Lady MacDiarmid never slipped. "I can assure you, Finella is much better prepared than I was."

Lady Theo rose. "We've had a lovely time, but I'm afraid we must be leaving."

Mrs. Cameron, their hostess, had a look of unfettered relief on her pleasant countenance. "Thank you so much for coming by, my lady." Her gaze included Mary and her friends. "It was a pleasure to meet you. I suppose I'll see you this evening."

"You will indeed." Theo marched out, leaving the rest of them to follow like a flock of chicks after their mother hen.

"What do you think that was about?" Caro whispered to Mary.

"I have no idea, but I have a feeling we'll find out."

Once they were in the carriage, Lady Theo's lips tightened, and after several moments she said, "I had hoped she'd wait, but apparently she thinks nothing of auctioning off her daughter the same as she was."

Mary and everyone else remained quiet.

"Morna was a diamond when she came out. A beautiful, silly young thing. My brother, Simon, the baby of the family, fell in love with her. As did almost every other eligible man, and some who weren't. He thought she returned his affections. In fact, he was sure of it. Then she was married off to MacDiarmid. He was fifty years older than her if he was a day, but he had the title and more money. He'd been married four times before with no issue to show for it, yet nine months after the wedding, she gave birth to Cormac." Lady Theo closed her eyes for a moment. "He's the image of Simon. There is no way to be sure who fathered Finella, but it could well have been my brother. He left for America before the girl was born and hasn't been back since."

The carriage rumbled over cobblestones before turning onto the smoother macadam. Lady Theo's gaze bore into Mary. "It pains me to say it, but none of them are to be trusted. Morna will be looking for the largest purse she can find for both of her children."

Mary swallowed. For the first time in almost an hour, her need for a chamber pot receded. "I understand."

Not only must she take care, Kit would have to be put on his guard as well. Perhaps she should just agree to marry him. It would keep both of them safe from fortune hunters, but would it provide the life she needed?

Kit glanced at his pocket watch for the tenth time in as many minutes. The hands still hadn't moved much. It was almost four o'clock. He glanced out at the hall of Lord Titus and Lady Theo's house. A half hour ago, Kit had to send the carriage back to the stable. There would be no excursion to-day. Where the deuce had the ladies gone? They should have been back hours ago.

"Featherton, will you stop pacing?"

Rather than leave the men to their own devices, Lord Titus had remained with them even as he worked on a paper he was preparing.

"I had an outing planned. The ladies should have been back before now. You don't think anything has happened, do you?"

"We don't have a fashionable hour to promenade. Morning visits make up for it."

Kit wished he'd known that before. They'd have to prepare for the evening's entertainment soon. A carriage came to a stop in front of the house. Thank God, they were back.

He strode to the front door intending to escort Mary up the stairs, when she dashed past him without saying a word. Was she avoiding him?

"I love you, Gervais, but not now," Caro said as Huntley reached out to kiss her. Anna and Phoebe rushed past as well.

Kit stared after them. "What is going on?"

"I wish I knew," Huntley responded, gazing up the staircase.

Lady Theo paused, her hand on the newel post as she mounted the curtail step. "Their first morning visits."

"As long as I'm not at fault, I don't care what it is." Rutherford joined Kit and the others. "We'll find out soon."

"Be sure to tell me when you do. I have the distinct feeling Mary will not wish to speak of it." Only because they were neither married nor betrothed. Even more reason to forge ahead.

"Mama, I don't want to be here." Finella fiddled with the fringe on her shawl. "I want to come out with Cait, in two years."

"If you don't stop, you'll ruin that shawl." Morna lightly slapped her daughter's hand away from the fringe. She hated having to pretend she wanted her daughter to marry so young rather than waiting to come out with her closest friend. Yet if Fee was to have a better life than Morna's had been, it meant getting her daughter married to a gentleman who could protect her. The only good thing old MacDiarmid— Morna had never thought of her late husband by any other name—had done was die before he could arrange a match with one of his friends. Unfortunately, her own father had been talking about husbands for his granddaughter, and, until her son Cormac was of age, Father was Fee's guardian. Regrettably, her son had another year before he attained one and twenty. Even then, Morna's father could cause trouble and probably would. "You know Cormac has said he'll choose a bride as soon as he attains his majority. You'll be much happier living in your own home after that."

"I suppose so." Fee's words did not match her woebegone face.

"Fee, my heart. I want you to be able to fall in love. Yet, if we wait much longer, that choice could be taken from you." Morna's throat closed and she turned away, not wanting her daughter to see her tears. If only she'd been allowed to wed the man she loved. How different her life would have been. She fought back her anguish. The most important thing now was to take care of Fee. Thank God Father wasn't in Edinburgh.

The outer door to the town house they had leased for the Season opened and closed. Booted feet pounded on the stairs, then her parlor door burst open. "Mother"—Cormac strode into the room with all the vigor of his youth—"did ye go on yer morning visits to-day?"

"Aye, we did." He smiled, and for a moment she thought she was looking at Simon. "Don't stand there grinning like a loon. Why do you ask?"

"There is a Sassenach lady staying with Lady Theo. Have ye met her?"

"Aye," Morna said slowly.

"Is she as pretty as they're all saying she is?"

"I don't know as I'd—"

"Oh aye, Cormac," Fee interrupted, "she is. All the London ladies are beautiful, and dressed so fine."

"Well then"—he tapped the end of his sister's nose as he had since she was a babe—"I'll give you the pleasure of introducing me." He glanced around as if he would share a great secret, then said, "And I'll introduce you to a fine London gentleman looking for a wife."

Fee's eyes grew round. At least the girl wasn't immune to men. "Is he handsome?"

"Better looking than my horse, and you know how beautiful Ivarr is."

She punched her brother's arm. "And does he have a long blond tail?"

Cormac coughed. "No, lass, ye'd be nay wanting a devil."

"That's enough foolishness from both of you. Cormac, you know better than to speak in such a brogue here."

He gave Morna a wicked smirk, so like his father's used to be. "Perhaps the English lady will like it."

The devil. She cast her eyes at the ceiling. "It's past time to eat our dinner and dress for the ball. I understand both the lady and gentleman will be there."

Glasgow, Scotland

Lord Simon Cavendish stepped gingerly down the gangway onto the dock. His body swayed as if it were still out at sea. It would most likely take a few days for the feeling to go away. It was the same each time he spent more than a week onboard. "Where are we spending the night?"

"The Tontine Hotel, my lord," his valet, Hailing, answered. "Mr. Oxley's gone to get a hackney, and I've arranged a cart for the trunks."

Simon nodded. His groom would also arrange for a strong pair of horses. It had been over sixteen years since Simon had set foot in this country. Sixteen years since he vowed never to return. Yet the fact that he had two children—if the second lived—and knew them not, had eaten at him every day of each month, of each year. And Morna. Holy God, he'd tried to stay away from her, but after the last time, when she'd caught with child again, he knew he couldn't continue to give her children to be raised by that bastard MacDiarmid. Despite her protestations of loving only him, she had not met him the night he sailed.

How young and stupid they'd been to think they could trick her father and old MacDiarmid. If only they'd run away, or said their vows in a church instead of an inn. Simon gave a harsh laugh. If only he'd not been too noble to hold her to hastily made promises, or so naïve he didn't know a lie when he heard one. It wasn't until long after he'd left that he discovered that under Scottish law they'd been legally married. The question now was, had she known?

It mattered not. She'd rejected him and could go to hell. He was here to claim his children, and no one would stand in his way.

"Did you say something, my lord?"

"No, Hailing. I was just thinking how odd it was for a man who hates sailing to own a shipping line."

"You've made a good job of it though, my lord."

"That I have." Simon wondered if his son would like to take over the business in a few years.

He was relaxing with a glass of smooth Scotch whisky in his hotel room, when Oxley knocked on the door and entered. "My lord, I've hired a yellow bounder for the journey to Edinburgh. It won't be comfortable, but it will get us there almost as fast as the mail. The company sent word to have horses ready for the changes. We'll be but one night on the road."

"Does that include our little detour?"

"Yes, my lord."

"Well done, Oxley."

"I'm right glad to be home. Almost there, in any event."

Simon fought the urge to run a hand over his face. "As am I. I'd forgotten how much I missed it."

"When do we leave for England, my lord?"

"As soon as I finish my business. I'll not stay a moment longer. The ship should be waiting in the Edinburgh harbor to take us to Hull when we arrive."

True to the coaching company's promise, two days later, as dusk was beginning to fall, they arrived on the outskirts of Edinburgh. He took out the most recent letter he'd received from his sister before his departure. "Tell the driver we're going to Charlotte Square. Wherever the hell that is."

He hoped Theo was home, and trusted that she'd be so happy to see her youngest brother she'd forgive him for failing to tell her he was arriving. Nevertheless, she'd know what was going on and where he could find Morna and their children. And this time, he'd take what was his.

CHAPTER TWENTY

"My lady, stop fidgeting." Mary took a deep breath. It had been so long since she'd attended a ball. She felt the tug of the last tape of her gown being tied. Why was this taking so long? Mathers hadn't even got to her hair yet. "What time is it?"

"Time for you to sit at the dressing table so I can finish you up."

"What did Madame Lisette say the color of this gown was? I've never seen anything like it."

"I don't know, my lady. It reminds me of a periwinkle."

Mary managed, just barely, to remain still as Mathers threaded a strand of pearls through her hair. She wore the pearl and sapphire necklace she had loaned Aunt Eunice for her wedding, and pearl earrings hung on gold wires that swung when Mary moved her head. Mathers handed Mary a lovely delicate brisé fan painted with gold and a shade of blue that matched the gown she wore. "I don't remember purchasing this."

"You didn't. Mr. Featherton sent it."

Mary slanted her dresser a look. "It's amazing how he knew the perfect colors."

Without batting an eye, Mathers nodded. "It is. He's an astute gentleman."

Pulling on her long kid gloves, Mary then added two bracelets as she thought about the trouble he must have gone to in order to have the fan painted. "You may very well be right."

"I usually am, my lady. You have fun this evening, and be careful not to let any gentlemen take advantage of you."

Mary kissed Mathers's cheek. "I will."

"I've told you before, my lady. You shouldn't be doing that."

"And I've told you that no one takes care of me the way you do. You've been the one constant in my life."

"You go now. That nice Mr. Featherton is waiting for you."

Not only Kit, whose capital had just risen vastly, but many other men as well. She frowned as she thought about the ladies who had set their caps for him. Harrumph. What exactly would this evening entail? She opened the door and ran straight into the gentleman in question.

For a bare moment they stood, bodies touching. Her errant senses went wild with longing and desire. She could do it now. Reach up and kiss him.

Then he moved back a half step, and cool air replaced his heat.

He placed his hand on her shoulder. "Are you all right?"

Breathe. "Yes. It was just a shock to find you here." That didn't sound good. "I mean, I wasn't expecting anyone to be right outside my door—"

His warm voice washed over her. "I've missed you to-day."

Her heart thudded harder. "I felt the same." A footman rushed by carrying a bowl of water. Why were servants always around when she didn't want them to be? "We'd better go to the drawing room."

Kit didn't move. "I wish to request the first waltz, and the supper dance. Will you grant them to me?"

Was he finally going to do something to the purpose? She bit her lips to keep herself from saying something stupid. "Yes, gladly."

He let out a breath. "Do you like the fan?"

She reminded herself he was nervous about her. "I do." She smiled, wanting him to know she would welcome his attentions. "It's perfect."

"Thank you. I did hope it would be." His lovely blue eyes reflected his words.

He placed her hand on his arm and escorted her to the drawing room as he'd done so many times before. Yet to-night was different somehow. She gave thanks to fate and the Deity. She was finally making progress.

Theo and Titus were in the drawing room awaiting their guests, when her butler, Reed, knocked and entered. His voice held a breathless note. "My lady."

"Is something wrong?"

"No, my lady. You have another visitor . . ."

Simon strode into the room, and all the air left in his wake. "I think I may have startled your butler."

Oh my God! She held her hand to her mouth, unable to speak.

"Theo." He grinned roguishly. "At least say you'll welcome your prodigal brother."

She flew into his arms. "Oh, good Lord, Simon. Could you not have given me some warning? I'm getting up in years, I might have had apoplexy. Does Papa know you've returned?"

His arms came around her, hugging her as he used to. "You can't give me more than seven years, and I'm quite certain that's not on death's door. Whether Father knows depends on whether he reads his mail."

Titus was next to her, hugging both of them and slapping her brother on his back. "Welcome home, young'un. I can't tell you how glad we are to see you."

Tears filled Theo's eyes, and she was so happy she didn't care if he'd not written. "We are just about to dine."

Simon held her back. "And going to a ball afterward, if I'm not mistaken."

"Yes, but you'll want to rest."

"Devil a bit." He sobered. "Is she here?"

She waited. Debating whether to tell him or not. It didn't matter. He'd discover any lies soon enough. "Yes. With her son and daughter."

He paled. "Daughter. A girl."

"That is what a girl is normally called," Theo replied more tartly than she'd meant to, then gentled her tone. "Her name is Finella."

He nodded twice. "Give me time to change, send dinner on a tray, and I'll accompany you this evening."

What was he thinking of doing? "Simon, are you sure?"

"I've never been more sure of anything in my life." He turned to go, then stopped. "I heard the old man is dead."

"Yes, going on two years now. It is amazing he lasted that long, but her father is still alive."

"You let me worry about him," he said in a grim tone.

For the first time since Morna married, Theo wondered what had actually occurred between Simon and the woman he claimed to love.

The door opened and her guests strolled in, laughing and talking. She made the introductions, then left Simon to his own devices. He'd changed from the happy-go-lucky boy she'd known. Still, perhaps that was not surprising considering what he had gone through. It was time to see what kind of man he was now.

She signaled to her butler. "Send a tray up for Lord Simon, and tell him we leave in two hours."

Kit raised his brows for a moment as Lord Simon left the room, then whispered to Mary, "Do you know anything of the brother?"

She kept her voice equally low. "Yes. I'll tell you what happened to-day as soon as I can." After accepting glasses of sherry from Lord Titus, Kit and Mary moved away from the rest of the group. She gazed at him as if she were particularly pleased. "I must say, I'm glad you enjoy innocent gossip."

He grinned. "And I never repeat what I've heard."

She paused, regarding him quizzically. "What a marvelous trait."

"And?"

"This is from the horse's mouth, as it were." She told him about the MacDiarmid ladies arriving and what Lady Theo said afterward.

"I am amazed she would confide in people she'd just met."

"As was I." Mary glanced over his shoulder. "Then she told us about her brother . . ."

"If they are all at the ball together, there may be fireworks." Normally he did not look forward to the sort of drama incidents like this caused, but for the first time since he had arrived at Rose Hill, Mary was thinking of something other than him and her. He could only pray it would ease the tension that still existed between them.

"Indeed. Lady Theo is coming." Mary fanned herself as her hostess strolled up.

"Lady Mary, Mr. Featherton." One of Lady Theo's brows rose. "You seem to be having an interesting conversation."

"We are," Kit answered. "We're discussing the sites we wish to see while we're in your lovely city."

Thankfully, Mary smiled brightly and nodded. It occurred to him that, other than when she'd had to make up the story about the birds, he'd never heard her prevaricate.

"Well then. You must let me know when you wish to trek around Edinburgh, and I'll arrange to have Lady Mary home in time for an excursion."

"Thank you, my lady." Kit inclined his head.

"Yes. Thank you," Mary said.

Once Lady Theo ambled away, Mary gave a sigh. "I'm glad you're quick on your feet. I never have been, except in the literal sense, that is." That didn't surprise him, and he found it refreshing. "Mary, I—"

"My lords, ladies, and sir, dinner is served."

From the corner of his eye, he saw Lord Titus approach, and quickly said, "May I escort you to the dining room?"

"I'd like nothing better."

Kit tucked her hand in the crook of his arm. He almost laughed as Lord Titus quickly reversed direction, making his way back to his own lady.

All was right with the world. Now they had only to get through the rest of this evening. He didn't like the idea of Mary dancing with other men, but there was nothing he could do about it. If he stood next to her and refused to leave her side, as Marcus had done with Phoebe, Kit would only cause talk.

Two hours later when they arrived at the ball, his worst fears were confirmed. It was as if everyone present moved en masse toward them. He did his best to keep Mary with him without creating a scene, but was all too soon separated from her as the Scotsmen clamored for an introduction to her and a place on her dance card. Kit congratulated himself on his forethought in securing his sets.

Before he knew it, he was surrounded by ladies as he had never been before. He bowed and smiled as his hostess introduced him to the young women.

"Oh, Mr. Featherton," Miss Macintyre said, fluttering her eyelashes, "I'm so glad to finally meet you."

He bowed, taking her proffered fingers in his hand. "Entirely my pleasure."

A tall, striking lady whom he'd already been introduced to edged her out. "Mr. Featherton, I wanted you to know I have some sets free—"

Kit struggled to keep his jaw from dropping. Dear God. Was she actually going to ask him to dance?

"Kenna," Miss Macintyre said sharply, "Mr. Featherton was speaking with me."

Someone needed to take these young ladies in hand.

"Mr. Featherton?"

He turned gratefully to Lady Theo as his hostess pulled the two young females aside.

"My lady?"

She smiled at him before turning to the young lady at her side, who blushed bright red. "Miss MacDonald, allow me to introduce Mr. Featherton, who is visiting me from England. Mr. Featherton, this is Miss MacDonald."

He bowed. "A pleasure to meet you."

She curtseyed, and said in a voice so faint, he almost couldn't hear her, "Pleasure."

"It would be my honor to stand up with you if you have a dance available."

She held out her dance card. The only name on it was a D. Mac-Donald, most likely a relation, for the opening set, which was a waltz. He took the pencil dangling from her wrist and scribbled his name next to the second set, a country dance. He was surprised to note only two waltzes were planned for the evening. Fortunately the second one was the supper dance.

"The second dance then."

"Thank you," she whispered.

"Never thank a gentleman for offering to stand up with you," he said gently. "It is always his honor."

She smiled shyly.

The sounds of the musicians readying themselves could be heard. Kit bowed. "I must collect my partner."

He swore softly as a gentleman bowed to Mary, and Kit reached her just in time to elbow the man away.

The Scot growled, and Kit raised his quizzing glass, giving the man his most innocuous look. "I'm terribly sorry, but Lady Mary is promised to me for this set."

Her eyes danced as he bowed. "My lady."

She inclined her head. "Mr. Featherton." As he led her to the dance floor, she lowered her voice. "You remembered."

"Why would you think I mightn't?" *Good Lord.* It wasn't possible, was it? "Don't tell me I once requested to stand up with you and forgot?"

Her laughter tinkled like bells. "No, of course not. Though, with the other gentlemen surrounding me, I did think that you might not think me in need of a partner and . . ."

Was that how she saw him? Someone who only danced with ladies requiring a partner? Yet wasn't that exactly what he had always done? When was the last time he had asked a lady to dance for the pure joy of having her in his arms? It shocked him that the answer was never. Mary was the first.

They took their places, bowing and curtseying with the rest of the crowd.

He took her small hand in his, and placed his fingers on her waist. "You may not have needed to dance with me, but I definitely needed to dance with you."

"What a lovely thing to say."

She was as light as a feather in his arms, and he didn't think he'd ever partnered a woman who moved as fluidly with him, as if they were one.

Kit's palm burned into her waist. Mary had known he was an excellent dancer. After all, he could make the clumsiest lady appear graceful. What she hadn't realized was how well they fitted together. It was as if they were made for one another.

She caught several ladies glancing their way, and she didn't believe it was because they looked so compatible. They probably wished they were with him. She hoped he'd hold her closer. "We seem to be drawing attention."

His grip on her waist tightened. "I feel like a Royal Menagerie exhibit."

She couldn't help but giggle a bit. "A suitable analogy."

His eyes turned bluer as he gazed down at her. She'd never enjoyed waltzing so much. All too soon the set came to an end, and he escorted her back to Lady Theo, where Mary was once more besieged. Before he left, he looked at her dance card. "Thank you for adding my name."

"How could I not? You did request the sets."

Unlike her first Season, when her eyes sought him out and he never responded, she was pleased to find him searching for her as well.

Her partner for the fourth dance led her to the floor. "Lady Mary, you are the most beautiful woman here."

"Thank you, my lord." She wanted to roll her eyes. In addition to being forward, all the gentlemen said the same thing. It was nothing but flummery. She almost wished to be complimented on her garden . . . by anyone but Kit, that was. When he told her she looked well, he was sincere. Mary turned her attention back to the young peer whose name she'd already half forgotten.

Sometime later, Mary stole a surreptitious glance at her dance card. Thank God. Only one more set until the supper dance. Soon a middle-aged gentleman bowed before her. "My lady, I believe this is my dance. However, if you'd rather stroll the room, I'm perfectly happy to oblige."

She fanned herself. Despite the doors and windows being open, the room was stuffy and hot. Now if only she could remember his name without having to peek at her dance card. "I'd like that extremely."

"Mr. Grant," Lady Theo said, "as you are not joining this set, would you be so kind as to arrange glasses of lemonade for Lady Mary and me?"

"My pleasure, my lady." He walked away, hailing a footman.

"You do not want to consider him, my dear," Lady Theo whispered in her ear. "He is a widower with five thousand a year and four children. All girls. The first one comes out next year."

Mary bit her lip to keep from laughing. "Thank you for your advice. I shall keep it in mind."

Mr. Grant returned her to Lady Theo just before Kit came to fetch her for the waltz. Once he took her hand, she felt as if she were in a different world. Did he feel the same? She desperately wanted him to. Yet how to know? He was as polite as always, but she wanted more.

Simon had waited in a shadow by the stairs to the ballroom until he saw Morna, his son, and his daughter enter. His stomach clenched as if he'd been struck. Cormac was tall and strong, just as Simon thought he'd be. Finella reminded him of Morna when she was younger. Sixteen, to be exact. He made the mental calculations. Finella was barely the same age. What the hell was Morna doing bringing their daughter out now? The girl was too young. He took a closer look, and Finella appeared ill at ease. This might not be her first adult entertainment, but it would certainly be her last for at least two years. No daughter of his would be allowed to marry at sixteen.

Wanting to see the shock on Morna's face when she saw him, wanting her to suffer as he had over the years, he'd thought to approach her boldly when she arrived. Yet he hadn't considered how the rest of Edinburgh's Polite Society would respond, or the embarrassment he could cause his sister and her guests. Therefore, he skirted the edge of the room as his family made their way through the crowd, and waited.

His son approached Lady Mary and was introduced, only to be turned away as she gave him a polite smile. Apparently, Cormac had not arrived in time to obtain a dance. Other gentlemen, the vultures, began to gather around Finella as Morna smiled and performed introductions. It was all Simon could do to stop himself from dragging his daughter away.

He crossed the ballroom, moving behind the pillars which separated the center on each side from small alcoves, potted palms, and enough cover to take Morna unawares.

While his wife stood off to the side, his children had partners and were forming the set for a country dance. When he was close enough to almost touch her, he placed his lips close to her ear. "Morna, I've come for you and our children."

Her head whipped around, and her eyes grew wide. She opened her mouth, and promptly swooned. Simon caught her before she slid to the wooden floor.

Theo was there in an instant. "Why in the name of heaven," she said in a disgusted tone, "could you not have approached her from the front? At least it would have given her a little time to accustom herself to your being here." He lifted Morna into his arms. "For the love of God, Simon, I don't think you've changed a bit." Theo glanced around. "Come through this door. There is a parlor, and I pray it's empty. Carrying her through the ballroom will cause talk."

"I don't care," he growled. Claiming his family was the only thing that mattered, and that included his wife. Damn him for an idiot. He loved her as much now as he ever had.

"You may not," his sister snapped, "but I do. Follow me. What were you thinking? Or were you?"

"I didn't want to give her a chance to deny me."

Ignoring him, Theo strolled toward a door painted with the same mural that covered the walls of the entire room. He held Morna tightly as if she'd awaken and jump out of his arms.

Theo opened the door, shoved him in, and glanced around. "Put her on the chaise. I'll procure some water."

The door closed, leaving him and his wife in the dimly lit parlor. He chafed her hands. "Morna, come back to me, my love."

Her lashes fluttered. A moment later, her lovely green eyes, the color of new leaves, opened. "It is you, Simon? I thought I was seeing a ghost."

"Mayhap a ghoulie?" He stroked her jaw and leaned down to kiss her. She smelled of heather and rosemary, as she had before. All thoughts of revenge on her were forgotten as he pressed his lips to hers.

"Ye do not understand, Simon." Tears filled her eyes. "I thought ye were dead."

CHAPTER TWENTY-ONE

"*Dead!*" Simon raked his fingers through his pitch-black curls. "Where did you get a daft idea like that?"

Morna reached out, stilling his hand. She quickly gave thanks that he was back in her life. This time, she wouldn't let anyone separate them. "When ye disappeared, that's what my da told me."

"I didn't disappear." His deep blue eyes flashed with anger. "I sent you a message asking you to come with me to America."

Her throat closed so tightly, she had to force the words through it. "I should have known it was a lie." She brushed angrily at a tear traveling down her cheek. "I swear to you, Simon, I would have come. I've loved you since I first set eyes on you."

He cupped her face in his hands. "I should have listened to the voice in my head that told me to fetch you. Instead I allowed my foolish pride to think you'd rejected me."

"Oh God, Simon. Never in a million years would I stop loving you." She threw her arms around him, pulling him down to her.

His lips touched Morna's. Gently at first, but long-denied desire surged within her, and she needed more. She clutched the back of his neck. Opening her mouth, she trailed her tongue along his lips, sucking the lower one.

Simon moaned. "God, Morna. I've missed you."

Stretching out on the chaise, he half covered her as she explored. He tasted of finely aged, smoky Scotch whisky. She pressed one palm to his chest. It was so much harder than before. She wanted the waistcoat and shirt gone. "Where are you staying? I'll come to you."

"There is something I must tell you."

His tone was so serious, her heart squeezed as if she'd been dunked in a cold loch. Surely nothing could keep them apart now. "What?"

Before he could answer, the door slammed against the wall.

"What the devil is going on here?" Cormac closed the door before striding toward them.

Morna struggled to sit up as Simon rolled gracefully to his feet. Her son, their son stopped and stared. His eyes widened in recognition. After all, the boy had been shaving for a couple of years now. "Who are you?"

"I'm—"

"Simon," she begged, "don't. Please, not here—"

"He has my face, my love." He kissed her hand then turned back to Cormac. "I'm your father."

His countenance flushed. "Ye mean I'm your bastard, don't ye?"

"Not at all." Morna was surprised at how calm Simon was being. "Your mother and I were legally married nine months before you were born."

Morna was thankful she was sitting down. If not, she would have fallen over. Yet how could that be, and why hadn't Simon said anything before? Why had he left her . . . ? *Twice!* "We cannot be wed."

"Nevertheless, the fact remains that we are." He motioned Cormac to a nearby chair, sat next to her, and held her hand as he met her gaze. "My only regret is that I didn't know it until a few months ago."

A throbbing had started behind her eyes. "I don't understand. My father told me it wasn't legal."

A look of undisguised hate passed over Simon's mien. "As he told me. Unfortunately for us and our children, he was more interested in the outcome he wanted than the facts. A couple of months ago in New York, I ran into a couple who were at the inn when we married. They asked about you, which led to a conversation regarding Scottish marriage laws. I did some research, and they were correct. Our marriage was and is legal." He brushed his thumb over her brow, soothing the pain that had started in her head. "It amazes me how gullible and stupid I was."

What a fool she'd been as well. "Ye weren't the only one," she said in her driest tone. Her heart ached thinking of all the years they'd lost. Disgust curled her stomach. The next time she saw Father, she would spit on him. If she ever consented to have anything to do with him again. "I even told old MacDiarmid, hoping he'd not take me to wife. The old bastard just laughed."

Cormac paced the small room—it hardly seemed large enough for father and son—and finally he stopped. "A fine mess this is." He ran his fingers through his hair as Simon had done not long ago. "The question is, what do the two of you plan to do about it?"

Simon raised a brow, and in a deadly calm voice, responded, "I intend to claim my family."

Kit made his way across the crowded ballroom toward Mary. As she had been years ago, she was surrounded by a group of gentlemen. However, this time nothing would stop him from claiming her.

"Mr. Featherton." His hostess placed her hand on his arm. "Would you be so kind as to dance with Miss Innes?"

He shook his head and said what he should have done years before. "I'm sorry, my lady, but I have already engaged a partner for this set."

Leading Mary out to the dance floor, he ignored other gentlemen as they muttered. He twirled her in his arms, being careful to keep the proper distance between them.

"Are you having a good time?" she asked.

"I am now." He hadn't been able to keep his eyes off her all evening. "And when we danced before." She blushed, but didn't say a word. "Other than that, it appears as if I'm expected to do the pretty with all the other ladies here." He lowered his voice, ensuring only she could hear him. "I am amazed at how forward even some of the young women are."

"I've noticed the gentlemen are the same. It must have to do with the weather."

His jaw tightened. "If any of them behaves inappropriately, I'll be happy to refresh their manners."

It would please him even more to rearrange their features for them.

Her gaze focused on his, and he was lost in her molten silver eyes as she smiled. "Thank you. I shall keep your offer in mind."

"Shall we make plans for to-morrow?" There might not be a promenade, but he wouldn't put it past some rogue to ask her to go riding.

"Let's do." She smiled. "Shall we visit Holyrood Palace?"

"I think that is a wonderful idea. We must tell Lady Theo so she can return you in time." Still feeling ill used over the last time they'd made plans, he continued. "I had no idea morning visits would take so long."

"Neither did I." Mary grimaced. "It presented problems I was not prepared for."

So he'd heard. Anna had voiced her disapproval to her husband about the experience. "Perhaps we should make the tour in the morning. That way we won't have to rely on anyone remembering to return you to the house."

She nodded as he fought his urge to hold her closer, tighter as they made the turn.

"I don't believe I'll be missed on the rounds."

Which meant, if he planned it right, he could have her for the whole day. If only he could monopolize her evenings as well.

With Finella in tow, Theo returned to the parlor. She glowered at Simon for a moment before taking a chair and pointing to another one. "Sit, lass."

Finella's large green eyes, exact replicas of her mother's, flicked from her brother to Simon, as she sank onto a chair next to the chaise. Simon wondered if she was always this quiet, or if it was merely the circumstances. He could murder Morna's father for having robbed him of the chance to know his children.

His son stood stock still, staring at the wall, until he refocused his gaze on Simon. "I remember you." Cormac dragged a chair over close to the chaise. "You were the man who taught me how to tickle a trout and skip stones."

Simon's throat tightened as he fought back tears. "You were so young. I never even allowed myself to hope you'd recall."

"My love." Morna's soft voice stole into the moment. "Mayhap we should tell your sister and Finella, and then figure out how we're going to handle this."

He made quick work of the explanations.

His sister covered her eyes for a few moments before saying, "I should have known."

"How could you?" Simon asked. "I didn't know until recently."

A soft smile graced her countenance. "I should have known you'd never take advantage of a girl. It's so easy to marry here, yet it never occurred to me to ask the right questions."

Brows drawn together, Finella gave every appearance of listening thoughtfully. Finally she focused on her mother. "This means I don't have to marry right away, and I can go home, doesn't it?"

"Home is a bit of a problem at the moment." Cormac grimaced. "I suppose we'll have to find and contact the rightful baron . . . as it's not me."

"Where will we live?" Finella asked.

"I have some ideas." Simon smiled at her. "However, until the legalities can be worked out, we'll be safer at my father's estate near Hull."

"Aye." Cormac nodded. "My grandfather will be fit to be tied when he hears about this."

Several moments passed in silence before Morna rose. "For the time being, we should go back to the town house I leased, and decide how to deal with all of this."

Theo stood, shaking out her skirts. "Go out through the door next to the fireplace. That will lead you to the hall. I'll make your excuses." She glanced at Morna. "If it's all right with you, I'd like to spend the day with Finella to-morrow while you sort this out."

Simon watched his wife, wondering if she'd know that was his sister's way of welcoming Morna and the children to the family.

"Thank you," she replied. "It would be a great help, and she should come to know her father's side of the family."

Once in the hall, Cormac called for the coach.

As they waited, Simon stood next to his son. "I'm sorry to be the cause of your losing your title."

His son shrugged in resignation. "It seems to me it was my grandfather and the old devil's fault. They had to have known your marriage was legal. I'm more worried about how it will affect Fee. There is bound to be a major scandal."

"My family is highly placed, and from what I understand, you have all lived quietly. Wherever we go, we won't remain in Scotland; somehow we'll find a way to minimize talk."

Cormac quietly studied the marble floor for a moment, then glanced up at Simon. "Who *am* I now, though?"

"Your name is Mr. Cormac Cavendish. Grandson of the Duke of Gordon. Who you are is whoever you wish to be."

The next morning, Kit handed Mary into his curricle, then dashed back into the house for the all-important guidebook.

"Where have Kit and Mary gone?" Kit heard Huntley ask from the breakfast room.

"I believe they are viewing Holyrood Palace to-day," Caro answered.

"What the deuce is he trying to do? Bore the woman to death?" Caro's laughter floated on the air. "No, my love. He's trying to keep her away from all the other gentlemen."

Kit was indeed. The only problem was he didn't know if Mary liked his company as a suitor or merely a friend. The latter was not what he wanted. Somehow he'd have to make her see him as a potential husband.

Forty minutes later, they reached the palace.

"It's beautiful," Mary said, staring up at the façade.

"I've heard the French renovated the King's chamber when the Count d'Artois was here. Did you know he used the abbey sanctuary to avoid his creditors?" Thankfully, Kit had read the guidebook.

"I did hear something about it, though I was too young to understand it at the time." He lifted her out of the curricle. "I love that they allow debtors to remain there and not go to prison."

"I take it you do not agree with the current law."

"Definitely not. It seems to me to be grossly unfair."

He led her through the main door, and handed the porter the entrance fee. "I agree. The inability to manage one's funds should not be a crime. What would you like to see first?"

"The Queen's chambers. I hear they are magnificent."

They spent the next two hours touring the inside of the sixteenth-century palace, before strolling through the courtyard garden. He was surprised, and pleased, to find almost no one else present. "Mary, I believe there is to be a drum this evening. Will you save me the same waltzes as last night?"

"I'd be delighted to." She glanced up at him, mischief twinkling in her eyes. "Won't the hostess be upset?"

He held back an exasperated growl. "They'll have to make do."

As they were about to stroll back to the carriage, the sound of tittering could be heard. "Don't look now, but I think we're about to be invaded." He tightened his grip on Mary. "Whatever happens, don't let go of me."

Kit seemed so appalled Mary wanted to chuckle, until she saw the trio approaching. The one in the lead was the young lady she had attempted to warn off yesterday.

"Oh, Mr. Featherton!" A girl dressed in a profusion of lace and ruffles quickened her step. "How unexpected to see you here."

Unexpected, my foot. The two ladies with the girl giggled, giving lie to her exclamation of surprise. How on earth did they find him? They must have learned where she and Kit were during morning visits.

He bowed. "Indeed, Lady Mary and I were just leaving. Enjoy the gardens."

The girl's face fell ludicrously, and it was all Mary could do not to laugh as Kit steered her quickly down the path toward the palace. If she had acted like that during her first Season, no wonder he hadn't given her the time of day. "One would think they'd still be engaged in morning visits."

"Obviously"—he shuddered—"someone forgot to lock them in, and they escaped."

"Oh dear." She fought to force down the burble of laughter. "I never thought to hear you say anything like that."

"I've never been chased quite as diligently as I was last night." Kit gave her a rueful smile. "One young lady even attempted to follow me to the gentlemen's retiring room. It's enough to put one off the Season." Fortunately, they didn't have to wait long for the curricle to be brought around. "I have much more sympathy for my friends who've had ladies set their caps at them." Once they were seated on the bench, his brow furrowed as he threaded the ribbons through his fingers. "I can't imagine how hard it's been for you, dodging your cousin."

Surprisingly, Mary hadn't thought about Gawain in several days. "I'm glad that appears to be over."

What *was* bothering her was the thought that some female might manage to compromise Kit just as they seemed to becoming closer. She straightened her shoulders. Obviously it fell to her to protect him. Yet how to do that when they were both expected to dance and spend time with others?

Rose Hill, Northumberland, England

Eunice held a cup of tea in her hands as she gazed at the handsome countenance of her husband. They had been married just over a week. "When do you wish to move into our own home?" Brian looked up from his plate. "As soon as you have everything the way you want it." His eyes sparkled wickedly. "It's the bathing tub that's calling to you, is it not?"

"Naturally, what else could it be? Although I believe a vessel that extravagant should have a grander name."

His lips twitched. "Perhaps we should call it Venus's pool."

She met his smile with one of her own. "Seriously though, the staff has been hired, and all the changes we discussed are completed. I had thought to wait until my mother arrived, but we can easily have them directed to our home."

That was wonderful to be able to say. The house she'd lived in with Roger had been part of his father's estate, and not theirs. Yesterday she and Brian had visited the solicitor, and Brian had ensured that if he predeceased her, she would receive the house and a generous income for the rest of her life.

"To-morrow then?"

She nodded. "I'll send word to-day and have most of our trunks taken over."

"When," he asked, "will the rest of your things arrive?"

"There is not that much, but I expect them in a week or so. I've received letters from my children. I imagine some of them will find an excuse to visit."

"Ah yes. They'll want to inspect me. We could always invite them."

She shook her head. "No, I'm going to have too much fun listening to the reasons they come up with to visit."

"You're a wicked woman," he said in a fond tone as he finished the last of his breakfast. He rose, then kissed her. "I must be off to the church. By the by, don't forget you're now in charge of the schedule for the altar flowers, and head of the Committee for the Betterment of the Poor of Our Community."

And, she was sure, anything else that could be given to her as well. Strangely, she was looking forward to all of it. "I know. I put the meetings off until next week."

He raised his brows. "Still hoping your mother will show up soon?"

"She is close. I can feel it in my bones. I just wish I knew what was going on with Kit and Mary."

"Well, that makes two of us." He kissed her again. This time instead of a peck on her cheek, he lifted her into his arms, tilted his head and plundered.

Her blood heated as his hand cupped her breast, and she wanted nothing more than to drag him back to bed. Suddenly, he broke the kiss. "There, that should keep you until this evening."

"You . . . I can't believe . . ." Before she could get out a coherent sentence, he patted her derrière and left the room, laughing.

Oooh, two could play at that game. He'd be very sorry he had left her wanting.

Later that day, as Eunice was changing for dinner and planning her revenge on her husband, the sounds of coaches and stamping horses drifted from the front of the house. "My love, we have company."

He strode out from the dressing room he'd been using. "Sounds like *a* company, if not a battalion. You stay here. I'll find out who it is."

"I'll come." She fastened her earring. "It may be Mama. She is long overdue, and I've begun to worry a little."

They reached the bottom of the main staircase as Simons opened the door. One footman in Bridgewater livery handed out the Dowager Lady Featherton, while another supported Mama.

Eunice hurried forward. "What took you so long?"

Her mother kissed her cheeks. "The ogre."

Lady Featherton grinned. "We finally lost the blackguard. Now where are the children?"

"Gone with their friends to Edinburgh." Eunice linked her arm with her mother, leading her into the drawing room, as Brian escorted Lady Featherton in and closed the door behind them. "I believe the thinking was that Mr. Featherton would have an easier time courting Mary there rather than here."

"Oh my." Lady Featherton pursed her lips. "I take it all did not go as planned."

Eunice raised a brow. "If you mean, you thought she would give up all her fantasies about a Season, and being courted, and falling in love ... No, it did not go as planned." She glanced at the door. "Be careful what you say around the servants. They believe Kit and Mary are wed. I'll ask Cook to hold back dinner for a half hour so that you can refresh yourselves."

When they reached the top of the stairs, Mama looked at Brian as if she were just seeing him, and stopped. "And who might you be?"

He bowed. "Mr. Brian Doust, rector, Your Grace. I take it you're my new mother-in-law."

"Well, at least someone got married," Mama groused. "I want to hear all about it over dinner."

Simons looked at Eunice. "Which bedchambers, my lady?"

"The Blue Room and the Green Room. We've been keeping them ready. I'll show them up. Please see to places for their servants."

"Yes, my lady."

Two hours later, she, Brian, Mama, and Lady Featherton sat in the drawing room sipping tea.

"There you have the whole story." Eunice, eschewing tea for wine, took a sip. "Brian and I have been waiting for your arrival before moving to our new house."

Lady Featherton slowly shook her head. "We made a mull of this one, Constance."

"We'll come about," Mama said. "Though I believe we should stay here for two or three days before traveling to Edinburgh."

"Perhaps you should wait until we receive word that Lady Mary and Mr. Featherton have wed," Brian suggested. "I'm afraid neither of them is happy with you at the moment."

"We shall take your advice, Mr. Doust," Lady Featherton said. "Better to let them work it out from here. I don't wish to distract them from each other."

Mama frowned. "We'll see. I'm concerned about Tolliver though. I'd like to make sure he's nowhere around Mary."

"I'll write to Mary and ask how she is enjoying the Season," Eunice suggested. With any luck at all, they would receive good news. "In the meantime, do not become too comfortable here. Brian and I are moving into our home to-morrow, and we'd like you to stay with us."

He glanced at her, a look of longing in his eyes. Ah well, even if they were not able to be alone, at least they'd have the bathing tub.

CHAPTER TWENTY-TWO

Morna awoke to the somewhat odd and very pleasant sensation of being cuddled next to Simon as he snored softly. This was only their second full night together, the last being their wedding night.

Yesterday evening they'd returned to the town house in mainly pensive moods. All except for Finella; she had been as happy as a grig. Morna wondered how the change would affect Cormac, yet she had the feeling Simon might know what to do better than she did. This morning was also the first time in years she'd felt completely happy. There would most likely be a scandal, but she didn't care for herself, and it would all be over by the time Finella came out. Now that Simon was here, there was no reason to rush her daughter.

Simon brushed a kiss on her hair. "You're awake?"

"I am." She snaked an arm across his broad chest, holding him tightly to her. "Where do we start unraveling this mess my father caused?"

"I have an appointment with my brother-in-law's solicitor to-day. He was to attend me in Charlotte Square, but instead I'll go to his office. The first thing to do is end your father's guardianship of the children."

"Will it be difficult?" she asked, trying not to be distracted by the black curls covering his chest, and failing.

"No, I have proof of the marriage." He rolled her on her side, snuggling up behind her, as if they were two spoons. "Your father tried to have the documents destroyed, but the innkeeper was a wily old man and hid the originals. I've also got a statement from the couple who witnessed our marriage."

She wiggled her bottom against his growing erection. "I'll leave it to you then."

"All you need to think about is where you'd like to live. We'll go to Hull in a day or two, but we won't remain there. I've been considering Bristol."

Morna only half listened. As long as her family was together, she didn't care where they resided. Right now, she wanted Simon, and even her thoughts of moving, or committing patricide for Simon having been taken away from her, couldn't stop her rising desire for him. Moaning, he slid into her, and Morna focused her attention on enjoying her husband.

An hour later, Simon, Cormac, and Finella kissed Morna farewell. Simon held her for a few moments. "After Cormac and I take Finella to Theo, we'll visit the docks, then the lawyer. You should start packing. We will depart in a day or two."

"I shall. Will we remain here until then?"

"We can discuss that this afternoon."

Morna kissed Simon one last time, and stood in the doorway as they hailed a hackney, trying not to remember the last time he and she had parted. There was no point in being maudlin. Everything would be fine now, and she had a great deal to do if they were to leave soon.

Later that morning, after having the trunks pulled down from the attic, and putting her lady's maid and two of the other maids to packing, Morna was in the garden, enjoying a rare bit of sunshine, when the butler, Oliphant, whom she'd hired for the Season, came out on the terrace.

He bowed. "My lady, there is a Lord Freskin here to see you. He says he is your father."

What the devil was he doing in Edinburgh? A cold breeze touched her spine. She debated denying him entry and making him come back after Simon had returned, then decided she'd hear the man out. There was nothing more he could do to hurt them. Still, she'd need to be canny. There was no point in giving him any information he wasn't already in possession of. "I'll meet with him out here. Please bring tea."

A few moments later, her father, a large, barrel-chested man, stomped out onto the terrace. "You should have told that butler who your father is."

She kept her eyes lowered. "I didn't think to see you here."

Tea arrived, and she poured, handing him a cup.

He scowled at the cup. "Woman's drink. I'll have a whisky."

If he thought she'd give him strong sprits, he must believe she was either stupid or daft. A meaner drunk she'd never met. "Then you'll have to go visit someone else. I don't keep it in the house."

"Don't lie to me, lass." He glared. "I'll find it myself."

Pretending a calm she didn't feel, Morna sipped her tea. "And I'll have you shown out."

Her father settled back in the chair, but it was clear his temper was on a short tether. "Call Fee down. I've come about her, in any event."

Morna stiffened. *Damn him to hell!* Thank God her daughter was with Lady Theo. "She is visiting a friend. Whatever you have to say, you will discuss it with me first. I am her mother."

"And I'm her guardian. A fact you'd do well not to forget. I'm at the town house. I'll expect the both of you there at four o'clock sharp to-morrow to drink tea with me. I've a gentleman I'll have her meet. Now that I think of it, since I'm here I want you and the children to move in with me. I'll have my servants pick up your trunks in the morning."

Morna's stomach clenched. Even though he had no power over her anymore, she bit her lip to keep from bursting out in tears. "I've paid the lease for the Season. We are perfectly content to remain here."

"If you want to keep the girl with you until she's wed, you'll do as I say." He stood and walked back into the house, bellowing for his hat.

Morna took a deep breath. Thank God Simon had arrived in time, but would it be enough? Her father was not a man who liked to be crossed.

Simon and Cormac sat in the solicitor's office, waiting as Mr. Kennedy read over the marriage lines and the statement.

"It's all in order. There is no doubt at all that you are legally married." He rubbed the side of his jaw. "I'll file to have Lord Freskin's guardianship terminated, but you should know, he is a powerful man in Scotland."

Simon's hands closed into fists. "But I am my children's legal father, and thus their guardian."

"Aye, and eventually the court will have to decide for you." The lawyer placed his elbows on his desk. "On the other hand, being as you, your wife, and your children are English citizens, his lordship would not have any luck at all trying to enforce the will appointing him guardian anywhere other than in Scotland."

Simon sat back, stunned. Of course they were. Morna became an English citizen upon her marriage to him, and, because he was their father, Cormac and Finella were English as well. "What you're telling me is that you'll file the court case to clear the record here?"

"And also to keep his lordship busy. He has a certain reputation for being difficult." Mr. Kennedy stood. "Might I suggest that you head south at your earliest convenience, or before your wife's father gets wind of the case? I'm sure Lord Titus can handle matters for you here. If you'd like, I'll send a power of attorney over to Charlotte Square for your signature."

Simon and Cormac rose at the same time. Simon shook the lawyer's hand. "Thank you for your advice. I had already made plans to go to England."

They strolled back to Morna's town house. Simon was disappointed that Freskin's guardianship wouldn't be immediately void, but he'd read law at Oxford and understood the legalities. It was a damn shame he hadn't been able to study Scottish law; that would have done him more good.

Cormac had been quiet during the whole conversation with the lawyer. He glanced over now and asked, "Everyone in the world seems to know about Gretna Green. How was it you believed my grandfather when he said ye weren't wed?"

Now older and much wiser, Simon had wondered himself how he could have been such a stupid fool. "I was seventeen when your mother and I met. We fell in love the first time we set eyes on each other. She knew her father was ready to betroth her to MacDiarmid, so I suggested we marry quickly, and we did. The following morning her father found us. He dragged her out of the inn, and I followed, certain that he'd have to recognize our marriage and allow me to take her back. Then he argued that as she was already engaged to Mac-Diarmid, and the marriage agreements had been signed, our marriage wasn't valid. I went home to England and asked my father for help, but he maintained that I was probably not legally married. I went back to university. Before I left for America, I came here to visit my sister and met your mother again. We tried, but couldn't stay away from one another."

"That's when Finella was conceived?"

"Yes, and when I taught you to tickle trout. Your mother knew within in a few weeks that she was carrying again. I sent a note asking her to come to America with me. I waited long past the hour the ship was to have sailed, but she didn't arrive. I thought she'd decided to stay with MacDiarmid. I left the next day. I never should have done so. I missed years with you, Finella, and your mother. Time none of us can ever get back."

Cormac shook his head. "I don't know if you would have made it out of the house with me. I remember an old groom who was always with me whenever I went outside, even with my mother." They walked together in silence. "I wonder what to do with myself now."

"Have you finished university yet?"

"I didn't go. Neither my grandfather or my—the old man thought it would be helpful."

"If you wish to attend, I'll do what's necessary for you to be accepted." Simon placed his hand on his son's shoulder. "I have a majority stake in a shipping line. I was hoping you'd be interested in working with me someday."

Cormac's eyes brightened. "Would I get to travel?"

Simon grinned. Young men never changed. "If that is what you want."

As quickly as his son had smiled, he frowned. "I wish I knew what will happen to the tenants and others dependent on the MacDiarmid holdings."

Simon was pleased his son took his responsibilities to heart. It boded well for Cormac's future. "I was under the impression there is a cousin."

"Aye, but I think he was as old or older than MacDiarmid."

"If he is dead with no heirs, and if you want it, I'll see what I can do to have the title and estate granted to you." For once Simon's father might be able to help. He had Prinny's ear.

"Can we wait until we know if there is an heir?" Cormac asked.

"Of course. We'd have to, in any event." Another issue Simon would ask Titus to look into it on Cormac's behalf.

When they reached the house, the butler opened the door and bowed. "My lord. Her ladyship would like you to attend her as soon as you returned. She is in the morning room." The old servant appeared to think for a moment before continuing. "It is down the right corridor at the back of the house."

"Thank you." Simon wished he'd discovered the butler's name before he left this morning. "Is anything wrong?"

"I believe it may have something to do with her ladyship's father. He visited earlier."

Simon held back the string of curses hovering on his tongue. "That old man could make a saint sin."

The butler inclined his head. "Indeed, my lord."

"Tell me your name," Simon said.

"Oliphant, my lord."

"You're a good man, Oliphant."

"Thank you, my lord."

Cormac led the way to the morning room.

When Simon entered, Morna rushed to him, grabbing his jacket. "My father wants me to bring Finella and move into his house. He has some man he's picked out to marry her. Tell me he's not her guardian anymore."

"I wish I could, but that is not yet clear." The blood drained from Morna's face, and she swayed. Catching her around her waist, he drew her to him. "Whether he is for the moment or not, he will not marry her off. You have my word."

"Will you fight him, Da?"

Simon's chest puffed out a bit. He thought he'd have to wait much longer before Cormac called him *Da*. "He'll have a fight, son, but not a physical one. Arguments and fisticuffs will not solve this. As Mr. Kennedy said, you, your sister, and mother are English citizens." Why that legality had never occurred to Simon before the lawyer mentioned it, he didn't know. "We are merely going to my father's main estate." He stepped to the desk, took out two sheets of pressed paper, and a pen that he was surprised to find sharp. He wrote a letter to his sister and Titus telling them to keep Finella at their house, and informing them he would be there with the rest of his family later that evening. The second missive was to the representative of his shipping company, telling the man that Simon was sending several trunks down to wait for the ship to arrive. He sealed the notes, then tugged the bell-pull. The butler entered the room. "Have this taken to Lord Titus's house in Charlotte Square. Tell the footman to wait for an answer. The other goes to Cavendish and Partners Shipping at the port."

The butler bowed. "Yes, my lord."

"And do not, under any circumstances, allow Lord Freskin past the front door."

"With pleasure, my lord." His butler bowed, and turned sharply on his heel.

Simon kissed Morna lightly on her lips. "How close are you to being packed?"

"I think it's almost done."

"Good. Except for what we will require for the next few days, we shall send everything to wait on the ship."

She shivered in his arms. "Where are we going?"

"For the time being, to my sister's. She and Titus will not allow your father past the front door. As soon as the ship arrives, we'll sail to my father's."

Cormac's face split into a wide grin. "I've never been on a ship."

Simon hoped his son loved sailing as he never did, but no matter; going by water would stymie Lord Freskin.

"Cormac, go out, if you would, and find a hackney. Have it pull around to the mews."

"Yes, Da."

Simon kissed Morna again. "Please make sure your maid has packed overnight bags for you and the children, then meet me behind the house."

She reached up and touched her lips to his. "I'll be as fast as a rabbit."

He hoped his ship arrived soon. If not, he'd have to arrange passage on another one. If Freskin knew what Simon and Morna were about, he didn't put it past the old man to abduct Finella.

Later that evening, Kit joined Huntley against one wall of the open room that had been given over to dancing. He snagged a glass of wine from a footman. "Where's Caro?"

His friend motioned with his head to a grouping of sofas and chairs where several ladies were involved in a comfortable coze. "I thought you'd be dancing."

"I managed to avoid this set." Kit blew out a breath. "I'm getting damned tired of being Mr. Perfect."

"I commend you for keeping it up for this long." The set ended. Huntley tossed off the rest of his drink and straightened. "I'm off to reclaim my wife."

Kit glanced around. Mary's partner was escorting her to Caro as Lady Theo was absent this evening. "I'll come with you."

"When are you going to ask her to marry you?"

"When I'm sure she'll accept." Kit didn't know what he would do if she rejected him. What he did know was that he didn't like the looks of Mary's latest dance partner. "Who is the man she was dancing with?"

"I don't know. Perhaps Lady Theo introduced them at one of the entertainments," Huntley said as they maneuvered their way through the crowd. "Munro, I think."

"I didn't see you during the last set." Mary smiled as Kit joined her.

"No." He slid in next to her, placing her hand on his arm. "The only lady I wished to dance with was already taken." If they were engaged, he could stand up with her more than twice. In fact, he could monopolize her all evening. That thought brought on others, of her in his arms and in his bed, golden hair spread out on the pillow. Her eyes turning silver as he pleasured her. *Blast and damn!* Huntley was right. Kit needed to ask her soon.

"Really." She raised one perfectly arched brow. "Who was that?"

He took a glass of lemonade from a passing footman, handing it to her. "You."

Mary regarded him over the rim of her glass. "Thank you. I greatly enjoy when we dance together."

Still, that didn't tell him if she liked standing up with other gentlemen as well. One in particular seemed to be trying to make a push in her direction. He led her out for the last waltz of the evening. "Would you mind if we leave after supper?"

She curtseyed as he bowed and placed his hand on her waist. "No, not at all. Truth be told, I'm a little tired."

Soon Mary was in his arms again, but it wasn't enough. He forced himself not to close the distance between them during the turn. It was taking all the self-control he had to keep from grabbing her hand, pulling her outside, and kissing her senseless.

Thus creating exactly the type of scandal his long-dead half-brother had caused. Kit couldn't do it. Somehow he had to find a way to keep his vow and convince her to become his wife.

An hour later, Mary and Kit arrived home to find Huntley's aunt and uncle still up and in conversation with Lord Simon and the woman she had met during morning visits the other day. A young man she'd been introduced to the previous evening was there as well.

"Do you know who the young lady and gentleman are?" Kit whispered.

"I do." She turned so that her back was to the rest of the company. "They are the ones I told you about. See how the younger man resembles Lord Simon?"

"Please join us." Lord Titus hailed them. "Help yourself to wine, brandy, or whisky. The others are in the nursery with the babes. Apparently the poor things are fussy."

Kit handed her a glass of sherry and remained by her side as they approached the group.

"Lady Mary," Lady Theo said, "you have met Morna. It turns out she and Simon are married after all." When the tale was finished it seemed to resemble something out of a romance novel rather than real life. Including them sneaking out of their town house and arriving here after Morna's father tried to gain entrance to the house. "They will be staying here," Lady Theo continued, "until passage can be arranged to England. I must ask you not to mention that fact to anyone."

"No indeed," Mary promised.

Next to her Kit squeezed her hand. "I'm sure none of us will say a word."

She couldn't imagine being married to someone old enough to be her grandfather or anyone she didn't love. A shiver slithered down her spine. Yet that was exactly what would have happened if she hadn't had the support of her family and been able to escape her cousin. Her heart went out to Lord Simon's family for all they'd suffered due to the selfishness of others.

She tightened her fingers around Kit's much larger hand. He was always either with her or waiting for her. They'd had so much fun sightseeing to-day, and no one waltzed better than he did. He wasn't as romantic as the heroes in the novels, but he was strong and steady. Although she would like a bit more romance, Mary could not imagine spending her life with another man. Kit was the gentleman she wanted to marry.

If only he'd ask her.

* * *

The next morning, Caro sat with Phoebe, Anna, and Theo around the breakfast table. Phoebe's and Anna's eyes were heavy as they sipped their tea.

"Where is Mary?" Phoebe asked. "I thought she'd be down by now."

"Down, eaten, and gone." Caro grinned. Mary's bedchamber was up the corridor from hers, and Caro had heard Mary leave. "She and Kit are taking in more of the sights."

Anna raised her eyes to the ceiling and shook her head. "Why is it taking so long for them to come to a decision?"

Phoebe pulled a face. "Sometimes it's not easy."

Dropping her head in her hands, Anna said, "I'm sorry, but you had a reason to be concerned. Kit, on the other hand, has never done anything even questionable."

Caro swallowed her bannock. "You must remember, Mary has not known Kit for as long as the two of you have."

"They are also both afraid of being rejected," Phoebe added. "If only we could think of something to show them they want to marry each other."

"You're both right," Anna said. "Ignore me. I'm just tired."

Theo poured another cup of tea, a knowing expression on her countenance. "You might be interested to know, I have put a scheme in play. Give it another day or so, and I believe we'll have a betrothal."

And then, Caro prayed, a quick wedding. According to the letter she'd received from her mother, there was a great deal of talk and speculation about Kit leaving Town during the Season.

CHAPTER TWENTY-THREE

The old traveling coach lurched to one side and stopped. *Damn it to hell.* Gawain pounded on the roof. "What happened?"

His groom's boots hit the ground. "I'm lookin'." A few moments later, Whitely appeared at the window. "Broke the wheel."

Bloody hell! They were so close. "Where are we?"

"We passed Alnwick a ways back. If you want to stay here, I'll go and find help."

Gawain opened the door and jumped down. "Help me unhitch the horses and you can ride back."

Fortunately, the horses had been broken to the saddle. His father had always said it might be useful someday. What Father actually meant was that they couldn't afford to take a chance that they wouldn't need the horses for both.

"Yes, sir."

An hour later, Whitely had returned with another man who inspected the wheel. "I got something in my wagon that will get you back to town, but it'll be a few days before we can get it mended."

Gawain wanted to shout at the man. Unfortunately, he didn't have the funds to argue or try to bribe him into fixing the wheel any faster. "Thank you."

The man gave him a strange look, as if he'd been expecting to be given more of a problem. "All right."

They lifted the heavy carriage, replacing the wheel. Once the horses were once again in their traces, he climbed back in the coach.

Gawain hated not having wealth. He detested not being able to afford one pair of horses for driving and others for riding. Maybe that's the first thing he'd do when he married his cousin. He'd even be able to buy a matched team.

As the other man drove away, Gawain asked Whitely, "Did you find an inn for us?"

"Yes, sir. It's clean, and breakfast and dinner are included in the price."

"When I'm rich, we'll stay in the best inns and order tradesmen to have the repairs done right away."

"I look forward to it, sir. Won't be long now."

"No. We'll find her direction in Edinburgh." Ever since his conversation with his mother, Gawain's sense of urgency had grown, and he needed to make Mary his wife before something came along to spoil his plan.

That evening, Theo stood next to her husband as the gentleman, using the term loosely, asked Lady Mary to dance.

"Who the hell introduced Munro to Lady Mary?" Titus snarled.

"I did." Theo braced herself for his disapproval. Even after all these years, she hated arguing with him. Not that she wouldn't give as good as she got. One did have to keep a tight rein on Scotsmen.

"And do not swear around me."

Titus scowled at her. "You'd trust an innocent like her with that rogue?"

"One of us had to do something." She shrugged one shoulder. "And I am the only one with the right connections."

"The bravura, you mean." *Gall* is what he really wanted to say.

She waved her fan languidly. "It is clear as day that Lady Mary and Mr. Featherton need a bit of a push. If Gavin Munro can't make Mr. Featherton jealous enough for him to lose some of his famous reserve, I'll eat my turban."

Titus slid her a cynical glance. "You'd better have Cook boil it for a long time and season it well."

She tucked her hand in Titus's arm. "Have a little faith, my love. Besides, Gavin knows that if he crosses the line with Lady Mary, he'll answer to me, and that he does not want to do."

"You have that much faith in yourself, do you?"

"Indeed I do."

"Well then, let's have a little wager," Titus said smugly.

As God was her witness, Theo would wipe that superior look off his face. "I have already wagered my turban."

"Aye, but you didn't mean it."

She raised her chin. This was going to be fun, and she may get something she wanted as well. "What do you want?"

He chuckled. "To see you eat your hat, of course, feather included."

She smiled. He was truly going to regret this. "And I want you to accompany me to Hull and perhaps even London."

"Do you now?" He raised an arrogant brow.

She almost laughed in his face. He might be a Scottish marquis's son, but she was an English duke's daughter and had learned to negotiate with the best. "I do."

"You've got yourself a wager, my lady. I'll make sure to tell Cook to order more spices."

As far as Kit was concerned, the evening was a complete and total failure. He'd got to dance twice with Mary, but neither was a waltz. Lady MacDonald, whose entertainment it was, still considered the dance to be scandalous. He watched Mary as Mr. Munro led her to the set forming for a Scottish reel. There was something about the man Kit didn't like. Probably because Munro kept looking at her as if he'd like to have her in his bed. As soon as it was over, Kit would ask her to take the air on the terrace with him. It was time to propose.

He just prayed she'd accept him.

"Mr. Featherton."

He glanced at his hostess. Accompanying her was a young lady who could not be more than seventeen. The girl wore thick glasses and looked as if she'd like to flee. *Damnation!* All he wanted to do was stay here and keep an eye on Mary and the Scottish rogue she was standing up with. Instead he pasted the expected smile on his face and inclined his head. "Yes, my lady."

Lady MacDonald smiled a bit nervously, almost as if she were afraid to approach him. "Miss MacGregor, I'd like to introduce you to Mr. Featherton. Sir, Miss MacGregor."

Stifling the sigh he wanted to heave and the urge to walk away, he bowed. "Miss MacGregor, it would be my pleasure if you would allow me to partner you for this dance."

A tentative smile trembled on her lips, and he knew he'd made the right decision. Why did parents allow their daughters to come out before they were ready? He'd make sure none of his did. If Mary accepted him and they had children.

"I'd be pleased to accept."

Unfortunately, by the time they took their places, he was at the other end of the dance floor from Mary.

A half hour later, Kit had never been so glad for a set to end. He escorted the young lady back to his hostess, who was fortunately not too distant from Lady Theo. Snagging a passing footman, he took one glass of wine and another of lemonade, then strode forward to collect Mary. Except she wasn't with Lady Theo. Where the devil was she? He scanned the room and saw that scoundrel Munro leading her to the other end of the ballroom.

Bloody hell! The blackguard was taking her outside, probably for no good purpose. Kit dumped the glasses in the potted palm next to him. Quickening his pace, he kept to the edge of the room so as not to be waylaid by his hostess or anyone else. Munro and Mary were already on the balcony when he arrived.

Although the light was dim, Mary seemed to be backed up against the stone balustrades, and the cur was standing far too close to her. Munro bent his head down as if he would kiss her. In the moonlight Mary's complexion was a waxy green, and her eyes wide with fear as she tried to retreat even further. The problem was there was no place for her to go.

Resisting the urge to grab the blackguard and pitch him over the side, Kit calmed himself. As angry as he was, he would not create a scene.

Clipping the end of each word, he growled, "Get. Away. From. Her."

Mary's gaze switched to him, and he thought he saw relief in her face as their eyes locked.

The other man glanced up and raised his brows in a look of distain. "And what is she to ye, Sassenach?"

He clenched his jaw. If the rogue wanted a fight, he'd get one. He hadn't spent all those hours at Jackson's Salon for nothing. "She is mine."

Mary sucked in a breath, her eyes shifting from him to the Scot and back to Kit.

The other man rose to his full height, which was about the same as Kit's, and crossed his arms. "Is she now?" Munro's Scottish burr became more pronounced as he glanced for a moment at Mary. "Then what's she doing out here with me?"

She opened her mouth but didn't seem able to speak. Kit reached his hand out to her. Just as their fingers touched, the Scot stepped between them. "No so fast there, Bobadil."

Kit smiled to himself. The cur thought he was a braggart, did he? He quickly assessed their positions. They were close in height and weight, and therefore probably evenly matched. Unless Kit wanted a prolonged fight on his hands, which he refused to subject Mary to, he'd have to hit Munro hard enough to put him over the low railing, which only came to the Scot's upper thighs.

Kit kept his hands from forming fists and giving his plan away. "You have one last chance to leave this terrace alone and by the door."

"Or ye'll do what, Englishman?" The Scott sneered. "You're likely too afraid ye'll ruin your fine cloths to do naught to me. I—"

Grabbing Munro's shoulder, Kit swung the man around, and plowed his fist into the Scot's jaw. Munro's jaw swung up as he stumbled back and toppled off the terrace into the bushes below.

Without thinking, Kit crushed Mary to him and her lips to his. What would have happened to her if he'd not been there to save her? What the hell was he doing now? His behavior was no better than Munro's, but he couldn't seem to stop himself. He softened his mouth, lightly nibbling her full bottom lip, cupping her face in his hands, before slanting his head and demanding she respond.

God, he'd never tasted anything as good as Mary, sweet and tart, just like the lady herself. He needed her with him for the rest of his life.

Thank the heavens, Kit had come when he had. Ignoring the low groan from the garden below, Mary threw her arms around his neck. His lips were warm, but firm and masterful. Nothing like what she had experienced when Gawain or the other rakes had tried to kiss her. He smelled clean, and very male. To think she had thought he had no passion. How so very wrong she'd been.

Mary gave herself over to Kit as he trailed his tongue along the seam of her mouth, and when she opened her lips in a sigh, he conquered her. She tentatively touched her tongue to his, and he pulled her closer, exploring the cavern of her mouth, tangling his tongue with hers in a strange intimate dance. How had she ever thought he wasn't interested in her?

"*Mine.*" His voice was a low growl.

Joy filled Mary's entire being. This was all she'd waited for and had almost given up on. It was even better than in the books.

Her words emerged in a breathy whisper. "Yes, yours."

His hand moved over her back, to her derrière. Cupping it, and lifting. She pressed forward, trying to get closer, but they were already flush against one another. All she wanted to do was climb on to him. This was so much better than she had ever imagined a kiss could be.

His lips moved over her jaw. "Marry me."

Hmm. Not exactly the proposal she'd looked forward to, but just having him kiss her made it worth it. She'd never suspected Kit could be so ardent. "Yes."

He took her mouth again, claiming her, this time giving no quarter. She moved her hands to his cheeks, cupping them as he devoured her. She gave, then took from him as well.

Suddenly he jerked his head up, breaking the kiss as if the magic spell had been broken. "No."

"No?" *No what? He doesn't want to marry me? After he kissed me like that?* This could not be happening.

He ran one hand through his perfectly coifed locks. "This is not the way to do it."

Do what? She wanted to pummel him, yet he still held her against his chest. "I don't understand you."

Taking her hand in his, Kit dropped down onto one knee. "Mary, my love, before I even saw you in my house, I knew I wanted you to be in my life forever. I love you and cannot imagine my life if I don't spend it with you. Would you do me the great honor of becoming my wife, my friend, my lover, and the mother of my children?"

He stared up at her as if he wasn't sure what her answer would be. How could he doubt her? Mary's throat closed, and she had to blink back a sudden rush of tears. A watery chuckle burbled out. "Yes, Kit. More than anything I want to be your wife and everything else you said. I love you too."

Then she was in his arms again, yet this time he pressed his lips gently to hers, teasing her to join him. She leaned into him, clutching the back of his neck with one hand and placing the other on his cheek. "I love you."

Someone coughed.

Kit broke the kiss, but didn't release her, and Mary peeked around him.

"It is almost time for the supper dance." Marcus raised a brow. "A brave guest finally convinced Lady MacDonald to allow a waltz. I assume you are now able to partake."

Mary's face flamed. Why hadn't she thought they'd be caught? Thank the Lord it was their friends and not someone else.

A large smile split Kit's face, and instead of looking at Marcus, Kit gazed down at her. "We are. In fact, I may never again dance with another woman. You may wish us happy."

Oh my. She had so many thoughts running through her mind. Everything from what it was like to have him gaze at her as if she were the most important person in his life forever—and it was wonderful; she had never felt so cherished—to feeling sorry for the young ladies and hostesses who would no longer be able to rely on him. Perhaps she could allow him to dance with some of the young ladies, but no waltzes. They were all hers.

She was smiling so broadly her cheeks began to ache. Finally, she had everything she'd ever wanted. No romance-book hero could match her Kit. "Yes, you may."

Suddenly all their friends were crowding in, congratulating them. Phoebe, Anna, and Caro had knowing looks on their faces as they took turns kissing Mary's cheeks and hugging her. The men slapped Kit on his back and shook his hand.

All the fear and tension she'd been feeling for years had slipped away. This was right. The way it was meant to be. Mary's throat tightened as she blinked back tears of joy.

"If we are going to take our places"—Phoebe linked her arm with her husband's—"we had better go in now."

"What did you do with the other man?" Rutherford asked.

Kit glanced toward the garden. "He decided he'd rather commune with nature."

Huntley barked a laugh and Caro smiled.

"Good place for him, if you ask me." Rutherford twined Anna's arm with his. "I didn't like the look of him."

Mary refused to allow anything to ruin her mood, yet Rutherford was right. There was something awfully smoky about Mr. Munro. She shook it off. She was betrothed to the man she loved, and her closest friends were here. Nothing could go wrong.

They arrived on the dance floor as the music began. Kit held her closer than usual. "Are you happy?"

Why did he even need to ask? "I am perfect."

The doubt left his eyes and he grinned. "You certainly are."

Theo glanced over at her husband. "I believe a journey to England is in the making. I shall instruct my maid to begin packing."

Titus narrowed his eyes. "I think you're counting your chickens before they hatch, my lady. You'll be eating that turban yet."

Stubborn Scots. "Hmm. Just where do you think Munro is right about now?"

Titus glanced around. "In the card room, most likely."

"If you wish, we can wager on it."

"And just where do *you* think he is?" Titus's jaw tightened. A sure sign he knew he was going to lose. Papa had taught her all about tells.

"I believe he is picking himself out of the holly bushes below the balcony."

"Ha!" Titus scoffed. "As much as I admire Mr. Featherton, he'd never be able to take Munro."

Theo suppressed her smile. "You think so, do you?"

"Aye." The syllable was short and curt.

"Well then, if I'm right, you buy me that diamond necklace I've been admiring, and if you're right . . ."

"We don't go to England."

That was only to be expected. After seventeen years, he'd still not forgiven her father for attempting to stop their wedding.

"Done." She thought for a moment. "Let's sweeten the pot."

His eyes narrowed. "What are you thinking?"

She widened hers. "If they marry within the next two days, you'll spend Christmas with my family."

"And if they don't, you'll agree to pack up and go on the next expedition. In two weeks."

"I agree." She slid a look at her husband and wondered how badly he would take losing their wager.

CHAPTER TWENTY-FOUR

Late that night, after everyone else had retired, Mary sneaked out of her bedchamber, along the corridor, crossing to the other wing of the house where Kit's room was located. They may have to wait another few weeks to wed, but she longed to be with him now.

Padding to the last door on the right, she stopped, took a breath, and opened it. Kit stood before a small writing desk reading a letter. She closed the door, and he turned, dropping the missive to the desk and hastily tying the cloth belt of his robe. He stared at her but didn't utter a word.

Now that she was here, Mary wondered what she'd been thinking. Perhaps she should go back to her chamber. Yet they were betrothed. Everything she'd planned to say died on her lips.

In three steps, he was with her, and his arms were around her. "My love?"

Oh God! Now what? Her throat dried. She could see his chest again, but this time she knew how hard it was. "I—I wanted to be with you."

Kit's forehead creased, and when he spoke, his voice was full of regret. "I'd like nothing better, but we cannot." Lifting her in his arms as if she weighed nothing at all, Kit carried Mary to a large, stuffed chair. He sat, holding her on his lap as he stroked her hair.

"I don't understand. We are marrying."

"More than anything, I want to make you mine in all ways tonight. You have no idea how often I've dreamed alternately of tearing your gown off or undressing you slowly, kissing every inch of you. For weeks, I have fought taking you in my arms and making you mine. You are the most beautiful woman I've ever seen."

Oh dear. Her breath shortened. She'd never expected him to say all that. How stupid she had been. "I thought you didn't want to kiss me."

Kit chuckled. "I was convinced *you* would slap my face."

"To think of all the time we wasted, but why *did* you wait so long?"

"I vowed not to kiss you until we were betrothed. Then this evening when I saw Munro and how pale you were, my last coherent thought was getting him away from you."

Mary touched her forehead to his. "I think my friends were right, I should have kissed you first." Still, now they were engaged. He had always been proper, but... "We are to be married soon." Warmth rose in her cheeks. "Many couples anticipate their vows."

"They do, and by the birth dates of their children, some of our friends have as well." He settled her more securely in his arms. "Yet I once promised I'd never be part of ruining a lady, and if by some strange occurrence, something were to happen to me before we wed, that is what you would be. Mary, I love you too much to take the chance."

Her heart was in her throat. No one, she was certain, loved her as much as this man. She laid her head against his shoulder. Someone or some occurrence must have affected him deeply. "What happened?"

Kit groaned and kissed her hair. "I once had an older brother, half-brother actually. My father and his mother married when they were very young. Crispin was the only child they had before she died. A few years later my father married my mother. Crispin never forgave my father. He was ten years older than I and extremely wild. I shall never forget the pain he caused both my parents. Even though my mother had not given birth to him, she loved him as if he were her own." Kit paused for several moments. "Crispin died after seducing a young lady who was engaged to another."

"Did he love her?" Mary asked, afraid of what the answer was likely to be.

"No." Kit shook his head. "He did it for sport, because he didn't like the other man, and he could. The girl did not mean a thing to him. Her betrothed called him out, and Crispin died in the duel. I was fifteen and vowed that I would never give my parents any cause to be ashamed or worry about me."

Oh God! And here Mary was tempting him to do just that. There was nothing for it, they'd have to wait. "Very well, I cannot argue with you. If only we could reason with my uncle."

Surprisingly, the corners of his lips lifted in a smile. "We may not have to. The letter I was reading when you entered was from my father. Your trust has been ended. He sent along the court order and the settlement agreement he and Barham worked out."

She tried to straighten in his arms, but he held her tightly. "You were sure of yourself."

"No." Kit kissed her lightly on the lips. "I was only hopeful. My father ended up going to Barham. You should read the documents. If there are any changes you'd like to make, we can have Lord Titus's solicitor wait on us in the morning. Or you can send them to your solicitor."

Mary wondered how much of what she'd included in her stipulations to Barham the settlement agreement entailed. Though more than that, this was her chance to have what she wanted, and she refused to wait. For the first time, her happiness was in her hands, and she would seize it. "In that case, I'll read the proposal now." She kissed him as she slid off his lap, setting her feet on the lush carpet covering the floor. "I wish to wed as soon as possible."

He led her to the table, pulled out the chair, and lit a branch of candles. Mary perused the letter from his father, one from her brother, and the agreement. She couldn't believe what she was reading: Other than funds set aside for any daughters, all her money was exactly as she'd told her brother she wanted, and Kit had given her Rose Hill. Tears started in her eyes again, and this time she couldn't hold them back.

"Mary." Kit's voice was full of love and concern. "Are you all right? As I said, if there is anything you wish to change . . ."

She chuckled wetly. "It is perfect. Just as you are." She rose, nestling her head in his shoulder as his arms came around her.

"Happy tears?"

"Yes. Immensely joyous tears."

"My love, the only thing in the world I want is to be your husband."

She sniffed, wishing she'd brought a handkerchief, then one was pressed into her hand and she wiped her nose. "In the morning you shall be."

Kit pulled her up, kissing her as he did. "As much as I hate for you to leave..."

"I know." She sighed. "I must return to my bedchamber."

She nuzzled his neck, then kissed him, not wanting to let him go. Kit groaned as he returned her caresses.

Later she crept back the way she'd come. After sliding between the now cool sheets, she lay awake, making plans for the morning. Finally she would have everything she had always wanted: a husband who so truly loved her, he cared not at all about her dowry or anything but her, and he thought she was beautiful. One more night, and she would be with him for the rest of her life.

Rosebury, Northumberland

"Brian, wake up." He fought the gentle tugging on his shoulder until he could no longer ignore it. He rolled so he could look at Eunice. "What is it?"

"Mama is getting ready to leave."

Damn! "Can the woman not listen to reason? Kit and Mary are better off figuring this out on their own."

"The only thing I can tell you is she is not listening to me."

Blasted old woman. "And you think I can change her mind?"

Eunice shrugged. "I have no clue, but you can try."

"Keep her here until I get down."

She nodded, and it was then he realized his wife was completely dressed.

"I shall." She climbed off the bed. A moment later, the door opened and shut.

Brian rubbed a hand over his face. How much would the Lord punish him for locking the dowager up until Kit and Mary returned? A better question might be how much his wife would punish him. This was the reason God gave man woman: to earn their keep on earth.

Heaving himself from his nice warm bed, he saw the wash water set up. His valet had laid out his shaving gear. In less than fifteen minutes, he was in the hall.

"I must leave," the Dowager Duchess of Bridgewater said to Eunice.

"Mama, I thought you agreed to wait until we heard from Mary."

"No, that was what Lucinda agreed to."

"Really, dear," the Dowager Vicountess Featherton said. "I think we should wait, but if you do have a feeling . . ."

"I do. Otherwise I'd not drag you out again."

Brian drew Eunice aside. "My love, I've dealt with enough old ladies to accept that when they get *a feeling*, nothing will keep them from their purpose."

Lips pressed together, she nodded. "You're most likely correct. I just hope they don't ruin everything."

She had a point there. "Kiss your mother farewell. Something tells me we've not seen the last of her."

Finally, Eunice smiled. "You're right, again." She turned back to her mother. "We want you to come for a longer visit on your return trip."

The dowager hugged her fiercely. "We shall."

"At least we know we will be welcome here," Lady Featherton said.

Eunice would love to be in Edinburgh to see how Mary and Kit responded to seeing their grandmothers. Eunice glanced at Brian. He shook his head and mouthed, "No."

She'd better attempt to warn them in any event. A few minutes later, she and Brian waved as the coaches left, then she went to her parlor.

> *Dearest Mary,*
> *I hope this letter finds you well. I thought I'd warn you that Mama and the Dowager Lady Featherton are traveling to you. Please do not be too hard on them.*
> *Best regards to all,*
> *Eunice*

She sealed the letter and handed it to her maid. "Please see that this goes out immediately. I can only pray it will reach Edinburgh in time."

On his second day in Alnwick, Gawain was eating luncheon when his groom entered the inn's common room. "Any news on when the wheel will be ready?"

"Another hour or so, the wheelwright said."

He kicked out a chair, indicating Whitely should sit. "We'll leave as soon as we can. It's still one hundred and forty miles to Edinburgh."

The groom pulled a face. "Four days unless we can afford to have the horses changed."

Gawain took a pull of his ale. "If I knew for certain we were headed in the right direction, I might spend the brass."

"Those old ladies lost us good." Whitely ordered a pint and stared out the window. "*Bloody hell!*" He jumped up and dashed out of the inn. Moments later, he ran back in. "I just saw them."

"The dowagers?" Gawain couldn't believe his good luck.

"The very same. Recognized the coach right away." Whitely grinned. "We won't catch 'em at the speed they're goin', but we're headed the right way."

Gawain drained his mug and ordered another. An hour later they were on the road toward Edinburgh. His plan would work after all.

Kit woke as the sun crested the horizon, and smiled. Finally, in a few hours, he'd be wed to Mary. Hopping out of bed, he tugged the bell-pull. Fortunately, Piggott was an early riser and would already be awake.

Piggott entered carrying a pitcher of water. "You're up betimes."

"It's my wedding day."

"Would you like a bath?"

Only if Mary was in it. "Not at present. Please have Lady Mary's maid wake her. I shall also require—" Kit had to think. Who would least object to being woken at sunrise? "Lord and Lady Huntley." Surely the others would forgive him for allowing them to sleep; after all, the children had been fussy. "They will need to attend her ladyship and me."

Piggott nodded. "I shall see to it."

An hour later, Kit, Mary, Caro, and Huntley met in Lord Titus's study. Mary and Kit signed the settlement documents, and their friends witnessed the signatures.

Caro hugged Mary. "This almost reminds me of when Gervais and I wed."

"Absent a marquis who should have been in Bedlam," her husband commented dryly.

Caro smiled softly. "As bad as he was, without him we would not have married."

Huntley's arm snaked around her waist. "Very true, and I would not have the most wonderful wife in the world."

Mary glanced at Kit and grinned. No lady could be a better wife for him than Mary. "When do you think the church will open? I'd rather have a more regular wedding."

Piggott knocked, then entered. "I have ascertained that one of the clergymen at St. Giles's Cathedral will be expecting you."

Someone had been busy on their behalf. Kit wondered if it was Lady Theo. At least he knew where the church was. He and Mary had toured it. "We will depart in a moment."

His valet bowed. "The carriage will be waiting." Piggott paused for a moment. "You also have chambers at the King's Arms, not far from the church. Lady Theo left a message saying your wedding breakfast will be held to-morrow."

Kit had his answer, yet why the hotel? Then the light dawned. This was Scotland. The marriage had to be consummated. Mary had been bold last night, but he didn't know how she would take being with him for the first time when she was aware that the whole house would know what they were doing. The hotel was a good idea.

"Thank her ladyship for me." He took Mary's hand. "Are you ready?"

"Yes." She nodded, pulling her bottom lip between her teeth as she did when she was nervous. "I am."

They made their way to the coach waiting in front of the house. Kit had a sudden feeling of rightness. No matter what happened, he and Mary were meant to be together.

The carriage traveled through the busy streets, until they reached the sixteenth-century gray stone church. One of the footmen accompanying them hopped off the coach, went to a small wooden side door, and knocked. A few moments later it opened a crack, then opened wider.

"Here we go." Kit jumped down and gently lifted Mary to the pavement.

They were ushered in, and the quiet of the place stunned him. Other than the church they'd stopped at on their way up, he'd never been in one that was so empty. Even the day they'd visited, there were people around. Their steps echoed, adding to the gravity of the union they were about to enter into.

"Good morning to you." A young, rosy-cheeked man greeted them. "I'm one of the vicars. I hear you wish to wed."

The juxtaposition of the old church and the young rector struck Kit. What he and Mary were about to do was new to them, yet as old as time. "We do."

"If you're ready, I'll begin."

"Do you not need our names first?" Kit asked.

The man seemed taken aback. "You're Mr. Christopher Adolphus James Frederick Featherton, are you not?"

"I am."

The rector turned to Mary. "And you are Mary Elizabeth Constance Gertrude Isabel Tolliver. Is that correct?"

"It is."

"Gertrude?" Kit whispered.

"Don't remind me. She was an aunt."

"I have nothing against the name at all. In fact, that was the name of the aunt who left me Rose Hill."

Mary's eyes widened. "Truly?"

"On my honor," Kit replied. He wondered briefly if she were one and the same. Odder things had been known to happen. He'd have to ask his grandmother, if he ever decided to speak to her again.

"Shall we begin?" the vicar asked.

Mary and Kit faced one another. Her fingers trembled a bit, but he pressed on them, comforting her. Although the vicar was right next to them, she had trouble hearing him over her pounding heart. Then Kit smiled, and promised to love, honor, and cherish her all the days of their lives, and she believed he meant every word. He held her gaze with his as she said her vows to him.

She'd forgotten all about the ring until he slipped it on her finger, and whispered, "My mother sent more. You can choose another if you'd like."

Mary didn't want another one. It was perfect. Rubies and diamonds set into a wide gold band, and Kit had selected it for her.

"Sir, could you please repeat, 'with this ring I thee wed'?"

"Sorry." He grinned. "With this ring I thee wed, with my body I thee worship."

That was the part she wondered about. She must have missed the rest, because a few moments later, they were pronounced man and wife.

Mary, Kit, Caro, and Huntley signed the register.

The vicar shook Kit's hand. "I wish you a long and happy life."

"Thank you."

As they left the church through the same small side door, he wrapped his arm around Mary's waist.

She had no idea what to say. Fortunately, Caro came to her rescue. "I realize it is early, but I think champagne is in order. Shall we repair to the hotel?"

"Excellent idea, my love." Huntley placed her hand on his arm.

Kit held Mary's hand as they walked the two blocks to the King's Arms.

They entered the massive lobby. Marble columns and a carved ceiling added to the feeling of space. The carpet was thick, cushioning their steps.

A tall, slender man dressed in black greeted them. "Mr. Featherton and Lady Mary, I presume?" Kit gave a curt nod. "I am Mr. Maitland. If you will please follow me."

He led them up one set of stairs to a room with a large parlor. Although it was not that chilly, a fire blazed in the hearth. On a round table, champagne, fruit, cheese, and bread had been laid out. He handed Kit the key. "There will be a runner stationed in the hall if you are in need of anything. He will call your servants, who have rooms at the end of the corridor."

"I had no idea hotels were so opulent," Mary said as she took in the furnishings.

"This rivals the Putney," Kit responded. "I'll pour the champagne."

He pulled out a chair for her, as did Huntley for Caro.

Mary took a plate, placing cheese, bread, and strawberries on it. "I'm famished."

"As am I," Caro responded, taking some of the food. "It's too bad they do not have chocolate."

The cork popped. Kit handed her a glass. Once the others had theirs as well, Huntley raised his flute. "To Kit and Lady Mary Featherton, may your married life be as happy as mine."

Caro punched him playfully in the side. "We wish you much happiness. The more I saw you together, the more confident I was that you belonged with each other."

"Here, here." Huntley raised his glass. "As one more of us falls to the parson's mousetrap."

"Indeed?" Caro arched a brow, and probably would have clobbered him if he hadn't been looking at her with so much love.

Kit slid his chair closer, putting an arm round Mary's shoulders. "I, for one, am glad to be caught. I cannot imagine a lovelier bride."

"Nor I a more handsome husband."

They toasted again, and ate. Once they'd finished the wine, Caro and Huntley took their leave.

Kit leaned over and kissed Mary. "Are you happy?"

"Never more so."

"Come, my lady."

CHAPTER TWENTY-FIVE

Rising, he lifted her into his arms, carrying her into the bedchamber. Her body slid against his when he lowered her to the floor. Mary swallowed, and her nerves flared. This, them going to the bedroom, was all going so fast. Though she hadn't been worried last night, she was now. She prayed he didn't expect her to know what to do.

Kit cupped her cheek, spreading his fingers so that his thumb could graze her lips. "I love you."

She could do this. Everything would be fine. "And I love you."

His lips teased and cajoled as they had last night. She opened her mouth, and his tongue met hers. Mary slid her hands over his broad shoulders and around his neck as his arms pulled her against him. He tilted his head, delving deeper into her mouth, possessing her as if he could not get enough.

She gasped as her bodice loosened. "I'm a little afraid."

Nuzzling her neck, he said, "I understand. I'll be as gentle as I can." He gazed down at her. "Has anyone spoken with you about what goes on between a man and a woman?"

Mary fought the blush rising in her cheeks. "No."

Although she'd been raised in the country, Mama had forbade her from being around the pastures during breeding season, and her father and brothers had continued to enforce the rule.

Concern and consternation showed in his face. "Let's take this a bit slower."

Unable to speak, she nodded, grateful she didn't have to say more.

All Kit wanted to do was sink into Mary and make her his. Part of him wanted to forge ahead without explaining what would happen, and just ensure her first experience was good enough that she'd forgive him for any pain. Yet it was her body, and she deserved to know what he'd do to her. What they'd do together.

Clothing off first.

Kit bent his head to Mary's, taking her lips again. Without breaking the kiss, he removed his cravat, then started to shrug out of his jacket.

"I want to help." She pushed the sides apart, shoving and pulling his jacket off, then unbuttoned his waistcoat. He hadn't planned on her wanting to be involved, but it might give her more confidence if he allowed her to remove his garments and set a precedent for him to remove hers.

Soon his chest was bare, and Mary slid her palms over his stomach and torso, seemingly mesmerized. Her curiosity was good. He carefully removed her hair pins, placing them one by one on the night table. Running his fingers through the fine silky strands, he'd never felt anything so soft and fine. He almost groaned. It shimmered gold, curling and reaching to her waist. He took her lips again, untying her stays and the ribbons holding the shoulders of her chemise, then pushed them slowly down, uncovering her breasts.

"Beautiful."

"Am I?" Her voice was higher than usual. Reminding him she'd need reassurance.

"Never doubt you are the most exquisite woman in the world. From the first moment I saw you, I wanted you."

"What are you doing?" she asked in more of a squeek.

"Worshipping you."

He nibbled his way down to her nipple, taking the furled nub into his mouth. Mary moaned. God, she tasted so sweet, so good. He had to remind himself this was for her. Cupping the other breast, he rolled the nipple between his thumb and forefinger. She pressed into his hand. How easy it would be to lose himself in her and forget she was an innocent. As quickly as possible, he divested them of the rest of their garments, all the while distracting her with his mouth and hands. Her light mews were a symphony to his ears. He lifted her, laying her on the bed.

His hands trembled a bit, knowing he was the only man who would ever touch her. He kissed and licked her body until her fingers speared through his hair, gripping his head. He had to tell her now, before they went any farther.

Mary writhed against him. "Why are you stopping?"

Kit took her hand, placing it on his shaft. "This is my member."

She touched it gently, running her fingers down it. "It's soft and smooth, almost like a baby's bottom." He clenched his teeth as she caressed him. "What does it do?"

Unable to take any more of her ministrations, he removed her fingers. "It has a couple of functions. The one that concerns us now is mating. I will enter you, using my member. That is how babies are made."

Her forehead pleated. "Where does it go?"

Nothing like having to give one's bride a lesson on anatomy before making love to her. "Have you ever seen a male dog on top of a bitch?"

"Once, but my governess took me away immediately."

Now, how to explain it? "When you have your courses—" She nodded. "It fits in that same passage." Or it would. "It will be tight at first, and there is usually pain associated with the first time."

She sucked in a breath.

Damn, he'd scared her. There should be a book or something to explain this to a lady. "Don't be afraid. I'm told the discomfort does not last long."

Her eyes grew wider. "Do you mean you've never done this before either?"

God help him. "I have, but not with a virgin." He kissed her. "If I could do this without hurting you in any way, my love, I would. As it is, I'll do my utmost to make it as pleasant for you as possible. Trust me, please."

What choice did Mary have but to trust Kit? Why hadn't her mother told her? If only she'd asked her friends. They all seemed to enjoy their husband's attentions. "I do."

"Relax and allow me to pleasure you."

His hands roamed her body as he plundered her mouth. When he sucked her breast she arched up against him and thought nothing could feel better, then he kissed her all over, heating her skin, lighting fires in her veins. He moved inexorably lower, and when she pushed against him, his mouth took hers again.

Mary grew hot and achy, tension thrummed within her, and she wanted him and wished she knew what to do. Then he stroked her mons, and the growing tension in her body coalesced there. When he inserted his fingers, she arched against him. Soon it grew until she couldn't stand it any longer. *Oh God, what was he doing to her?*

"Let it go," he murmured. "Trust me."

His hand gently squeezed her breast, and she spun out like fine glass in a fire. Just as she thought she'd die, an inferno swept through her, and Kit was over her, bracing on his arms, kissing her again.

Suddenly he was buried inside her. She cried out at the sharp pain, and he stilled. "What happened?"

His fingers brushed her hair from her face. Kit's face was tense as he touched his forehead to hers. "I entered you. It will only hurt for a little while."

But why did it have to hurt at all? "I don't understand."

"Your maidenhead tore. I'm sorry, my love, I didn't want to cause you pain. Sadly there is no way around it."

She'd heard of a maidenhead, but never knew what it was. "Does it always feel like this?"

"God no. As I said, only the first time. How are you feeling?"

The twinges receded, and all she felt was him. This must be what was meant by becoming one. "It's better. What do we do now?"

"We're not finished yet." He kissed her hair. "I'll make it good for you. I promise."

His lips roamed over her face and neck. She grabbed his head and kissed him, trying to forget the pain and possess him as he had her. She caressed his tongue with hers, and he groaned. Then he moved inside her again, and gradually the sting was replaced by the fire she'd had before.

"Wrap your legs round me."

Mary did as he asked, then clung to him as he thrust harder and deeper. Their bodies were slick, and her hips reached up to meet him, as if she already knew the strange, intimate dance. From deep within, she began to tremble again and forgot the pain, only concentrating on reaching the peak as she had before.

Just as the flames took her, she called out for Kit, and he shouted her name.

For a few moments, their hearts beat a tattoo, then he rolled off to her side, but brought her with him, slipping one arm under her, holding her as if she would break.

Kit felt like the worst scoundrel in the world. He wouldn't blame Mary if it took her a long time before she wanted to try it again. He waited for her recriminations; instead she was so quiet. Still, she'd come for him twice. Perhaps she wouldn't think it was so bad. He stroked her back, waiting for her to do something, anything. If only she'd forgive him. "I'm sorry."

"No, don't be. It wasn't all dreadful. In fact, at the end it was quite nice." Mary rolled slightly, placing her palm on his chest. "What is what we did called?"

"Lovemaking." Kit settled her more firmly against him. "It is pleasurable, or will be the next time."

He glanced at her, and was not surprised to find her unconvinced.

Mary drew her brows together. "You are positive it only hurts the first time?"

"Yes." He'd make damn sure she never experienced pain again. "You may be sore for a day or so, possibly less." If only he knew what else to tell her. "I'm sure Phoebe or Caro could elucidate it more fully than I am able to."

He wished to God someone had had the foresight to explain matters to Mary. It would have made this so much easier, for both of them.

"What shall we do now?"

Not engage in more lovemaking. He was glad Lady Theo had thought of the hotel, but it was a bit awkward now. "We'll order baths. The warm water should help you feel more the thing. Give me a moment." He rose from the bed, looked at her and . . . blood. How could he have forgotten? Taking a linen cloth from the wash stand, he knelt next to Mary.

She rose up on her arms, and stared at him. "What are you doing?"

"Cleaning you." He carefully wiped between her legs, and she winced.

"For what reason? I thought we were bathing."

"There is blood, from when your maidenhead tore."

Her face turned scarlet. She held out her hand. "I can do it."

"No, please. Let me take care of you."

She huffed, but lay back down, her cheeks still aflame.

After rinsing the cloth, he continued. "I am, after all, your husband."

If he didn't do something, he was going to lose her. Tossing the linen aside, Kit climbed onto the bed.

Mary slid across the bed, as if she'd flee. "What are you doing?" "I'm going to cuddle you." He flopped down, pulled her close, and wrapped his arms around her. For several moments she lay rigid against him. Eventually, her body began to soften. "This isn't too bad, is it?"

She nuzzled her head on his chest. "No, not at all."

While Mary dozed, Kit tried to come up with what to do next. She wasn't the only one who required more information about their first time. He should have asked some questions as well. Such as, how long would he have to wait before they could make love again? She was still skittish, and he must ensure she enjoyed herself before she'd want to engage in marital congress on a regular basis.

Other than bathing and eating again, what were they to do for the rest of the day and night? Play chess or cards? He heaved a sigh. It was time for reinforcements.

Theo smiled into her tea-cup as she waited for Titus to come break his fast. He'd been sleeping soundly when she'd left their bed-chamber early this morning, ready to step in if the course of true love between Mr. Featherton and Lady Mary looked to be deviating from the proper course.

As soon as she'd arrived home last night, she'd written to the rector and hotel, ordering her footmen to await answers.

Lord and Lady Huntley had returned not long ago, and Theo encouraged them to return to bed, promising a full breakfast would be delivered when they wished it. The other ladies ate with their children. She didn't expect to see Simon, Morna, and the children for another hour or so. Theo was so pleased all was turning out well, she almost couldn't contain herself. All in all, this was turning into an extremely good day.

Her butler entered and bowed. "Here is the package you requested, my lady."

She did not even try to keep the smile from her countenance. "Thank you, Reed." The sound of Titus's boots sounded in the hall as he turned down the corridor to the breakfast room. "You may bring his lordship's coffee, and another pot of tea."

She glanced at the door, and her husband filled it with his broad shoulders, the same ones that, as a younger woman, had made her want to swoon. Truth be told, she wasn't unaffected now. A jaunty grin split his face.

Coming forward, he kissed her cheek. "Good morning, my dear."

"Good morning, my love."

The coffeepot arrived as he took the seat across from her. She poured and handed him his morning libation.

"Ah, thank you." Titus reached for his newssheet, and stopped, staring at the velvet box atop the paper. "What is this?"

"The diamond necklace. I thought you'd want to give it to me yourself."

His eyes narrowed. "Are you not being a bit precipitant?"

Theo took a sip of tea. "Not at all. Mr. Featherton and Lady Mary were wed this morning, and are now enjoying a room at the King's Arms."

Ignoring his coffee, Titus sat back and crossed his arms over his chest. "How the devil did you manage that?"

"You failed to account for young love."

He shook his head, grinning again. "Apparently. What did happen to Munro?"

"Mr. Featherton knocked him over the rail into the holly bushes, just as I suspected. Did I fail to mention that he spars with Jackson?"

Titus handed her the box. "Congratulations, my love. Well played. When do we leave for England?"

"Thank you, my dear." She took a bannock. "Simon is waiting for a ship he expects any day to dock. I sent a message to the port this morning. Now that Lady Mary and Mr. Featherton are married, I believe the rest of our guests will depart in the next day or two. Isn't your paper due this week?"

"It is. I'm waiting for another piece or two of information. You're worried about your brother."

"I'm concerned Lord Freskin may attempt to stop them from leaving Scotland."

Titus reached across the table, taking her hand. "He'll have to get through us to do it. The old devil may be good at fooling young men, but he will have a difficult time with us."

"I trust you are correct. In the event he discovers Morna and the children have left the town house she leased, I've made sure he is to be denied admittance here."

"He'll discover she's gone and he'll try to track her, but I doubt if he'll think of looking on a boat."

"That is what I believe as well. Pray God he doesn't either discover Simon is here or think of the port."

Mary leaned back in the copper tub, thinking about what had happened between her and Kit earlier. She was sore down there, but not inordinately so, and although it had hurt at first, all the parts before and after were quite nice. Especially when he'd touched her breasts, and the way he'd kissed her was better than anything she'd ever expected or imagined.

Oh my, just thinking about it, her nipples ached, and she was getting that feeling between her legs where Kit had touched her. Her father had always told her to get back on the horse when she had fallen off. This might not be exactly the same, but the principle was.

Rising from the tub, she reached out for the towel, but it was too far. "Mathers?"

The door to the bedroom opened. Kit strolled around the screen dressed in his banyan. Only this time it was not pulled together at all. "She's gone to fetch something."

Mary couldn't drag her eyes from him. He was beautiful. This was what Lady Cooke must have been thinking of when she denigrated the Elgin Marbles as not being impressive specimens. Mary didn't know who her ladyship was comparing them to, but Kit certainly took the shine out of the statues. Her mouth dried. His member, which had been sort of dangling, rose to greet her.

"My love, what did you need?"

Was that a hint of laughter in his voice? She glanced up, but he was not smiling at all.

"Mary?"

The apex of her thighs dampened and throbbed. "You."

He shook his head. "I'm here."

"No." She wasn't making any sense at all. "Help me out."

When he gripped her waist, she swung her arms around his neck, breathing in his scent. He smelled of musk, and him. "I want to make love."

Kit shifted her, placing his hand under her derrière, and what a delicious feeling that was. "You'll be sore."

"I need you now."

He stopped arguing. The screen toppled over as he strode to the door, locking it, then took her to the bed. He laid her down gently, before divesting himself of his robe.

This time she knew what was going on and where everything went, and planned to enjoy every bit of what he could give her.

CHAPTER TWENTY-SIX

Mary stood in the copper tub as it glinted in the afternoon sun, looking like a nymph emerging from the sea. Water droplets glistened on her creamy skin. Kit had been tempted to debate the merits of waiting a while longer before making love again, yet when she had stared at him and his shaft answered, he had to have her. He lifted her from the vessel placing her feet gently on the floor, then picked up the towel from a nearby stool and slowly dried her before carrying her to bed.

He let down her hair, fisting the curls in his hand and burying his nose in them. Kissing her eyelids, the corner of her lips, his other palm roamed freely, paying close attention to which spots elicited the deepest moans and breathiest sighs.

They'd got off to a rough start, but he prayed they were making up for it now. Mary mumbled something about riding a horse, which didn't make a lot of sense, but gave him an idea. This time he'd let her control the penetration. He lifted her on top of him.

She straddled him, her hot, wet core touching his nether parts. "Can we do it like this?"

"There are a great many ways to do it." He took advantage of his position, cupping her breasts. She cried out when he licked each one, and began rocking on him.

"I want . . ."

"I know." He lifted her up, slowly lowering her onto him, until she could manage it herself. "Better?"

Biting down on her lip, she nodded. Her divine face was a mask of concentration. His love for her hit him like one of Jackson's punches. She was everything. His life, his home, his future. No mistress or lover had made him feel as possessive as he did now. How he'd thought he could have a companionable marriage, he didn't know. All Kit wanted was Mary's happiness, and he would do anything for her. He touched her tender nubbin.

Waves of pleasure washed through Mary. This time she could feel Kit as she convulsed around him. Tears of joy pricked her eyes. Just as he had in driving the carriage, he encouraged her to take what she wanted. Yet he knew exactly what she needed at the right moment. She trembled and fell over him as he finally took his own relief. His arms enclosed her, holding her tightly. She'd known she loved him; still, this lovemaking brought them together in ways she'd never dreamed of or known about. She couldn't imagine her life without him, and knew she'd fight for him and their family.

His fingers winnowed through her hair as he kissed her forehead and the tip of her nose.

Against her head, his lips curved. "Have I told you lately that I adore you?"

Snaking her tongue out to lick his nipple, she smiled when he groaned. "No, I don't think you've ever told me that."

"I do, and I will forever." He moved her off his chest, brushed her hair back, and kissed her. "You are the best thing that has ever happened to me. I might even forgive our grandmothers. Though, if you'd come to London, I would have courted you without all their machinations."

"Would you have?"

"Indeed. I'd already been searching for Barham to ask where you were. You were the only lady who never left my mind."

She kissed him. "I had no idea. My first Season, I held dances for you, yet you never asked."

"I thought you hadn't noticed me."

Mary reveled in the feel of his hard body against hers. Them, together, was so incredibly delicious. "And you believe you would have courted me this year?"

"I'm older and wiser." He grimaced. "But I can understand why our grandmothers might not have believed I'd do it." He touched his lips to hers. "What I'd like to know is how long they had been planning for you to go to Rose Hill."

"Hmm. You know, that is a very good question."

His stomach rumbled. "Are you hungry?"

Even if she weren't, she would have said yes, only because he was. "I am."

Kit pushed himself off the bed. "Wait here." Grabbing his banyan from the floor, he padded into the other room. "We have been provided for." A few moments later, he returned with a large tray. "At least they were not going to make us ask for food."

Cold meats, more cheese, fruit, and fresh bread were arranged on the tray. He placed it on the bed, then went back to the parlor. This time he came back with wine and lemonade.

She picked up a serviette and realized she had no clothing to protect.

"Whatever you drop on yourself, I'll be more than happy to clean off." Kit gave her a wicked smile, his deep blue eyes warm with desire.

Oh my God! That's what it was. All the times he'd looked at her, and she hadn't understood. Even to the point of thinking she had spilled something on her gown. What a pea goose she'd been.

Plucking a grape from the bunch, he held it out to her.

She took the fruit between her teeth, chewed, and swallowed. How decadent this was, being naked in bed with him while eating, but she couldn't bring herself to feel the slightest bit of shame. "I'll do the same for you."

When she remembered how coldly she'd behaved toward Kit at times, Mary was amazed he had continued to court her. She believed now that he would have wooed her if she'd come to Town, and for reasons she didn't understand, that gave her more confidence.

To-morrow, when they returned to Charlotte Square, she must remember to ask Anna about her book. Kit might like it as well.

For the second day in a row, Simon woke with Morna in his arms. He'd never allowed himself to think of them having a life together, and now he would fight to the death for her and their family.

She was still young enough, and she'd always got pregnant so easily, he wondered if they'd have a third child. One they would raise together. Not that it could lessen the love he had for Finella and Cormac. Simon's heart was tied to them in ways he still didn't fully understand.

"Good morning." Beside him Morna smiled and stretched. "What time is it?"

"Around nine o'clock." He debated making love to her again and delaying the day a while longer, or getting up and ensuring they left Scotland before her father could cause them problems. Duty won. "We have a lot to do to-day."

Her countenance shifted from happy to solemn. "You're right. There are things I'd like to get from MacDiarmid Keep. Do you have any good ideas about how I should go about it?"

"If you trust your lady's maid, I'll send my groom to help her arrange the packing and transport."

She gazed at him, a seductive glint in her eyes. "And what, my lord, will I do for a maid while she's gone?"

Simon pulled her to him. "I've always been held to be a quick study."

"That you are." She raised her brows. "I'm well aware you can get me out of my gowns. The question is, can you get me into them?"

He rolled her under him. "We won't know until we try."

A knock came at the door. "My lord. Her ladyship asks you to attend her in the breakfast room."

"We'll be down as soon as we're dressed."

"Very good, my lord."

"This will have to wait until later," he said, slapping her gently on her bottom. He rolled out of the bed before he got distracted again.

Twenty minutes later, Simon and Morna were in the breakfast room. Theo handed him a letter. He opened the seal, spreading the sheet out. "My ship is in Musselburgh."

"Why there and not at Leith?" Titus asked.

"There was a problem with the mainsail, and the captain pulled in there." That might have been a better choice at any rate. Freskin would definitely not look in the small fishing village. He'd have to have the trunks sent down there.

Simon read down further, looking for when the ship would be ready to sail again. "He expects to be ready to sail in two days."

"I'd hoped to be gone before then," Morna said.

Simon placed his hand over hers. "I as well. By this afternoon, your father will know you and the children are not at the town house."

They fell silent for several minutes.

Finally, Theo set her cup down. "I have an idea."

Titus groaned. "The last time you had an idea, it cost me a diamond necklace and a trip to England."

She raised her brows. "That was your fault for not believing I could do what I said."

Simon dearly wanted to know the story behind the necklace. "England?"

"We shall meet you at Hull."

She rang the small silver bell on the right side of her plate. Before she put it down, Reed stepped into the room and bowed. "My lady?"

"Ask Lord and Lady Huntley to attend me. It's time they were up and about in any event. We have a busy day ahead of us."

The butler bowed again, closing the door behind him as he left.

"Morna," Theo said in a sharp tone that had Morna jerking her head up. "Have you got everything from the house here?"

"We have, but there are some items I'd like from MacDiarmid Keep. Simon talked about sending my maid, as she's known there, and his groom to fetch what we want."

Theo nodded. "Make the list and send them off. They can meet us at Carberry Tower."

"My love." Titus's forehead furrowed deeply. "You do know the Elphinstones are in London for the Season?"

"I am aware of that fact. However, our families have been friends for so long, I am sure of our welcome for a few nights. Even if they have only a skeleton staff." She signaled a footman. "Bring me my writing paraphernalia."

By the time the Huntleys entered the room an hour later, Theo had written to Carberry Tower, sent Morna's maid and Oxley off to MacDiarmid Keep, written another note to Mr. Featherton and Lady Mary informing them it was time to return to Charlotte Square, and drunk two pots of tea. As Lord Huntley took a chair next to his wife, Theo ordered a fresh pot.

"Now then." She addressed Huntley. "We have a bit of a problem here. I'd love to have you remain longer, but we must all depart in two days."

Glancing at Simon, Huntley took the cup his wife gave him. "I don't foresee a problem. Is there anything we can do to help you?"

Before she could answer, the butler entered. "Lady Simon, this has come for you."

Simon grabbed Morna's cup before the liquid spilled across the table, and held out his hand. "I'll take it."

When he tried to hand it to her, she shook her head. "You open it."

He perused the hastily written missive. "Your father attempted to gain entrance not long ago. Oliphant sent him away, telling him you were not receiving until after noon."

Morna laughed. "I'd have loved to see that!"

"You're not the only one." The old bastard would likely take his ire out on anyone left at the town house. "How many servants do you have there?"

"Ten, no eleven, not including Cormac's valet and Fee's maid."

"Are any of them from MacDiarmid Keep?" Simon would be damned if he'd call the place Morna's home.

"Only our personal servants."

"Send a messenger to the house and tell the butler I'll hire anyone who wishes to work for me." He glanced at Theo. "Where can they go until it's time to leave?"

"You may as well put them on the stagecoach and send them to Hull. You won't require more than your personal servants until you have a place to live."

"I'll send them in private coaches. That way I'll know they'll all get there." He looked at the footman. "Take my valet with you. He and Oliphant can make the arrangements."

"Yes, my lord."

"Now—" Theo placed her serviette on the table. "Simon, you and Morna may attend the wedding breakfast I'm having for the Feathertons in a few hours."

"You are as bold as brass, my love," Titus said admiringly. "What about your children?"

"They shall be on their way to Carberry Tower."

Morna's eyes flew wide. She opened her mouth, then closed it, flicking a glance at Simon.

His sister did nothing without a reason, but damned if he could figure it out. "What are you thinking?"

"When Lord Freskin discovers you are here, he'll come looking for you. The children will be safe away, but he won't know it because you will still be here. I shall put it about during the breakfast that Titus and I are traveling to London when our guests leave. It has been a long time since I've visited my family."

"When will the children depart?" Morna asked.

"During the breakfast. When there are so many carriages and coaches in the area no one will notice."

"Wait a moment." Simon held his hand up in a useless attempt to slow things down. "You said *when* Freskin finds out. Don't you mean *if*?"

"No, I meant what I said. You, my dear brother, have a spy in your midst."

Morna gasped, her hands covering her mouth.

Simon had the sudden urge to strangle whoever the person was. "Who?"

"Fee's maid." Theo had a smug smile on her face. "Yesterday I told Fee that she must remain in the house unless she had my permission to go out, including not going alone into the garden. This morning, she asked permission to go for a walk in the square. With everything going on, I told her if she needed air, to sit on the terrace and I'd station a footman with her. Not long afterward, one of the grooms who had helped bring your servants over here saw Fee's maid leave through the gate to the mews. He followed her to Lord Freskin's town house, then came right back and told the head groom what he'd seen." She looked at Morna, whose complexion had paled. "It's my belief the girl planned to take Fee to her grandfather. The maid's satchel was already packed. I added enough money that she'll be able to get home. However, she will not be allowed in this house again. I expect to see your father either before the entertainment begins, or afterward. Even he's not stupid enough to court the scandal he'd create by attempting to drag Fee out of here. Did your servants know about your trip to England?"

"No," Simon said. "We—I wasn't sure who we could trust. If they overheard us, and Freskin finds out we are planning to leave, he'll be watching the port in Leith."

Huntley cleared his throat. "You may use my coach to take Cormac and Fee to wherever they are going."

Simon nodded tersely. "Thank you. It will serve to further confuse anyone watching the house."

"Good morning to you. Or is it?" Cormac entered the breakfast room and stood near the door, looking uncertain. "If you're discussing something you'd rather I didn't hear, I will leave."

"Not at all." Simon pulled out the chair next to him. "You're involved."

His son strolled forward and kissed Morna's cheek before settling in the chair next to Simon. "Is it bad news?"

"Some of it is." Simon couldn't keep the gravity from his tone, then he grinned, because no matter what, he was that much closer to having his family out from beneath Freskin. "And some of it's not."

It would have been too much to hope that Simon would be able to tell the story his way. It was, after all, Theo's plan, and she'd made most of the arrangements. At the end, she beamed at them all, and for the first time he had a good idea how much she'd worried about him, Morna, and the children. His sister wanted nothing more than to fry Freskin in his own fat, but would settle for her family being safely away in England.

"So then," Cormac said. "Which one of us gets to string the old man up first?"

CHAPTER TWENTY-SEVEN

Kit leaned against the doorway as Mary's maid put the finishing touches on her hair. He'd scandalized poor Mathers by insisting he be present during Mary's toilet. What would the maid do when he insisted on watching his wife being dressed?

God, she was divine, and to think she was finally his.

Mathers began to pack Mary's remaining items. Everything else had been sent to Charlotte Square earlier. Kit moved to Mary. "Are you ready, my wife?"

Her smile was the best thing he'd ever seen in his life. "I am, my husband."

There had been several hours when he'd doubted the wisdom of remaining at the hotel, but somehow it had worked to their advantage. He couldn't imagine being more in love than he was now. Still, after having watched his parents for the past several years, he knew his feelings would deepen and Mary's would as well.

She placed her fingers in his hand. "I suppose we should go. There are only a few hours until the wedding breakfast."

He bent his head and kissed her. If only they could remain here, in their own little world. "If it weren't for the fact that I want to show you off to everyone as my wife, I'd be content to cry off."

Mary placed her small palm on his face. "As would I, but I need to show all those Scottish ladies that you truly are not looking for a wife."

"Looking for a wife?" He couldn't believe what she'd said. "Why would anyone have thought that? The only woman I wanted was you."

"Lady Theo put it about." Mary linked her arm with his. "After I saw what the ladies here were like, I resolved to protect you."

"I am eternally grateful you did, and extremely effectively."

She slapped him playfully on his arm. "You probably didn't even notice."

"My only focus was you. I wanted to punch every man who danced with you."

"If only I'd known." She laughed. "I would have found excuses not to dance with them."

Kit drew her into his arms. "If you'd known, we would have been wed long before this."

Wrapping her arms around his neck, she rose up and kissed him. "Yes, we would have. I cannot believe how awkward we were around one another."

"Huntley and the rest of them told me to kiss you."

"Anna suggested I seduce you."

He laughed. "I'm amazed we finally got together."

"Love has a way of sorting one out, don't you think?"

"Yes, I do. Let's make a pact. Whenever one of us feels slighted by the other, we must tell the other person. I don't want any more misunderstandings between us."

She held him to her. "I absolutely agree. We both of us take the actions of the other too much to heart at times."

"It looks as if our servants have gone. Shall we walk, or take the carriage?"

Mary shrugged. "How far is it?"

He kissed her lightly on the lips, then linked her arm with his. "Less than two miles."

"Let's walk. I have a feeling we'll be back in a coach soon enough."

They left the chamber, strolled down the main staircase, then out the door onto the street. He dismissed the coach waiting for them. "I think you're right. At least it gives us some more time alone."

They'd been walking for several minutes when Mary asked, "Where shall we go when we leave Edinburgh?"

That was a good question. "Would you rather return to Rose Hill, or journey on to Town?"

He glanced at her as she frowned. "Before I would have said London, but now I'm not sure. It would be disastrous to meet Diana Brownly. If she knew we were in Town, I don't think she could help but mention us."

"My mother has an idea to explain our marriage. The only thing is, I don't know her plan."

Mary stumbled, and he held her up. "Oh dear, I haven't even considered how your family would take all of this."

If only they were not in public, he could kiss her silly. "You have no need to worry. The moment my mother discovered my grandmother's part in the scheme, she wrote to me. As far as she is concerned, you are as much of a victim as I am, and welcomed you to the family with open arms." He smiled at Mary. "Although I must say, I don't feel at all like a victim now. You are the most precious person in my life."

She glanced up at him, her eyes full of love. "I know exactly what you mean. I never thought to be so happy."

"Let's go home to Rose Hill. We can make it truly ours."

Sliding him a roguish look, Mary said, "But won't the hostesses miss you?"

Kit tucked her closer to him. "I think I'm done being Mr. Perfect for the *ton*. I'd much rather be my wife's perfect husband."

"I do wish we were not on the street."

"Why is that?"

"Because I'd take you in my arms and kiss you."

The hell with the rest of the world. If they wanted to talk, they could. He and Mary were walking through one of the many squares, when he brought them to a halt, turning her to him. "Then do it."

A lovely rose appeared in her cheeks, yet she reached up and touched her lips softly to his. Wrapping his arms around her, he slanted his head, deepening their kiss.

Someone tsked, then an older woman said, "Liam, do you remember when we were like that?"

"My dearest love, we still are."

Kit and Mary strolled past the couple, who must have been the same age as their grandmothers. She leaned in and whispered, "Will we be like that at their age?"

He glanced at the couple once more. "I'll guarantee it."

Mary couldn't believe how much she loved Kit, being with Kit, being married to him. She felt dizzy, as if she'd drunk too much champagne. They seemed to agree on everything. Not only had they decided to put off going to Town until the Little Season but resolved to invite his family to Rose Hill. From what he'd told her about his parents, she was sure she'd love them.

They had just rounded the corner into Charlotte Square, and were at the bottom of the steps to Lady Theo's house, when a large, middle-aged man stepped down from the door, fuming.

"*You!*" He pointed at them. "Tell the witch who lives there Lord Freskin wants his grandchildren and daughter back."

Kit raised one brow. "I shall tell her no such thing, and I suggest you find a way to control yourself and speak to her in a civil tone."

As the older man approached, Kit whisked Mary behind him. Lord Freskin stood only a few inches in front of her husband, assuming what would have been a threatening posture to anyone but Kit.

In a bored drawl, Kit asked, "Do you want something?"

Lord Freskin swung his fist up, and the next thing Mary knew, the man was on the ground cradling his jaw.

Turning to her, Kit shook out his hand. "Shall we?"

Mary glanced at his lordship, then back to her husband. She may not have been allowed to see animals breeding, but she had seen her brothers engage in fisticuffs, and that was the best flush hit she'd ever witnessed.

She placed her hand on his arm. "Indeed."

Reed had the door open as if nothing untoward had occurred. "Welcome back, my lady, sir."

"Thank you, Reed," Kit replied as they entered the hall. He bent his head to her. "I'm sorry you had to witness that."

"Thank you, but my brothers were much worse and not nearly so skilled. Your science is wonderful."

"You mean that display didn't shock you?"

"Not at all. Quite the contrary. I actually love a good match."

His palm cupped the back of her waist as they mounted the stairs. "You are an amazing woman."

A footman showed them to their new chambers. "Her ladyship wishes to see you."

"Thank you." Mary removed her bonnet and glanced around the room. It was about the same as the one she'd had before, except for the bed. That was much larger. Well, Kit did take up a great deal of space.

He wrapped his arms around her. "I'd much rather remain here with you, but if we find out what Lady Theo wants, we might be able to carve out some time alone."

"I think that is wishful thinking, my love." Mary reached up and kissed him. "Did you forget the wedding breakfast?" She couldn't help but giggle as he heaved a dramatic sigh. "Give you one night away from social obligations, and you've already become spoiled."

Kit gave her a wicked grin. "It is you who make me not wish for them."

His hand slid down over her derrière, and her breathing hitched. "Once we're back at Rose Hill, we'll have a great deal of time together. After all, your family won't come until after the Season is over."

"I'm not sure a lifetime of being with you is going to be enough." His other hand caressed her breast as he nibbled her chin.

Never in her wildest dreams—well, perhaps in her very wildest ones—had she imagined being the sole desire of any man. That it was Kit made it all the better. The more time they spent together the more comfortable they became with one another, and the sillier all her previous doubts seemed. "You're an evil man for attempting to seduce me when we must see our hostess."

"You mean I haven't accomplished it?" His voice was low and sensual. "I could swear your heart is beating faster. Perhaps if I slide my fingers between your lovely legs . . ."

Oh God! She was ready to fall into bed with him. They'd never get where they needed to be at this rate. "Cease." Reluctantly she stepped out of his embrace. "Let's see what she wants."

They arrived in the breakfast room to find all their friends, and Lord Simon's family, present.

"I'm sorry for your confrontation with Lord Freskin," Lord Titus said. "We knew he'd be angry when he was denied admission to the house, but I never thought he would attempt to assault one of our guests."

Kit shrugged. "You can't be responsible for his actions. How do you plan to get your brother and his family away?" After they told him what they'd decided, he said, "I believe you should allow Cormac and Finella to appear at the breakfast. Enough people will be here that they can slip away unnoticed while one of you creates a distraction, perhaps by having another round of toasts, giving them time to change into traveling clothing and sneak out the back."

"You might even disguise them as servants," Mary suggested.

Caro leaned forward. "A different hat and cloak would be all that is needed. Huntley and I can go out with them, as if they worked for us, and put them in the carriage."

"Have the luggage on it," he added, "and send outriders. After all, no one wishes their possessions to be stolen."

"Armed outriders," Simon said in a grim tone.

Mary glanced at Marcus and Phoebe, who were in quiet discussion. They seemed to have come to a decision, and Marcus said, "Instead of bringing the coach back here, we can rearrange our travel to compensate for the lack of one carriage and meet up with it at the tower."

"That would certainly draw less attention if the house is being watched," Huntley agreed.

"One more thing." Marcus turned his attention to Lord Simon. "How many people know you have returned?"

He shook his head. "Hardly anyone at all. I was not announced at the only entertainment I attended, and we left early. What are you thinking?"

"This scheme would be better served by you not attending the wedding breakfast. It will make it easier for you and your wife to leave undetected. Otherwise, you'll be the main focus of attention."

Lady Theo fiddled with the strand of pearls around her neck as she took in the suggestions. "I'd almost think you had done this type of thing before, my lord."

Marcus gave her an enigmatic smile, and Kit whispered in Mary's ear. "He worked for the foreign office during the war."

After several moments, Lord Simon nodded. "I believe it will work."

A half hour later, Kit was finally alone with Mary in the small parlor next to their bedchamber. Her tub was being filled, and he thought back to the day she'd seen him in the corridor after his bath. He'd have to order a much larger bathing vessel for Rose Hill.

She laughed lightly as he slowly pulled her to him. "How much time do you think we have?"

"I'm not sure." A teasing smile graced her lips as she rubbed her palms over his bare chest, where the banyan was unfastened. "Did you have anything in mind?"

He covered her mouth with his. "When it comes to you, I always have ideas." No other woman had ever made him want her so badly. She was his sun and his moon. He walked her back to the desk. "I thought you might like to learn something new."

"My lady, your bath is ready."

Hell and damnation.

Mary sighed. "I'd better go. We don't have much time to change, at any rate."

He held her fingers until they slipped away.

"Sir?" Piggott poked his head in the room. "I've got your tub set up in the dressing room."

Kit strode out of the parlor. He couldn't wait to get home and have Mary to himself. If he hurried, he could watch her being dressed.

Forty-five minutes later, he swore as he threw down another neck-cloth, missing the pile on the floor. He was getting as bad as Brummell had been.

Piggott handed him another one. "Sir, if I might suggest you calm yourself."

"I am calm," Kit ground out.

"I think Piggott is right."

Kit glanced around. Mary stood with her back against the door. All being in a hurry had done was cause him to miss seeing her dress. "You are beautiful."

As she strolled forward, two champagne glasses in her hands, the sheer overskirt embroidered with white thread was unable to hide the way in which the pale-yellow silk gown outlined her hips. The bodice, also embroidered in white, sparkled as it caught the sunlight. "They look like diamond chips."

"Nothing so extravagant." She chuckled. "They are paste." Her gaze roamed over his body, and his muscles tightened, wanting her. She touched the front of his shirt. "I must say I like the look, though I think some of the older ladies might be scandalized."

Kit grinned as Piggott's complexion deepened. "You didn't wait for me."

She raised her brows, looking at him as if he were daft. "*I* didn't wish to be late. It is *our* wedding breakfast." Mary made herself comfortable on the dressing-table chair. "Please continue."

Kit took a breath. This one would have to be right. Wrapping the wide cloth around his neck, he proceeded to tie it, then lowered his jaw down slowly a few times.

Next to him, Piggott frowned. "I don't recognize that one."

Glancing at Mary, Kit grinned. "No? It's Featherton's Amour."

Piggott gave a sigh of relief and placed a ruby and diamond tiepin in the snowy folds. After Kit's jacket was on, he added his pocket watch and quizzing glass.

Mary rose, giving him a glass of champagne. "Congratulations, Mr. Featherton."

He inclined his head. "Thank you, my lady." Tossing off his champagne, he held out his arm. "I think we should be on our way."

They'd been excused from the receiving line in order to make a grand entrance into the ballroom, thus allowing Finella and Cormac to slip away unnoticed.

Later, as they were mingling, Huntley caught Kit's eye, nodded and raised a glass. Kit bent his head, pressing his lips close to Mary's ear. "They're away."

She smiled, as if he'd whispered a sweet nothing to her, and the couple they were speaking with made a jest about new love.

They ambled around the ballroom until Mary said, "I think Lady Simon might need help."

Kit glanced over. An older man with a stern scowl appeared to be almost to the lady. "I wonder if he's a friend of her father's."

"I don't know, but if we can assist her, we should."

He and Mary arrived in time to hear the gentleman say, "I don't see your father here."

Lady Simon raised her chin. "You should know he and Lord Titus are not friendly."

The man's jaw moved as if he were chewing a cud. "Where are your children? I haven't seen them."

She glanced around as if searching for them. "They are here somewhere. I specifically tasked Cormac with taking care of his sister. If you see them, you may send them to me. We should be leaving soon."

The older man inclined his head. "I suppose I'll see you at some of the entertainments."

"We have decided to go home. Neither my son nor my daughter is having a good time. I believe they are both too young for what the Season has to offer."

The gentleman's face reddened. "I'll talk to your father about that."

Kit and Mary approached as the man left. Kit snagged a glass of champagne from a passing footman and gave it to Lady Simon. "Who was he?"

"A friend of my father's. From his reaction, he may be expecting a match with Fee."

"He—your father"—Mary swallowed—"could not think to see her marry a man that much older than she is."

"He did it to me." All the color had drained from Lady Simon's face.

For a moment Mary also appeared as if she'd be ill. Kit hailed another footman and took a flute of champagne from his tray, pressing it into her hand. "Drink some of this."

She stared at Lady Simon. "That's monstrous!"

"I agree." Kit tightened his grip on her arm. "You're quite pale, my love. Perhaps Lady Simon would escort you to the ladies' retiring room?"

"What a wonderful idea." Mary took the other woman's arm.

He walked with them to the corridor. "Take your time. When you haven't returned in five minutes or so, I'll tell Lady Theo you're not feeling quite the thing, and make our excuses." Mary frowned. "She'll understand when I tell her Lady Simon went with you."

Squeezing her hand, he whispered, "Go now."

CHAPTER TWENTY-EIGHT

The corridor was empty as Mary and Lady Simon made their way to a door leading to the servants' area. Once there, they took the back stairs up to the first floor.

"Thank you for your help," Morna said. "I'm afraid he'll be watching me."

"You're welcome, but it was my husband's idea. We are more than happy to aid you and your family." After all she'd been through with her cousin, Mary was surprised she was able to keep her voice even. "I've had my own problems with family members." Once they reached Lady Cavendish's chamber, Mary took the other woman's hands in hers. "If there is any way we can serve you, please do not hesitate to ask."

Morna blinked several times. "Thank you. You have all been so kind to us. Perhaps we'll see you in London?"

"I look forward to it. We'll be there for the Little Season."

After Mary reached her room, she tugged the bell-pull.

Several moments later, Mathers answered. "Are you all right, my lady?"

"I was a little faint, but I'm fine now. Please help me change. I have a feeling I'm going to need a walk."

Mathers gave her a look, but did as Mary asked.

A half hour later, Kit entered the parlor. "Lord and Lady Simon are going to require a bit more help."

"After she had that conversation with the older gentleman, I thought that might be the case. What is our role?"

"You need to take the air with your maid. I'll join you before you reach the end of the garden. Lord Simon will be waiting in a coach right next to the garden gate."

She donned her bonnet. "I'm sure we'll be fine."

Kit pulled her against him. "After looking for you for a year, finding you, then almost losing you due to our misunderstandings, I'm not taking a chance of anything happening to the only woman I could ever love."

If it was anyone but him saying that, she would not have believed him. "The only one?"

"Yes." His lips grazed hers. "When we return, I'll show you how much."

The sounds of guests leaving the party drifted back to the garden as Mary leaned slightly on Lady Simon, who wore a plain muslin cap and drab woolen cloak, as they made their way to the gate.

They'd almost arrived, when Kit joined them. "The streets leading to and from this side of the square are fouled with carriages. One more won't be noticed in the crush." He opened the gate and stepped out. A coach stood right where it should be. Mary bit her lip as Kit jerked the door open, then let out the breath she'd been holding, when Lord Simon appeared in the opening, holding his hand out to his wife.

"Thank you." He nodded to them.

Once Lady Simon was seated, she gave the first smile Mary had seen on her face. "I thank you as well. I hope we meet again."

Kit closed the door, tapped on it twice, and the carriage started down the mews. "A good day's work."

"I do hope we hear from either them or Lady Theo that they arrived in England safely."

Snaking his arm around Mary's waist, he grinned. "That was extremely inventive of you to feign illness."

"I'm not as clever as you think. I suddenly thought of what would have happened if my cousin had ever got hold of me. He may not be old, but the prospect was equally nauseating."

"Which reminds me, I need to write to my father with our marriage announcement, and you should write to your brother. I daresay he would like to know you've wed."

A burble of laughter escaped her. "Poor Barham. He's been kept so much in the dark, he's completely baffled. I received a letter from him after your father wrote to him, and never did write back." The marriage announcement was somewhat problematic. "What will you put in the *Post?*"

"Only that we have wed. As you know, my mother has been putting around a story about my leaving Town. I have no idea what she's said, but knowing her, it will have been vague enough to match any ending."

Her mother-in-law sounded like a splendid lady. "I look forward to meeting her."

He held her a bit closer. "She dearly wants to meet you as well. I almost wish we could go straight to Town."

"No, it's better to wait until the Little Season. There will not be so many questions, and Diana Brownly will be either safely married or back home."

Kit and Mary had reached the terrace and entered through the library. He held the door open for her. She stepped in and stopped.

"Uncle Hector, what are you doing here?" Mary exclaimed in the loudest, most strident tone Kit had ever heard her use.

Lord Titus and a gentleman around the same age, or perhaps a bit older, rose.

Lady Theo glanced between Mary and her uncle. "Hector is a petrologist. I meant to tell everyone we'd have another guest, then with all the bother concerning my brother, I must have forgot. I take it you are related?"

Kit pulled out his quizzing glass to intimidate the man if he proved to be a problem. Mary's uncle was a tall, slender man in his middle age. Touches of white interlaced with the light brown hair at his temples. A pair of spectacles perched on the end of his nose. He glanced up from a map they had been studying. As innocuous as he appeared, this was the man who was responsible for making his wife's life hell during the past few years.

Hector Tolliver pushed the glasses up onto the bridge of his nose. "Mary." He smiled benignly. "How wonderful to see you." His brows pulled together slightly in confusion. "But why are you here, my dear, and not in London for the Season?"

Mary's chin rose defiantly. "I recently married."

His brow cleared, and he smiled again. "That's wonderful, and about time it is. Not that I would want you to wed just anyone to see it done. Did you marry Lord Huntley? Is that the reason you're here?"

"No no, Hector," Theo interpolated. "Huntley wed Lady Caro

Martindale last autumn. Mr. Featherton, Viscount Featherton's eldest, is Mary's husband."

Kit gave a shallow, stiff bow. "We married yesterday."

"Splendid. I shall instruct my man of business to wind up the trust." He nodded several times, more to himself than anyone else. "Still, I don't understand why Barham didn't contact me."

Mary's jaw dropped, then she shut it so hard her teeth clicked. This whole conversation was deuced odd. The man acted as if nothing unusual had occurred. Kit cleared his throat. "The trust was ended last week, and the marriage settlements have been signed."

"Eh?" Tolliver's brows snapped together. "Did I miss your birthday, Mary? I thought the trust wound up next year. If so, I'm terribly sorry. I meant to particularly remember this one."

"No, sir." Kit had heard academics were forgetful, but this was outside of enough. "The trust was ended by court order. I imagine your solicitor will have sent word."

Tolliver cocked his head to one side, reminding Kit forcibly of a large bird. "I don't understand. What court case?"

"Oh dear," Lady Theo said, rising. "Why don't we all move to the sofas, and I shall ring for tea, and . . . perhaps something stronger."

She tugged the bell-pull and shooed them all to the area near the fireplace. Kit and Mary sat on a loveseat, which faced a larger sofa.

He placed his lips close to her ear. "I have a feeling this is not at all what we thought."

"I think you're right," she responded in a whisper. "Uncle Hector appears completely baffled. What could have been going on?"

Lord Titus passed around a decanter of finely aged Scotch whisky, and one of sherry. Kit poured a sherry for Mary and Scotch for himself.

Once tea was served, Tolliver fixed Kit with a confused look. "There appears to have been a great deal going on that I'm not aware of. I'd appreciate it if someone would enlighten me."

Mary slid Kit a glance and nodded.

"Well, sir, it appears quite a lot of chicanery has been going on in your name . . ."

More than half an hour and several cups of tea later, many of them laced with Scotch, Uncle Hector, as he'd asked Kit to call him, dragged a hand down his face. "I must humbly beg your forgiveness,

Mary. I had no idea all this was happening. Please trust me when I say, if I had, I would have put a quick stop to it."

She squeezed Kit's hand. "None of it ever made sense to me. It just never fit with what I remembered of you."

Uncle Hector picked up the whisky then placed it back down again. "Nevertheless, I was remiss. I'd like to say I have no idea where Gawain could have come up with such a foolish notion that I would want him to marry you, or that your fund would go to me if you wed against my wishes. He has a trust that is more than sufficient to command the elegancies of life, and has no need of your money. It is strange that, as far as I know, he has not drawn from it. Then again, he lives at home. The plain fact is that if Barham agreed the suitor was a good man, I would have had no objection. I believe it all worked out splendidly in the end."

"*Grandmamma!*"

The Dowager Duchess of Bridgewater entered the parlor under full sail.

Mary was half out of her seat when Kit pulled her back down, and rose. "Don't act rashly."

"I must say, I agree."

Kit groaned as his grandmother followed closely behind.

"Remember, keep your temper," Mary said in an under voice, all the while smirking.

He bowed, and Lady Titus greeted the ladies. "My dear duchess, and Lady Featherton, what brings you here, or need I ask?"

"Our grandchildren, naturally," the Dowager Duchess of Bridgewater responded.

Kit's grandmother glided up to him, stood on her tiptoes, and bussed his cheek, then patted it. "We were sorry to miss the wedding."

Lady Theo rang for more tea, and the dowagers took the chairs on either side of the loveseat where Kit and Mary were sitting.

"We would have been here sooner," Lady Bridgewater said, "but we stopped at Rose Hill hoping to throw Gawain off the track."

His grandmother frowned. "Despite everything we tried, I believe he may already be here."

When she turned her attention on Uncle Hector, Lady Bridgewater's blue eyes turned to shards of ice. "I never would have believed such underhanded dealings from you, Hector. What do you have to say for yourself?"

He blinked, then hung his head, reminding Kit forcibly of a chastised child. Then again, he wouldn't like coming under her fire either. "I—I was not aware of what was going on. I've been so busy with my studies. In fact, the only reason I'm here is that Lord Titus and I are cooperating on a paper for the Royal Society."

"It's true, Grandmamma," Mary said. "He really did not know. He, Lord Titus, and Lady Theo have been traveling from site to site for two years. We just finished telling him all that has occurred."

They were quiet for several moments until his grandmother pursed her lips and said what at least some of them had been thinking. "It was probably Cordelia. She always was a little strange. Fey, I would call it."

"You might have something there, my lady," Hector said. "She always thought my brother would die, leaving me the earldom. I never could convince her it was not what I wished for, but she dearly wanted a title. Sometimes I wonder why she married me at all."

"Greedy, if you want my opinion." The duchess scowled.

Uncle Hector's face turned beet red. "Here now, that is my wife you are talking about."

Mary straightened her shoulders, and her chin firmed. "That is quite enough."

Kit pressed his lips together but couldn't keep one corner of his mouth from twitching up as their eyes turned toward Mary.

She made a sharp cutting motion with her hand. "It's done. I agree that some people need to be dealt with, but that is for Uncle Hector to do. Name-calling will not help anyone."

"Well—," the duchess began.

Mary glared at her grandmother. "Not another word unless it is to congratulate Kit and me or to tell us how Aunt Eunice and Brian are doing."

"We do congratulate you." Kit's grandmother smiled gently, her eyes appearing suspiciously damp. "Your aunt and Mr. Doust are getting along famously. They have already moved into their new home, and we were privileged to stay a few days with them."

The dowager duchess lifted her cane as if she'd pound it on the floor, and stopped. "Mary, the only thing I have ever wanted is the happiness of my children and grandchildren. I cannot tell you how pleased I am you and Kit have married."

The storm that was threatening blew over just like that. Kit shook his head, unable to believe how Mary had taken control. Give her a Season or two and he had no doubt she would be on her way to being one of the *ton*'s leaders. "When did you arrive and where are you staying?"

"We are at the King's Arms. It is the only hotel worth our custom," Mary's grandmother said.

His grandmother rolled her eyes. "We arrived to-day, dear, and came directly here. How much longer will you remain in Edinburgh?"

"To-morrow is our last day. Mary and I will repair to Rose Hill for the remainder of the Season."

His grandmother turned her most engaging smile on Mary. "A wonderful decision. After all, young people in love should have time together. I am so happy to welcome you to the family."

Mary's stern countenance transformed into a friendly smile. Quite frankly, no one could resist his grandmother when she wanted to please. "Thank you, my lady."

"Oh, my dear, you must call me grandmamma. I foresee we will become great friends."

"Very well, Grandmamma Featherton."

His grandmother beamed. Mary's grandmother, however, did not appear as pleased. Kit remembered something his mother used to say about honey and vinegar.

The dowager duchess rose, and everyone else hopped up as well. "We would be pleased if you would join us for an early dinner."

Apparently Mary had forgiven her grandmother for she grinned. "We'd love to, Grandmamma."

On the other hand, Kit had absolved his as well. He and Mary had what they'd wanted all along. "We shall meet you at five o'clock?"

"Excellent." His grandmother turned to Lady Theo. "I saw your father recently. He misses you."

"Thank you for telling me. He'll see us shortly. We have plans to depart for England when our guests do."

His grandmother gave her "all was right with her world" smile. "You do know, he only wants for you to be happy."

Lord Titus glowered, but Lady Theo grinned. "It has taken many years, but I understand that now."

Kit vowed his children would never doubt that he loved them and wanted what was best for them.

He and Mary escorted their grandmothers to the front door. "We'll see you soon."

His grandmother kissed him again. "We are looking forward to it." The dowager duchess embraced Mary. "I am so very happy for you, my dear."

Once the door was closed, she turned to him. "I cannot believe how easily I forgave her."

"I know. I feel the same about mine." He grimaced.

Mary's eyes opened wide. "Oh, but your grandmother is a darling."

He raised a brow. "My grandmother is the most manipulative female I have ever had the pleasure to meet, and she does it all charmingly. There is no standing against her. Even my mother cannot remain angry at her. She is completely lovable."

Shaking her head, Mary chuckled. "She is that. They are so opposite. I wonder how they became such good friends?"

"Perhaps we should ask them." They entered their chamber, and he glanced at the clock. "Please tell me that is not the correct time."

She looked at her watch brooch. "I'm sorry to tell you it is slow. We have just enough time to change and leave. They must have planned dinner before they asked us."

Damn! At this rate, he'd never have time alone with his wife. "When we get to Rose Hill, I'm barring the doors."

"I'll help you."

She rang the bell-pull and soon her dresser and his valet were attending them. Now that everything with her uncle had been settled, Mary seemed to dismiss the cousin. Yet if their grandmothers thought Tolliver was in Edinburgh, Kit would have to be on his guard. After all, few people knew he and Mary had wed. He wouldn't put it past the blackguard to try to abduct her.

CHAPTER TWENTY-NINE

Mary would rather have walked, if only to spend more time with Kit, but her thin silk-and-kidskin slippers would have failed, at least twice, and one could not attend a dinner wearing half-boots.

He handed her into one of Lady Theo's small town coaches. Once he'd taken his seat, he put his arm around her shoulders, and they sat in companionable silence during the short ride to the hotel.

Suddenly Mary had a thought. "I wonder what they would have done had they found us at the King's Arms?"

Kit barked a laugh. "Ordered champagne and danced a jig, is my guess."

She grinned. "You're probably right. I know we've decided to forgive them, but I would still like to know what prompted it all."

His head moved, as if he was gazing at her. Unfortunately, her bonnet blocked her view of him. "I'm not sure I wish to know what goes on in their brainboxes. It might frighten me." Kit tightened his hold on her. "But by all means, ask. It might be interesting to know how ladies who should be in Bedlam think."

Mary was still chuckling a few minutes later when the coach came to a stop at the hotel. Kit waved aside the footman waiting to assist her, and handed her out himself. A surge of love speared through her as she remembered all the small, caring gestures he'd made toward her that she'd mistaken as mere courtesy and not signs of his regard. For the first time she wondered if Kit had attempted to court her in Town, whether she'd have been aware enough to notice. He definitely wouldn't have punched a gentleman there. *Hmm.*

They were escorted to their grandmothers' apartments. The rooms made the ones they'd had look small in comparison. The parlor was larger, and flanked at each end by bedchambers. They even had a balcony with a view to the garden in back of the hotel.

Her grandmother bussed her cheek, then held out her hand to Kit, who bowed over it. His grandmother hugged and kissed Mary and Kit.

"Kit," her grandmother said, "you may pour the drinks."

"Yes, ma'am."

Under the watchful eye of her grandmother's butler, the hotel's servants bustled in and out preparing the table. Their conversation centered on their travel to Edinburgh until the butler announced dinner. Once seated, with only Grandmamma's servants in attendance, the conversation grew more interesting.

"I suppose you are aware of Meg's love interest," Grandmother Featherton said.

Kit's lips pressed together. "I am. The best I can say for him is that he seems to care for her and has no ulterior motives. A bit of a bore, in my opinion."

Mary wanted to pinch him under the table, but he'd been seated across from her. She couldn't even reach to kick him. How could he not know he'd just given their grandmothers permission to interfere?

"I agree, Kit," Grandmother Featherton commented. "He's not up to her weight."

He shrugged. "There is nothing for it. It's her choice."

As he applied himself to the soup, their grandmothers exchanged an almost surreptitious glance.

"Speaking of potential mates," Mary said, giving them a wide-eyed, innocent look. "Exactly when did the two of you decide Kit and I would make a good couple?"

"Not *good*, my dear," Grandmother Featherton said. "Excellent. Constance and I have always striven for brilliant matches."

"And not what the *ton* normally considers brilliant," her grandmamma added. "Life can be a very long time. Even lengthier if one is unhappily wed."

Kit held his serviette to his mouth as he made a small choking noise.

"Are you all right, my dear?" his grandmother said as she slapped him on the back. "For instance, look how happy your parents are."

He glanced up, his eyes suspiciously red. "You matched them? To hear it from my mother's point of view, they fell in love."

"Of course they did," Grandmamma Featherton responded in an insulted tone. "We simply threw them in each other's way and ensured they had sufficient opportunity to get to know one another."

Frowning, he was quiet for a moment. "What about my father's first marriage?"

His grandmother slowly shook her head. "He met her at a house party not far from Gretna Green. Before we knew he was wed, it was over and done."

Mary's grandmamma's lips formed a thin line. "Bad blood. Madness ran in her family."

He rubbed his forehead. "I thought she died in child-birth."

"She died," Grandmamma said, "jumping off the parapet of her family's home with the child in her arms."

"Your father was devastated," Grandmother Featherton added. "That was when Constance and I decided to make sure none of our children suffered a bad marriage again. Most of the matches were fairly easy. You and Mary, however, provided an unusual challenge. You were both so reserved, and then Gawain began his harassment. We were almost at our wits' end."

"I don't understand." Mary stared at Lady Featherton. "How did you know to put us together, and how did you think of your idea?"

Her grandmother gave her the same look she'd give a slow-witted child. "Sometimes a person needs the opposite to complete them. At other times, such as with your Aunt Eunice, they need the same type of person. You and Kit appeared to require mates who would think alike. What made it more difficult, Mary, is that you are also a romantic who has had little experience with men."

That was true enough. Would she have fallen for a complete rogue, thinking his advances were love?

"On the other hand"—her grandmother smiled—"for all his experience with the *ton*, Kit had never wooed a female. He'd spent his time not giving the young ladies any reason to think he was interested in them."

"The year you came out—" Grandmother Featherton smiled beatifically. She really was good at this. "We watched the two of you watch each other. Then nothing. Finally, during a conversation with Bridgewater's steward, Constance discovered the steward's cousin was at Kit's estate."

If he'd been another man, Mary was sure Kit's jaw would have dropped. "How—how long did your preparations take?"

"After that," his grandmother said in a cheery voice, "not long at all. We needed the year for Mary to feel safe, so she could be receptive to your courtship, and we wished to ensure that your heart was not otherwise engaged."

A cold chill ran down Mary's spine. "And if Kit's heart had been?"

Her grandmother smiled kindly. "You would have left Rose Hill none the wiser. Miss Brownly would have had to come here for her Season."

"Remarkable," Kit commented faintly. "I was firmly convinced you'd both lost your minds, but, and I say this with strong reservations, it appears as if you know what you're doing. I believe Mary will agree with me when I tell you we are remarkably happy together."

She nodded her head. "I agree wholeheartedly, yet what of Diana Brownly?"

Lady Featherton grinned. "The last we heard, a very nice gentleman from Cornwall has her interest. He is a country-bred baronet and only in Town to find a wife. He is quite smitten with her as well. She has also been told that your marriage has been undisclosed from the *ton* for various reasons which cannot be revealed. Kit, your mother has assured Miss Brownly that all is proper and sworn her to secrecy."

That was sure to appeal to Diana's sense of romance.

They had moved from the dining table to a cozy group of chairs and sofas. Grandmamma glanced at Kit. "Get me a brandy and your grandmother a sherry. We will not have tea served. I expect to retire soon."

He did as he was told, and shortly thereafter they bid their grandmothers a good evening. Once in the carriage, he said, "That was an illuminating conversation."

Mary removed her bonnet. "Especially for you. How do you feel about their revelations concerning your father's first wife?"

"It explains a great deal. My older half-brother was never allowed around the younger children as babies. Not that I think he cared. Even when he was with me, there was a groom or nurse present at all times. The older he got, the wilder he became."

She snuggled into him. "It's sad."

"Yes." Kit put his arm around her shoulders. "I must say, I don't think them nearly so mad."

"Nor do I." Mary wondered who their grandmothers would try to match next and was very much afraid it would be Kit's sister.

It was their last day in Edinburgh. The city had managed to endear itself to Kit. Mayhap he and Mary would visit again. They were strolling with the Eveshams, Rutherfords, and Huntleys through the squares making up part of the city's New Town. The ladies walked ahead, chatting, as the gentlemen entertained Arthur and Ben. Kit had never been so happy and at ease, knowing all was right with him and Mary. He hoped they would soon join the others in parenthood. Even now, she could be carrying his child.

Next to him Marcus tensed, and Kit looked at their ladies. A man, dressed as a gentleman, stood directly in front of them.

Kit and his friends approached as casually as they could under the circumstances. Phoebe's hand stole into a pocket in her skirts, and Anna took a few steps to the side. Caro remained next to Mary.

"Gawain, what are you doing here?" Mary asked.

"I've come for you. What did you think, that I'd let all that money go? I never took you for a fool."

Phoebe and Anna might be capable of defending his wife, but she was Kit's to protect. He made his way to Mary, standing behind her. Raising his quizzing glass, he asked in a bored drawl, "Who might you be?"

Tolliver glanced briefly at Kit, then said to Mary, "You may as well come with me now. You wouldn't want anyone to get hurt."

She leaned into Kit the slightest bit. "Really?" Her tone was haughty and dismissive. "Who do you think is going to hurt all of them?"

"I have men," he said, looking at the group. "They know how to fight."

Kit wanted to laugh. There was no one in the square but a few children and their maids. Instead he said, "You and me. Now. Unless, that is, you're afraid to fight a man."

Tolliver stared at Kit as if noticing him for the first time. "I don't know who you are or why the hell you're concerned. This is between my cousin and me."

"I'm her husband." He raised a brow. "And I don't particularly care for scoundrels who swear in the presence of my wife."

Tolliver stepped back as if struck. "You're married?"

Kit inclined his head.

The idiot began to laugh. "Your birthday isn't until next year. It's all mine. I've won!"

Kit supposed they should have left it at that, but he couldn't. "You've won nothing. Your father is here."

The man's face paled and he lunged at Mary.

Kit reached out to push her behind him, but before he could succeed, Mary drove her fist into the man's nose. Blood sprayed out, and Tolliver went down with a thud.

"Ow!" Mary cradled her hand. "Why did no one tell me that would hurt?"

Kit couldn't help but grin. "For your first time, you did a wonderful job. Would it be too much to ask that next time you allow me to strike the blackguard?"

"If I'd had any idea I'd injure myself, I would have let you do it this time."

Kit wrapped her hand in his handkerchief. "You need to ice it immediately."

He turned to Marcus and Rutherford, who had picked Tolliver up. "I suppose the best thing to do with him is take him to the watch until his father can fetch him."

"Probably something that should have been done a long time ago," Marcus agreed. "Huntley's already gone to find a constable."

Later that afternoon, after her hand had been iced and the swelling reduced, Kit snuggled next to Mary in bed. She wore a silk confection the likes of which he'd never seen before. "Where did you get that?"

"Caro. She brought it from Italy."

Although he dearly wanted his wife, some things had to be discussed first. "I had looked forward to smashing your cousin to pieces."

"I'm sorry, but despite the pain, it felt amazingly good to hit him."

"What do you think Tolliver will do when he discovers his mother is delusional?"

"Find his own way. I never really liked him, but it is a shame his mother filled him with all that nonsense."

"And his father was not around to counter it."

Mary glanced at him with sadness in her eyes. "That's true. I wonder who they would have married if our grandmothers had been involved."

Kit groaned and pulled Mary on top of him. "I don't think I want to know."

"They have been extremely successful."

"Don't tell me you now support what they've done!"

Mary nuzzled his chin, then moved her lips to his and nibbled. "They did put us together."

Kit wondered what his wife would do if he tore the silk from her body. Then he decided he was over-thinking this. He grabbed the neck, gave her a wicked smile, and tore it apart.

Not giving her time to protest, he blanketed her mouth, wanting her to struggle catching up with him. She met him, parrying her tongue with his. "Ah, my love."

Kit fluttered kisses down her body until he reached her hot, wet core. "Mine."

She arched against him. "Yes, yours."

Mary screamed with pleasure as he entered her. Bright lights impaired his vision as she convulsed around him.

He saw heaven and knew it was Mary.

Dawn came all too early. Before he could even think of making love to his wife again, there was a knock on the door.

"Sir, you need to awaken."

Kit groaned. "Give me a few minutes."

Mary turned in his arms. "How much time do we have?"

"Not enough for me to love you properly."

She smiled, flicking her tongue against his nipple. "What about improperly?"

CHAPTER THIRTY

Dunwood House, Mayfair, September 1817

Mary hugged Phoebe as she and Kit entered the drawing room. "It is wonderful to be back in Town."

"We're so happy to see you," Phoebe said. "It's been too long since you were able to join us."

Marcus brought Mary and Kit sherry. "You look well. I take it married life is agreeing with you."

Kit grinned. He did that a lot lately. "It is." He slid his arm around Mary's increasing waist. "We shall have a happy event in February."

Huntley entered with Caro, each of them carrying a small bundle. Mary peeked at both babies before carefully embracing her friend. "They are lovely! Have you decided on names yet?"

Huntley grinned. "We have."

"Though it was a bit of a battle with our fathers," Caro added. She motioned to the baby her husband held. "May I present Giles Andrew Douglas Ingram, Viscount Rushdon, and this"—she kissed the head of the baby she held—"is Lady Emily Charlotte Meraude Noel Grevill."

Grace Worthington slowly made her way to them. "What beautiful babies!" She rubbed her hand over her burgeoning stomach, and addressed Mary. "Congratulations to you as well!"

"Thank you." Mary smiled.

"Where are Eugénie and Will?" Grace asked.

"I almost forgot to tell you," Phoebe said. "I received a letter yesterday. She gave birth to a boy. They didn't have the name yet."

"Have you heard from Lord Simon and his lady?" Mary asked Caro.

"We have. They are doing well. It looks as if they will buy a house in Town and another property near Bristol. Lady Simon asks that her thanks for Athey be passed along. She is doing a wonderful job as Finella's lady's maid."

Marcus replaced the sherry with champagne. "A toast to Huntley, Caro, Will, Eugénie and the new babies."

The Rutherfords entered the room, and Anna hugged everyone. "I take it you've heard about the Wivenlys' new son?"

Huntley made his way over to Kit. "This is it. You won the wager."

He was still for a few moments. "The one we made at Beaumont's wedding, you mean?"

"That was the only one I know of. You were the last one married."

"No, Rupert Stanstead was there and he is still not wed."

Huntley pulled a face. "He is too young to be thinking of filling his nursery."

"I believe you might be wrong about that." Kit grinned. "Care to wager?"

"What wager?" Robert Beaumont joined them. "Not on my daughter."

Marcus rolled his eyes. "Is that all you think about?"

"No, I think about Serena." Taking a glass of champagne from Marcus, Robert smiled. "When are you and Phoebe going to have another? I am here to attest, daughters are the most engaging children known to man."

Marcus glanced at his wife. "It's too early to say, but we hope for another one next year."

"The wager," Huntley said, bringing them back to the topic. "I say Rupert will not wed for another few years."

Kit grinned. "And I say he'll be wed before year's end."

"My cousin Rupert?" Robert asked.

"How many other Ruperts do you know?" Huntley said in a dry tone.

"I say he finds a young lady and marries," Marcus added.

Robert's eyes twinkled with mirth. "I think I'll pass. Rupert will do what he wishes and might surprise everyone."

Ella Quinn's bachelors are quite sure of what they want in life—and love—until the right woman opens their eyes . . .

After a painful heartbreak, Rupert, the handsome young Earl of Stanstead, has decided that when it comes to love, avoidance is best. Until he meets a woman who makes him forget his plan—and remember his longing for a wife and family. Yet he senses that she too has been hurt, though she attempts to hide her feelings—and more—in the most baffling and alluring way. Intrigued, Rupert is willing to play along, if winning her is the prize . . .

Crushed by her late husband's scorn, Vivian, Countess of Beresford, believes she is monstrously undesirable. Sadly childless, she has moved to London resigned to a solitary life. Still, when she encounters Rupert at a masquerade ball, her disguise as Cleopatra emboldens her. Convinced he doesn't recognize her, she begins an after-hours affair with him, always in costume—while allowing him to innocently court the real her by day. But when Rupert makes a shocking choice, will Vivian be able to handle the truth?

**Please turn the page for an exciting sneak peek at
Ella Quinn's next historical romance
LADY BERESFORD'S LOVER
coming in July 2015!**

CHAPTER ONE

End of August 1817, Beresford Abbey, England

Vivian, the widowed Countess of Beresford, sat at her desk in the morning room of the dower house in which she'd been living for the past year, plotting her escape. A beam of bright afternoon sunshine shot along the gold and blue Turkey carpet, interrupted only by the supine form of her gray cat, Gisila.

In truth, plotting was probably too strong a word, though Vivian liked how it sounded, and she did feel as if she was escaping; not only the dower house, but Beresford Abbey itself. In a few short days her period of mourning would end.

Her hand clenched as if she could strike her dead husband and everyone else in this hellish place. Soon she would leave and vowed never to return to this estate, or the market town where everyone had known of her late husband's deceit and had pitied her, but had said nothing to her. Not that Vivian had ever been given the opportunity to be a real wife. Soon after her marriage, Edgar, who at the time was still the heir, couldn't stand the sight of her, in or out of the bedchamber. Mrs. Raeford had that honor, if it could be called such, absent the ring and title of course.

Vivian should not have had such great expectations of her marriage, but Edgar had been attentive and charming while their fathers arranged the union. Father had assured her this was a good match and a dutiful daughter would trust her papa, like the good puss she was. After all, he had said in a kind tone, Vivian was no great beauty, too blond when the fashion was for dark hair, slender to the point of skinny, when men preferred voluptuous ladies, and too bookish. Although, if someone, anyone, would have told her about her future husband's lover, Vivian was sure she could have brought herself to refuse the match, for one of her many failures was too much pride.

Vivian waited for the familiar rage to rise, but after a year of waiting to be released from her duty to her husband, there were no more tears and the pains in her stomach had finally ceased.

She would never again allow herself to be so naïve, or so trusting.

Giving herself a shake, she opened the weekly letter from her mother.

> *My darling Vivian,*
>
> *I am so pleased to hear you are going to Town with Cousin Clara. As you were aware, we had not planned to arrive for another several weeks. However, there has been a new development. Your father has taken it into his head that he needs a new hunting bitch, and nothing will do but he must have it immediately. All else has been forgot in his search. You may well imagine my frustration, but Papa will have his way. Consequently, it appears we will not attend the Little Season at all.*
>
> *Have a wonderful time. I look forward to your letters concerning the entertainments.*
>
> *Give Clara my best.*
>
> *With much love,*
>
> *Mama*
>
> *VB*

Poor Mama. Did reasonable men even exist?

"My lady." Hal, who'd been her personal footman since her come out, hovered in the open door. "The new Lord Beresford asks if you'll receive him."

What could he possibly want? Since the reading of the will, Vivian hadn't had much to do with her husband's cousin and best friend who'd come into the title.

Well, whatever it was, she would not allow it to stop her from leaving.

"I'll see him. Please bring tea and ask Miss Corbet to join me." Silvia Corbet, the vicar's eldest daughter had been Vivian's companion for the past year, and during that time Vivian had come to love Silvia like a sister.

"Yes, my lady. I'll get her first."

"Thank you. That would be best."

Vivian was not completely conversant concerning the rules of being a widow, but she could not think they would allow her to be in the same room with a gentleman who was not a close relation. Or perhaps that was incorrect. She had heard that some widows took lovers. Still, she did not want to be alone with the man. He had nothing to say that would interest her.

A few moments later, Silvia entered the room. "Hal said we had a visitor."

"Indeed, the new Lord Beresford." Vivian moved to the sofa. "Thank you for coming so quickly."

"I was on my way to you in any event." Silvia's demeanor had changed her normal friendliness to barely suppressed anger upon hearing his lordship had come. She chose a chair in the corner of the room near one of the windows, took out her embroidery, and gave a short nod.

As soon as Vivian's companion had settled, his lordship was announced, and the tea tray set in front of her obviating the need for her to stand and greet the man. "Good afternoon, my lord."

He glanced at her, bowed, and smiled, apparently not even noticing that Silvia was in the corner. "Good day. I hope I find you well."

"Yes, thank you, quite well." And she'd be even better when she left this place. What she did not understand was how the man could fail to notice Silvia. However he hadn't glanced her way. What could he want that had him so focused on Vivian? "Would you like some tea?"

"Please. Two sugars and milk, if you would."

The Queen Anne sofa, opposite her, groaned as he lowered his large muscular frame onto the delicate piece. Vivian winced, expecting it to splinter at any moment. Nothing in this parlor was made for persons of his size and weight. Finally satisfied the sofa would not break, Vivian handed him the cup.

He took a sip, focusing his solemn brown gaze on her. "Have you made plans for what you will do after your year of mourning is over?"

Vivian glanced up, then lowered her eyes. By any standards, he was a handsome man with thick sable hair, a straight nose, and well above medium height. However, his resemblance to her late husband was too strong for her to be comfortable in his presence, and she had no intention of telling him of her cousin Clara's invitation. "Have you need of the dower house?"

"Of course not," he assured Vivian hastily. "You are naturally welcome to remain as long as you wish." He set his cup down, clearing his throat. "There is, however, a proposition I'd like to place before you, if I may?"

He probably wanted her to act as his hostess until he married. She should tell him she was not interested. Vivian wanted no more dealings with anyone by the name of Beresford. Unfortunately, curiosity had always been her besetting sin. She raised her brows and returned his gaze. Praying she presented the image of a calm composed widow, when in fact her stomach churned as it had when facing her husband. "Go on."

"I'd like to propose a marriage between us."

Marriage!

In the year Lord Beresford had been at the abbey, he hadn't once sought her out, and now he proposes marriage? Did he think she was simply to be a piece of property to be traded at will? Fury pierced her like lightening during a summer storm. After what his cousin put her through, he must be mad. It was all she could do to maintain her countenance. How could he think she would exchange one Lord Beresford for a newer version? Not only would she never even consider such a suggestion, if she did, she'd be made a laughingstock among the servants and the villagers. If his expression hadn't been so serious, she would have thought he was playing a sick joke.

When she didn't respond, he continued, "You are, after all, familiar with the Abbey and the area. It would not be a love match, but neither was your union with my cousin. I believe I can promise I will never embarrass you or cause you any distress."

As her husband had done when she'd discovered his long standing affair with a local farmer's wife. She took a few shallow breaths, attempting to gather her wits and find a way to end this conversation civilly. "We barely know one another."

For some reason, that seemed to hearten Lord Beresford. "A state which may be easily remedied. The fact remains that I am in need of a wife, and you fit the bill. I can give you children."

Vivian's cup rattled. She was that close to throwing cup, saucer, and pot at him all at once. The next thing she knew, the delicate china was being taken from her hands. Silvia put her arm around Vivian's shoulders, and sat next to her.

Beresford jumped to his feet as if a bee had stung him. "What are *you* doing here?"

"Why am I not surprised?" Silvia replied in a voice of icy distain. "Apparently you have forgotten I am Lady Beresford's companion. Now, *my lord*"—her tone took on the manner of a queen—"I believe you've said quite enough, and it is time to take your leave."

He flushed, strode to the door, opened it, and fixed his fierce look on Silvia. "You may leave. I wish to speak with her ladyship alone."

"Over my dead body," Silvia mumbled just loudly enough for him to hear.

He opened his mouth, and Vivian decided to step in before all-out war could ensue. She knew nothing about his lordship's manner, but, as much as she appreciated her companion's championship, she'd never seen her companion so exercised or rude.

In a calm, but unapologetic tone, Vivian said, "I asked Miss Corbet to remain with me."

He glared at Silvia as if he'd argue.

"However," Vivian continued firmly, "I do not believe I need to hear any more of your proposition, my lord. My answer is no. I have no desire to wed you. In fact, I have no desire to marry anyone ever again. Once was quite enough, thank you."

As he stalked out of the parlor, he glanced over his shoulder. "I'll speak to you again when you are in a better frame of mind, my lady."

"Not if I have anything to say about it," Silvia spat at his retreating form.

His shoulders hunched then the door snapped shut behind him.

"What gall!" Vivian picked up her tea-cup, and took a sip of the now tepid liquid. "That was as unexpected as it was unwanted."

"He's an impossible, arrogant man." Silvia fumed. "And always has been. He hasn't changed at all. Having inherited the earldom will probably make him worse."

"I'd forgot you and he were acquainted."

"Unfortunately." She scowled at the door. "He spent much of his childhood at the Abbey, and was always trying to tell my sisters and me what to do. How dare he stroll in here and think he could make a proposal like that!"

Vivian's lips twitched. Suddenly the whole preposterous situation was humorous. After all, he couldn't make her marry him. "I do recall that he did not call it a proposal, but a proposition."

"Who made whom a proposal?"

Standing just inside the room was a tall woman in her late middle-age with bright red curls dressed in a gown the same color as her hair. Her large bonnet appeared to hold a nest of birds. Although her clothing was in the latest fashion, the hat, although new, was clearly from the style of the previous century.

"Cousin Clara!" Vivian jumped up and rushed to hug her relative almost tripping over the greyhound hovering next to her cousin's skirts. "I didn't expect to see you until next week. We didn't even hear you arrive."

"It's all right, Perdita." Clara picked up the dog and soothed the greyhound, petting the dog and cuddling it. "I told your footman not to announce me." Setting Perdita down, Clara returned Vivian's hug. "I assume this has something to do with the young man I saw stalking out of the house in a rage."

"The new Lord Beresford apparently thought I'd make a good wife for him as I'm used to being Lady Beresford. Silvia sent him away with a flea in his ear. Oh, pray forgive my manners." Not that Vivian had had much of a chance to use them in the past six years. "Cousin Clara, this is Miss Corbet, who has been acting as my companion. Silvia, my cousin, the Dowager Marchioness of Telford."

Silvia curtseyed. "I'm so glad to have finally met you. Vivian tells me you have great plans for her for the Little Season."

"And for you as well." Lines fanned out from Clara's eyes as she smiled. "I understand that without your company this past year would have been unbearable for Vivian."

"I don't know about that." Silvia glanced at Vivian. "We've always got along well, and I was happy to help her. Since my father's remarriage, he was pleased I was out of the house." Silvia's fine dark brown brows furrowed. "Yet, I cannot accompany you to Town."

Clara's eyes opened wide. "Why ever not? I sincerely hope it is not because of your father, I already have his permission, and you are no longer acting as a companion. Therefore, there is no reason you should not have a come out." She waited a moment for the news to sink in. "Besides which, I've made all the arrangements. We'll have such fun. I've never had the opportunity to bring a young lady out. Sons are not at all the same." She removed her bonnet, and sat down on the same sofa recently vacated by Lord Beresford. "I wish to leave in two days' time."

"That soon?" Silvia gasped. "I don't even know what to bring with me. I'll require new gowns—"

"There is nothing to worry about." Still holding the dog, Clara took a place next to her hat. "From what I see, both you and Vivian need new wardrobes. In fact, I think we shall leave in the morning. There is no need to waste time. Besides, Perdita is ready to be home. All this traveling has upset her nerves."

Or, Vivian thought ruefully, give her former companion time to find an excuse not to go. She, on the other hand, was more than happy to quit Beresford as soon as possible.

Vivian didn't know how her cousin had arranged everything or why, but she was happy Silvia would finally have the Season she'd never had. Her younger sisters were already married. One to a wealthy young man of good lineage and fortune and the other to his friend the heir of a viscount. Although, Silvia's sisters had offered to sponsor her for a Season, she had declined stating that someone must remain with Papa and take care of him. An excuse she no longer had.

More tea arrived, and she busied herself fixing a cup for Clara. Vivian's thoughts turned to Lord Beresford's reaction to her companion and Silvia's behavior in response. Sparks had definitely flown, and he had seemed not only angry, but embarrassed that she was present. Was there something between them other than childhood animosity? If so, why had he proposed to Vivian?

The greyhound remained close to Clara, peeking out every once in a while from under her skirts. "Cousin Clara, when did you get a dog? I've never known you to have one before."

Clara stroked the small animal. "We always had hunting dogs, but one of my nephews brought her back from the Peninsula and asked me if I wouldn't mind keeping her until he found a new owner. They stayed with me for a few weeks while he sorted out his business. She and I just took to each other. I don't know why I never had a house dog before. She's an excellent companion."

"I hope she likes cats. You know I've had my Gisila for years and cannot go anywhere without her." Speaking of her cat, Vivian glanced around and found Gisila under the desk.

"I'm sure they'll be fine. Perdita normally remains under my skirts. It's amazing I don't trip over her." She turned her attention to

Silvia. "Miss Corbet, as you will be residing with me, I believe I would prefer to address you as Silvia, and you may call me Cousin Clara."

Silvia appeared slightly startled, not a state that happened often or easily. "Yes, ma'am."

"You may think this is a strange start on my part." Clara smiled gently. "But I knew your mother when she was a child and your grandmother was a close friend of mine."

"I had no idea."

While her cousin and Silvia chatted, Vivian strolled to the window seat. For the past few months, just the idea of going to Town again had occupied her mind. She had not attended a Season since her first one, and was both excited and frightened. It had been much too long since she'd been around the *haut ton*. At first, she thought merely to attend the smaller entertainments and the theater, now with Silvia coming out, Clara would insist on being present at the large balls. Perhaps Vivian would be better served by remaining with the chaperones and older matrons. That would be easier and less fearsome than worrying about dance partners.

The other business she must be about was finding a small estate. Her mother had offered to bring Vivian home after her husband died, but she'd a feeling then that she could not go back to her parents, and nothing had happened to change her mind. It was time to strike out on her own. To have a home where what she said was the law, and the sooner the better. After all, that was all she could expect from her life.

Departing on the morrow was easily done and for the best. She stepped into the corridor, and found one of the maids. "Please tell my maid and Miss Corbet's maid that we shall require our trunks packed immediately. Also, have Lady Telford's bags placed in the green room, and inform Cook we'll have a guest for dinner."

The maid bobbed a curtsey and hurried off.

Vivian slipped back into the morning room.

If only she was the type of widow who could take a lover, but what sane man would want a lady with a deformed body? Her husband's cousin could not possibly know about her problem, otherwise he would never have suggested marriage. She supposed she should be glad Edgar had not discussed it. Thankfully, her clothing covered the worst defect. No, other than as dancing partners, gentlemen had no place in her life or rather they would not want her in theirs.

Made in the USA
Monee, IL
02 April 2023

31154312R00173